The Killing Doll

Live Flesh

Ruth Rendell

arrow books

This edition published by Arrow Books in 2005

Copyright © KingsMarkham Enterprises 2005

The right of Ruth Rendall to be identified as the author
of this work has been asserted by her in accordance with
the the Copyright, Designs and Patents Act, 1988

The Killing Doll copyright © KingsMarkham Enterprises 1984
Live Flesh copyright © KingsMarkham Enterprises 1986

Arrow Books
The Random House Group Limited
20 Vauxhall Bridge Road, London, SW1V 2SA

Random House Australia (Pty) Limited
20 Alfred Street, Milsons Point, Sydney,
New South Wales 2061, Australia

Random House New Zealand Limited
18 Poland Road, Glenfield
Auckland 10, New Zealand

Random House (Pty) Limited
Isle of Houghton, Corner Boundary Road and Carse O'Gowrie,
Houghton, 2198, South Africa

The Random House Group Limited Reg. No. 954009

www.randomhouse.co.uk

A CIP catalogue record for this book
is available from the British Library

Papers used by Random House are natural, recyclable
products made from wood grown in sustainable forests.
The manufacturing processes conform to the environmental
regulations of the country of origin

ISBN 0 09 191106 0

Printed and bound in Great Britain by
Bookmarque Ltd, Croydon, Surrey

THE KILLING DOLL

FOR SIMON

Chapter 1

The winter before he was sixteen, Pup sold his soul to the devil. It was the beginning of December and dark before five. About two hours after that, Pup collected the things he wanted and went down on to the old railway line. Dolly had gone to the hospital – there was visiting between seven and eight – and Harold was nowhere about. Possibly he had gone to the hospital too; he sometimes did.

Pup carried a cycle lamp. He went out of the gate in the fence at the end of the garden and climbed down the slope through the trees and bushes. Here the old railway line lay in a valley so that the gardens looked down on to it, though in other places the grass path where the lines and sleepers had once been ran along a raised embankment. It ran over bridges and under bridges, four or five miles of it, so overgrown in the summertime that, from the air, it must have looked like a strip of woodland. Now, in the winter, the birches and buddleias were bare, the grass thin and damp, clogged with rubbish, sodden paper and rusty tins. Between the clouds a misty moon glowed, a sponge floating in soapy water.

To the left of him rose the brick arch over which Mistley Avenue passed. It was more than a bridge and less than a tunnel, a damp, dark hole through which a light or two could vaguely be seen glimmering. In the middle of it, someone had once dumped a

1

feather mattress from which the down was still leaking. There were always feathers everywhere inside the Mistley tunnel, stuck to the bricks or ground in the mud or floating like white insects in the dark air. Pup shone his torch and its beam showed him the tunnel's greenish walls, running with wetness. He squatted down among the feathers and lit the candle he had brought with him. He had also brought a small kitchen knife and a cup. His soul, he had thought, must take some visible, tangible form for him to hand over. The knife was quite sharp and needed only a touch to the ball of his thumb to bring the blood welling. A drop of blood, two or three in fact, fell into the cup, and Pup contemplated them by the light of his candle. Now he had gone so far, he hardly knew what words to speak.

Up in a tall chestnut tree in one of the back gardens an owl cried. It was no hoot that it made, still less a tu-whit-tu-woo, but a cold unearthly cry. Pup listened as it was repeated, that keening eldritch sound, and then he saw the owl, a big, dark, flapping shape silhouetted for a moment against the inky reddish sky at the tunnel's mouth. He was suddenly aware that he was cold. His blood was flowing in single sluggish drops down the shiny white inside of the cup. He stood up and held out the cup and said:

'Devil, O Devil, this is my soul. If you'll give me everything I ask for, you can have my soul and keep it for ever. Take it now. In exchange you've got to make me happy.' He paused and listened to the utter silence. A feather floated down from the roof and was caught and burned in the candle flame. Pup wondered if it was a sign that his soul had been received. He decided to take immediate advantage of it. 'Make me grow,' he said.

It was two weeks before he told Dolly about it and then he told only part of it.

'You what?' said Dolly.

He was doing Marlowe's *Faustus* for 'O' level. 'It's in a play we're doing at school. I thought I might as well try it. After all, my soul's not much use to me, is it? You can't see it or feel it or do anything with it, so I thought I'd sell it to the devil.'

'Sell it for what?'

'Well,' said Pup vaguely, 'just good things to have. Everything I want really. I asked him for things.'

'You might have asked him to stop Mother dying,' said Dolly as if she were talking of someone offering up prayers.

'I don't think that's the kind of thing he does,' said Pup thoughtfully, taking a second chocolate éclair. Already, a little prematurely assuming maternal care of him, she was feeding Pup up on rich cakes and encouraging him to take plenty of sugar in his tea. Building him up, she called it.

Harold, in front of whom any conversation, however private, could be conducted with impunity because he never heard a word when he was reading, had his book propped up against the pot of Tiptree pineapple jam. He was eating sliced tomatoes and egg-and-bacon pie with a fork, American fashion, putting down the fork to lift his cup, keeping his left hand free for turning the pages. Dolly never drank tea. When the visit was over, up in her own room, she would have her nightly ration of two glasses of wine.

'You going to come with me, Dad?' she said. He gave no sign of having heard, so she tapped on the back cover of *The Queen That Never Was*, a life of Sophia Dorothea of Celle. 'I said, are you coming with me?'

3

'It's a very painful thing, going to that hospital,' said Harold.

'She likes to see you.'

'I don't know about that,' said Harold, using a favourite phrase of his. 'She wouldn't if she knew how painful it was.'

There was no chance of his going. She went on her own as usual. After she had gone and Harold had departed for what he called the breakfast room, though no one within living memory had ever eaten breakfast in it, to spend the evening with Sophia Dorothea, Pup went up to the first floor where his bedroom was. There were three floors but they hardly used the top one. Pup's room was at the back, looking out on to the old railway line, the backs of the grey stucco houses in Wrayfield Road, Mrs Brewer's garden next door and the Buxtons' garden next door on the other side. He drew the curtains. These were made of very old pink and fawn folkweave and had belonged to Harold's mother when this house had been hers. On the bedroom wall Pup had marked out, with the aid of one of Dolly's tape measures, a column six feet high, divided on one side into centimetres (because he had learnt the metric system at school) and inches on the other because feet and inches were still more familiar to him when referring to a person's height.

He took off his shoes. It was a month since he had measured himself. He had last measured himself on 18 November and then he had still been four feet eleven. For months and months he had been four feet eleven, and now as he stood up against the gradated column, tension pulled at his stomach. He shut his eyes. What was he going to do if he stayed four feet eleven for the rest of his life?

'Devil, O Devil . . .' prayed Pup.

He marked where the top of his head reached. He

4

turned round and looked. Four feet eleven and a half. Was he deluding himself? He didn't think so. If anything, he hadn't stretched his knees the way he usually did and his hair was flatter than usual, it had just been cut. The new mark was beyond a doubt half an inch higher than the last mark. Four feet eleven and a half. Anyone weak enough or vain enough to stretch a bit would have made it five feet. Had the devil done this for him? On the whole Pup thought it unlikely – it was mere coincidence.

All the Yearmans tended to shortness. Harold was a small, spare man, thin as a boy at fifty-two, a just respectable five feet six. Let me be a just respectable five feet six, prayed Pup, looking at himself in Grandma Yearman's spotted mirror. Six-and-a-half inches, please, Devil. Faustus had not asked for – or been offered – personal beauty. Perhaps he was handsome enough and tall enough already. Pup had the long Yearman face, domed forehead, long straight nose, wide mouth, the Yearman yellow-brown hair and the Yearmans' yellow eyes which those who were kind called hazel. Neither he nor Dolly had inherited Edith's red hair, Edith's pale bright blue eyes, a redhead's pink freckled, tender skin. He would be happy enough with his appearance, he thought, if he could grow six-and-a-half inches.

Dolly would never be happy with hers. Dolly's appearance was something else altogether, though she never spoke of how she felt about it to anyone, not to Pup, not even to Edith. She had not written the letter to the magazine, though it might have come from her. 'Disfigured, Stockport' seemed to have precisely what she had. Coming home from the hospital – they had told her they doubted her mother would live to see the New Year – she sat on the bus reading the magazine with her right cheek against the dark window. On buses she always sat on the right-hand side for that reason and if there was no right-hand seat vacant she waited for the next bus. Of course she seldom went on buses. It was not as if she had ever gone out to work.

'Being attractive to the opposite sex does not depend on being pretty in a physical sense, you know. Think how many plain women seem to have a host of admirers. Their secret is self-confidence. Cultivate your personality, make yourself an interesting, lively person to be with, try to get out and meet people as much as you can and you will soon have forgotten all about your birthmark in the excitement of making new friends.'

Dolly had no friends. Edith had sheltered her and now she wondered what she was going to do without Edith. As soon as she was sixteen, Edith had got her to leave school. There was no question of her having a job. She stayed at home, helping her mother, in the way girls did years ago when Grandma Yearman was young. They used to go out shopping together and Edith got Dolly to take her arm.

'You're not helping that girl, treating her like an invalid, Edith,' Mrs Buxton had said. 'There's girls with worse disfigurements than hers get married and lead normal lives. There's a girl I often see about when I go to my daughter's in Finsbury Park, she's got a mark all over the lower half of her face, not just the cheek like Dolly, and I see her about with her baby in its pram. Lovely baby and not a mark on it.'

'We took her to one specialist after another,' said Edith. 'There was nothing to be done. Harold spent a fortune.'

Dolly never said a word. She sat at the sewing machine, learning to be a dressmaker under Edith's instruction. They never went anywhere but they were always dressed as if about to be taken out to lunch, trim homemade dresses, sheer tights, polished shoes, their hair shampooed and set, Dolly's, of course, carefully combed so that a curtain of it hung across the cheek. The highspot of their day was Pup coming home to tea.

For seven years it had gone on like that. Dolly was twenty-three.

'It's just as well I never went out to work, if you ask me,' she said to Pup. 'At any rate I learned how to look after you and run this place.'

It was a big house, furnished much as Grandma Yearman had left it. Most of the others like it in Manningtree Grove had been divided up into flats. The Yearmans' house was shabby and rather dark. Squares of old carpet were islanded on its floors in seas of linoleum or stained boards. The plumbing was antique and the wiring unreliable. Harold and Dolly and Pup were not interested in homemaking or housekeeping. They did almost nothing about celebrating Christmas. Pup put up some paper chains in the dining room but no one bothered to take them down and they were still there in March when Edith died. There was snow on the ground and it lay untrodden, virgin, a gleaming white avenue of it, on the old railway line. Dolly fed the birds with cake crumbs that she put on an old bookcase outside the kitchen window and threw a brick at Mrs Brewer's cat when it came after them. She didn't hit it but would one day; she hated that cat, all cats, and one day she would get that one.

Mrs Buxton came in, wearing Wellington boots that had to be cut at the tops, her legs were so fat.

'I just wanted to say how sorry I am about your mother, dear. I know what she meant to you, she was more than a mother if that's possible. And your poor

7

little brother, I feel for him. Fancy, you've still got paper chains up in March.'

Pup had been sixteen in February but you felt he was younger than he was because he was so small. He was quiet and kind and polite and made no demur when Dolly got him to kiss her before he went off to school and kiss her again when he came in. The mantle of Edith's maternity had slipped on to her shoulders and she was suddenly more maternal than Edith had ever been. She worried over him, wondering why he was so contained and reserved.

He had measured himself on 18 January and 18 February and each time he had grown a little. On 18 March he was five feet one inch tall. He bought himself a paperback he saw on a stand about how to do magic. Faustus had been able to make gold, conjure apparitions, perform feats of trickery. More and more these days he was identifying with Faustus, though a healthy scepticism went on telling him his new growth was just chance.

'I shall never get over it,' Harold said after Edith's funeral at Golders Green. 'She was all the world to me. I shall never get over it.'

Dolly got him a new biography of the last Tsarina out of the library but it was twenty-four hours before he felt able to start on it. He refused to sleep in the bedroom he and Edith had shared but moved into the other first-floor front one and said he was going to have *her* room kept exactly as it was. This was what Queen Victoria had done for Prince Albert when he died. Dolly had to make the bed up and turn down the sheet and drape one of Edith's nightdresses across it, although Edith herself had never lived like this, had rolled her nightdress up under the pillow and often hadn't made the bed at all.

Mrs Collins, for whom Dolly was finishing a dress

Edith had started before she went into hospital, said it brought tears to your eyes to see him. Entering the house, she had surprised Harold going off upstairs with a book about the Almanach de Gotha, had supposed it was the Bible and his destination his late wife's room. Mrs Collins was religious in a curious sort of way, a member, indeed a leading light, of the Adonai Church of God Spiritists at Mount Pleasant Green.

'He ought to come to us,' said Mrs Collins. 'She's bound to want to come through to him from the Other Side.'

'She's more likely to want *me*,' said Dolly through a mouthful of pins, going round Mrs Collins' hem on her knees. 'You ought to ask me.'

'We do ask you, dear,' Mrs Collins said. 'We invite all human souls,' as if Dolly were some kind of freak who could just lay claim to that definition.

Pup got off the bus at Highgate tube station and walked home along the old railway line. In one hand he carried his school briefcase, in the other a plastic carrier containing the paper and paints and drawing pins and Blu-tak he had bought in Muswell Hill. It was 18 July, a fine summer's day. Pup wore clean blue jeans, a clean white shirt and a lightweight grey zipper jacket. Dolly would have liked him to wear grey flannels but Pup, who was easy about most things, insisted on jeans. Nor would he let her make them for him. Levi's, they had to be like others wore, or FUs or Wranglers. He had come this way because he liked the old railway line but also to avoid the company of his friend Dilip Raj and certain others who went to his school and also lived in Manningtree Grove or its environs.

There were a lot of people on the line this afternoon, mostly children sitting on the parapets of

9

bridges, but grown-ups as well: a young man who walked along kicking a tin, finally kicking it over the parapet at Northwood Road and down into the street below, and women walking dogs. Pup paused to stroke the noble head of a Pyrennean mountain dog being walked from Milton Park to Stanhope Road and back. The sun shone in a bland, hazy sky and all the buddleia bushes were in flower, a mass of long purple spires on which here and there alighted a peacock or small tortoiseshell butterfly. They were getting rare, those butterflies now, but sometimes you saw them up on the old line when the bushes were in bloom.

Just before the Mistley tunnel he climbed up the bank through the long grass and hawthorn seedlings, the yellow flowering ragwort and the pink flowering campion and the paper and Coke cans. He let himself in by the garden gate. Dolly was waiting for him, like a mother or a wife, holding out the unmarked cheek for a kiss. He kissed her. He would have kissed the other cheek, for he felt no revulsion. Dolly picked up a stone from the heap she kept on the window sill and hurled it at Mrs Brewer's cat.

'You ought to throw earth,' said Pup. 'You might hurt it.'

'It walks all over my plants,' said Dolly, though there were no plants in the garden worth mentioning, only Solomon's seal and enchanter's nightshade and, in their season, some anaemic Michaelmas daisies. 'What did you do at school today?' Dolly often asked him this, believing it a mother's duty to ask and forgetting he was sixteen.

'Differential calculus,' said Pup gravely. He had very little idea what this was but hearing that sort of thing made Dolly happy. He had begun, half-consciously, half-unconsciously, on a course of keeping Dolly happy.

10

'It sounds difficult. Is that what your homework is?'

'That and Finno-Ugrian languages,' said Pup, applying himself to salami, Cornish pasty, piccalilli, cole slaw and Battenburg cake.

Bags in hand again, he was going down the cavernous hall (the walls painted dark green to the halfway mark and pale green at the top like an old-fashioned hospital or even workhouse, the floor quarry-tiled in red and black) when his father let himself in at the front door. All the years of his marriage, the first thing Harold ever said when he came in was that he was worn out. Pup greeted him in his usual polite, friendly way.

'Hallo, Dad. Had a good day?'

'I don't know about good,' said Harold. 'I know I'm worn out.'

Pup went upstairs to his room. It was hot and stuffy and he opened the window. He took off his shoes. Today he felt no very great trepidation, for he could tell by the shortness of his jeans that he had grown, but even he had not hoped for five feet three. Five feet three. He was really growing and was no longer the shortest boy of his year. Dilip Raj and Christopher Theofanou were both shorter than him.

He put his shoes on again and took the drawing materials out of the bag. With the magic book open before him at a page of diagrams, he began to outline a crescent shape on one of the sheets of cartridge paper. He had four sheets of paper, one for each of the four elements, one to go on each wall of the room on the top floor he had marked out for his temple.

He was going to be a magician.

11

Chapter 2

'Will you make me a robe?' Pup said.

'D'you mean a bathrobe?'

Pup shook his head. 'Come upstairs. I want to show you something.'

'I see,' said Dolly like a cross mother. 'I suppose it's that room you won't let me go in. I know you locked the door and took away the key. Now his lordship thinks it's time to open up, does he?' She tossed her head. 'I don't know if I can spare the time.'

Pup gave her his sweet smile. 'Yes, you can, dear.' Sometimes he called her dear and she loved it. The caressing word melted her. 'You know you'll come. You'll like it.'

'Oh, all right.'

They seldom went up there. Or rather, Dolly corrected herself as they climbed the last flight, *she* seldom went up there. Once these top rooms had been servants' bedrooms, or so Edith had told her, but had anyone in Crouch End ever had servants? It was Dark Ages stuff to Dolly. There were five rooms, low-ceilinged, the walls all papered in strange faded patterns (bunches of pallid sweet peas on spotty mauve, daisies tied with blue ribbon on yellowish stripes), the floors lino'd, pink or fawn or blue, odd bits of furniture standing about, a bed, a pier-glass, a wardrobe on legs with an oval mirror. She ran a mop over the floors twice a year, flicked a duster. That was how she knew he had locked the door of one of the rooms at the back. It was strange having these empty, scarcely known rooms in one's own house, as if it wasn't one's own. A shadow crossed Dolly's mind. Sometimes she had these premonitions.

Pup unlocked the door of the back room. Dolly gasped. The daisies on the yellow stripes were gone. Pup had painted over them in matt black. The ceiling was red. Under the window Dolly recognized from its shape an old bamboo card table that had been in the sweet pea room, but Pup had covered it with a black cloth. Each of the four black walls had pinned to it a sheet of paper with a design on it. On the north wall was a yellow square for earth, on the east a blue circle for air, on the south a red equilateral triangle, apex upwards, for fire, and on the west a silver crescent for water.

'They are *tattwas*,' said Pup. 'They are the symbols of the four elements. I'm going to do magic.' He could tell by her face what she was thinking. 'Not conjuring tricks, I don't mean that, not rabbits out of hats.' One by one, he took his books off the table and showed them to her: Eliphas Levi, A. E. Waite, Crowley. 'It's a kind of science,' he said, knowing that would get her. 'It takes years of study. I think I might have a gift for it.'

Dolly said nothing. She had opened one of the books at random and was reading the words of an incantation so esoteric and abstruse, so protracted and complex, that it seemed to her a person would have to be an intellectual giant to comprehend it.

'You can forget it if you don't want to know,' said Pup. 'You don't have to be in on it.'

'Oh, I want to be in on it,' Dolly said hastily. 'If it takes years of study, d'you have to go to college?' She was ambitious for him; she didn't want him to go into the business with Harold. This might be the answer. 'What can you *be* when you've done it?'

Pup nearly laughed. 'It's not what you'll be, it's what you can do. You can get yourself what you want, anything you want.' Doubt and hope were mingled in Dolly's expression. 'So will you make me a robe? I want a golden robe with a black sun and moon and stars sort of stuck on it.'

'Appliquéd,' said Dolly. She suddenly realized he was taller than she. It must have happened very recently. She felt a tender pride in him. 'Let's go down and see what I've got. I've got a dress length of gold polyester I got in John Lewis's sale. That might do.'

Dolly was at the machine in the front-room window, stitching the side seams of the golden robe when she saw Myra Brewer walking along the pavement on the other side of the privet hedge. Myra was going to visit her mother as she always did on Thursday evenings. Passing under the overhanging branches of the two ginkgo trees which grew in the Yearmans' garden, she put up her hand and plucked off a handful of the maidenhair-fern-shaped leaves. Myra was one of those people who are unable to walk under overhanging leaves without snatching at a bunch of them. Those Brewers, Dolly thought, including the cat among 'those Brewers', were always damaging her property. She banged on the window but Myra had already gone by. No one had hair that red, not even Edith's had been that red, Myra must put henna on it. Dolly heard the next-door door slam as Myra let herself in.

'I thought you were never coming,' said Mrs Brewer as her daughter made a pot of tea she wouldn't put herself out to make.

'You always say that. You always say, "Aren't you late?" or "I thought you were never coming."'

'If I say it, it's because it's true. You always are late except when he brings you in his car. Where is he tonight? Home with wifey, I suppose.'

Myra could have cried when her mother talked to her like that. It was all true. He was at home with wifey and she was thirty-seven and her hair looked awful if she didn't put henna on it. She had been in the ladies' loo at West End Green on the way here and there had been this graffiti on the wall that said: 'The quietest thing on earth is the sound of hair going grey.'

'It's no good looking like that,' said Mrs Brewer, putting cream in her tea the way she had done when a girl in Devonshire. 'It's no good getting down in the mouth. You can talk all you like about the second half of the twentieth century and all that but human nature doesn't change. You should have seen the writing on the wall when his boys went to boarding school and he didn't divorce her then.'

Myra said nothing. She had had enough writing on walls for one day.

'There's that little bitch with the birthmark throwing stones at Fluffy again,' said Mrs Brewer.

Fluffy was a long-coated tabby that Mrs Brewer called a Persian. Sometimes he sat on the post between the Yearmans' front fence and the house next door. Mrs Brewer had the ground-floor flat and the people on the next floor and the people on the top floor all had cats, though only Fluffy sat on the post. Dolly said there were more cats in Crouch End than in all the rest of London put together.

'Well, there are more mice in London than people,' said Pup who knew about things like that.

Edith used to tidy up the front garden in the autumn, cut down the Michaelmas daisies, pull out the enchanter's nightshade and sweep up the leaves. Dolly supposed she would have to do it now. Wearing the cotton gloves that had been her mother's, using Edith's secateurs and Edith's small red-and-silver painted trowel brought her mother most forcefully back to her. She could almost see her when she closed her eyes, that thin, pinched face, that fiery red hair, and smell the lemon verbena toilet water she used. The tears came into her eyes. She began furiously digging out weeds.

Fluffy came tightrope-walking along the fence, did his claw-scraping act up the side of the post and then sat on top of it. Dolly looked up at him while he was scraping and again when he settled down. Manningtree Grove was long and straight and fairly wide in spite of the cars parked nose-to-tail along it, and motorists used it as a through route between Crouch End Hill and Stroud Green. Cars went down it very fast, especially the ones driven by boys of seventeen and eighteen. Dolly heard a car coming as it bounded over the hump where Mistley Avenue went across. She knew what she was doing and yet she did not quite know; her intention was half-fantasy. She leapt to her feet, clapped her hands and shouted out. Fluffy jumped off the post and fled across the road.

Dolly heard the car roar by, without a pause, with no sound of brakes. It had been going very fast; they thought nothing of driving at fifty down there. She waited for Fluffy to come back, to scrape the post and then sit on it. She even selected a stone to throw at him. After a little while she laid down the trowel and got up and went down the path, through the gate, out on to the pavement and looked. Fluffy lay near the gutter on the opposite side of the street between the front bumper of a red Datsun and the rear bumper of a green Volvo. Dolly went across the road. He was dead, limp, though still very warm. A little blood was coming from the corner of his mouth but otherwise he was unmarked. The impact had killed him and flung him there. Dolly felt rather sick. She went back indoors and washed her hands.

Mrs Brewer had been out at the time. She found the corpse during the evening and sat down and cried. She tried to get Myra on the phone but Myra was out somewhere with the married man. Dolly, who seldom drank before the evening, not before 5.30 anyway, had to have a glass of wine and then another after the Fluffy incident. An Indian woman called Mrs Das who lived in the flat above Mrs Buxton had heard Dolly yell and seen Fluffy flee and she told Mrs Brewer about it. This was not because she liked cats – indeed, where she came from they outlawed cats, believing their bodies to be inhabited by the spirits of dead witches – but because Mrs Brewer was one of the few people in the neighbourhood, apart from other Indians, who condescended to speak to her. Dolly never spoke and Mrs Das wasn't to know Dolly hardly ever spoke to anyone.

There was no way of proving it and nothing overt Mrs Brewer could do. But she told everybody she knew.

'Her mother was as nice a woman as you'd meet,' said Mrs Buxton. 'Your Myra reminds me of her in a way.'

Myra had never seen Edith Yearman. She had already been ill before Mrs Brewer came to live there. 'In *what* way?'

'The hair for a start. The eyes. Of course Myra's a lot heavier built, she'd need to fine down a bit.'

'Charming,' said Myra to her mother. 'That's the pot calling the kettle black.'

Mrs Brewer took no notice. 'She must be sick in her mind, murdering a person's pet.'

*

17

It seemed to Pup that he had probably stopped growing for good. He had been seventeen in February and five feet seven and he was still five feet seven. No Yearman, as far as he knew, had ever been so tall and he was satisfied. In the golden robe, appliquéd with sun, moon and stars, he made quite a commanding figure.

According to Eliphas Levi, author of *The Doctrine and Ritual of Transcendental Magic*, the magician may buy a knife for use as his dagger, providing he uses this knife to manufacture his other elemental weapons. Pup bought a knife in the big ironmongers in Muswell Hill and painted the hilt of it with the name Lucifer and also with the archangelic name of fire. He could use the knife to make his wand and perhaps his pentacle but he was doubtful about carving a cup.

On the old railway line, the bushes and the branches of the trees were still bare. It had been a cold spring. Harold had had the flu and Dolly had had it mildly and it had swept through Pup's school and now Mrs Brewer had it. Mrs Brewer was fat and ageing and her flu turned to bronchitis. Myra came to stay. She kept on with her job as part-time receptionist to a dentist in Camden Town, but she was there in the evenings and overnight. It was years since she had worked full-time. The afternoons were the best times for the married man to get away.

'He won't miss you,' said Mrs Brewer, wheezing. 'He'll have a chance to catch up on things with wifey.'

'I don't know why you're so cruel to me after all I do for you,' said Myra.

'There's a saying in the Bible about being cruel only to be kind. You've got nothing, d'you realize that? Not even a roof over your head. That little bitch with the birthmark that murdered Fluffy has got more than you have and she's half your age. At least that's her father's house.'

'He owns that great place? All of it?'

'All of it, miss. And a nice little business in the Broadway. Hodge and Yearman, Typewriters and Instant Print. I'm surprised you haven't noticed it when you've been passing through in *his* car.'

'All right, Mother, for Christ's sake. Now you've started yourself off coughing.'

Very early in the morning Pup and Dolly went together down on to the old railway line to find a tree branch for Pup's magic wand. Eliphas Levi, said Pup, suggested that the wand should be a perfectly straight branch of almond or hazel, cut at a single blow with the magical pruning knife or golden sickle, before the rising of the sun, at that moment when the tree is ready to blossom. He had with him his dagger with the painted hilt, ready for cutting the wand from the tree.

It was a cool clear London morning and the old railway line was as green as a country lane. The grass and the budding trees were drenched with bright, cold, glistening dew. Dolly had hardly ever seen the dawn but she guessed that, just as the sky is flooded with gold after the sun has set, so it may be before the sun rises. Between bars of darkish cloud, the sky was livid. Birds had been singing, a concentrated, unmusical twittering, since long before they climbed down the embankment.

Pup knew when the sun would rise, he had a sense about these things. Neither of them was entirely sure they could tell an almond or a hazel tree when they saw one, though Pup said it was faith and love which counted more than accuracy. They walked through the Mistley tunnel and along the channel between the weed-grown platforms which were all that now remained of a station that had once been there –

Mount Pleasant Green. They had plenty of time and they walked nearly all the way to Tollington Road, over bridges and through tunnels, on the dewy turf, before they found a tree Pup said must be a hazel. From this tree, as the yellow of the sky began to brighten, he cut with a bold sweep of his arm a slender wand hung with golden catkins.

They walked back the way they had come. The air was not yet tainted with the fumes that would soon come drifting from the traffic passing under and passing over. Along the old railway line you could smell pale green tree flowers breaking into blossom, you could smell the new grass and the cow parsley that sprang up to cover the rank wet newspaper, the empty cans, the broken bottles, the feathers and the cigarette ends. It was cool and fresh, the sun blazing now but cold as midwinter.

Dolly wore her lion's mane hair in a style designed half to cover her face. She had a tweed suit on and a red wool jersey, both homemade (though few would have guessed it), and sensible brown hide walking shoes. From time to time she glanced at Pup, who carried his wand like a pilgrim's staff, with love and pride and hope. He had the same lion hair as her but he wore it just to the tips of his ears and this gave him a look of earnest innocence. His face was a long oval and he had the long straight nose and full lips of a saint or perhaps merely a bystander in certain medieval paintings. He was very thin and light on his feet. Although he wore jeans and a sweater and a jacket he somehow gave the impression, so contained and neatly made as he was, of being dressed much more formally.

It was just after half-past seven when they turned the corner into Manningtree Grove. Dolly had not wanted to risk her tights on the embankment again, so they had got off the old railway line by going up the steps in Mount Pleasant Gardens. Harold must have come out to take the milk in, for he stood on the front garden path, a milk bottle cradled like a child in each arm, like twin babies, talking over the fence to Myra Brewer.

With an instinctive gesture that was almost a reflex, Dolly drew the curtain of hair across her cheek. She looked but said nothing. Myra Brewer was wearing a bright green blouse and a green-and-navy check skirt and her gold watch and some gold chains and had on her full panoply of make-up, enough, in fact, for going on a television chat show under powerful lights.

'Good morning, Myra,' said Pup who had never been introduced to her but who happened to know what her first name was.

Myra said hallo. Pup smiled gently at his father, gave Dolly the hazel wand to hold, and took the milk bottles out of Harold's arms as if they were too heavy a load for him or an impediment to his continued conversation. Later that day, after school, he stripped the catkins and the leaf buds from the hazel branch and painted it yellow. He painted a black spiral round it and inscribed upon it the name of Lucifer. Dolly gave him a glass tumbler, the last remaining one of a crystal water set, and he used this for the cup, painting the name of Lucifer on it and the archangelic name for the element of water. The pentacle was more difficult. At last he found a shop in Hornsey where the man agreed to cut him a plywood circle. Pup told him he wanted it for backing a mirror.

Dolly was invited to attend the ceremony of the consecration of the elemental weapons. At his request, she brought him a glass of red wine, a slice of bread and a saucerful of salt. He needed a rose too but they had none in the garden, so Dolly waited till it was dark and stuck her hand through the fence and picked a bud from Mrs Buxton's Rose Gaujard which was just coming out. Pup made his own holy water. Facing towards the north, standing to the south of his altar, he extended his hand over the saucer of salt and chanted:

'May wisdom abide in this salt and may it preserve my mind and body from all corruption. May all phantoms depart from it so that it may become a heavenly salt, salt of earth and earth of salt. May it feed the threshing ox and strengthen my hope with the horns of the winged bull! So mote it be.'

He had got it out of a book but he had learned it by heart. Mixing the salt and some joss-stick ash into the water made it holy. Dolly sat on a cushion on the floor, watching him, feeling a deep thrill of excitement. Pup walked round in a circle with the glass of holy water, sprinkling it to the four quarters of the temple. He lit a joss stick and walked round again, saying:

'And when after all the phantoms are vanished, thou shalt see the holy formless fire, that fire which darts and flashes through the hidden depths of the universe, hear, thou Voice of Fire.'

There was a great deal more. It went on for two hours and Dolly loved every minute of it. As he raised his arms and the golden sleeves hung like pennants, Pup's face was rapt, his eyes glowing with hieratic fervour. He was obsessed with magic these days, he admitted it himself. He read nothing but books on magic which might have accounted for his failure to get more than three poorish 'O' levels and made it seem unlikely that his 'A' levels would be much better, always supposing he stayed on long enough to do them. The word 'magician' had a frivolous or even charlatanish ring to it, so Pup called himself a geomancer.

'Can you be a geomancer without "A" levels?' asked Dolly who seemed to think it was something like going into computers or being a physicist.

Pup did not disillusion her. He was beginning to see that by Edith's death he had lost a cook and housekeeper and gained a mother. It seemed a long time ago now that he had cut his thumb and parted with his soul to the devil, a very long time since he had asked for anything. Wearing the robe, holding the dagger in his hands, he stood before his altar and asked for his own version of what Faustus had desired: a successful career, magical powers, wealth, Helen of Troy – but a Helen many times multiplied and to have, not merely to see and snatch at in vain.

Chapter 3

In a house at the Stroud Green end of Mount Pleasant Gardens, facing what remained of the old green and opposite the meeting place of the Adonai Church of God Spiritists, Diarmit Bawne sat in his room on the top floor. It was a so-called double room because it contained two beds, though it was no more than ten feet by fifteen. The other bed had been occupied by a kind of family connection of Diarmit's called Conal Moore, and when Conal had gone away he had promised to come back, but he had still not come back after three weeks and Diarmit was waiting for him anxiously. Diarmit had no work and no home but this room and knew hardly anyone in London. Fortunately, there was the Department of Health and Social Security to keep him and pay the rent of the room.

These days Diarmit spent a lot of time sitting at the window looking down into the street and at Mount Pleasant Green across which he expected Conal Moore to come because that was the direction in which Crouch Hill station was. The green was deserted and had been for some time except for the pigeons, and the Dalmatian and the mongrel collie that half-heartedly chased the pigeons and scavenged from the litter bins. Diarmit made himself a cup of tea in a mug with a teabag and powdered milk. Conal had left two large tins of powdered milk in the room and three large boxes of teabags and some noodles and curry stuff you added hot water to to make a meal but he had left nothing else of his, not even any of his clothes. Diarmit wished he would come back because he was growing more and more frightened of being alone. He knew no one in the house and it was several days since he had spoken a word to anyone or anyone had spoken to him. He sat in the window and drank his tea, watching the Dalmatian and the collie, watching the chestnut leaves falling on to the wet green grass.

He was twenty-four, the youngest of twelve children. When he was nine in County Armagh, his mother had been killed by a bomb intended for a Member of Parliament whose house she cleaned. Diarmit saw the bomb go off and he saw what happened to his mother, though he was not injured, or not apparently injured, himself. His father, long before, had gone to America 'to see what it was like', had seen and never come back. Diarmit's brothers and sisters were scattered about the British Isles. First he went to his eldest sister in Dublin but she had seven children of her own and an extra one was too much for her, so he was passed on to divide his time between his two sisters in Liverpool.

He had a brother in Belfast, a butcher with his own shop, the most successful and well-to-do of the Bawnes. When he was sixteen, Diarmit was sent back to Belfast to live with his brother and learn his trade. He was there two years. Then the whole street, including the shop, was bombed one day and the opposite side reduced to rubble. Neither the butcher nor Diarmit was hurt but Diarmit vanished and was found some days later, wandering in the countryside twenty miles away, having lost the power of speech and his memory.

After that he spent nearly a year in a mental hospital, though he was never certified. He came out, returned to Liverpool and resumed the existence of moving from one sister to the other. Neither wanted him. Family conferences were held to discuss the big question of what was to be done with Diarmit, what permanent job could be got for him, where was he permanently to live. The army was considered as a possibility, work on the land, bus driving, security officer, traffic warden. His mental history was against him; there was that black-out, that year in the hospital, that loss of speech that had afflicted him on several later occasions. He lived more or less always on the dole. Sometimes he had doubts as to whether he actually existed at all, and these were particularly strong when his speech failed him or when his sisters, exasperated, ignored his presence or their children acted as if any room in which he was was an empty room.

Conal Moore was his sister Mary's brother-in-law. He lived in London and worked for Budgen's on the delicatessen counter. Everybody in the family and everybody connected with the family was rooting for something for Diarmit, just to get him off Mary's back, so it was welcome news to hear from Conal, though it was no great surprise. Conal said he could get Diarmit a job on the butchery counter, after all that was Diarmit's line, and if he liked to come down he could share his place for a bit till he found somewhere.

Diarmit had come to Mount Pleasant Gardens and found a note waiting for him and the key to the room. The note and the key were on the table in the downstairs hall where all the tenants' correspondence was put. Diarmit could read his own name on the note but nothing else. He was better with print, for instance he could make out a lot of what was in a newspaper, but handwriting defeated him. He had let himself into the room and ever since then he had been waiting for Conal to come back and he had been wondering what was in the note.

The note was in his pocket. He carried it about with him. He had a sister living in London. Her name was Kathleen, she was married and she lived in Kilburn. Every day Diarmit meant to go and see Kathleen so that she could read Conal's note to him and so that he might have someone to talk to and be with. But every day it became harder and harder for him to do this, a now nearly impossible feat of effort and endurance. He had been to Kilburn, it was easy to get there from Mount Pleasant Green, you took the train from Crouch Hill to Brondesbury, it was easy to get there and he had got as far as walking along the road where Kathleen lived but he had not gone up to the house to knock at the door. He was too afraid. Sometimes he thought it would be better if he walked there instead, it would not be so quick and sudden as going by train.

When he had finished his tea he put on his jacket and went downstairs and out of the house. He walked across the green towards Crouch End. There was a Budgen's supermarket at Crouch End and another at Muswell Hill but neither had a butchery counter. Perhaps there were others he didn't know about, he couldn't ask, he didn't know what to ask or how to frame the words.

It was a coldish, dull, negative sort of day in autumn. He went into Budgen's and bought a single item, a loaf of bread. It puzzled him that there was no butchery counter, only a section where pre-packed cuts of meat were on sale. He said thank you to the girl at the check-out but she said nothing to him. He wondered if she could see him or hear him, and he thought of giving a sudden loud shout but he was too afraid to do that. Never before had he been alone like this, but somehow always involved, for good or ill, with his large family.

He came out once more into the raw grey afternoon. There were a lot of people in Crouch End Broadway, slouching along or scurrying or marching fast, regardless of the small and timid in their path. Their faces were sullen and hostile or indifferent. Now he had bought the loaf he knew he wouldn't go to Kathleen's, he would go back to Mount Pleasant Gardens and wait for Conal Moore.

A woman in a fur coat walking ahead of him dropped a plastic carrier bag into the litter bin attached to a lamp-post. Diarmit turned his head this way and that to see if anyone was looking and then he took the carrier bag out again and put his loaf in it. It was a shiny olive-green bag with the name 'Harrods' written on it in gold. He walked back across the green, carrying a small, sliced, wrapped white loaf in a Harrods bag and the pigeons flapped and scuttered out of his way.

Chapter 4

At the end of the autumn term, Pup left school. He left on a Thursday and on the Monday set off with Harold in the morning to work at Hodge and Yearman. Jimmy Hodge, who Harold had been in business with for thirty years, had just retired.

Dolly was cross about it and disappointed. She wanted him to get his 'A' levels and go to a university. He had read so many books and learned so much and spent so much time in the temple and now it would all go to waste.

'It won't go to waste,' said Pup. 'I shall do it in my spare time, I shall do it in the evenings.'

While he was at work, Dolly borrowed some of his books and tried to read them. The subject was immense and her brain reeled. The Philosopher's Stone, the Ancient Mysteries, the Qabala, Dr Dee and Helena Blavatsky, Magnetism and the Golden Flower – from all this she was able only to isolate and establish that the adept, the magus, once he had learned it all, might achieve anything he desired and have anything he wished. It was a science right enough, thought Dolly, to whom this signified a study that required protracted concentration and the learning of thousands of facts. What other science could be so complicated and so taxing to the mind? Dolly read about the magical Order of the Golden Dawn, that group or circle of magicians, founded in 1888, to which, it seemed, all the great names that figured in this pile of books had belonged. She imagined him one day as another Waite or Regardie, world-famous as the author of some such weighty textbook as one of these.

Pup himself was as keen as any student might be, embarking on the long training for a professional career. He and Harold came home from work together, sometimes calling in at the Haringey Central Library to change Harold's books; they had their tea and then, when Harold retreated to the breakfast room with the memoirs of a princess of Thurn und Taxis or went out on one of his mysterious trips, presumably to a pub, Pup would go up to the temple. He was obsessed with magic, it was an all-absorbing craze with him as football was to some of his contemporaries. The occult had him in its grip. He could hardly wait to get into the golden robe and begin an incantation or make divinations with the tarot cards or settle down to the study of etheric projection.

He cast horoscopes and he made talismans. He went back to the shop where the man had cut him the plywood for the pentacle and got him to cut out in metal two small polygonal shapes and pierce a hole in each. Dolly was a Venusian subject, so her talisman was a seven-sided pendant which he painted green and the letters on it red as was correct. For this, he had to use 'virgin' instruments, unused before, bought new for the purpose, the brush, the paint, the thong.

'And I'm a virgin,' said Pup.

Dolly nodded her head vigorously. That was how it should be. The magical powers were enhanced by virginity. Time after time, instructions in the books for performing a certain evocation or banishing ritual stressed that the magician should be chaste. It made Dolly happy that Pup never looked at a girl. He had friends of his own sex, sometimes he went to their homes, he went out for a drink occasionally with Chris Theofanou, but he had no eyes for girls. Carefully, almost reverently, she hung the talisman he had made her round her neck. It would keep away harm, he said, it would protect her from evil powers.

Quite often he invited her into the temple to watch him perform a particular rite. She covered some cushions in scarlet and gold and black material and on these she sat, watching him with awe and admiration. But he didn't always want her there and she never invited herself, she wouldn't put herself forward. It was enough for her to know he was making progress, that he was not like so many other boys of his age but was up there, quietly applying himself to his studies.

Sitting downstairs in the front room, pinning on a pattern or working the sewing machine, Dolly thought how proud their mother would have been if she could have seen him and known what he was doing. Perhaps she could see and did know. It was missing her mother that made Dolly go to the Adonai Church of God Spiritists.

Mrs Brewer had a new cat, a ginger-and-white kitten that was too wise ever to go near the road or even into the front garden. It stayed in the back, prowling across conservatory roofs and hunting on the old railway line. Dolly kept a pile of stones on the old bookcase outside the kitchen window to hurl at it when it came into her garden, just as she had done in the days of Fluffy.

She wore her talisman for her first visit to Mount Pleasant Hall. Although she knew by sight many of the people who attended and could see that not one of them had any claim to elegance or style, she dressed herself with care. Dolly felt that if she could only be well enough dressed, well enough groomed, there must come a point where people would observe this alone and the naevus pass unnoticed. She wore the dress and coat she had just finished making for herself in tweed of a smart olive-drab shade. At the neck she tied a little vermilion silk scarf and hung on the pendant so that it showed between the lapels of the coat. She had chosen the tweed and the scarf particularly to complement the talisman.

No one in Manningtree Grove and its environs dressed as well as her except perhaps some of the young black girls going off to catch trains in the mornings. And yet, as she seldom went out, all this elegance was wasted on shopping in Crouch End Broadway or down the Holloway Road. This was the first time she had been out in the evening for she didn't know how long.

Before leaving she had drunk a tumblerful of wine to give her courage but, even so, being out alone at this hour filled her with unease. She had those agoraphobic sensations not uncommon in house-bound, withdrawn people. She felt exposed and vulnerable and threatened. The people who were about in the evening were a different set from those she encountered shopping in the mornings and they seemed to her to have more curious eyes and less guarded expressions. Dolly had no friends. Pup didn't count, he was her child. Her mother had been her friend and her mother was dead. She wondered how she would feel when, in the next hour or so perhaps, she heard her mother's voice.

But in the event it was very different. No more than a dozen people came for the seance and that included Mrs Collins and her daughter Wendy and the medium. The hall was a not very large room with a small curtained-off stage at one end. There were green roller blinds at the windows and coconut matting on the floor. Mrs Collins was wearing the navy blue suit she called a costume that Dolly had made her. She smiled in a way Dolly knew that wearing it was meant as a compliment to her. Wendy was fat and long-chinned and well over thirty but she had no birthmark on her right cheek.

They all sat in a row on rush-bottomed tip-up chairs. Mrs Collins switched off the uncompromising, high-wattage overhead light and turned on the table lamp she had brought, plugged in on yards of lead to somewhere at the back of the stage. The medium was an old woman, fatter even than Wendy, and had a somewhat more comfortable chair in which, as soon as everyone was seated, she went promptly into a trance.

After a while, people began to come through with messages: an old friend for Wendy Collins, an aunt for a Miss Finlay. They spoke through the medium's lips in strangled whispers. It was not frightening, not exciting, not even *believable*. Edith's voice didn't sound like Edith. It was too soft and lugubrious.

'Dear daughter, I am always near you, I watch you taking care of Peter and my beloved husband . . . '

Edith had never spoken like that. Dolly felt indignant that the medium should be such a fraud, callously deluding people, and then, simultaneously with that thought, there came to her a breath of perfume, of lemon verbena. She almost cried out, so powerful for a brief moment was this scent of her dead mother.

It was gone in an instant, the medium was waking and the Adonai Spiritists were preparing to leave. Dolly was trembling from the shock that scent had given her. It seemed to prove the truth of what she had read in Pup's books.

During the seance it had grown dark outside. The

yellow and white street lamps were on and a single white lamp shone in the centre of Mount Pleasant Green. It would not have occurred to her to feel frightened to walk home in the dark on her own. But in the little vestibule where the notice boards were between the inner glass doors and the outer doors, a woman touched her sleeve, said she was Miss Finlay and might they walk home together? Dolly nodded and followed her out. At the touch she had smelt lemon verbena again. It was Miss Finlay's scent, that was all, it was Miss Finlay's lemon scent that she had smelt all the time.

Miss Finlay scurried along as if pursued and Dolly had to take long strides to keep up with her. As they walked Dolly thought about that scent and about her mother's voice sounding so soft and low-pitched and Miss Finlay talked about how wonderful the seance had been and how amazing the medium.

'It must be marvellous to have powers.'

Dolly felt affronted. 'My brother has *real* powers. He does magic.'

'What, like sticking pins in a wax image?'

'Of course not, nothing like that. He's a geo-mancer, it's scientific.'

Miss Finlay giggled. Dolly was very offended and when Miss Finlay said she was looking for a dressmaker, she wanted a velvet skirt made, she merely shrugged and said she was in the phone book. They were outside the Yearmans' house and Dolly pushed the gate open. Nervous Miss Finlay had another half mile to walk up to Crescent Road all on her own. Dolly said good night absently. This was not the companion she was looking for, the friend that would make her forget her birthmark in the excitement of their meeting.

Pup must be in the temple. The landing light on the top floor was on. Dolly let herself into the house and without taking her coat off, went straight to the kitchen. There was an open bottle of Soave in the larder and she needed a glass of it. The second shock of the evening was when she opened the door and found the light on and Harold sitting at the table with Myra Brewer, two cans of Double Diamond and two bags of crisps between them.

Harold gave Dolly a sheepish grin.

'Tell her our news, Hal,' said Myra.

He did so. Dolly listened to the halting, embarrassed, rather shamefaced announcement in silence. She was going to say she didn't believe it but that wasn't true; she found she had no difficulty at all in believing it. Still without speaking, she went back into the hall and closed the kitchen door.

Then, having taken a deep breath and clenched her fists, she ran upstairs to tell Pup.

Chapter 5

'The top floor,' Myra said, 'would make quite a nice flat for Peter and Doreen.'

Harold was unused to hearing his children called by their given names and he almost had to think who it was she meant. They were walking about the house, thinking what changes would have to be made when they were married. Or Myra was thinking of these things. Harold had supposed he and she would simply go along to some register office, presumably the Wood Green one, and get through the requisite very few words after which he would be a married man again. He was used to being married, found it difficult to sleep without a woman in his bed and hoped to resume the state with the minimum of upheaval. He considered what Myra had said and it seemed to him a tremendous step, comparable to changing one's trade or emigrating.

'I don't know about that,' he said. When he used this phrase he meant not that he was ignorant on the subject but that he had doubts of its wisdom or feasibility.

'It seems so peculiar, a grown-up son and daughter living at home.'

'I lived at home till I got married.' And after, he might have added.

'Well, in those days . . .' Harold was fifteen years older than her, and she thought of herself as a girl;

'He's a widower, he's got children practically my age,' she was inclined to say when speaking of her future husband. 'They could have a bedroom each and the front room for a lounge. I don't see why we shouldn't put in a kitchen, a sink and water heater really, that's all that's needed. I don't mind paying, I'll use my Unit Trusts.'

'You'll have to tell them. I can't.'

Harold avoided everything disagreeable. It was to this negative aim that he devoted his energies. Walking half a mile to work, poking about in the shop all day (he knew a great deal about type-writers), going home again – he did not object to any of that. He liked having a big house to spread himself in, though he never spread himself much, mooching between the kitchen, the breakfast room and the once-sacred bedroom. He liked living in the house in which he had been born, the only place he had ever lived in. His leisure he devoted to reading what he called 'history books', biographies of the more colourful characters in history such as Mary Queen of Scots, Nell Gwynn and the Prince Regent (never Cromwell, Robespierre or Palmerston) and the memoirs of princelings and princesslings of nineteenth-century European minor royal houses. As a result of this, he was actually an authority, not, as he believed, on history itself, but on the myth and legend of history.

In the end he had to tell them. Myra wasn't there to do it. She was packing up in West Hampstead, telling the married man she had had a better offer, thank you very much, and when he had gone, crying herself to sleep.

Dreading it, loathing the idea of it, working himself up to a pitch of fear and shame, which was the exaggerated state he always got into if he had to exert himself or be candid, Harold falteringly told his daughter that Myra wanted her and Pup to move upstairs. As is generally so in these cases, Dolly took it much better than had been expected. She didn't scream or cry or attack him but was merely haughty.

'I wouldn't want to live in the same place as her anyway. I'd rather go up there. At least we'll be on our own, we'll be independent. I don't want to associate with her more than's strictly necessary.'

'Don't be like that, Dolly,' said Harold feebly.

'I will be like it. You said you'd never get over Mother, that's what you said.'

'We'll be all right on our own,' said Pup when he got home from work. 'It'll be nice.'

'Yes, it will. It'll be lovely, just you and me. We'll be all right, won't we, Pup? We'll be happy, just the two of us.'

'Of course we will, dear,' said Pup.

Dolly wasted no time. Next morning she lugged up to the top floor everything she wanted, chairs and tables and mirrors and a cabinet and a desk, table linen and bedlinen and china and glass as well as Edith's sewing machine. Harold scarcely noticed. He never required more than a chair to sit on and a bed to lie on. Myra didn't care, she was going to get new anyway. Mrs Brewer had not been accurate when she said Myra had nothing; she had her Unit Trusts and her National Savings, getting on for £1500, the way it had mounted up over the years.

They were married in March. Harold came back from his honeymoon in Newquay to find Pup and Dolly moved upstairs and the house so silent as to give a false idea that it was occupied solely by his wife and himself. Myra made real coffee in the filter pot she had bought in St Ives and open sandwiches with hard-boiled egg and tuna. Harold would have preferred Walls' pork pies and tomatoes and a pot of tea but he was not a man who complained. He sat quietly reading the memoirs of Princess Marie-Louise for the third or fourth time.

Next day his son and Pup met in the shop just before 9.30. Pup was as kindly and polite as ever. He had run the business in his father's absence and had run it efficiently, even keeping the books for the VAT. Harold was teaching him how to service and repair typewriters and when he knew enough he said he was going to do outside servicing, visiting homes and offices. No other company in the vicinity was willing to do that and it was just the fillip they needed in this recession.

They went home together. On the way they called at the library and Pup carried Harold's books home inside his coat because it had started to rain. Myra ran from the kitchen to kiss Harold in the manner of a brand-new wife. There was a spicy smell of something made with peppers and curry that was as new to the house as Myra was. Not yet back at her job, she had had all day in which to cook and to beautify the place and herself, beginning as soon as Harold had left with a fresh application of henna to her hair.

During their long affair, the married man had given Myra a lot of fairly good jewellery. She hung it on herself liberally and, when she was dressed up, without restraint. She was wearing the navy blue acrylic blouse and emerald-and-navy-and-white check skirt which formed part of what she called her 'trousseau', and round her neck, half-a-dozen gold chains from which were suspended a gold wishbone, a gold four-leaved clover, a gold and ivory dice and other such toys. She had her best gold watch on and her charm bracelet and her former lover's ring with the fire opal that quite eclipsed Harold's wedding band.

Pup stood in front of her, smiling first at his father

39

and then at her, as if giving them his blessing in a paternal way. Myra wondered if he was quite right in the head. He put out his hand and lifted the gold chains which hung over the large well-braced promontory of Myra's bosom. She jumped at Pup's touch; she couldn't help it. Pup gave her another smile, reassuring this time. He examined the wishbone, the four-leaved clover and the dice as if they interested him greatly, and he lifted Myra's hand and looked at the charms on her bracelet. Myra began to feel nervous and uncomfortable and she nearly said something sharp, when a diversion was created by the workmen descending the stairs. These were the men she had got in to install a sink and a water heater in the smallest of the five rooms on the top floor. She snatched her hand away from Pup and the gold chains flew about, jangling.

'That's the lot then,' the plumber said. 'I'll pop in in the morning and check your taps.'

'I was thinking,' Myra said in the rather shrill way she had when she was not at ease, 'while you're here, why don't we go the whole hog and have a bathroom put in for Peter and Doreen?'

'I don't know about that,' said Harold.

'It's not very civilized, is it? To be perfectly honest, it's not ideal, is it, having just the one bathroom in a house this size?'

'Planning permission'd have to be got,' said the plumber. 'Planning permission is essential prior to the installation of your water closet.'

'All right. Why not? How d'you go about it?'

The only possible convertible room was his temple. Pup said in his gentle way, in his soft, low voice, 'Dolly and I don't need our own bathroom, thank you very much. For such a short time –' he smiled at Myra, '– it would be a waste of money.' He said,

40

'Excuse me,' to the workmen and walked past them up the stairs.

'What do you think Peter meant by "such a short time," Hal?' said Myra, dishing up stuffed peppers. She called her husband Hal because no one else had ever done so and it had a dashing ring, rather out of keeping with Harold's appearance. Pup's remark had made her think. In fact, he had only meant by it that he intended to share a house with her for no longer than he could help, and as soon as his ship came in, he would move out.

'Ask me another,' said Harold. He took the plate and said, 'I thang you!' after the manner of Arthur Askey which he thought and believed Myra would think a witty and sparkling rejoinder.

'You don't suppose he's thinking of getting married himself?' said Myra, asking him another.

'Don't make me laugh. He's only eighteen.'

'It would be the best thing really for all of us, though I don't suppose there's much chance for poor Doreen.'

Harold said nothing for a moment. He was still overcome at the conversion of the horrible, dark, dirty, old dining room into a reasonable place to eat in. The looping up of the port-wine-coloured velvet curtains with lengths of red ribbon and the provision of a few blue scyllas in a Denby-ware honeypot, which would have struck most people as pathetic, seemed to him only awesome. He had never before tasted green peppers and he didn't think he liked them much. There was a napkin with a bit of lace in one corner but he felt it would be going rather far to wipe his mouth on it.

'Dolly?' he said. 'I don't know about that.' Harold wanted to impress his wife with his wit but the only way he knew how to do this was by being facetious or coarse. From some old stock of such phrases he dredged up a metaphor: 'You don't look at the mantelpiece when you're poking the fire.'

'What an awful thing to say,' said Myra coldly. 'Does that go for your own married life, too?'

Harold nearly said he didn't know about that. Hastily he brought out instead something about her being too young and pretty for him really, people would call him a cradle snatcher. The truth was that while embracing Myra on the previous night, not in the Newquay hotel but for the first time in the matrimonial bed in the sacred bedroom, her resemblance to his dead wife, at first so seemingly attractive, had unnerved him. The room was dark but not absolutely dark, for the light from a yellow street lamp penetrated the olive-coloured curtains, shedding a pale green luminosity. Myra's face had looked glaucous and gaunt while her red hair spread out over the pillow just as Edith's had. A certain amount of guilt had been affecting him – not much but a little – over his failure to visit his dying wife during her last days. He could imagine how she must have looked, though. With Myra he had been unwise enough to look at the mantelpiece while he poked the fire and he had had the horrible notion he was making love to a corpse. Much more of that and he wouldn't be able to do it at all.

'Can I give you some charlotte russe?' said Myra.

Dolly had made no fuss about moving upstairs because anything was preferable to sharing living space with Myra. At first she was stunned by what had happened and happened so quickly. In spite of the reassuring things she had said to Pup, the things a dispossessed mother says, she had felt helpless. She had felt lost or as if all her security had been knocked from under her feet and left her floating towards danger and want. It was now that she needed that friend to confide in and consult for advice. Wendy Collins might have been that friend, for a day or two Dolly thought she could be, but it was strange, whenever she opened her mouth to talk to Wendy about Myra, to explain what it was like to be deposed and pushed out, to have Myra down there, the words remained trapped inside her and what came out were things about the weather and the price of food.

She tried to get on with her sewing but it was neither so easy nor so pleasant up there. Mrs Collins, who had been her best customer, had varicose veins and refused to climb all those stairs for fittings. There was no way out of the house except through the hall whether Dolly sought the street or the old railway line. She got to know when Myra went to work, Monday and Wednesday and Friday mornings and all day Thursday, and she tried to pass through the hall only at those times herself. Thursdays she longed for, just to feel herself alone and free in her own home again. The rest of the days she took to spending more and more time in the temple, just sitting in there and being quiet. Or she would sit on the cushions, reading his books, with a single joss stick burning. Unlike her father, Dolly had never been a reader of fiction. Fiction was about beautiful women and handsome lovers and adventure and the great world, about which Dolly knew nothing and which frightened her. It was about people who had friendships with other people.

The books were always back in their right places when Pup came home from work. Like a wife, she had ready for him the food he liked: cold barbecued chicken, pork pies, turkey roll, tomatoes, potato crisps, tinned peaches and evaporated milk, real dairy-cream-filled sponge, chocolate digestives, dry roasted peanuts. She always offered him a glass of her wine but he nearly always refused. He spent all evening in the temple and she was mostly invited to be with him. But like a wise mother she knew better than to obtrude into his life to that extent; she knew when to say no.

'I don't think I will tonight, Pup,' she would say and go and sit in the dormer window, her left cheek turned to the street. On the windowsill there and on her bedroom windowsill at the back she kept a little mound of stones to throw at Gingie. But he never sat on the post as Fluffy had done or ventured into the Yearmans' back garden. Those evenings she sometimes drank a whole bottle of wine.

'She's practically an alcoholic, that girl,' said Myra to her mother. 'You should see the bottles. I shall have to get a second dustbin. You should see that house! I'd no idea. To be perfectly honest, it needs thousands spent on it. She never cleaned it and I don't suppose the first wife did. I've got my work cut out there for years to come.'

'Marriage isn't all roses,' said Mrs Brewer. 'You've got your hubby and now you're paying the price.'

'For Christ's sake, Mother, there's no pleasing you.'

'Got married to please me, did you? You can tell your little bitch of a stepdaughter if she lays a finger on my Gingie, I'll have the RSPCA on her.'

Myra had married principally to have a home of her own. She saw a future in which she gave little dinner parties or even quite large cocktail parties, in which the cavernous drawing room was furnished dashingly with stripped pine and Korean canework, corner units and glass tables with upholstered surrounds. That was the way she imagined the interior of the house in Hampstead Garden Suburb, home of her dentist employer and his wife. It was a little dream of hers one day to invite George and Yvonne

Colefax to Manningtree Grove, to a home she need not be ashamed of.

Already she had livened the place up with some of her own pieces from West Hampstead, the Athena Art Van Goghs, the gold chrome spotlights, the reproduction wine table. Her plastic apron had on it a map of the London tube system. If Peter and Doreen didn't want a bathroom of their own, she might as well spend the money having a really super Wrighton kitchen put in here. She called to her husband.

He came into the kitchen, still holding the open copy of *Her Grace of Amalfi* by Grenville West which was providing him with a little light relief from a life of the Princess Frederick, mother of the Kaiser. Myra put a tube-map dishcloth into his hands. Before his second marriage and during his first he had never dried dishes but had rinsed cups and plates under the tap and left them to drain. Plates had never got sticky because he had lived contentedly off Cornish pasties and Scotch eggs and apples and tomatoes and tubs of ice cream, foodstuffs which scarcely need plates at all.

Dolly, in her window, watched them go off down the road for a drink in The Woman in White or perhaps to bingo. Harold had never played bingo before, but Myra had and Mrs Brewer had frequently. Pup was in the temple, performing a Lesser Pentagram ritual as an opening for a piece of practical work. He had told Dolly nothing of what this practical work might be but she guessed it was something to do with the changes he was bringing into being at Hodge and Yearman. Already he had had the sign over the shop altered to 'Yearman and Hodge', the Hodge part in very small letters. The name of the company had been changed, he told

Dolly, but she didn't follow that, she wasn't interested.

She looked down on Myra who was dressed as usual in her favourite green, the emerald blouse tonight with all the gold chains, black cotton satin trousers and black patent sandals. Dolly had very good taste herself, she had a fine colour sense, and she knew that people with Myra's colouring should never wear bright greens and blues but rather shades of stone and brown or even pink or the red of their hair. It exasperated her, but her face, to any passer-by looking up, gave no sign of this. Long ago she had learned to control its natural movements so that an observer's attention might not be drawn to it. Like Diane de Poitiers – her father might have told her – she never smiled and never frowned.

She was holding the talisman so tightly in her hand that the rather sharp-sided heptagon made a red imprint on the palm. From the other side of the wall, Pup's voice could be heard maintaining a low regular chant. He was invoking archangels. Dolly refilled her wine glass, stood up against the wall with her ear to it and listened to Pup.

'*Ateh malkuth ve-geburah ve-gedulah le-olam . . .*'

He was conjuring strength for himself to make something come to pass. What seemed irrelevant. Was there a limit to what could be accomplished? She put up her hand and touched the surface of the naevus . . .

> 'Before me, Raphael,
> Behind me, Gabriel,
> On my right hand, Michael,
> On my left hand Uriel . . .'

The walls were thin in these big houses.

Carrying the glass of wine, she walked back to the

window. There were blobs and streaks of orange light on the walls and ceiling now and the sky was parrot-coloured, scarlet and grey, with sunset. Up here Dolly felt herself cut off on a limb of loneliness. The room was stuffy and close and Pup's voice droned behind the wall. She would have liked to break things, smash a window and shout out. Down in the street, trotting fast towards Hornsey Rise, came Miss Finlay, moving as she had done that evening in the winter, as if hastening away, without actually running, from some peril behind. Dolly had heard no more about the velvet skirt, wanted none of Miss Finlay, yet as she saw her scurrying along, going about her business whatever it might be, she felt a pang of resentment, of jealousy almost – though jealousy of *what*? – that Miss Finlay had no more desire to have her as a friend than she had to know Miss Finlay better.

Had she perhaps said something to offend her? Dolly thought back. Their conversation relayed itself to her from the whiff of lemon verbena to the parting at the gate. And then, her father and Myra in the kitchen ... She had told Miss Finlay about Pup's magic, mentioned it and his powers, and Miss Finlay had said something silly, something about sticking pins in wax images. It had seemed silly at the time. Dolly recalled it in detail. Circumstances alter cases and time alters them.

She had no wax. She would hardly have known how to handle it if she had. There were materials in the room she knew how to handle. She searched through the old fibre trunk, the cardboard crate in which she kept remnants and cut-offs of material. She went into her bedroom and fetched a pair of very light-coloured tights that had a ladder in them. It was going to be a longer job than she had thought at first. For one thing she had never done anything like

47

this before. She would need kapok and that meant going to the shops tomorrow. Taking a sip of her wine, she outlined a shape on the tights with french chalk, and then she began cutting.

When Pup came home on the following evening she showed him the doll. It was about fifteen inches high, a rag doll with knitted nylon skin and rust-coloured wool hair and a face embroidered in lipstick red and rouge pink and eyeshadow green. The doll's chest was the fattest and most prominent part of it. It wore a bright green blouse and a navy, green and white check skirt and round its neck and over the bulging chest Dolly had hung gold chains. In the ironmongers in Muswell Hill she had found some plumber's chain, the sophisticated sort that is composed of tiny balls joined by links, the whole being of gilt rather than silver metal.

Pup laughed. 'Our wicked stepmother,' he said.

'You can see it's her, can't you?'

'It's exactly like.' He gave the doll back. 'What did you make it for?'

Dolly told him. He looked rather grave.

'I do white magic.'

Even implied reproof made Dolly angry, even when it came from him. Especially when it came from him.

'You sold your soul to the devil!'

'Come on,' said Pup. 'I was a kid.'

He walked out of the room and went into the temple and closed the door. There, having put on the orange robe, he began to perform one of the rites of the Pentagram, a Lesser Banishing ritual. It was of a kind specially evolved for the banishing of disturbing or obsessing ideas. Pup had been more and more afflicted with these lately and they had nothing to do with Myra or effigies of Myra.

Tears had come into Dolly's eyes. She clenched her

fists. After a moment or two she got her pin box and stuck pins all over the doll, into its legs, its body, its bosom and its embroidered face. It had taken her all day to make, all last evening and all day, about ten hours' work. She picked it up and hurled it against the wall.

Chapter 6

A postcard came for Diarmit after Conal Moore had been gone for about three months. The picture on it was of the Cliffs of Moher in the west of Ireland. Conal had printed Diarmit's name and the address. He knew who it was from only because one of the other tenants picked up the card and said, 'It's from Conal,' though whether she had said it to him, Diarmit could not be sure, certainly she did not look at him when she spoke, she might merely have been thinking aloud.

What Conal said on the card, Diarmit never found out. Perhaps something about paying the rent, for next day the landlord spoke to him and said Mr Moore owed a month's rent. This time Diarmit was in no doubt that he was being addressed, though he did not feel, so vague and fidgety did the landlord seem, that he was being spoken to as a real, solid, flesh and blood person but rather as a guessed-at presence or a shape just discerned at the end of a dark room. He paid the back rent and some rent in advance out of his accumulated Social Security. He had plenty of money; there was nothing to spend it on.

Conal's postcard joined the note in his pocket. It puzzled Diarmit terribly as to what Conal meant by offering him that butcher's job. It had been a firm offer, surely, but it had all been done by word of mouth, and now Diarmit could not positively remember if the name Budgen's had actually been mentioned by Conal. Perhaps Mary had said Budgen's as people say Hoover when they mean a vacuum cleaner. It might have been some other supermarket – Tesco, Finefare, Sainsbury's, Spar, International, Safeway. Diarmit knew the names so well because he had taken to walking about all over north London looking for the supermarket where the job was waiting for him. It bothered him that they might have been angry because he had never turned up for it. He went into supermarkets in Holloway, Crouch End, Muswell Hill and Wood Green, wondering which it could have been but never actually asking, hoping that somehow, when he came to the right place, he would know.

He was an unobtrusive person, neither tall nor short, with darkish brown, dusty-looking hair, features that might have been roughly moulded from putty with careless fingers, grey puzzled eyes. He had brought with him all the clothes he possessed: Hong Kong-made jeans and shirts, a thick grey duffel coat, a quilted nylon jacket. In a secondhand shop in the Archway Road he had bought himself a pair of dark wine-red cord trousers and he wore these most of the time with a dark red shirt which did not show the dirt. He carried the olive-green bag with Harrods printed on it in gold about with him in his other pocket (the pocket which did not contain the card and the note) in case he bought anything.

After he had been, for the third or fourth time, into Sainsbury's at Muswell Hill, looking in vain for a butchery department, as if it might be hidden in some corner of the store he had not yet penetrated, behind the cigarette kiosk, for instance, or in the corner between the vegetables and the turkeys, he crossed the road and went into the big ironmongers where Pup had bought his magic knife and Dolly her gold chains. There he selected, as nearly as was possible in a domestic hardware store, the implements of a butcher's trade: a steel cleaver for chopping and two long knives. The girl on the checkout was talking to a friend of hers and she did not look at Diarmit or speak to him except to say, 'Seventeen pounds, forty-five.'

From Woodside Road he walked all the way back along the old railway line, carrying the knives in the Harrods bag. It was warm and sunny and there were red and black butterflies on the purple spires of buddleia between Highgate and the old Mount Pleasant Green station. Being in possession of the tools of his trade made Diarmit feel a little better. He would be ready now if the job were to present itself. How this might be he hardly knew, though he had vague ideas of someone coming to the door in Mount Pleasant Gardens and asking for him or of Conal coming back.

Back in the house, he used the pay phone for the first time. To do this was a tremendous effort for him, an act of will comparable in anyone else to braving naked an icy river or confronting a savage dog, for by now he had gone a long way along the road towards a split-off from reality. It was as if one of those knives, grasped and held poised, was waiting to strike and cleave a great chasm between himself – whatever 'himself' might be, for that was already fast becoming lost – and the natural, normal, real world where others lived their natural, normal, real lives. But he used the phone. He phoned his sister Kathleen in Kilburn, having held her number in his memory for many months. As the bell rang he trembled, he trembled as the pips sounded, for suppose he should put his money in and speak but Kathleen not hear him?

His five-pence piece went into the slot and he spoke on a drawn breath.

'It's Diarmit, it's your brother, Kathleen. I'm here, not far from you, at Conal Moore's.'

A man's voice. He hadn't seen her for years and she had married since he had seen her. 'She's got a lot of brothers.'

'She has. I'm Diarmit, I'm the youngest. Now I don't recall your name, what would your name be?' Diarmit went on desperately because there was no answer, 'Are you there? Will Kathleen be there?'

'She's at work.'

'She's lucky, then, lucky to have work.' Diarmit experimented with a pleasant laugh. 'I could do with work myself. When do you expect her back now? This is her brother, you see. This is her little brother Diarmit. Where is she now? Could I ring her at her work?'

'She'll be home half-five.'

The phone went down. At least he had heard his voice, Diarmit thought, he had known who he was. And Kathleen really lived there, she lived in Kilburn, at where that number was, it was all right, it was true and real. Instead of going back into his room, he left the house again with the note and card in his pocket and the Harrods bag in his hand and went down the steps that had been cut out of the embankment to the old station. The rosebay willow herb was in bloom and the white campion. There were pink and white and yellow weeds flowering among the green grass and the rusty cans and the blown feathers. It was warm and hazy, it smelt of cow parsley and diesel fumes. Diarmit walked along the edge of the platform and jumped down and walked on the grassy bed where the track had been.

A woman was coming along with a white Pyrennean mountain dog on a lead. As big and incongruous as a polar bear it looked to Diarmit. He spoke to the woman courteously.

'Good afternoon. A lovely afternoon.'

She made no acknowledgement of this. Her eyes were fixed rigidly ahead. He spoke again, 'Lovely sunshine . . .' and this time, as if to confirm that she could neither see nor hear him, she bent down and whispered something to the dog, fondling its head. He stood still, watching her go. She tripped along fast, hauling the dog behind her up the steps. Diarmit walked along the old railway line, swinging the Harrods bag, singing as he went like Bottom the Weaver who sang so that others might know he was not afraid. Diarmit would have liked to sing Irish songs but there were none he could remember, so he sang 'God Save the Queen', the only verse he knew over and over, that others might know he was not afraid and for himself too, to know that the sound came from something and that that something was himself.

He got off the line at Stapleton Hall Road and walked to Crouch Hill Station. There was a real railway line there and a real train that would take him to Brondesbury near his sister Kathleen's. It was nearly six when he got there. He walked along the concrete path and up the two concrete steps and rang at the door.

Kathleen had just come in from work and her husband had just gone off to work. Before he went, he had told her that her brother Diarmit had been on the phone, on the scrounge too by the sound of it, no work, on the dole, and hadn't they had enough of her family, for God's sake? Kathleen didn't know what to do. She was tired, she was pregnant, and they hadn't got a spare room anyway. And everyone knew what Diarmit was, going to Mary for a fortnight and stopping three years. He had been funny ever since that bomb.

For all that, she meant to have him in, she meant to talk to him and explain. It was the sight of him and the stink of him that unnerved her. He looked as if he hadn't had a wash for a month and he smelt of old vegetables. Dressed in dirty dark red, his face pale like clay, a carrier bag over one arm and the other hand stretched out towards her waving a paper, he frightened her so much that she stood there staring and quivering for a moment in silence. She smelled his smell and the heartburn she had came up and scalded her throat. She pushed the door and shut it in his face and leaned against it, breathing hard.

Diarmit knew she had not seen him because he did not exist any more. He had had that feeling before, that he did not exist, after the bomb in Belfast. But since then he had recovered his being more or less consistently, only occasionally had he doubted that he was there. Now he knew for certain he had become invisible and inaudible, no one could see or hear him and it had been going on at that level ever since the morning when he went hunting round Sainsbury's for the butchery department. They had tried to take away his existence so that they wouldn't have to give him a job, and they had succeeded if Kathleen couldn't see him, if his own sister didn't know him.

And now, as once previously, he was aware of how large the things of the world were. He felt very small. Most people, even children, were much bigger than him, buses and cars were enormous, seeking to mow him down, roaring at him, as he crossed Kilburn High Road. It was useless to attempt to go back by train. The man would not hear him ask for a ticket, even supposing he were tall enough to reach the ticket window. He would walk. Though it was a long way, six or seven miles, on this fine sunny evening he would walk. He felt the hard sharp edges of his knives through the green plastic and they comforted him. With them he would defend himself if the big people, not seeing or hearing him, tried to trample him underfoot.

Up in his room, Conal Moore's room, he felt safer. He was like an insect, safe in its cranny in the wall but in peril when it has to run across the floor. An insect can sting feet with the knives in its belly. Diarmit held the Harrods bag close against him as he climbed the stairs.

Two people came running down from the top, laughing, making a noise. He flattened himself against the wall so that they should not bowl him over and sweep him down as they passed. Inside the room it was better. He made a pot of tea, he slept. But after that he began to feel besieged and threatened. He felt that his life was in danger; what ego he still had which he knew he had but which the others, the Conal Moores and the supermarket people, discounted, that was in danger. During the day he was aware that the house emptied, it was a hive only by night. He went down listening outside doors for sounds of life within. It was entirely silent but for music coming from behind one door.

The Dalmatian and the mongrel collie ran about the green, scavenging from litter bins. They looked very large to Diarmit even from this distance. Next to Mount Pleasant Hall they were pulling down a row of old houses and the air was yellow and thick with plaster dust. Next they would pull this one down. Diarmit understood how it would be. There was no one in the house but himself and he was as invisible as an insect, so they would pull the house down around him, not knowing he was there or not caring.

They would care no more for him than they would for the wood-lice and mites and spiders and silver-fish that also lived in the house. He would be crushed in the rubble, overwhelmed by a cloud of yellow dust. He sat in the window and trembled.

By night it was safe. The workmen did nothing after five, he had observed that. He could come back to the house at night and hide there all night but by day he must be gone, taking whatever he valued with him. He might come back and find that the house had disappeared but that was a risk he must take.

Next day, after they had all pounded out of the house, banging doors, laughing, crashing down the stairs, they made enough noise for devils in hell, he crept out with his knives in the Harrods bag. He carried them as a wasp carries its sting or a security guard his gun. There was no doubt in his mind where he was going; he had it all worked out. Down the steps in Mount Pleasant Gardens and on to the old railway line where it spread out wide in a grassy valley, on to where it narrowed at the old Mount Pleasant Green station, and thence to the Mistley tunnel.

The tunnel was as dry as it ever got inside. It had an earthy oily smell and there were feathers everywhere. That mattress must have contained a million little white and grey feathers, for thousands had come out and blown away, had embedded themselves in the clay or adhered to the curved roof or lay in quivering heaps, yet the old torn mattress was still cushiony, still padded with down. Diarmit sat down on it and took his knives out of the bag.

From where he sat, well back under the curve of the roof, he could command a view of both the tunnel's openings. He could assess what kind of a threat presented itself. As for himself, no one could see him, so there was no need to be hidden. But after a while he raised the mattress up on its side edge, making it into a curving wall which he propped in place with a roll of rusty wire netting and an oil drum. It was not for concealment but protection. He squatted behind it, as in a dugout or behind a windbreak, and it did protect him. Three or four people came through the tunnel, one walking towards Highgate, the others to Mount Pleasant, and although they were giant, lumbering, hostile creatures, their bodies nearly filling the tunnel space, none of them even brushed against the mattress and he was safe.

Diarmit understood then that he had found a way to live. Each night he could sleep in the room but by day he must come here, wary and armed, and station himself behind his barricade.

Chapter 7

The doll, Mrs Collins said, was exactly what Wendy wanted. No, she didn't think ten pounds too much, ten pounds was very reasonable. Wendy wanted it as a birthday present for the little girl whose godmother she was. The doll was very obviously a little girl itself with a pink smiling face and yellow plaits and scarlet shirt and blue checked pinafore dress. Dolly had made several, all different, since the Myra doll and had had no difficulty in selling them.

Mrs Collins gave Dolly a ten-pound note which Dolly, crossing the road from Mrs Collins' little terraced cottage in Orchard Lane, spent on stocking up with wine at the off-licence. Five bottles, wrapped in tissue in two carriers.

It was a dull warm, white-skied summer day. Dolly climbed up the steps and got on to the old railway line by the bridge in Northwood Road. A woman was walking along with a white Pyrennean mountain dog on a lead. Dolly was wearing a pink and yellow and brown plaid cotton dress with a wide brown belt, tights and low-heeled sandals. The tights were new, on for the first time, and to protect them she decided not to climb up the embankment but to go through the Mistley tunnel to the station and up the steps.

It was absolutely dry underfoot; there had been no rain for a fortnight. Usually it was a bit muddy inside the tunnel but not today. Footprints and cycle tyre marks were etched in the hard, pale, feather-strewn clay. Dolly walked through the tunnel, carrying her bags of wine bottles. Someone had stacked the mattress up on its side and propped it up with an oil drum and some wire. Perhaps, rather, the council or the railway people or somebody or other were collecting up the rubbish in here at last before taking it away. Dolly nearly went over to the mattress to see, at closer quarters, if it did look as if some genuine tidying work had been done, but she thought better of it. The bags were heavy, and the smelly dirty old tunnel was no place in which to linger.

She mounted the steps. In Manningtree Grove, outside the house, she paused for a moment. Myra had lost no time in revitalizing the garden. The Michaelmas daisies and Solomon's seal were all gone and in their place she had planted annuals – lobelias and tagetes and petunias – and these were in flower. Dolly was not one of those people who think all flowers beautiful and here she thought the juxtaposition of cobalt blue, orange and shocking pink particularly inharmonious. Gingie, for once, was sitting on the post.

'Get off!' said Dolly and clapped her hands. The cat fled.

She let herself into the house but not quietly or cautiously. It was a Monday and Myra worked till lunchtime.

'Doreen!'

Dolly froze. The door to the front room opened and Myra came out, wearing jade green dungarees and a navy-and-white striped T-shirt.

'Caught at last,' said Myra but not unpleasantly. 'I always seem to see the tail end of you disappearing. Now I've got you, come in here and give me the benefit of your advice.'

'Why aren't you at work?'

These were practically the first words Dolly had ever addressed to her but Myra gave no sign that she realized this. 'I've started a fortnight's holiday, my dear. I'm going to begin on the painting tomorrow. Now don't look like that!' Dolly hadn't looked like anything. Her face, as usual, was expressionless. 'Yes, I mean me with my own two hands,' Myra said. 'To be perfectly honest with you, I spent so much on converting your kitchen I can't afford to have the men in again.'

'They only put a sink in,' said Dolly, 'and we didn't want that.'

Myra gave her tinkling laugh. 'Oh, well, that's frank if you like. We won't argue about it. I didn't bring you in here to argue. I want you to tell me what colour scheme you think I ought to have.'

This was something Dolly had plenty of ideas about. For a moment she forgot her hatred of Myra. 'It's a light room. You could have a strong colour. You could have a white ceiling and brilliant white paintwork and deep russet walls. That would tone in with the carpet and those chairs.'

Myra was astonished. She had spoken to Dolly because she had genuinely thought it would be better to be on speaking terms with her. But in answer to her question she had expected some such rejoinder as 'I don't know' or 'whatever you like'. 'I'm not keeping that filthy old carpet or those chairs,' she said scornfully. 'I'm having haircord and stripped pine. And I think a natural beige for the walls, there's a shade they call papyrus.'

'Suit yourself.' Dolly shrugged her shoulders. It was still early in the day but she suddenly felt she needed a glass of wine badly and she made for the door.

Myra had hoped for an offer of help which she

now saw she wasn't going to get. She remembered, though, the original purpose of accosting Dolly. 'Want a coffee? I was just going to have one.'

Coffee was no substitute for a tumblerful of Spanish burgundy. 'No, thanks.'

'Well, if I can't twist your arm, I can't. Come and inspect the work, though, will you? I hope to have a good bit done by Friday. Come and have a look and tell me what you think. We ought to be friends, Doreen, two girls living in the same house.'

Instead of putting up the real objections to Myra as usurper and iconoclast, Dolly chose a less obvious impediment. There was little she had to be proud of but she was proud and jealous of her youth. While she had her youth, miracles could still happen, her blind prince might come or some genius find a cure. 'You're older than me,' she said.

'A little bit,' Myra said, going red.

'I'm twenty-six. How old are you?'

The flush deepened. 'When I'm asked that I usually say "somewhere between thirty and death". To be perfectly honest with you, I'm thirty-eight.'

'I thought so.' Dolly picked up her bags and went off upstairs.

She poured herself a big glass of wine and sat down to drink it. Four dolls sat on the mantelpiece, two little girls with yellow plaits, Myra and an Indian boy doll in a silk turban. Dolly sipped her wine, watched by the dolls.

'Sunbeach' was the name of the colour Myra chose for the living room, a compromise between her choice and Dolly's. She thought Dolly might come down and see how she was getting on but Dolly did not. She worked every day and when she had finished the living room she started on the dining room, bought cheap but smart-looking brown haircord to carpet the floors and a three-piece suite in pine with brown-and-white check cotton upholstery. Pup looked in sometimes to give her a kindly word of encouragement, and occasionally Harold, conscious of the huge sacrifice he was making on the altar of marriage, turned his back on the shabby delightful solitude of the breakfast room and sat reading his book in a chair by her stepladder.

After that initial nasty feeling that he was indulging in necrophilia, Harold had only twice made love to his wife and neither time had been particularly satisfactory. For a while he was uneasy about denying her what he thought of as a wife's right. He lay in bed waiting for the touch or the question, and when neither came but instead a cheerful 'Good night, Hal', he felt he had been given another night's reprieve. But in fact, though he knew nothing of this, Myra had not married him for love, still less for sex. She had had all the sex, and indeed all the passion and fulfilment, she had wanted with the married man. She was a trumpery, shallow, insincere woman was Myra, but she had her happinesses and her miseries like anyone else and for her, all the happiness of love had gone when the married man went. In a husband, in Harold, she wanted a man to go about with and be seen with, someone of the opposite sex to talk to, and a provider of a big house and the security it brought.

She was not dissatisfied with her bargain, and all the better if she could honour her part of it with her skills and her savings rather than a pretence of sexual enthusiasm.

By daylight, Harold was proud of his wife's appearance. When they went out together, it gratified him to be seen arm-in-arm with her. Harold was one of those men who like to say they don't understand women, women are a mystery. His mind ranged sometimes over the incomprehensible women of history – Messalina, Catherine de' Medici, Anne Boleyn, Charlotte Corday – their unaccountable behaviour lending weight to his convictions. Women were an enigma and his own wife as great an enigma as any. He derived an almost complacent satisfaction from thinking this way. It absolved him from having to consider why Myra accepted his lack of ardour so equably, why she was wearing herself out painting and why, instead of having a bit of hush now the dining room was done, she should wish to invite people to eat in it.

Myra couldn't catch Dolly in the hall again, so she went upstairs and tapped on the door. Dolly guessed who it was, snatched up the dolls and put them in the remnant box out of sight.

'We're having a few friends in for dinner on Thursday week,' Myra said in her best suburban wife manner. 'I hope you and Peter will join us.'

'I've got to go to a meeting.' The Adonai Spiritists were holding another seance and Dolly had almost decided not to go but she would now. 'What friends? Dad hasn't got any friends.'

'Quite frankly, Doreen, I think I'm a better judge of that than you are. Of course he's got friends. If you must know, we're having my boss Mr Colefax and his wife and a very nice couple Hal and I got to know at bingo. If you won't come, I expect my mother will.'

The dining room had apple-green walls now, beige Dralon curtains, haircord on the floor, aluminium-framed Constable prints, and on the table Ravenhead glass and stainless steel cutlery and tablemats of British game birds.

Pup didn't refuse the invitation. He performed an Elemental ritual and went out and bought himself a suit, grey flannel, plain and elegant, and a grey shirt with a small pink and white pattern on it. He thought it unnecessary to mention this to Dolly or that he had cast the I Ching and it had told him that the desires of the superior man are not thus to be pacified.

He came out of the temple, wearing his robe, and kissed Dolly who was just leaving for her seance. Just as she closed the front door behind her, Miss Finlay came tearing along at her usual pace. There were police everywhere, she said, and did Dolly know what it was about? When she, Miss Finlay, had tried to get on to the old railway line down the steps at Crescent Road, a policeman had turned her back. There was nothing in the evening paper and she hadn't got television. Dolly hadn't got television either, though Myra had just bought a colour set. They walked down Manningtree Grove towards Mount Pleasant Green and in that short time two police cars passed them with blue lights flashing.

Myra's guests all had television and they had all had their radios on while getting ready to come out. When they were having their pre-dinner drinks in the pine and cane living room they talked about nothing else, not that it wasn't a horrible thing to talk about, a horrible thing to happen, the man who did it must be a monster, no better than an animal.

'I've yet to hear of animals cutting each other's heads off,' said Mrs Brewer.

Pup said nothing. He was sorry it had happened on the old railway line and inside that very tunnel where, long ago now, he had performed the first ritual of his career. On a fine summer evening like this one it was hideous to think and talk of murder. He was looking at Yvonne Colefax, a very pretty blonde who wore a white dress made of some clinging pleated material. What would make a man want to kill a girl – a *girl*, of all possible victims – and then sever her head from her body with a hatchet?

'Unresolved aggression,' said George Colefax as if Pup had spoken aloud. 'A hatred of women whose challenge he can't meet.' He said it with an emphasis that seemed heartfelt and his wife gave him a glance. 'Cutting off the head would silence a mocking tongue and make certain the eyes could no longer see him.'

Myra came in to announce dinner. They trooped into the dining room. Harold had never before sat down to a three-course meal at 8.30 in the evening. All this talk of decapitation made him feel queasy, especially as he was halfway through a book mostly concerned with the torture meted out to Madame de Brinvilliers. He had to sit between Mrs Brewer and Eileen Ridge, the bingo friend. Myra wore a long green polyester skirt with black daisies on it and a very tight, sleeveless, black polo-necked sweater and all her gold jewellery. Mrs Brewer, in blue Crimplene, picked at her food and actually sniffed a dish of courgettes in cream sauce. Besides the courgettes, Myra had cooked strange food in elaborate ways, chicken with walnuts, potatoes gummed together with egg and cheese, cabbage that had bits of bacon and caraway seeds in it. George Colefax picked all the caraway seeds out of his very white, even teeth with a gold toothpick. He was a doctor of medicine as well as a dentist and had no compunction (did not even realize such talk might be distasteful) about explaining to the company what a difficult job cutting someone's head off would be and how the perpetrator, whoever he might be, would have needed knives and perhaps a saw as well as a hatchet. Myra brought in raspberry Pavlova cake.

'It was a woman with a dog found her,' said Mrs

Collins outside the hall after the seance was over. 'She's a woman who lives in Stanhope Road that's got that great big white dog, great big white Pyrennean something. She was on the old line and the dog started sniffing at something and she saw it was this girl without a head. Then she saw the head a little way away. They took her into hospital for the shock.'

'What an experience,' said Miss Finlay. 'It would haunt you to your dying day.' Today she smelt, Dolly had noticed, only of Pear's soap.

'You'd never get over it. Who'd do a thing like that? Only an animal, an absolute animal.'

Dolly was tired of hearing about it. She stood by the gate, picking leaves from a bush of lemon mint which grew there, crushing them in her fingers and smelling the scent. Her mother had not appeared during the seance, had spoken no word. The leaves had a pungent lemony scent.

'My mother used to use cologne like that,' Dolly said, holding her fingers under Mrs Collins' nose.

'Brings her back, does it? You don't get over losing your mother. I know I never have. You don't want to go off on your own, you two, not after what's happened today. You'd best wait here with me, my daughter's coming for me in the car and she'll drop you both off.' It was barely dark yet. Miss Finlay looked fearfully along the street and across the green. 'We can expect you both, I hope,' said Mrs Collins, 'for Mrs Fitter's seance on the fifteenth of next month. You've heard of her, haven't you? She's wonderful. The tickets are going like hot cakes. Five pounds a seat but you can take my word for it, it's cheap at the price. Oh, that lemon scent is strong, isn't it, dear?'

When Wendy Collins dropped off Dolly, the party was still in full swing. She went straight upstairs and just avoided encountering Yvonne Colefax who had gone to the bathroom to dab herself with more Balmain's Ivoire. Back in the living room, Yvonne sat on one half of Myra's new two-seater settee. Pup hesitated, remembering the I Ching and the Penta-grammic Banishing ritual, and then he went and sat next to her. At a loss for what to talk to her about, he offered to tell her fortune. He had overheard Myra regaling his father with details of the Colefaxes' private life, so he was able to give her a very accurate assessment of her past. She thought he was amazing and said so, looking into his eyes.

'How *could* you know I lost my first husband when I was only twenty-one?' said Yvonne, having forgot-ten she had imparted this fact to Myra during the previous week.

'Your eyes told me,' said Pup gracefully.

'Load of wicked rubbish,' said Mrs Brewer.

'Excuse me, but everything he said was the absolute truth.'

Mrs Brewer's face was very red as if she were going to have some sort of attack. Yvonne could hardly take her eyes off Pup, was looking at him as if he were a seer or guru, and Pup felt quite weak and faint. He had to keep telling himself how precious and requisite was the retention of virginity to a young geomancer. Yvonne smelled wonderful and her white silk thigh, the whole smooth slippery length of it, was pressed softly against his own. She had a rather breathy, childlike voice, full of wonder, a wide-eyed voice if that was possible. And although she must have been seven or eight years older than him, she seemed younger.

It was half an hour since he had heard Dolly come in. He ought to go, it would be wise to go. Myra was telling her guests how she and Hal were planning an autumn holiday in Cyprus.

'I don't know about that,' said Harold. 'It's the first I've heard of it.'

'Oh, darling, you and your memory!'

'I must be going now,' said Pup. 'Goodbye. Thank you for the delicious dinner.' Some impulse made him go up to Myra, lift her hand and kiss it.

It was a signal for everyone else to make a move. Myra could have killed him. Mrs Brewer wanted Harold to accompany her next door, put all the lights on and search the flat in case an intruder had got in in her absence. Like the man who cut off heads, for instance. Pup went upstairs. Dolly was in their living room, drinking rosé. Often on summer evenings, instead of putting the light on, she lit a candle. She was sitting in the half-dark with her single candle burning, looking down from the window at Ronald and Eileen Ridge getting into their car.

'Pup,' she said, 'did you hear about the girl on the old railway line?'

He nodded. 'We don't have to talk about it, do we? How was your meeting?'

'It was all right. Listen, we've got a physical medium coming in three weeks' time, what they call a materialization medium. You will come with me, won't you? You have to say by tomorrow because the tickets are going to sell like hot cakes.'

'I never knew anyone actually buy cakes when they were hot, did you?' Her puzzled, slightly offended expression made him smile. 'Of course I'll come, dear.'

After Harold had left her, Mrs Brewer began to feel very ill. She thought she had indigestion as a result of eating Myra's strange food. It had begun as heartburn while she was still next door, sitting in one of the uncomfortable pine armchairs. Now this had intensified into a deep pressing pain down her left side, paralysing her left arm and clamping her as if in an iron cage. It might have occurred to Mrs Brewer that she was having a heart attack except that she believed women never have heart attacks and no one had told her that this immunity ends with the menopause.

Gingie came and lay on her bed. She passed an uncomfortable night and felt so tired that she stayed in bed all day and the next day, but when Myra came in on Sunday, she was up and about again and she said nothing of her illness.

Chapter 8

One hundred and four people passed through the tunnel before the fateful one. Diarmit counted them. Three or four a day they came, occasionally more, and he had been stationed behind his barricade for twenty-three days before the attack came on the twenty-fourth.

By then he was becalmed in a false security. Huge though they were, they kept to the centre of the tunnel and he was just outside the range of their sweeping strides and great stamping feet. But the girl on the twenty-fourth day left the path and came juggernauting towards the mattress. She was in search of something, he thought in his terror, the roll of wire perhaps or the wooden cask or the old chair with which, through the weeks, he had bolstered his fortifications. Her head reached the roof, and her great flailing arms, swinging above the mattress, made a gale in the air. He jumped up in his fear, though he knew himself too small and too faint in substance to be seen, but he jumped up with a spurt of courage, a knife in each tiny feeble hand to defend himself.

The sound she made was a screaming roar of fury. He almost quailed at that, he almost yielded. It was as much as he could do to keep on his feet, not to shrivel into the ground and scuttle, certain prey for her foot. But he remained there with unflinching bravery, stabbing his sting at her, his double sting, pounding into that vast threatening mass, until the weight of it subsided, sinking on to him, a bloodied hulk.

He had done it, he had won. He struggled free. He stepped back, gasping, looking at the thing at his feet as a knight might have looked at a slain dragon. His hands were red and sticky with blood. In death his attacker had shrunk rapidly. Her body was no bigger than an ordinary girl's now, a small young girl. Diarmit marvelled that such things might be, that courage and defiance might reduce a powerful aggressor to this little dead thing.

Perhaps he should reduce it more. After all, he knew all about dismemberment. Wishing he had a saw, he got to work with the cleaver, then the knives. He abandoned the task because he got tired and, as he heard in the distance by the chiming church clock, it was 5.00 now and safe to go home.

The sunshine felt as strong as at noon. A warm curtain of it met him as he came out of the tunnel mouth, carrying the hatchet and the knives in his Harrods bag. The buddleias and willow herb and marguerite daisies were thronged with bees, a white butterfly pursued its waving, fluttering flight, and a ginger cat walked along the edge of the old station platform, but he met no one and passed no one until he had gone up the steps and was in Mount Pleasant Gardens.

Although he was covered with blood, the splashes and great soaked areas did not look like bloodstains on the red shirt and the red cords. In any case, no one looked at him, he remained invisible. On the demolition site beyond the green the workmen had knocked off for the day and the dust had settled. There was very little left of the houses; there were only bricks and rubble and an empty site. Diarmit went upstairs, up and up and up to his top floor. There was one bathroom for all the rooms on the top and in the mornings and the evenings it was always occupied but it was empty now. He took the cleaver and the knives out of the Harrods bag and washed them under cold running water. Then he turned the bag inside out and washed that.

In his room he felt more safe and sound than he had done for a long time. He made himself a pot of tea and sat drinking it by the open window. The Dalmatian and the collie lay on the grass, sleeping in the sunshine. How good it would be if Conal Moore were to come now! Diarmit felt somehow that his existence, his selfhood, was seeping back; first, the act of defence in the tunnel, then the warm sun, then the tea – all this was bringing him out of limbo, out of nothingness. Conal would see him, know him, he felt sure of that. Kathleen would know him if he went to her door now. The brave stand and the shed blood had made him recognizable, solid, whole.

I kill, therefore I am.

It was not until the next day that the woman with the Pyrennean mountain dog found the girl's body and not until two days after that that Diarmit knew it had been found. He saw a newspaper which someone had left on top of a pile of them on a dustbin in the side entrance. The photograph was of that face which, hugely enlarged and violently coloured, had loomed over him in the tunnel and had let out those terrible sounds. He sat on a bench on the green and deciphered the headlines, then the text, working very slowly and moving his forefinger along the lines of print. It was then that he understood they were calling him a murderer. 'The Headsman', they called him.

That was like calling a soldier in a war a murderer! If anyone came and asked him why, he had his explanation ready. You see how you would feel, driven out of the only home you've got by a threat of being buried under tons of rubble, only allowed home during the hours of darkness, forced to take shelter out of doors and barricade yourself in lest the stampeding hordes trample you. You try it and see how you'd feel when a huge scavenger threatens to crush you. You'd lash back with all your poor little strength, wouldn't you? If you had the nerve, if you were brave enough.

They had not worked on the site the day before and no workmen had appeared today. Diarmit sat on the bench and watched the site and the house where his room was. The weather was still warm and sunny and the stains on his clothes began to give off a hot fetid reek. The Dalmatian came and sniffed at him. A woman, passing, pushing a bicycle, wrinkled her nose, stared at him and turned away. These evidences of his existence pleased Diarmit, but after a time the dogs annoyed him, the Dalmatian and the collie had been joined by a rough-haired mongrel, and all three sniffed him and followed him. They followed him to the door of the shop where he bought his bread and milk and teabags and they followed him back across the green to his doorstep.

Diarmit took off his clothes for the first time for many weeks and washed them in the bathroom, using Camay soap for he had nothing else. It was Sunday tomorrow and he could stay in. No demolition was ever done on a Sunday. His clothes dry – he had spread them over the windowsill and closed the sash on them – he put them on and watched for Conal. A strong presentiment told him Conal would come back today but the hours passed and still no Conal and the sun departed in a long, slow sunset, followed by a long, smoky-violet dusk, and he had not come. When it was dark Diarmit tore up the note and the postcard and flushed the pieces down the lavatory in the bathroom.

Next morning he was dressed and ready to leave when there came a sharp knocking on the room door. That would be the men come to tell him they were about to begin demolishing the house. They could see him now, they could be aware of him, he had a real existence. He opened the door.

Outside on the landing, in plainclothes, were two policemen.

They told him their names. They were a detective sergeant and a constable. Diarmit let them come in and they stood, looking about the room. The longer and larger of the knives lay on the table where he had used it to cut a slice of bread.

The sergeant said, 'We're anxious to know the whereabouts of Conal Patrick Moore.'

Diarmit smiled at them. He felt how much he liked them, how grateful he was that they had said nothing about the girl in the tunnel. Their eyes had rested with indifference on the knife.

'So am I,' he said. 'So am I anxious. I don't know where he is at all.'

'And who might you be, sir?'

Diarmit told them his name. He told them his story, how he had come to London to Conal and a job but there had been no Conal and no job. To speak and be spoken to was enjoyable, to exist and be recognized. He talked on and on because it was such a novelty. The sergeant had to stop him.

'Don't you want to know what we want him for?'

This had not crossed Diarmit's mind. He didn't much care, no. He savoured only the delight of being addressed as 'you', of being able to communicate, of being treated as a normal ordinary person.

'There've been a lot of robberies from shops in this

75

area,' said the sergeant. 'They stopped round about the time you say Mr Moore went away. Now there's a similar pattern of robberies in a district of Birmingham. Would he go there?'

'He might,' said Diarmit. Mary's husband and his brothers had an old father in Birmingham. He told the sergeant this. He was shocked. The Bawnes and their family connections had always been law-abiding, respectable people. 'You'll be letting me know when you find him?'

'And you let *us* know if you hear anything.'

They left. Diarmit reflected on what they had told him. Of course, no supermarket would give a job to a friend or relative of a thief, he could understand that. It was a blessing, too, that Conal had been gone before he came. He had no wish to be associated with a criminal. So the room was all his now. He was free. He felt strong and brave and young and free and, stretching up his arms, he capered about the room, doing a little dance of freedom and happiness. What a clearing and cleansing of his life had taken place these past few days!

The realization that today being Monday might be the day for starting demolition of the house sobered him. He was pretty sure they would know of his presence and come to warn him but he ought to go out and be on the safe side. Besides, it was a fine morning. He took up the Harrods bag with the knives in it and ran down the stairs. No point in leaving valuable things to be buried under rubble.

Once he was out in the street, a daring idea came to him. Why shouldn't he try to find himself work? Why not start looking for a job?

Chapter 9

From her bed, lying there propped up on pillows, Mrs Brewer could see the green valley through which the old railway line ran. At previous times when she had been ill, she had liked to watch the people coming and going, using the green track as a short cut – schoolchildren, dog walkers, young people who seemed to spend so much of their lives aimlessly wandering. Since the murder no one used it. Only Gingie could be seen, stalking through the long grass, in quest of real or imaginary prey.

It was August, red-hot, sultry, dry as a bone. Mrs Brewer was going to get up at about twelve in time to think about lunch. This gastritis or whatever it was knocked you sideways; she didn't know when she had felt so tired. And it wasn't as if she was old yet, only sixty-four and good surely for another twenty years.

She would have to get up in a minute to open the window, the heat in here was getting unbearable and the sweat was beginning to roll off her. Mrs Brewer had always been proud of not sweating much and had sometimes boasted of this to Myra. Perspiration was so unfeminine. She began to wish Myra would come in. Thursday was her day off and there was nothing to stop her. For God's sake, it was her duty and she only lived next door!

Gingie had appeared outside the window, making

soundless mews, or soundless no doubt because he was on the other side of the glass.

'All right, I'm coming,' said Mrs Brewer and she pushed back the bedclothes and put her feet over the side of the bed and got them on to the floor. Another wave of heat washed over her and she broke into sweat.

The phone was in the living room. She would have to phone Myra. But should she try to reach the phone first or open the window to Gingie first? Fresh air might be what she needed. She could walk – just. Very slowly she shuffled towards the window. Gingie was on the sill, screaming silently.

'I'm coming, boy,' said Mrs Brewer.

Suddenly she was filled with passionate tender love for the little cat and it seemed to her that never before, not for long-dead John Brewer or the infant Myra, had she felt as she now did for this mewing scrap of orange fur. Her love made her pant and gasp. She wanted to feel Gingie against her, to squeeze him in her arms. She struggled with the window, the heavy sash bar, while the cat's face grew enormous, a huge open mouth of misery and frustration. The iron vice and the iron claws which had grasped her on the evening after the party clamped again, resuming their grip. Her love burst inside her like a shower of needles. She hung on to the window but her knees and then her whole body gave way and drooped to the floor in an agony no one could endure for long.

It was not long before Mrs Brewer ceased to endure it.

Myra had rather disliked her mother but it was a shock to see her lying there, so great a shock as to make her feel faint and have to sit down with her head between her knees. Later that day, when the doctor had been and the undertakers, when the body had been removed to the undertakers' chapel of rest and Gingie had been taken home with Mrs Buxton, Myra sat down with a glass of sherry and realized that *her mother was dead.*

She had thought her mother would live for twenty years. Her mother had even seemed quite young as mothers went. Now she would never again be told that Mrs Brewer thought she was never coming or that she had made her bed and must lie in it or have her clothes and her manners and her cooking criticized. Harold was kind, made no complaint about being given a de-frosted TV dinner and kept saying, 'It's a bad business, a bad business.'

Dolly remembered how she had felt when her mother died, and though it went against the grain with her, she made herself go downstairs and say stiffly to Myra: 'I'm sorry about your mother.'

When Myra woke up in the morning, the first thought that came to her was that her mother was dead and the second, a new one, that the flat next door for which her mother had paid £30,000 two years before might now be hers.

She phoned George Colefax's home in Shelley Drive off the Bishop's Avenue. Yvonne answered.

'I shan't be in till Monday. My mother passed away yesterday. It's been quite a shock.'

'Your mother?' Yvonne's little girl voice rose an octave. 'But I was only talking to her last week,' as if this guaranteed Mrs Brewer could not have died, must be shamming. 'But that's incredible, Myra, that's really awful.'

'She had a very peaceful end,' said Myra. 'Very quick. She didn't suffer. Could you tell George, please, Yvonne?'

Yvonne said she couldn't because George hadn't spent last night at home, he had been working late so had stayed at the flat over the surgery, but she would phone him, of course she would do that. Myra had her own ideas about George working late and where he stayed but she was too preoccupied to think about that now.

During a quarrel some months before, indeed before Myra's marriage, Mrs Brewer had said she would get herself a will form and dispose of her property not to Myra, the natural legatee, but to the Cat Survival Trust. She even went so far as to look their address up in the phone book. Myra, enraged, bought the will form herself and gave it to Mrs Brewer next time she went over.

Had her mother ever filled it in and signed it and had it witnessed? It was unlikely but she must find out. Her mother had cooled down and come round, of course, and been very gratified about the marriage, but suppose she had made the will in the heat of the moment and never unmade it? Myra was in possession of a key to the flat next door. She went off and registered Mrs Brewer's death. She went to the undertaker and fixed up the cremation, and when she got home again, the police phoned her to say the coroner's officer's decision was that no inquest would be necessary. Pup and Harold came home and still she hadn't been next door. By now she felt sick with anxiety. She served Harold with his beef stroganoff and chocolate mousse, and when he had finished, she said she really thought she ought to pop next door and check everything was locked up and as it should be, et cetera. Her hand shook as she inserted the key in the lock.

Dolly and Pup had a pot noodle snack, Ryvita and Sainsbury's pâté, Waldorf salad, tinned peaches and cream. Pup changed into his best jeans, the pink and grey shirt and a new black velour sweat shirt. Dolly wore a dress she had just finished making for herself, a long-sleeved shirtwaister, the dark green material with a pattern of tiny strawberries chosen to go with her talisman. It was a very warm evening and there was as yet no autumnal chill in the air. The sky was a deep clear blue and the sun sinking in dazzling gold as they walked down Manningtree Grove towards Mount Pleasant Hall. Dolly had their tickets for Mrs Roberta Fitter's seance, at five pounds apiece, in her black suede handbag. She wore rather smart, lowish-heeled black court shoes. For most of the way Pup talked about magic, about self-initiation and spiritual exercises, about providing new insights into the psyche.

A corrugated iron fence had been put up round the demolition site. The plaster dust had subsided but it still clung like pale mould to the leaves on the shrubs in the hall garden, the laurel leaves and the rosemary and the lemon mint. The hall doors stood wide open. Dolly handed over their tickets.

The medium was late in arriving. The twenty-three people who had come to see Roberta Fitter do her stuff sat waiting patiently on the twenty-three rush-bottomed chairs Mrs Collins had assembled for them. Each bore a card with the intended occupant's name printed on it. Dolly and Pup were in the front row.

At the end of the hall in one corner a curtain rail had been fixed diagonally across, a little way down from the ceiling, and from this rail hung a pair of black curtains. Inside it was a chair with a padded seat and back and wooden arms, and behind the chair, another pair of curtains, dark green this time, hung flat against the wall.

Miss Finlay was sitting next to Dolly and next to Pup sat a very old man who wore, in spite of the heat, a raincoat and cloth cap. He was chewing tobacco, a habit Pup had never actually come across before. Miss Finlay pointed out to Dolly a big frog-faced woman sitting in the row behind them up against the left-hand wall.

'That's the lady who travels with Mrs Fitter. It's her job to look after her.'

'A sort of road manager,' said Pup but smiling so sweetly that no one could have taken offence.

'She's called Mrs Leebridge and Mrs Fitter's control is called Hassan. He was a sepoy that was killed in the Indian Mutiny defending a British officer from a maddened subahdar.'

From a room at the back of the stage, Mrs Collins appeared with her arms full of black clothing: a loose dress, a pair of knickers, a pair of tights and black velvet Chinese button-up slippers. These she dropped in Miss Finlay's lap.

'You have to pass them round,' Miss Finlay said. 'You have to check there's nothing concealed in them in case of fraud.'

Very painstakingly she pulled the tights inside out and stuck her fingers into the toes of the slippers before passing them on to Dolly. The frog-faced woman got up and closed all the windows and the room seemed immediately to become stuffy. She pulled down the thick dark green blinds and switched on the central light. The black garments went round from hand to hand, and when they reached the back row, Mrs Collins came on to the stage with a tall slight woman she introduced as Mrs Fitter. She said she wanted three ladies to come forward and watch Mrs Fitter dress herself. Dolly would never have put herself forward so far as to volunteer but Mrs Collins didn't wait for volunteers; she summoned Dolly and Miss Finlay and a Mrs Bullen.

In the room behind the stage, Roberta Fitter said

not a word as she stripped off her clothes. She was too important and her business too serious for idle chatter. Dolly thought how wonderful it would be if Pup could some day be revered like that. Mrs Fitter had a thin, brown, wrinkled body with breasts like pigskin purses and grey pubic hair. While they were waiting, Miss Finlay had told Dolly that at a recent seance someone in the audience had shouted at Mrs Fitter that she was a fraud and as a result the ectoplasm had rushed back into her body so rapidly that it had left a burn mark where it went in by way of her chest. Dolly, holding her hair instinctively across her own face, looked for the burn scar on Mrs Fitter's chest but she could see nothing except beads of sweat and a sprinkling of hairs.

When Mrs Fitter had dressed herself in the black clothes, she walked across in front of the audience and sat on the chair behind the open curtains. There was a red light on now from a table lamp on a plant pot stand about a yard to the right of the cabinet. Someone switched off the overhead light so that only the red one remained and this was very dim. It was just light enough to see that Mrs Fitter had gone into a trance. The curtains operated on cords and these Mrs Leebridge now drew to conceal Mrs Fitter from view.

Myra tip-toed in a reverent sort of way across the hall and into the living room. She had an idea she ought not to be in the flat, that she was perhaps breaking the law and that if a policeman or a solicitor were to see her she would be in grave trouble. This made her look uneasily about her, it made her keep on looking over her shoulder. A rolltop desk that had been her father's was her quarry. It wasn't locked. Myra opened it, lifted out a stack of yellow packets of holiday snaps and there underneath them, still blank, still untouched, lay the will form. Myra expelled her breath and momentarily closed her eyes. Then she went through the rest of the papers which Mrs Brewer had kept in an orderly way, found National Savings to the value of £3000 and a bank deposit book showing an accumulation of nearly £2000.

How long would she have to wait before she came into possession? Some months, she feared, remembering that when her father died intestate, letters of administration had had to be applied for. In that case, she might as well take her mother's fur coat with her, a very good ranch mink it was and only two years old. It would be a pity not to have the benefit of that next spring.

Harold was in the breakfast room. He had been doing a lot of serious reading lately – James Pope Hennessy's *Queen Mary*, no less, and a book called *The File on the Tsar* – so for light relief he had turned to an historical novel about the twin sons its author said Mary Queen of Scots had secretly borne to the Earl of Bothwell. He had just reached the point where one of the twins was about to rescue his father from the dungeons of Elsinore, when Myra came in wearing a fur coat. Harold stuck a finger in his book, half shut the covers and looked at her because it had been a very hot day and the temperature was still over seventy.

Myra took the coat off and threw it over the back of a chair.

'Well, Hal, I think you and I can count on being thirty-five thousand pounds to the good by next year. How does that grab you?'

'The old dear never made a will, then?'

'Of course she didn't. I knew that. It was all talk. Why bother when it'd naturally go to her only daughter? I think we ought to celebrate, we ought to have a bottle of champagne. It's not every day you come into money like that, we ought to have a real celebration.'

'I don't know about that,' said Harold. 'I don't fancy the idea of celebrating your mother's death.'

'We're not celebrating her death, don't be ridiculous, we're celebrating coming into money. It's not the same thing, surely you can see that?'

'Go down The Woman in White, then, shall we?'

'I'm not going there. Let people see me in a pub with Mother not even cremated yet! What a thing to suggest. Celebrate at home is what I meant, like civilized people do.'

Harold said nothing. He returned to the windswept ramparts of Elsinore. Myra looked in the cupboard in the dining room and found about a quarter of a bottle of sherry left over from her party and half that quantity of Dubonnet. While she was thinking what to do, she drank up the sherry direct from the bottle. It was a Friday, pay day, but because she had not been to work, her pay was still at the dental surgery. She had about forty-five pence in her purse.

'You could go to the wineshop and get us a bottle of sparkling white,' she said to Harold.

Harold laughed in an absent way without looking up. 'Good job you didn't take me up on my offer. I'm skint.' He pulled out his trouser pocket. 'Not a sausage.'

By this time Myra wanted a celebration very much indeed. An excited restless feeling had come over her. She was in that euphoric state in which one wants to dance about and sing, and as people do, she wanted a companion whose mood would match hers and who would dance about and sing with her. Harold Yearman was not ideally cast in this role but he was all she had. These days Myra seldom thought of the married man but she thought of him now, of how he had liked to enjoy himself and how wild he could be.

She stood in the hall which she was halfway through papering and which smelt of wallpaper adhesive, and she wondered if, considering the state of her current account, she dared give a cheque to the man in the wineshop. Even if she did dare, the shop closed at 8.00 and it was five to now. Myra looked up the stairwell. Doreen wouldn't miss a couple of bottles from that hoard of hers, probably didn't even know what she had there, and in any case Myra could replace them on Monday when she had been paid. Hal, she felt intuitively, wouldn't like the idea, so she wouldn't tell him. She went upstairs.

There were locks on some of the doors but none was locked. Myra opened the door into the living room and went in. The first cupboard she went to, in a shallow alcove beneath some shelves, was full of bottles of wine and she helped herself to two of Asti Spumante. Turning round, she nearly dropped them out of her arms. Four dolls were looking at her from the mantelpiece, two little girls with yellow plaits, an Indian boy and – herself. Though it was not flattering, though it was very nearly grotesque, she recognized it at once as herself from the hair, the bosom, the colours, the gold chains. Myra felt angry and a little afraid. She was glad she had taken the wine now, she didn't feel a bit guilty or apprehensive, she was glad she had thought of it.

Harold took it for granted that his wife had been the 200 yards or so down the road to buy the wine. He would not have involved himself in an argument over it or consented to the licensee of The Woman in White cashing a cheque or anything of that sort, but since she had got the wine and there was, after all, something worth celebrating, he put a bookmark into

Twins of Destiny and followed Myra into the dining room.

The french windows were open. The garden was green and leafy and full of shadows but glanced, too, with dark golden beams of sunshine. It was peaceful and still and very warm and a pigeon was cooing in the pear tree. Myra thought about the doll, pushed the thought fiercely away and poured the wine.

'To us! We're in business, Hal.'

'I don't know about that,' said Harold. 'There's many a slip between the cup and the lip.'

'How can there be when she never made a will? We can go to Cyprus for a fortnight now. First thing we'll do when we get the money is – buy a car!'

'You'll have to drive it then.'

'And have the kitchenette all done with pine units. And fitted carpet in our bedroom, a sort of amber colour would be nice.'

They talked for a while about what they would do with the money. The warmth of the evening and the wine spread through Harold, a delicious, languid calm. He answered Myra amiably while reflecting on the dismal fate of Mary Stuart. Presently Myra got up to close the windows.

'Or we'll have gnats in. There's one bitten me already.' She rubbed her thigh.

Harold said facetiously, 'Let's have a look.'

She had drunk the sherry before they had started and now she staggered a bit, lifting up her skirt to show him. Harold got hold of her and pulled her down on his knee. Her face was brightly flushed, that damask rose skin of hers, and he wondered why he had ever thought she looked like Edith; there was no resemblance. Plumped on Harold's lap, Myra was face to face with herself in the mirror on top of the sideboard. With the married man, she had sometimes looked at her own reflection in a narcissistic way and she did this now, suddenly seeing how beautiful she was, how young and voluptuous with her smooth skin and big round breasts, her mane of chestnut hair and her long legs in black spotted tights. For the first time she thought how lucky Harold was to have her for a wife, a beautiful young wife and he such a meagre little grey scrap of a man. Thinking of them like that, of her having so much to give and him unworthy but greedy to receive it, excited her. She put his hands on her breasts. She reached for her wineglass.

'D'you feel like a bit?' said Harold.

Normally she would have reproached him for his vulgarity. But she was sluggish, feeling sexier than she had done for nearly a year. 'Of course I do.'

'Better go upstairs then,' said Harold.

In Mount Pleasant Hall there was for a moment no human sound and it was dark but for the feeble red glow beyond the cabinet. You could make out the shapes of the persons sitting next to you and in front but no more. It was about as dark as it is in a theatre when the lights have gone down and the curtain not yet risen.

Mrs Collins, from her seat at the end of the front row, suggested they should all sing something. Hassan's favourite song was alleged to be 'Pale Hands I Loved Beside the Shalimar' but no one knew the words, so they sang 'The Volga Boatman' instead.

At the third repetition of 'Heave, my brothers', the curtains parted a little and a figure in a turban appeared between them. You could just make out the shape of the turban and a long white robe.

Miss Finlay whispered to Dolly, 'That's Hassan.'

'Sssh,' said Mrs Leebridge.

The figure spoke in a voice like that of the man

who kept the Tandoori takeaway shop in the Seven Sisters Road. 'Good evening, friends.'

There were murmurs from the audience and Mrs Leebridge said, 'Good evening, Hassan,' in a loud schoolmistressy way. 'Are you going to show us any spirit friends tonight?'

Hassan made no reply but disappeared between the curtains. A moment or two later his voice said:

'I have a lady here who passed on with a wound to her head, a car accident or something of that kind.'

There was silence. Dolly heard someone whispering behind her. Then a man from the row behind said rather hoarsely:

'Is it for me?'

Hassan said, 'That's the voice,' and the curtains parted to disclose another draped white figure, bulkier this time and with what looked like a bandage tied round its head. From behind Dolly came a sound as of indrawn breath. The figure spoke in a subdued girlish voice.

'It wasn't my fault, Michael.'

The man behind said, 'Let me see you close to.'

There was a mumbled something that sounded like 'too soon' and the figure glided back between the curtains. Dolly heard the man say, 'Oh, dear God,' in a voice tremulous with emotion.

'His wife was killed last year,' said Miss Finlay. 'She drove her car out into the road in front of a lorry. They lived next door to Mrs Bullen. Listen, Hassan's speaking again.'

'Is there anyone who has lost a gentleman who was in the forces perhaps? Anyway who wore a uniform?'

A girl from a row behind called out, 'Is it you, Dad?'

'That's the voice.'

From between the curtains came another white-robed shape. Mrs Leebridge said, 'Look, you can see his peaked cap.'

'Sssh,' said Miss Finlay.

Pup could see no peaked cap, only someone tall and thin, wrapped up in a sheet. The figure stood to attention and saluted.

'Isn't it wonderful?' said Mrs Leebridge. 'And you can see Mrs Fitter in the cabinet there lying in a deep trance all the time.'

Nothing in the cabinet was visible to Pup. It was too dark. He had looked carefully, though, as one taking a professional interest in something not too distant from his own line of country. The back of the hall, however, was a little less dark owing to one of the blinds having ridden up a fraction and let in a shaft of twilight. This was sufficient to show him the owner of the voice who had been claimed as his daughter by the figure in the peaked cap. It must be her, for everyone else (in Pup's own phrase) was as old as the hills. He saw the profile of a round youthful face, the plump curve of a cheek, an upturned nose and a mass of dark curly hair, and he was trying to see more when Mrs Leebridge got up and tugged down the blind.

The curtains closed quickly. Hassan's voice asked if there was anyone who had lost a four-footed companion. There were several replies to this, so it remained uncertain whose pet was the flickering white something that appeared briefly between the curtain hems or even what kind of animal it was. A bird materialized after that, or Mrs Collins said it was a bird, she said she saw it come out between the curtains and perch on the red table lamp. Dolly didn't see it but she was certain she felt its wings brush her face as it flew down the centre of the hall. A woman sitting next to the man called Michael claimed it as her dead budgerigar.

No more animals materialized but several more white figures came out, their robes reddened by the lamplight. The body of the hall was now totally dark because it had grown dark outside. There was a stillness and a quiet and then a fidgeting and whispering among the audience so that Dolly began to think the seance must be over. Hassan's voice made her jump.

'Are there a brother and sister sitting together in the front row?'

Dolly could not speak. It was Pup who answered.

'That's the voice!'

Dolly began to tremble and Pup took her hand and held it tight. A strong lemony scent drifted from the stage and pervaded the hall.

Chapter 10

The figure was tall and thin, faceless, a swaddled pillar of white sheet. The lamplight laid a red glaze on it, as on a cloth that has been used to wipe away blood. It swayed a little as it walked with mincing tread across the stage towards them.

'Is it you, Mother?' Dolly's voice was unsteady.

Hoarsely, as if its throat were constricted, it spoke. 'It makes me happy to see you two together.'

Dolly gasped. She reached out a hand yearningly. Then Pup too put out his hand and the apparition, swaying over them, clasped both in hers. Dolly felt thin bony fingers and a palm slippery with a clammy dew. In the darkness she tried to make out a feature, to recognize some defined angle of shoulder or hip, to sense the essence of her mother. The smell of lemons was overpowering. Pup raised himself up to look more closely, but immediately he did so, their hands were relinquished and the shape retreated. It glided away from them into the bloodstaining light, into the red air, and for a moment, before it disappeared between the curtains, its robes looked crimson. The curtains quivered and fell closed. Dolly gave a heavy sigh that made Pup turn and look anxiously at her, but she looked tranquil, she looked happy.

There were no more materializations. Hassan came out and said the medium had used up all her supply of ectoplasm and was in any case exhausted, that was enough for tonight, friends, and thank you very much. Dolly closed her eyes and breathed deeply. She felt as if her mother were still with her, still present in the hall. The central light was switched on and she blinked and sighed.

'Wonderful, isn't she?' said Mrs Leebridge. 'You've never seen anything like that before, I'm sure.'

Mrs Collins said it amounted to genius.

'There's not a doubt about that.' Mrs Leebridge went up to the cabinet and drew back the curtains and gave Mrs Fitter a cigarette.

There was a scraping of chairs as people got up. The blinds were raised and you could see the dark blue night, a sliver of moon made dim by the shine from street lights.

Dolly said in a vague dreamy voice, 'Mrs Collins's daughter is going to give us a lift home in her car.'

They filed out along the passage. The double doors were sheltered from the street by a porch with a gable and just inside the porch, beside the notice board, was standing the girl whose father had come out and saluted. In the quite bright electric light, Pup could see that she was a very pretty girl indeed. In fact she was not at all the sort of girl likely to be found in this company of the drab elderly, being about twenty and dressed in a very short navy blue dress with white coin spots, white tights and high-heeled red sandals. When she saw Pup she gave a nervous giggle.

'I know I'm a fool but I'm scared stiff to go out there in the dark.'

Mrs Collins was indignant. 'It makes me cross, that sort of thing. As if there was anything to be frightened of in our friends from the Other Side desiring a glimpse of their loved ones.'

'I can't help it, I'm scared.'

Pup made a decision. She was looking at him, her soft red lips slightly parted. There was no doubt in his mind what was happening. Like Coward's Amanda, his heart had always been jagged with sophistication, inexperienced though he was. The strange thing was that he hardly knew whether he was yielding to temptation or resisting it. All that was clear was that the time had come.

'Let me have the pleasure of seeing you home,' he said in his grave courteous way.

'*Would* you?'

'Of course.'

Dolly was too preoccupied to feel much resentment. Besides, she wouldn't be on her own, she would be in Wendy Collins's car, so there was no need to feel nervous about the 'Headsman', as the papers called him. Of her mother she could not be afraid, though that gliding presence had in any case slipped away.

The car dropped her outside the house. She unlocked the front door and let herself in. The house was in darkness and there was a draught blowing through from the back. Dolly hesitated and then she went through into the dining room where the draught was coming from and put the light on. The french windows were wide open and the breeze had blown Myra's new curtains so that one of them had wound itself round the standard lamp and the other been caught up on the back of a chair. There were two empty wine bottles on the ceramic top coffee table, which Dolly recognized as from her own stock, an empty glass and one half empty and on the floor by the window one of Myra's sandals and a pair of black spotted tights.

She closed the windows. She understood fairly well what had taken place and she shivered. The memory came to her very sharply of her mother in the white shroud and she seemed to feel again the damp coffin-cold hand. Somehow, although she knew her father was not really old, although Myra was quite young and what some would call attractive, she had believed the marriage had been made for convenience and companionship, what the French call a *mariage blanc*. Again she shuddered with disgust. On an impulse to admonish and insult, she stuck the heel of the sandal into the neck of one of the bottles and tied the tights round the other like a scarf round a snowman.

When she had done that, she was breathing like someone sobbing. All the joy and comfort of the evening was gone. She went upstairs, opened a bottle of wine and poured herself a tumblerful. If only Pup were there to talk to, if only he had come home with her! She had never discussed matters of that kind with him, he had seemed to her too young and innocent, but now she would not have been able to keep silent. Pup, though young, was wise; Pup had great ability to console. Thinking of the couple down below, directly below her, lying in a drunken satiated sleep, Dolly took her wine and sat in the window to wait for Pup to come.

Pup was in Hornsey. He was walking along slowly in the soft breezy late summer night.

'My girl friend got the tickets,' the girl was saying, 'and then she couldn't go. Well, she chickened out, if you ask me. I thought I'd go though just for a laugh. It was a laugh, wasn't it? My dad's alive and well and living in Slough. What's your name?'

'Peter.' Pup was digesting the implication of her last remark. 'You don't live at home then?'

'Me? You must be joking. I share with two other girls but they're away. They're students and their college isn't back yet.'

Pup took her arm to cross the road and did not bother to release it when they got to the other side. She said she was called Suzanne. Her rounded golden-skinned arm was covered with soft down which for some reason had become erect.

'You want to come in for a bit?'

They had arrived outside a house not unlike the Yearmans' but with a dozen bells by the front door. Suzanne's flat was a very large room and a very small bathroom and a tiny kitchen. The overhead light failed to come on when she pressed the switch and she groped for the table lamp. Pup touched her arm, shook his head and put a match to the half-burnt candle that was stuck in a wine bottle by one of the beds.

She giggled. 'I'm going to tell you something. I waited for you on purpose. There was an old woman offered me a lift but I said no.'

'I was looking at you all the evening,' Pup said. 'I was thinking how beautiful you are.'

'Were you really?'

Pup put his arms round her and kissed her. He felt he did it rather well, considering he had never done it before but only seen it done by couples in the street and on Christopher Theofanou's television. Suzanne responded so enthusiastically that Pup felt quite ill with excitement. What he would have liked and wondered if this was what all men would really like, would have been to tear all her clothes off and rape her in one minute flat. Impossible, of course. He said in a cool conversational tone: 'I've got news for you. I'm an innocent virgin.'

She stared. 'You're kidding.'

'No, it's the truth.' He smoothed back the dark curly hair, looked into her eyes. He let his hands slide to her shoulders and then enclose her soft full breasts. Pup had read a lot of books, including novels. 'But I'm young and strong. You'll have to teach me. Will that be all right?'

'Wow,' said Suzanne. 'You bet it will.'

Dolly waited for him. She re-filled her tumbler with wine. It was an hour and a half since Pup had parted from her to see the girl home. Of course the girl might live miles and miles away and perhaps they had had to wait for a bus and perhaps now Pup was waiting for a bus home. She might live in Wood Green or Hackney or almost anywhere in north London.

Pup was so small and slight. In the dark or at a distance he might easily be taken for a girl. The Headsman might take him for a girl. Dolly began to pace up and down but she was unsteady on her feet, the wine had done that for her. Midnight, half-past, ten to one. Suppose he had missed the last bus? Would he attempt to walk? Dolly poured herself more wine. She wanted to scream out her terror that something had happened to Pup. He might be walking home, he might meet the Headsman or that gang that roamed the council estate.

She longed for him. She began to count, one, two, three, when I get to a hundred I shall hear his key in the lock, I shall hear him coming up the stairs. Ninety-nine, a hundred ... The house was utterly silent, the world was silent, even the perpetual traffic seemed to have ceased. Dolly fell on her knees.

The Yearmans were not a religious family. God had not inhabited Dolly's childhood or done much more than nod in passing through school RI lessons. She found herself praying to the spectre that had swayed across the stage in Mount Pleasant Hall.

'Mother, protect Pup and bring him safe home to me ...'

She would never be able to sleep. What was the

use of going to bed? She finished the wine in the bottle, opened a second one. It was two o'clock. Another tumblerful finished her. She crept, she crawled, across the hall and fell on to her bed in a stupor.

At 7.30 on Saturday morning Pup came home. It was a beautiful morning and he felt jaunty and light on his feet and full of joy. As he let himself into the house it occurred to him that it would not behove him to show these feelings, so, with his story ready, nursing the secret knowledge of his date for six o'clock that evening – a story prepared to cover that, too – he came in a contained and rather diffident way up the stairs. He need not have worried. Dolly was still asleep. Harold was still asleep. Myra was awake and up and in the bathroom, taking aspirins, remembering what had happened. Her former lascivious feelings of exultation in sacrificing her beauty to grey old Harold had changed to revulsion, even shame. She pulled her bright green towelling dressing gown round her and tried to face the day ahead.

The day ahead was faceable for Dolly when she saw that Pup's bedroom door, which had been open when she went to bed, was now closed. Her head was pounding and she felt weak at the knees. Never before had she drunk so much wine at one go. She went down to the bathroom and had two aspirins out of the bottle Myra had left standing on top of the lavatory cistern. Her hair was all over the place. She damped it and combed it out and pulled a curtain of it carefully down to cover half her cheek. Instant coffee would help but she and Pup were out of coffee. She got her purse and key.

Myra was in the hall, her face haggard, her hair scooped up and pinned on the crown of her head. The green she wore looked iridescent to Dolly's morning-tender eyes, it was so bright. She pounced on Dolly.

'Surely it wasn't necessary to do that? I mean, go in there and shut the window, yes, but my sandal stuck there like that and my –.' Myra could not bring herself to say the word. Her face was red and working. Nor could she mention the doll. She had meant to, had planned to, but she couldn't.

'It was my wine,' Dolly said.

'Well, agreed, of course it was. And if you'd been at home I wouldn't have dreamed of such a thing without asking. I was going to put it back. First thing this morning, I was going to replace that wine and the fact is if you hadn't gone in there to shut that window, which to be perfectly honest was no damn' business of yours anyway, you'd never have known a thing about it.'

'A person likes privacy.'

'You'd better lock your doors then.' Myra had forgotten all about wanting to be friends with Dolly. She thought she could see in Dolly's eyes knowledge of what had happened on the previous evening, knowledge and scorn, so she lashed back in the way some people do when their antagonist has a disability.

'You don't imagine doing your hair like that hides that thing on your face, do you? Frankly, Doreen, it draws attention to it.'

No one, ever, had referred to Dolly's naevus in any fashion comparable to this. She could hardly believe what she had heard. But she had heard it and she was aware that she would feel the full pain of it later. Blushing deeply, she turned instinctively away; humiliated, she performed the more deeply humiliating act of presenting her 'good' cheek to Myra.

'Pancake make-up would be better,' Myra pursued. She loved giving cosmetic advice, advice on clothes, on 'making the best of oneself', and in doing so she forgot her original malice. 'Or even Leichner stage make-up, a greenish powder maybe. You'd need an expert in techniques for covering scars, that sort of thing, but that's not a problem, I mean, these people do exist.' She put out a hand and lifted the long lock of hair. Flushed with blood, the naevus burned a rich purple.

Dolly jerked backwards, pulled her hair out of Myra's grasp and ran out of the front door. It was cooler this morning, quite cool and fresh, and the breezy emptiness of the street was like her own loneliness. She hated Myra, that went without saying, she loved Pup. Yet last night, simply by staying out, simply by not being there as he always was, he had taken a step away from her. Dolly felt colder than the temperature warranted. She longed for a friend to talk to. Why couldn't a friend have come into the house instead of an enemy like Myra? When she reached the corner shop she realized she was holding her hair across her cheek, holding it with both hands, her shoulders hunched.

Myra never said a word about the doll. Perhaps she hadn't seen it when she went in to take the wine, Dolly thought, or perhaps if she had noticed it she hadn't recognized it, vain as she was, as representing herself. One afternoon when she had nothing else to do, Dolly made it an emerald green jacket from a scrap of material left over from a client's dress. Emerald had been a fashionable colour that summer.

The doll soon lost its companions. Miss Finlay bought one of the little girls with yellow plaits, Wendy Collins's best friend had the Indian boy and Mrs Leebridge wanted the other little girl.

Dolly took it to Mrs Leebridge's flat herself. This was in Camden Town, in a block not far from the tube station. Mrs Leebridge, large, flabby-fat, frog-faced, was perhaps the only person Dolly had ever known who could be in her company without reacting in some way or other to her naevus – without staring at it in fascination and then quickly looking away or ostentatiously not looking at her face at all ever or darting swift covert glances. Mrs Leebridge behaved with Dolly just as she did with everyone else, noticing her only as a sponge to suck up the stream of self-love and boastfulness which poured from her thick flapping lips and the almost equally effusive adulation of everything pertaining to Roberta Fitter.

The doll was paid for, glanced at, then set aside and ignored. Mrs Leebridge talked about how she herself had been privileged to see ectoplasm coming out of Mrs Fitter's chest and forehead in white streams. She showed Dolly photographs of spirit faces surrounded by ectoplasm and floating in the air and one of Mrs Fitter in a trance with a long white tube coming out of her chest and a man's face in a kind of balloon at the end of it.

'I hope you'll come to another of our seances, dear.'

Dolly said she would think about it.

'I hope you'll do more than think, dear. Only five pounds, that's nothing these days, that's less than you'd pay to go to a show in the West End.'

Dolly didn't much like underground trains. You had to sit facing people and people in trains had nothing else to do but look at other people. But Mrs Leebridge lived so near the station that it seemed stupid to hang about waiting for a bus.

It was just after 5.30. She was a hundred yards or so from the station entrance when she saw Myra ahead of her with her red bushy hair down on her shoulders and wearing the very sandals one of which

101

Dolly had stuck by its heel into the neck of the Asti bottle. George Colefax's practice was in Camden High Street and Myra must be on her way home from work.

Vaguely Dolly knew that Myra travelled by tube from Camden Town to Archway and caught a bus or more usually walked the half-mile or so home to Manningtree Grove. She disliked the idea of travelling home with Myra and she hung back a little until Myra had passed into the station and was lost to view.

Dolly wondered what Myra would say if she warned her off wearing that awful emerald green. No doubt it was all right for Myra to give people unwanted advice but not for them to give it to her. By the time Dolly came into the station Myra had disappeared and Dolly did not see her again until she came on to the platform.

There were a lot of people on the Barnet Line platform, though it was not densely packed. As usual, people had gathered themselves into groups, each separated from the next by a few feet, at the very edge of the platform. How they would know exactly where the doors would be when the train came in (for this was the reason for the mode of waiting), Dolly had never been able to understand. Myra was in the centre of one of these groups in her emerald green cardigan. At some point between Dolly's first sight of her and now, she had scooped up her hair in the way she often did, no doubt because of the heat – it was very hot down here in the tunnel – and had fastened it on to the back of her head with a large tortoiseshell slide Dolly had not seen before. It was interesting to someone fond of clothes and colour to notice how a fashionable shade such as that green would occur regularly in every crowd, when you half-closed your eyes you could see dozens of bright spots of it against a uniformly drab background. It had been the same, she remembered, a year or so back when purple grape was 'in' and during the months she called the 'yellow summer'. Dolly herself was wearing a sand-coloured coat and skirt, with a sand-and-blue-and-red check shirt and Pup's amulet tucked away inside it because it did not quite 'go'.

She made her way through the press of people until she was behind Myra and within four or five feet of her. On the left of her stood a tall businessman in a chalk-stripe suit and on her right a plump elderly woman. Their bodies slightly overlapped Myra's; she was a little nearer the edge of the platform than them. A bright segment of green cardigan, a scrap of green, white and navy check skirt, showed between their more sober grey and fawn, and this, as Dolly watched, was in turn covered by the slim shape of a young girl in the same fashionable green spotted with black. Dolly moved forward. The notice which announced incoming trains had lit up to indicate that the next one would be for Mill Hill East.

It seemed to Dolly that everyone was staring directly ahead, reading for perhaps the hundredth time the advertisement posters on the concave wall of the tunnel opposite or, as in the case of the man in chalk-striped grey, a folded newspaper held three or four inches from the eyes. Dolly hooked her handbag over her shoulder and looked down at her hands. She turned her hands over, palms uppermost, and looked at them. Images filled her mind: her mother shrouded and gliding across the dark stage, the rooms she and Pup now lived in, a pair of spotted tights lying by an open window, an amorphous greenness on which lay fiery hair. Suddenly she fancied she could smell lemons.

The girl in the green with the black spots on it stepped a little to one side. Dolly had not exactly pushed her but had thrust herself behind the man in grey and rather to the right of him so that the girl was obliged either to move or argue. She gave Dolly a huffy look and turned her head away. Dolly was aware of two more people, perhaps more than two, coming to stand immediately behind her and the girl. They pressed against her, not pushing, but standing very close. She could feel their warm breath on the back of her neck. It was very warm indeed in the tunnel and sweat prickled Dolly's upper lip.

No one but the girl could have seen what she did with her hands and the girl had turned her face away in offence. Dolly held her now shaking hands at waist height. She could not see the train lines, the rails on which the wheels ran or the electrified rail between them but she knew they were down there, in the deep gulf between the platform and the concave wall. Last week, Pup had told her, the line between Mornington Crescent and Euston had been closed for two hours because someone had thrown himself on the line. Not in front of a train but just on to the electrified rail, and it had killed him. Of course, for good measure, if you wanted to commit suicide it would be a surer way to throw yourself over just when the train was coming in.

The light up the track at the far end was green now, awaiting the coming Mill Hill East train. Dolly could hear it in the distance and feel the wind that blew ahead of it. She held herself perfectly still, her eyes on that bright, virulent, poisonous green, which was all she could now see, which had expanded itself into a great green field crowding all her vision. Her throat was constricted and dry. She unclasped her hands and raised them, the palms a spare centimetre from the green jacket, the woolly pile of it brushing her hands. The train burst out of the tunnel mouth into the station and Dolly braced herself to push.

The elderly woman in brown turned round sharply. The twitch or start Dolly had made must somehow have alerted her. She took in the position of Dolly's hands a second before Dolly snatched them away and her face, bun-like, motherly, one of those determinedly cheerful faces, was overspread with horrified disbelief.

The train stopped and the doors opened. There was a surge forward. Dolly turned and fought her way back through the crowd eager to get into the train. She pushed with her hands, with her arms and shoulders, coming as she retreated in a panic, face to face with Myra.

Chapter 11

She needed air. She sat on a wall, breathing deeply, feeling the damp breeze on her face. It was horrible to think of what she had nearly done, sent some stranger to her death by electrocution and under the wheels of a train. Myra had not even been at the front of the waiting crowd but well in the rear. Perhaps there had been some difficulty over her ticket or she had been delayed, talking to someone she knew. Whatever it was, the woman in the green coat that Dolly's hands had almost pushed over that subterranean precipice had not been Myra, though she had been almost more Myra-like than her apparent double, for Myra, when Dolly came face to face with her, stared at her, passed her speechless, had been wearing a tan-coloured skirt and her red fuzzy hair still hung about her shoulders.

And now Dolly thought of the pleasant bun face, briefly become horrified. Suppose that woman should pursue her, tell the police of her? Attempted murder, she thought, and she put up her hand to the naevus by which anyone who had seen her could identify her. She got up. She was afraid to go back into the station and began to walk rapidly up the Kentish Town Road.

A taxi came and she got into it. It was perhaps only the second taxi she had been in in her life, but she felt she couldn't face any form of public transport. She was overwhelmed with dread of the police coming and the bun-faced woman with them, of knowing herself identified and hearing her action described. As soon as she was home she poured herself a big glass of red wine and it comforted her, it gave her courage. The second glassful she took with her into the temple. She thought she would hide there if they came and tried to find her. Before settling herself on the cushions, she moved to the altar to look at the elemental weapons as she always did on coming in here. Amid her fear it brought her a separate feeling of unease to see a film of dust lying on the dagger's blade that Pup used to keep so bright.

The doorbell ringing fetched her out on to the landing. Her father went to answer it and she expected the deep sound of men's voices and the tramp of feet. But it was only Myra who had forgotten her key. Dolly re-filled her glass.

'I couldn't get in the first train that came,' Myra said crossly. 'It made me hours late. You'll just have to have an omelette or something.'

Harold would rather have had tinned ravioli or a pork pie but there were no such things in the house or not down here. He was obliged to accept what Myra called a 'soufflé' omelette, this being the kind in which the whites of the eggs are separately beaten into stiff peaks. Harold thought it was like eating peppered and salted cotton wool but he didn't let it bother him. He ate it with a fork held in his right hand, using his left to turn the pages of a reconstruction of the life of Henry II's paramour Rosamund Clifford, which he had propped up against the cruet. Myra, breathing hard, took away his plate and handed him a crème caramel she had made the night before.

'I thang you!' said Harold, continuing to read. He

had the lady encaged by the king in the middle of Woodstock maze.

Myra snatched the book and threw it on the coffee table.

'Steady on,' said Harold. 'You've lost my place.'

'Well, for God's sake, always reading at meal-times.'

Harold licked his spoon. 'I've finished now,' he said mildly. 'Want to go up The Woman in White?'

Myra shrugged. They went. Ronald and Eileen Ridge were in the pub but they had little to say and Harold never said much. Myra, who had rather more to drink than usual, was almost silent.

'What's up with you?' said Harold on the way back. 'You got your visitor, is that it?'

Myra shook her head. She couldn't be bothered to answer him, not even to tell him off for using vulgar euphemisms. She only wished she had got her 'visitor'. Thirty-nine was young to have the menopause but not out of the question, she supposed. Not long ago she had read in a magazine at the hair-dresser's that it was normal to have the menopause any time between thirty-eight and fifty-five. But she was such a young thirty-nine! She was so pretty and with a young girl's bloom on her, she couldn't be having the change, could she? She couldn't already be sliding into the grey sexless trough of middle age. Hair growing on the face, she thought, her waist thickening, hot flushes and all the rest of it. The other possible reason for a woman of thirty-nine missing a period she wasn't even going to consider.

It was pointless worrying about it. She was eagerly awaiting the arrival of the letters of administration so that she could get at her mother's bank account. Harold said it wasn't right for her to keep going next door taking what she wanted out of the flat; she ought to wait till she got the okay to go ahead. Myra didn't care. She seldom attended to Harold's wishes these days. In the meantime she finished doing up the hall and when the paint was dry and the carpet down she fetched in two rugs from Mrs Brewer's living room, a console table and a framed reproduction of *The Laughing Cavalier*.

Yellow leaves fell gently on to the yellowed grass of the old railway line. A sinking sun put forth mild gleams through the smoky autumnal haze. Pup and Suzanne walked along hand-in-hand. They had been to the cinema in Muswell Hill because on Saturdays the students spent all afternoon beautifying themselves and did not go out before evening.

From time to time, they stopped and kissed or stood embraced or simply stood still, hugging each other and gazing into each other's eyes. They behaved like all young lovers do who are suffering from temporary frustration, causing embarrassment to the few people who passed them and who had forgotten what it feels like to be nineteen or so and forced by circumstances to go to the cinema instead of to bed.

By six, the student who was going to see her mother would have gone and seven would see the departure of the student who was going out with her boy friend. Pup kissed Suzanne on the bridge at Stanhope Road and hurried her down the steps. They did not see Myra but she saw them. She had been down to Crouch End Broadway for an evening paper and a packet of Rennie's for her indigestion and she saw them as she was walking back to Manningtree Grove. Dolly was coming down the stairs as she let herself into the house and would have walked past Myra with averted eyes.

Myra said loudly, 'It's ridiculous you taking this

attitude, Doreen. What have I done, I should like to know? Tried to help you, that's all.'

Dolly opened the front door in silence.

'Let me tell you,' said Myra, getting closer to the bone than she guessed, 'you're going to need friends one of these fine days. When you're all on your own you're going to need friends. You won't always have your brother.'

Still Dolly did not speak but she hesitated.

'You won't always have your brother dancing attendance on you. He'll want to lead his own life, he'll want to get married, won't he? As a matter of fact I've just seen him walking along with a girl – hand-in-hand, to be perfectly honest with you. Rather a tarty-looking girl, I must say, but we'll let that pass. You didn't know? You actually didn't know, did you? Well, I'm sorry if it's been a shock but it's always better to know, isn't it? I can't honestly say it didn't look like they'd got a serious thing going because, frankly, it did.'

Dolly, as on the previous occasion, went quietly out into the street and closed the door behind her. A feeling of sickness which had nothing to do with what had just passed, which had in fact come over her in just the same way on the previous evenings, now overwhelmed Myra. She retched, clapped her hand over her mouth and rushed for the kitchen sink. Harold, sitting in the breakfast room in one of the few remaining old armchairs, looked up from Robert K. Massie's *Nicholas and Alexandra* at the sounds of vomiting. This was his last remaining sanctum but even here the wallpaper had been stripped from one of the walls and Myra's paintpots already stood on newspapers on the gateleg table. He got up, put his head round the door and called out that it must be the paint getting at her, maybe she had a paint allergy.

'You're just trying to stop me making the place look nice,' Myra shouted back.

It can't be true, it can't be true, a voice cried to Dolly. The voice was in her head but it was like her mother's voice. She had been going out for wine. Not to the shop in Northwood Road – since the Headsman she went there no more – but to the nearest place, the wine supermarket in the Broadway. She had one bottle left, she could get more tomorrow. She walked round the block, came back to the house and ran upstairs. On the top landing she thought she smelt lemons, just for a moment and then the whiff of it was gone.

Her mother's voice said quite clearly, out loud, 'It's true!'

Could she ask Pup? Would she dare? How could she ask him anyway, when she never saw him, when he was never there? It *was* true and she would lose him. She had never thought of the possibility of this before, that Pup might leave her for another woman. Somehow, without formulating it in words, she had believed he and she would be together, celibate and holding themselves apart, all their lives. She imagined him and this girl, hand-in-hand, walking home through the October twilight to her home. The mother opening the door to them, tea with the family, Pup the recognized accepted suitor. Oh, the pain of it, the unspeakable agony of it!

She opened that last bottle of wine and poured a tumblerful and drank it down like a thirsty person drinks water. If only he would come! If he came now, she thought she would have the courage to ask him. But he wouldn't come, he wouldn't come till the deep middle of the night. She tried to think of other things. Often she felt it should have weighed on her more, what she had done on the station platform at Camden Town, or what she had meant to do and

111

would have done but for the bun-faced woman. Her mind reverted to it and sweat broke over her as she thought of what might have happened.

But it was not a powerful enough diversion to distract her from Pup for long. The tears were running down her face. She took a duster into the temple and dusted the things on the altar, and as she worked she cried. Pup's golden robe hung neglected on the back of the door, a half-burned candle lay on its side in a heap of joss-stick ash. Dolly blew off the dust that had settled on the books, the four volumes of *The Golden Dawn*, the heavy tome that was *The Chaldean Oracles of Zoroaster*, the slimmer *Book of the Dead*, *The Key of Solomon*. She cleaned it all up and tidied it and then she sat on the floor and wept. Just before 8.00, she went out to buy more wine and, passing the bathroom door, heard Myra being sick inside.

In the hairdressers on Monday afternoon Myra read in a magazine an article called 'Those Different Pregnancies' which said that some pregnant women were sick in the evenings, not the mornings, they might even be sick or feel queasy all day long. Myra, under the dryer, felt hot already. Now the sweat broke from her and ran down her sides. She couldn't be pregnant, could she? It was seven weeks since she had had a period and five weeks and a bit since that stupid business when they had drunk the wine to celebrate her mother's money. But even so, she couldn't be pregnant by old Harold, it just wasn't possible.

With the married man she had been on the pill but it wasn't wise to stay on that indefinitely so, when she had come off it, sometimes she had taken care of that side of things and sometimes he had. Often she hadn't been very careful. A psychiatrist would say,

Myra knew from her magazines, that this was because she had unconsciously wanted a child. And maybe she had, maybe she had thought that would have fetched him permanently to her, in spite of his wife. Yet for all that passion, for all that love-making, two or three times in an afternoon sometimes, Myra had never even had a false alarm. And she had been young then, she thought sadly, and he young and strong, a big virile man who had fathered two children on his wife. It wasn't possible that she had never conceived in all those years, yet now be pregnant by puny old Harold.

Walking home from the station over the Archway bridge and down Hornsey Lane, she met Harold and Pup coming home from the shop via the library. Pup was carrying his father's books under his arm. That was something that maddened Myra – the idea of being married to someone who had to have things carried for him by a younger and stronger man. It was half-past five and she was starting to feel sick again.

'Not going out with your friend tonight then?' Dolly said as Pup walked in.

Pup shook his head. Suzanne had a week's holiday and, long before she had met him, had fixed up to go to Corfu with a girl friend – the same one who had chickened out of the seance – and she couldn't cancel it, she'd paid £100 in advance. Pup was wondering how he would get on without her. He sat down to his corned beef and Marks & Spencers ratatouille, a carton of tropical fruit juice and a rum baba.

All day Dolly had been screwing herself up to this, rehearsing what to say. And there was always the fear he wouldn't come home anyway. When at last she did speak, it was with apparent insouciance.

'This friend of yours, it's a girl, isn't it?'

Pup hesitated. He put down his knife and fork. He

113

knew very well, almost precisely in fact, how Dolly felt about him. She was even more possessive of him than Dilip Raj's mother was of her son. And Dilip Raj's mother didn't have a birthmark slapped on the side of her face like a great crimson pancake. Pup understood it all. 'Yes, it is,' he said gently, and then, 'How did you know?'

Dolly didn't answer. 'Pup, is it serious? You aren't thinking of getting married, are you?'

'Of course not,' said Pup with perfect truth.

Dolly had gone white but now her colour came back, though she was still breathless.

'"Of course not" to what? It isn't serious or you aren't getting married?'

'Both,' said Pup. 'Neither. Anyway, she's not here any more, she's gone away. Now you can tell me how you knew.'

She used his name for Myra. She was happy and she made a sound that was nearly a giggle. 'Our wicked stepmother.'

He shrugged at that. Dolly watched him eat the rum baba and drink up his fruit juice. She was drinking Mosel herself, just starting on the second bottle, and working on a new doll, a ballet girl with black hair and a tutu.

When he had finished, Pup went into the temple. It suddenly seemed very small. Virginity is an asset to a geomancer. Maiden virtue holds some special qualities that are dissipated by sexual experience. Pup had known this long before he yielded to temptation (or resisted the temptation to keep himself pure and aloof) because the price he was paying in avoiding sex was very high and his diffuse, urgent desires had to be constantly assaulted by invocation and banishing rituals.

But the effect of terminating chastity was dramatic.

He could no longer do magic. It was true, just as the books said, the gift was lost, the power vanished.

He stood in the temple and looked about him and saw a poky attic bedroom with streaky black walls and bits of rubbish lying on an old bamboo table. The idea of making holy water or burning incense seemed grotesque. He could not imagine chanting all that Hebrew mumbo-jumbo, at least not *seriously*. He had abandoned his chastity and the power had gone.

Or could it be that something more easily explainable had happened? Here Pup's strong vein of common sense asserted itself. Could it be instead that now he had discovered sex, the things which he had done before now seemed mere childish substitutes for it? Very likely. Most probably it was both these explanations which contributed to his feeling of boredom about the temple and what had gone on in it.

He looked regretfully at his collection of books. He thought of all the knowledge he had accumulated. It was a pity to waste it. Perhaps he need not waste it. Considering the enormous store Dolly had learned – had been taught, he thought, by him – to set on magic and the rituals and all the jiggery-pokery of it, it would be unkind and unwise altogether to abandon it. He loved Dolly. But, oh, how he loved this new glory that had entered his life! The two loves seemed incompatible unless he could achieve some compromise and achieve it through his lost magical skills.

Pup stood at the window in the temple, thinking of all this, holding the silly knife with its crudely painted handle, watching the blackened leaves drop from the fruit trees and float slowly down on to the wet grass. A plan, daring yet simple, was beginning to take shape in his mind.

Chapter 12

Dismay was what most women felt in the presence of Yvonne Colefax. If a woman knew she was going to see Yvonne, she would dress carefully and pay particular attention to her face and hair only to find that she was still inadequate, she was still not in competition. Yvonne inspired dismay and a resigned sinking of the heart. One remembered her as beautiful but generally as less beautiful than she was, so that each time one saw her afresh, it was with shock that she was so much lovelier than one had expected.

Two things about her consoled Myra. One was that Yvonne was nice, she was what people call 'always the same' and that sameness was to be simple, childlike and friendly, and the other was that the one person on earth Yvonne wanted to be noticed and admired by did not seem to see his wife as anything out of the ordinary. More than that, he seemed to prefer almost anyone's company to hers, and if there was ever a case of a man treating his wife like a servant and his home like an hotel, this was it. Myra wouldn't have put up with it for a moment, let alone five years or however long it had been that George and Yvonne had been married. Yvonne might have a Porsche to drive about in and a wonderful house just off the Bishop's Avenue but that, Myra reflected sententiously, was no substitute for respect and consideration. And here was Yvonne, being George's doormat again or at least his errand girl, running down to Camden Town with something else George had forgotten when she must surely have better things to do with her time.

Yvonne came up to the desk where Myra sat in the front hall. Myra had forgotten just how pale and fair and soft her hair was, like dandelion fluff. And how slim she was, slender enough to bring a pang to almost any woman's heart, and how aquamarine blue her eyes. She was never overdressed, never unsuitably dressed, but for all that she didn't dress like other people but rather like someone in a film or television play whose garments have been very carefully chosen by experts and whose accessories are all exactly the same shade. The expert was, of course, Yvonne herself and this morning she looked like the young Faye Dunaway dressed for the part of a woman from the East Seventies going shopping in Saks Fifth Avenue. Camel-coloured suit with a thin brown belt and tall, narrow, shining brown boots as bright as conkers and a rakish little white felt hat with a brown ribbon. The scent of Ivoire overcame that of the pine air-freshener with which they sprayed out the waiting room each morning.

'You look absolutely amazing,' said Myra generously. 'You off somewhere exciting?'

'Just out shopping,' said Yvonne as Myra had known she would. 'George rang and said would I get him a Higginson's and bring it in, so I have. Here it is.'

'A what?' said Myra but by that time she had unwrapped and exposed the long cardboard box labelled 'Higginson's Syringe'. 'What does he want that for?'

'He's got this patient swears it's her teeth and George says it's not, it's her ears, so he's going to syringe her ears out.'

'I could have popped out and got that,' said Myra. 'Want a coffee now you're here?'

'I'd love some coffee. You are kind, Myra. I'm afraid I'm just an awful nuisance, aren't I?' Yvonne said this with the air of one who is accustomed to being told she is tiresome and her jewel-like greeny-blue eyes sparkled as if tears always hung suspended in them. 'You look a bit pale. Are you all right?'

Myra thought how nice Yvonne was. Why couldn't Doreen be like that, friendly and down-to-earth and meeting you halfway? After all, if there was anyone with a reason for putting on airs, it was Yvonne, and yet here she was as natural as a child. For a moment she thought of confiding in Yvonne but she dismissed the idea. It was more than possible that Yvonne actually wanted a child and would have scant sympathy for a woman with an undesired pregnancy. So she only smiled and said she was a bit tired and they chatted about clothes for a while over their coffee and Yvonne told Myra how she had been all the way to Florence specially to buy her boots and handbag and belt and Myra didn't think she was too awful, did she?

Half an hour after she stopped work for the day Myra had an appointment with her GP. She had brought a specimen of urine with her but she knew it was too late to bother about that. She knew she was pregnant, eight or nine weeks' pregnant, and it was not confirmation she needed. She needed advice, consent or maybe, hopefully, only the making of arrangements.

Walking up the windy hill to Camden Town Station, Myra thought about the married man. She had been thinking about him a lot lately. It was in autumn that he and she had met and in autumn that they had parted. Myra thought of how she had stood in the bay window of her furnished room, watching for his car to come and for him to step out of it and slam the door and walk towards the house, walking with that supple grace of his, his head held high. He had stayed slim, never put on an ounce of weight, and the frosting of grey in his hair only made him look more distinguished. Every Wednesday and every Friday and most Monday evenings for year after year he had come and then one day he had told her there was no way he could desert his wife and she had rejoined that she had had a better offer anyway. Did he know where she was now? Did he ever think of her?

In spite of the appointment, she had to wait nearly half an hour to see her doctor. He examined her and confirmed the pregnancy. He began scolding her for not having come before; at her age early attention was vital, an amniocentesis would have to be carried out. Myra interrupted him. She didn't want a baby, she wanted an abortion. The doctor looked rather severe and Myra, made defiant, angry and unhappy too because fearful doubt is not at all the same thing as certainty, said aggressively that she thought any woman in England had the right to an abortion just by asking for it.

'Before we take any steps,' the doctor said, 'I should like to talk to you and your husband together.'

From that, in spite of her pleas of it being her baby, her body and her business, Myra could not move him. He would do nothing for her until he had spoken to Harold as well. Myra had never discussed with Harold the possibility of having children. It had no more occurred to her than it would to discuss men with Dolly or clothes with the perpetually sweatered and trousered Eileen Ridge. But now that she thought about it, she was not at all sure that

Harold would be as dismayed at the prospect of a child as she was. Lazy, slow, apathetic people often liked children. Harold, in a half-hearted way, seemed to like the children he already had. Suppose, when she told him, he were to react with thrilled excitement? Suppose he were to be, in one of his own phrases, tickled to death? Suddenly Myra knew beyond a doubt that this was how it would be – Harold thrilled, Harold flattered at this proof of his virility, Harold adamant when it came to discussing with any doctor the termination of the pregnancy.

Myra walked home up Crouch Hill. She reflected dismally that, no matter how frightened and fed up a woman might be, she still had to think about what to have for supper. She went into the shop that was part butcher, part delicatessen, and the Irishman with the peculiar eyes and the rubbery face served her with two pork chops. He never smiled, he never said much, he always seemed to be listening. Next door was a newsagent. Myra bought an evening paper. She was in search of an advertisement she had seen before, directed at women requiring abortions, and there it was, a box among the small ads.

She rang the number when she got home. The woman she spoke to was friendly and forthcoming and she said she must warn Myra that, on admission to the nursing home, before anything was done, a fee of £500 would be required from her. It was only fair to tell her this from the start. Myra put the phone down. There was £20 in her current account and this amounted to all her resources. The letters of administration had not yet come, might not come for weeks, and until they did, though she might drop in next door picking up unconsidered trifles, there was no way she could get her hands on her mother's money. These things always took ages. It was over two months already. Myra could remember precisely when her mother had died, for the date of that death was the day before the conception of this hated, unwanted child.

Pup had plans for the expansion of Yearman and Hodge. As soon as he had passed his driving test, they were going to buy a van. He had started going out servicing typewriters but it would be better when they had the van. These new electronic machines were the thing, Pup said to his father, big and efficient but light as a feather with all the works a mere microchip. They could still do well and make a profit if they took twenty-five per cent off for cash.

'You've got drive,' said Harold in the sort of tone one might use to inform someone he had a nasty cold.

'We'll have to think about photocopiers for the future,' said Pup. 'Photocopiers are the coming thing.'

He walked up to Queen's Avenue in Muswell Hill, though it wasn't a very nice day but wet and windy. When he got home, he resolved, he would do some magic for Dolly. To make her happy. Like in the old days, he would perform one of the great rituals with incense and wine and roses. He owed that to Dolly.

The girl who opened the door to him said she typed theses for people. She was in the middle of doing this philosophy thesis for someone seeking a PhD and the typewriter was sticking on the *g*. Well, the carriage return was sticking too. She had had it three years and it had never had a real service.

Pup set to work on it. It was an Adler and he knew all about Adlers. The girl watched him. She was rather a plain girl with a long face and a big nose but she had waist-length blonde hair and a very good figure. The figure was shown off to the best advantage in Lycra stretch jeans and a red T-shirt. Both looked brand new and Pup wondered if she had put them on because he was coming. They had met once before in the shop.

After a while she produced a bottle of Asti Cinzano. 'But perhaps you don't drink on duty?'

'I'm not a policeman,' said Pup.

'It's a well-known female fantasy,' the girl said, 'sort of day-dreaming what it would be like with the man who comes to mend the TV.'

'Or the Adler Gabrielle Five Thousand.'

'Well, if you say so.' She poured generous fizzy pink drinks. 'What's your name? I mean I know it's Yearman but what's your first name?'

'Peter. What's yours?'

'Philippa. How much longer is that going to take you?'

'About five minutes, Philippa.'

'Do you know, I suddenly got scared your father might come instead. I mean, I couldn't have fantasies about him, could I? Can I re-fill your glass?'

'Not if you don't want me to spoil this very nice expensive typewriter for good and all.' While he still had his chastity, Pup thought, he had been able to handle this sort of thing. It had sometimes happened and he had pretended not to understand. Ah, those were the days! Or were they? 'There you are, I don't think you'll have any more trouble with that *g*. Are you registered for the Value Added Tax?'

'What, me?'

'One mustn't take anything for granted,' said Pup, very close to her now. He lifted some soft locks of fair hair that clung to the front of the T-shirt. In spite of Suzanne he felt less than fully confident, so he used the ploy that had succeeded so well with her. 'For instance, you're probably acting in the belief that I'm an experienced man while the fact is I'm still a virgin.'

'That's unbelievable!'

'There are more things in heaven and earth, Philippa, than are dreamt of in all the philosophy you type on that machine.'

'Well,' said Philippa, 'you don't want to go on being one, do you? I mean you'd like to sort of put an end to it?'

'I should love to,' said Pup with fervour.

He felt a bit tired at the end of the day. Walking slowly homewards, he turned over in his mind the plans he had made to keep Dolly happy and give him a measure of freedom. Tomorrow night he had a date with Philippa and he meant to spend all day Saturday with Suzanne. Dolly, alerted by Myra, would never be made to believe he was spending all that time, half the day and half the night, with Chris Theofanou. He was generally free from vindictive feelings, but these days he felt quite savagely towards his father's wife. Pup had a special dislike of wanton malice.

An evening class or a club, or better still, a combination of both were what was needed. And a club-cum-class that would seem to benefit him in the one pursuit of his that interested Dolly. Pup had no qualms about telling quite ferocious lies in a good cause. He was pleased with his plan, it seemed to him foolproof.

Dolly began grumbling as soon as he got in. 'I hate being forced to live up here. I hate this poky room and having to go down all those stairs every time I want to use the bathroom. It's so unfair! People won't climb up here and it's not worth my while making their clothes if I've got to spend pounds on bus fares.'

'I've got something to tell you,' Pup said.

She had been putting food on the table in front of him, cold sausages, potato salad, a bowl of tomatoes, but she stopped, holding the bowl, the gesture arrested in mid-air.

'It's not about that girl, is it?'

'Of course it isn't. Have you ever heard of the magical Order of the Golden Dawn?'

She nodded, relieved. 'I read about it in one of your books.'

'Well, I've joined it. The Highgate branch. I thought I should. There'll be a lot to do, meetings and seminars and special courses, quite a few evenings every week, I expect, and sometimes weekends. But if I want to succeed as a geomancer I don't really have an alternative.'

In the relevant book, Pup recalled, it also said that the Order of the Golden Dawn, founded by Eliphas Levi, Crowley, Yeats and other like-minded dabblers in the occult in 1888, had under its later title of the Stella Matutina collapsed in the 1930s. He thought it unlikely that Dolly would wade through the innumerable dull passages in the book before this fact was reached. If she did, he could always say the Stella Matutina had been revived a few years ago.

Dolly's face was ardent. 'I think it's wonderful, I'm so glad. Did they ask you to join them?'

'Well . . .' said Pup, not exactly committing himself.

'They must have done. It'll be a help to you in your career, won't it? It'll put you on the road to success.'

As far as Pup thought about having a career, it was as one of the directors of an expanding business machines company. He started to eat his sausages. Like a woman conditioned by a patriarchal society – in fact, very much like Dilip Raj's mother – she never ate with him but waited on him and watched.

'I'm going to be formally admitted as a member,'

said Pup, beginning as he meant to go on, 'tomorrow night.'

After supper, remembering his resolution, he went into the temple and beckoned to her to follow him. She came joyfully, lit the candles and then sat on the cushion under the fire *tattwa*, gazing at him. Pup stood by the altar, looking at his elemental weapons and felt like groaning, the whole thing was such a bore. Why had he ever begun on it? Why hadn't he gone in for football or Tai Chi or stamp collecting?

'Well, then, what shall I do?'

'You're asking *me*?'

'I mean is there anything special you're embarking on? Any piece of work? Or anything particular that's bothering you? D'you want something invoked. I haven't got any holy water but I could make some.'

She hesitated. 'One day,' she said, 'you'll be a master, won't you? You'll be able to do anything, miracles?'

Her hand had not gone up to her cheek but he knew her meaning and he was aghast. A kind of panic rose in him, impatience with her and the whole business, self-disgust. Better to have told her it was finished, better to have destroyed the temple and thrown away the robe. But only let him think of something before she put that monstrous question directly to him . . .

'I know,' he said. 'We'll clobber the wicked stepmother!'

She was immediately diverted. She was surprised, presumably because he had shown such distaste before. As if it mattered, he thought, white magic, black magic, all quackery, all rubbish. Pup pulled the robe over his head and thrust his arms into the wide sleeves. The night was dark and moonless and the wind which had been blowing all day had sprung into a gale, whipping tree branches and driving clouds in black flocks across a sky lit red by the lights of London. It was nearly 9.00 and he was weary but Dolly was not. She went into the other room and came back with the Myra doll in one hand and a tumbler of red wine in the other. Pup very nearly laughed. He thought how shocked he would once have been at the idea of profaning temple and rituals with any alcohol except that used strictly in the ceremonies.

He drew the curtain. The temple was now lit to a suitable cabbalistic flickering dimness by the flames of four candles. The whole thing was going to be a bore and to satisfy Dolly he would have to go on for at least an hour. His father and Myra had already gone to bed, or at least his father had. He had heard the click of a light switch below him and the bathroom window had shed a rectangle of yellow light on the dark wet grass. Pup drew a circle in chalk on the floor and inside it he drew a pentagram. Something that would make this business less tedious was that he was no longer trammelled by rules and instructions. He could do what he liked, say what he liked, jumble it all up.

Dolly was sitting with the doll on her lap. With her legs crossed, her hair hanging forward over her bent head, the crude metal talisman dangling from her neck, she looked like a little girl. Pup felt a fierce yet exasperated pity for her, he felt she was like an albatross or a millstone around his neck. He put out his hand for the doll and dropped it so that it flopped on its back in the middle of the pentagram.

'Give her a pain,' Dolly said viciously. 'She's had a lot of trouble with her stomach lately. Give her – give her appendicitis!'

'That's a bit strong,' Pup said.

He turned to the east and made the Cabbalistic Cross and then he began on the Inscription of the

Pentagram. This was a Lesser Banishing ritual but he had forgotten the proper order of words and soon he was muddling it up with bits of consecration formulae and Hexagrammic rituals and invocations and all sorts.

For a short while at school he had done Latin. He recited the few declensions and conjugations he remembered. Then he abandoned that, prepared holy water and scattered it about, walking round and round the circle until he was giddy. His sleeve, falling back as he raised the wand in his hands, showed him the time by his watch. Ten-fifteen. He could stop soon.

When he had recited all the Hebrew names he knew and all the Egyptian ones and all the names of Greek gods and goddesses that he could remember, when he had said prayers frontwards and repeated them backwards, he seized the dagger from the altar. He held the dagger high above his head, a tall, commanding figure whose golden robe shivered and shimmered in the light from the candles.

Dolly gave a little gasp. Pup plunged forward in a swoop that was almost that of a *samurai* in its grace, and thrust the dagger's point through the belly of the doll with a sure stroke. For a moment or two the doll remained impaled on Pup's dagger and he had to draw it off with his other hand. Some of the stuffing came out and a fat worm of cotton wool like an entrail. Dolly looked as if she were going to clap but as if clapping would somehow be out of place. She got up, leaving the wounded doll where it lay. Pup pulled off his robe and blew out the candles.

Back in their living room, Dolly poured the last of the wine into her glass. The wind sang round the house and rattled the old window sashes in their frames. As she had come into the room after the ceremonies, her mother had spoken to her quite clearly and in her normal speaking voice:

'It's going to be a wild night.'

Edith had always been one to comment on the weather. 'Cold enough for you?' she would say or 'This rain will get rid of the fog,' or something like that. Now, as Dolly stood by the mantelpiece on which the ballet girl doll now sat alone, as she stood sipping her wine, Edith came very close to her in a breeze of lemon scent and whispered: 'I never did like a wind, I'd rather anything but wind.'

Pup came in and Dolly hoped their mother would speak again so that he could hear her, but Edith was silent.

'Can you smell anything?'

'Candles?' said Pup.

Dolly shook her head. 'Come on, I'll make us both a cup of cocoa.'

They were out on the landing, in the dark, and this time it was he who asked the question: 'Did you hear anything?'

'The wind,' said Dolly. She put out her hand for the light switch but could not find it.

'It sounded more like a cry,' Pup said. He put the light on and they went into the kitchen.

In there, the window was too small for curtains. The panes rattled with a monotonous regular thudding. Dolly began heating milk in a saucepan and got out the tin of drinking chocolate. The window rattled, the wind made a keening sound as it rushed through the old railway line, and downstairs from immediately below them came a slither and a heavy thud.

Dolly clutched Pup's arm. 'Whatever is it? D'you think someone's got in down there?'

'It was in the bathroom. The bathroom light's been on for ages. You can see it on the grass out there.' He went back to the landing and looked down the stairwell. 'I wonder if Dad's all right.'

'We'd better go down.'

The milk rose up in the saucepan and streamed down over the gas ring. Pup turned the gas off. They went down and tried the bathroom door. It was locked. The door to Harold and Myra's bedroom stood ajar. It was dark inside but Pup could make out a humped shape, a down quilt tucked round it, on the far side of the double bed. He went softly over to the bed, expecting to see Myra, and saw his father lying there, fast asleep.

Dolly was rattling at the bathroom door. Harold didn't stir. Pup went back upstairs, got a piece of wire and poked it through the keyhole on the bathroom door until the key tumbled out. He could see the key under the door and, inserting his wire, hooked it through.

Still the door would not open more than an inch or two. Something was pushing against it. Pup pushed too and the door opened enough to admit him and then Dolly and he saw that it was Myra whose head and shoulders had prevented the door yielding.

She was lying on the floor, wearing only the top half of a pair of green nylon pyjamas. Near her, on the marbled tiles, lay a small pool of cloudy water and a big tube thing with a nozzle on one end and a bulb on the other. Her face was white and stiff as wax and when Dolly, trembling, shaking and gasping, remembering some ancient recommendation of Mrs Collins's, unhooked the wall mirror and held it to her lips, there was no mist of breath on the glass.

'She's dead,' Dolly whispered.

'She can't be dead! There's no blood, there's nothing.'

Her eyes met his and hers were full of wonder, of a deep, almost incredulous admiration. 'Of course

129

she's dead,' Dolly said. 'Of course she is.' She drew
in her breath in a sobbing way. 'I'd better go and
wake Dad.'

'I'll do that,' said Pup.

Dolly picked up the tube thing and dropped it in
the basin. In lifting Myra's pyjama trousers she
uncovered what lay beneath them, a cardboard box
labelled: Higginson's Syringe. Something prompted
her to cover Myra's body with a bath towel. She
mopped up the pool of water and then she stood,
silent and trembling, looking down at the dead,
mummy-swathed thing on the floor at her feet.

Chapter 13

The doctor at the inquest said Myra had been ten weeks pregnant. She had tried to syringe out the uterus with a solution of water and shampoo and had continued pumping after the liquid was used up and there was only air left in the syringe. This had caused a bubble in her bloodstream, an air embolus, which, when it reached her brain had killed her. She would have felt nothing, known nothing, simply collapsed and died.

Pup, sitting with Harold, thought that it was not true she had felt nothing. He remembered that cry. It seemed strange to him that a woman could damage her brain and kill herself merely by introducing water and air into her womb, although the doctor said this was not uncommon among women trying to procure abortion. To Pup, it still seemed nearly incomprehensible that in big, vigorous, energetic Myra, life had hung so precariously. It was as if she had been struck down, not by a little bubble of air in her blood, but by some external force that took no account of strength and vitality and love of life.

Dolly did not attend the inquest or the cremation. She had always avoided as much as she could public places and gatherings of people. The funeral was at Golders Green Crematorium where Edith's had been. George and Yvonne Colefax came and a cousin of Myra's who had been a witness at her marriage to Harold. Apart from Pup and Harold himself, there

131

was no one else in the crematorium chapel but a tall, good-looking man with greying black hair who walked with an easy grace. He slipped in and sat at the back while they were struggling through the Crimmond Version of the Twenty-third Psalm. George Colefax knew who he was and nodded to him. It was George Colefax who had rung him up and told him Myra was dead. By the time they were standing outside looking at the flowers, the man had disappeared.

Harold went home in the black funeral car he and Pup had come in but Pup accepted a lift from the Colefaxes. George's car was a large silvery-white Mercedes Benz. He was going to drop Yvonne off at a friend's house in Muswell Hill, and since Pup also had a friend to visit in Muswell Hill, that would suit him too. George drove in grim silence. Yvonne sat beside him, crying quietly for Myra. She was dressed in a suit of very fine black wool and a ruffled blouse of black and white crêpe de Chine and on her thistledown hair she wore a tiny black hat with a veil. Pup, sitting in the back, wished he could still see her legs. Yvonne's legs and slender feet were miracles of sculpting in black gossamer stockings and black patent court shoes. She cried softly, sometimes saying what a fool she was to cry but she had been so fond of Myra, it wasn't as if she had all that many friends. George kept silent, his shoulders hunching just a bit more. The tears did nothing to Yvonne's Arthur Rackham fairy face but trembled on it like drops of dew. Pup hoped he and she might be allowed to leave the car together but Queen's Avenue was reached before Cranmore Way and he was obliged to get out, thanking them politely for the lift.

Without Myra the house was quiet and strange. It was an altered house, new and clean, and the cheap new furniture had a pathetic look. Once she had it to herself again and Harold and Pup were back at work, Dolly began moving things downstairs. She brought down her sewing machine and put it back in the living room that had been Myra's pride. She brought down the chest of remnants and the box of patterns and the ballet girl doll. The other doll, the Myra one, its body ravaged by Pup's dagger, she had removed from the temple some time in the small hours of that dreadful night. When she looked at it next day, her feelings had been strange ones – awe, wonder, guilt, remorse, triumph.

That same day she had destroyed the doll. No fireplace in the Yearman home had been used since Harold's mother died but the fireplaces were still there. Dolly lit a fire in the one in the room that had been hers and Pup's living room. Smoke billowed out and filled the top floor, unable to escape properly up the clogged chimney, but at last, set among Dolly's firelighters and screws of newspaper and bits of wood, the Myra doll was consumed. She opened all the windows to cleanse the place of smoke.

It was with a feeling of relief, almost of triumph, that she moved back into her old bedroom and moved Pup's things back into his. That evening they all ate together in the kitchen once more: tinned spaghetti, corned beef, granary rolls, St Ivel cheese spread, de-frosted chocolate éclairs. If Harold noticed this reversion to the old ways, if he was aware of an end having come to the reign of stuffed peppers and moussaka and eggs Florentine, he gave no sign of it. He read with his book propped up against the cruet, and when he had finished, he shuffled off to the breakfast room. Dolly had asked him if he would like her to clear it up a bit, do something about all those pots of paint, but Harold said no, to keep it just as Myra had left it.

Ron and Eileen Ridge, who had been on holiday in Spain at the time of Myra's death and funeral, paid a visit of condolence.

'I did it,' said Harold. 'I killed her.'

Ron was embarrassed. 'Don't say that.'

Harold spoke with lugubrious pride. 'I do say it. But for me she'd be alive today. We men have a lot to answer for in this world.'

'True enough,' said Ron.

Harold showed them the breakfast room, the gateleg table still covered with a dust sheet, the paintpots still standing on newspapers, Myra's brushes in a glass jar.

'How touching! It makes me want to cry.'

'It's the least I can do, Eileen,' said Harold, 'seeing it was me killed her.'

'He's no right to say that,' Dolly said to Pup, and then she said what he had been dreading to hear from her: 'It was you killed her.'

Pup held the living-room door open for Dolly and let her pass in ahead of him and then closed it firmly. He thought his face must have gone white, it felt very stiff and cold. Dolly had flushed. The naevus was a dark, sore-looking purple.

'You must not say that.'

'Why not? You made holy water, you said the words, you stabbed the doll with your dagger and she died. Half an hour later she was dead. You stabbed the doll in the stomach and it was that part of her killed her.'

'Dolly,' he said, 'it was a coincidence. Myra killed herself. She caused her own death by doing a mad thing to herself with that syringe. I told you what the doctor said.'

'Yes, and you told me you couldn't believe a bubble of air like that could kill anyone. You know it couldn't. It was your magic killed her, you killed her.

And why not? You've studied, you've got the power, I think you could do anything. You're as good as that Mrs Fitter. You're equal to her, you're in the same class as her and she's famous. You can be famous now. Isn't that what you want?'

There were a good many statements among what Dolly had just said whose accuracy Pup doubted. As for Mrs Fitter – he was on the point of telling her the truth about Suzanne's father but he thought better of it. Dolly had been strange since Myra's death, perhaps since before Myra's death, intense, preoccupied, sometimes seeming to listen or stare as a cat may do, erecting its fur at nothing. If Pup had pinned himself down to it, had really wanted to think of it, he would have said there was something disturbed about her and he might have gone even further. But he did not want to think about it. He did not want to think about Myra's death, about Dolly's loss of balance or about anything that was in any way connected with magic, the occult, the supernatural, ectoplasm, rituals, good and bad spirits, incense, archangels, Crowley or any of it.

What he wanted was to go upstairs and dismantle the temple. Put the dagger, the wand, the cup and the pentacle in the plastic bag for Haringey Council to take away, give the golden robe to Oxfam, sell the books down the Archway Road and paint over the black walls with some of Myra's 'Sunbeach'. Walking home from work, he decided to do this or some of this, once he had had his supper. But as soon as he saw Dolly, as soon as she had come up to him and put up her face for his kiss, he knew that, of course, he couldn't do it. Get rid of the temple, deny his powers, his commitment, and then what would become of the alibi he had used so successfully last night in order to see Philippa? He had probably gone too far already in refusing to accept responsibility for

Myra's death. Unless he could invent something else. Chess? Car maintenance classes? Cinema club? She knew he was interested in none of those things. She knew what interested him, what *had* interested him. Pup nearly groaned aloud.

Dolly was so close to him she could read along the line of his thoughts. Not read them, thank God, but read along the periphery of them.

'You've got a meeting of the Golden Dawn tomorrow night, haven't you?'

Pup nodded. He was going round to Suzanne's.

'Will you tell them?'

He looked at her. The question that came into his mind was, would a normal person ask that? 'Tell them what?' he stalled.

'How you did magic and made Myra die.'

His own steady sanity recoiled. Every word was an affront. He suddenly saw clearly what he wanted from life and meant to have: pleasure, joy, peace, material things, money, worldly success, women. And, looking hopelessly at her, he saw something else, too. It had all come about because of him. If he had never sold his soul to the devil, Dolly would never have heard of the occult, if he had done no magic, not made the temple, Dolly would have thought magic something conjurors did for kids at parties. He had begun it and for her sake as well as his own he couldn't let her down now. He smiled at her.

'We – you – can tell people I can harness certain powers. I can make things happen, if you like, but we mustn't tell them about Myra. Can't you see that, dear? You're not allowed to kill people, you know that, it's against the law.'

She nodded. When she spoke after a moment or two, he thought with relief that she had changed the subject.

'You've got your driving test tomorrow?'

'Yes. At ten.'

She laid her hand on his arm. 'Let's go into the temple and perform a Pentagram ritual for success.'

'I'm going to pass anyway.'

'Isn't that what you learn magic for? Isn't that what you sold your soul for? For success and getting what you want?'

How well she had learned the lessons he had taught her! He had run out of joss sticks but that was no excuse as she had bought some herself to keep in stock for him. She sat on the cushion with her glass of wine, watching him make the Cabbalistic Cross and utter the prescribed words for success in a coming venture.

The next day he passed his driving test as he had known he would.

'Now you'll be wanting us to get that van, I daresay,' said Harold.

'I'm taking delivery this afternoon.'

Harold, who had been in the middle of an account of the sorrows of Prince Leopold after the death in childbirth of the Princess Charlotte, a subject fairly appropriate to his own situation, stuck his finger in the book to keep his place. 'You haven't wasted much time.'

'What were you thinking of doing with the money you get from Mrs Brewer's flat?' said Pup.

'Now you wait a minute, you hold your horses, that'll be months and months.'

'Maybe. We should be able to get a good big bank loan on the strength of it, though. I want you to put it all in the business. We could take over one of those shops in Crouch Hill when the leases fall in in the summer and go into word processors. I've got it all worked out.'

'I don't know about that,' said Harold, turning pale. 'There's a recession on or hadn't you heard?'

'That's the time to expand. There won't always be a recession. I've got my eye on that new tower block going up at the Archway.'

'We're not moving into any tower block.'

'Of course not. It's something else I've got in mind.'

Harold gave him a hopeless look and returned to his reading. 'All this drive,' he said. 'I don't know where you get it from.'

'I don't know where we're going to go,' said Suzanne, sitting on her bed and handing Pup his cup of herb tea. 'They say they'll go in the bathroom for half an hour but I draw the line at that.'

'I've got a car,' said Pup. 'Well, a van. No windows in the back and I've bought one of those duvets.'

'You're kidding.'

'Come and see. I thought we might go up on the Heath.'

'You know, you're pretty amazing,' said Suzanne, twining herself round him.

They were putting up a block of old people's flats on the site at Mount Pleasant Green. It was so cold that the frost lay white on the builders' tarpaulins and stacks of bricks. The air was still but with a cutting edge to it and the sky sparkled with stars rarely seen in the London suburbs. There was a starry-eyed look about the lighted houses that surrounded the green as if surprised by the bitter cold that had suddenly clamped down on them.

'I always feel better once the winter solstice is behind us,' said Miss Finlay, scurrying along so fast that Dolly had to trot to keep up with her. 'You know the days are getting longer even if you don't feel it.'

A handwritten and hand-drawn poster advertised Roberta Fitter's seance. Dolly had paid her five pounds, she was coming willingly, but she rather resented that poster. 'They ought to have my brother here.'

'He's not a medium, though, is he, dear?'

'He could be. He's got amazing powers. I had this cold last week and he cured it. My colds usually go on for weeks but my brother did this special invocation and next day it was practically gone.'

Talking about him recalled to her mind how he had refused to come with her. Well, not refused exactly. He had a meeting to go to. But she felt the lack of his company. It had been so nice last time. He was always out now and she was always alone. That was why she had come here tonight, to see Edith again, if possible to bring Edith more positively back with her, to have more of her than an occasionally heard voice. And as she entered the hall she sniffed the air, hoping for an early foretaste of lemon scent, but the place smelt faintly of some kind of cleaning fluid and tonight Miss Finlay had used lavender water.

It was cold, in spite of the two wall heaters with their thin, glowing elements. The curtains to the cabinet were open and you could see a green and black tartan blanket thrown over the chair Mrs Fitter would sit in. This time Dolly was not asked to assist the medium with her dressing. Graciously, as to a favoured novice, Mrs Leebridge gave her the black clothes to hand round among the audience. Again Miss Finlay pulled the black tights inside out, her face drawn into a frown of concentration. Roberta Fitter was rather a long time getting ready, and a murmur of relief went up from the twenty or so people there when at last she appeared in the shapeless dress and the black Chinese slippers, crossed the stage with bowed head and hunched shoulders and sat in the chair, drawing the blanket around her knees.

'It's no trouble to her, going into a trance, is it?' Miss Finlay whispered. 'It's a knack I could do with. I find it more and more difficult getting off to sleep these days.'

'Sssh,' said Mrs Leebridge.

When the lights were turned off, it was much darker in the hall than it had been in August. It was so dark, pitchy black, that at first Dolly thought they would be able to see nothing. Then Mrs Collins put on the red lamp by the cabinet. It was a relief. The brief blackness, the icy cold blackness, had for a moment been alarming, bringing her a choking feeling of panic. Her hands, though in fur-lined mittens, still felt as cold as when she was walking along the street. She moved them about, rubbing the fingertips together. The red lamp gleamed but not warmly, not with the suggestion of a glowing brazier, but rather as a red warning light may shine in the darkness on a lonely road.

The curtains were drawn and the medium lost to view. Mrs Collins came on to the front of the stage and suggested they sing the 'Indian Love Call'. Miss Finlay put up her hand like a child in school and said she didn't think it was the right sort of Indian. So they sang the 'Volga Boatman' once again, out-of-tune elderly voices mostly, cracked voices but for Dolly's clear soprano, and after a chorus or two the curtains opened and the thin, turbaned figure of Hassan appeared between them.

'Good evening, friends.'

One or two people said good evening. The curtains seemed to move and he was gone, though it was too dark to see him go. The fidgeting among the audience ceased and there was silence, stillness, the

140

dark and the cold. Someone had switched off the wall heaters. Their light would have been a distraction but the air seemed to be growing steadily and rapidly icier. Miss Finlay, her hands in woollen gloves, was pulling the front of her coat down to cover her calves. Dolly glanced to her right and she could just see, now her eyes had become used to the dark, that the woman who sat next to her was holding hands with the man on her other side. They were not young or good-looking or well-dressed, they were just an ordinary, middle-aged, working-class, married couple, but they had each other and each had the other's hand to hold. Dolly hunched her shoulders, tense with increasing, incomprehensible alarm. If nothing happened in the next few minutes she wouldn't be able to stand it, she would have to leave. Someone coughed slightly, a nervous clearing of the throat.

Then, when it felt as if you could have cut the cold, tense air with a knife, Hassan spoke from the cabinet:

'Is there someone here who has lost a gentleman who liked growing things? A market gardener perhaps? A gentleman with green fingers?'

The audience was silent.

'He's waiting to come through,' Hassan's voice said. 'A florist, could it be?'

A woman behind Dolly piped nervously, 'My husband had his own greengrocery business.'

'That's the voice!'

The curtains quivered. A figure appeared in something whitish that caught the red gleam from the lamp. It suddenly struck Dolly, for the first time it truly came to her, how terrible and wonderful it was, how it changed your whole life and way of looking at things, to have spirits brought to you thus from the abode of the dead. She trembled and stared.

'Is it you, Stan?' the woman said. Dolly heard the

chair behind her creak and scrape as the green-grocer's widow got to her feet. Her voice was yearning. 'I've missed you so, Stan. Put out your hand to me, won't you put out your hand?'

The spectre extended a long thin hand that quivered. The arm, from which draperies fell back, passed in its own miasma of coldness close to Dolly's face and she gazed at it, that skinny, sinewy arm, very thin for a man's. The woman leaned forward between Dolly and her neighbour and reached out her own hand as if to try and touch the outstretched fingers but the spirit retreated with a slow twirling movement, glided away without even a whisper of sound from its trailing wrappings and slipped between the curtains.

The widow was still standing up, still half-leaning across the people in front of her. 'He didn't speak to me, he didn't speak a word. I wonder if he's angry. They say they know everything on the Other Side. I wonder if he knows I couldn't keep the business going. I did try but it was too much for me. Oh, Stan, why didn't you speak to me . . . ?'

'Silence, please, friends,' said Mrs Collins. 'We must have quiet.'

The woman's voice dropped to a whisper and then was hushed. People seemed stilled by the cold, paralysed by it. Dolly was so cold now she was hugging herself for warmth. But there seemed no warmth left anywhere to find and the cold as deep now as in the place where those shrouded figures came from and returned to.

Hassan's voice came hollowly from the cabinet.

'I have a lady waiting to come through. She's a lady who died before her time. An operation perhaps or a wound in the lower parts.'

Dolly kept absolutely still. Her mother had had two abdominal operations before she died. She waited for the lemon scent to come and, when there was no lemon scent, for someone else to claim the woman. Somehow she knew her mother would not come without that heralding breath of perfume. It was not Edith who waited there on the edge of the living world for Hassan to lead her over the threshold.

And now she was becoming afraid. Someone surely would claim the woman. Please, please claim her, Dolly mouthed silently.

'A young lady,' Hassan's voice persisted. 'There's somebody here who must have lost a young lady that passed over in November.'

Then Dolly knew no one would claim her, for she knew who it was and knew it was for her. Perhaps she had really known for a long time now and that was why she was shivering with cold. Her teeth would have chattered if she had not held them clenched.

She gathered her strength. Her teeth chattered as soon as she parted them but she spoke. 'Is it for me?'

'That's the voice!'

'Myra,' Dolly said, 'is it you?'

The curtains parted and Myra came out of them. She wore a long white robe like all the spectres did but the red light gleamed on her red hair, and when Dolly saw the dabble of blood on her skirts, the flickering spotting of red, she jumped up and screamed aloud. She couldn't help herself. The scream came involuntarily from her throat and she went on screaming until Mrs Collins seized her and clamped a hand over her mouth.

Myra had retreated swiftly. The cabinet was open and Roberta Fitter sat there, staring wildly about her like a madwoman. Someone in the audience called out:

'Put the lights on!'

'No, you don't,' said Mrs Leebridge. 'You'll kill her. Look at her! Look what that girl's done.' She went almost fearfully to the cabinet and took one of Mrs Fitter's hands in hers. 'The ectoplasm rushing back like that, it's a wonder she's not all burned up.'

Dolly broke away from Mrs Collins's grasp and ran out of the hall. She knew there was no escaping Myra now and Myra was waiting for her in the porch, not visible, not tangible – unless that tremor against her face was her cold touch – but a voice that spoke in Myra's accents.

'I may as well walk home with you, Doreen.'

Dolly pushed open the door and went out. It had begun to snow lightly, a fine icy powder. She began to walk home through the snow with Myra by her side.

Chapter 14

The cleaver and the knives, Diarmit Bawne's elemental weapons, lay gathering dust. They were still in the Harrods bag on the floor in a corner of the room and he never looked at them. They did not belong to him but to Conal Moore who had been a thief and a murderer and who, when the police were after him, had run away home to Ireland.

Conal Moore had a sister and brother-in-law in Kilburn who refused to speak to him and did not want to know him because of his criminal behaviour. For this reason, too, no one would have anything to do with him, would not recognize his existence, except the police. The worst of his crimes had been to hide in a tunnel on the old railway line and kill a girl who came through and cut her head off. After that, there was no help for it but to run away back to County Clare. But before he left he had had the sense to leave his room and some of his belongings in the care of a responsible citizen called Diarmit Bawne.

Only Diarmit knew he was in Ireland and knew he had killed the girl. Only Diarmit knew where the weapons he had used were. He intended to make a statement about all this to the police, lay all the facts about Conal Moore before them and hand over to them the Harrods bag of knives, but at the moment he was too busy to get around to it. Unlike Conal Moore, he was a responsible hard-working person with a job and he didn't have the time to devote to all these outside things.

Conal had been a mass of nerves, afraid of all kinds of things. One of the things he had been afraid of was that they would demolish the house while he was in it and he would be buried in the rubble. Diarmit couldn't help laughing to himself when he thought of anyone believing a thing like that. For one thing, the men would have seen him if he had put his head out of the window and shouted. He had been a small insignificant creature, Diarmit remembered, but not that small, not so small you couldn't see him. He, Diarmit, could wear his clothes, after all, did wear them every day. It wasn't that he much cared for the idea of wearing a murderer's clothes, especially the dark red trousers and shirts Conal had worn so that they should not show bloodstains, but it was a terrible waste not to wear them. Waste not, want not, as his mother used to say. Diarmit Bawne had no family now, he was alone in the world, standing on his own feet, but Conal Moore had a dozen or so brothers and sisters living all over Ireland and in London and Liverpool and Birmingham. He was their responsibility now, they must do the best they could for him, for Diarmit had done enough, looking after his home and his clothes and his possessions, not many would do as much.

It was only two or three weeks after Conal had run away that Diarmit had got himself the job in the Greek's shop that was part butcher's, part delicatessen. It was only a short walk from Mount Pleasant Green. The Greek could understand very little of what Diarmit said and Diarmit could understand about as much of what the Greek said, but this suited them both. Formerly the Greek had always employed other Greeks who talked all day to him in his own tongue. He wanted someone who would leave him to the quiet and solitude he liked. Diarmit never tried to talk to him much; they had nothing in common and he was busy with his own thoughts. He had begun thinking a lot about Conal Moore.

With his lazy ways, his nerves, the crazy way he had of thinking people were going to knock him over and trample on him, Conal would have made a bad impression on Georgiou, he would never have got the job. Probably he hadn't got a job at home in Ireland. People like that were always out of work, living on the dole or, worse, on the charity of their families. Conal had thought he was going to do that with his relations in Kilburn but his brother-in-law had been too tough a nut to crack. None of his family wanted him any more, they had had enough to last them a lifetime. It seemed likely to Diarmit that Conal would never be seen again. He would either disappear quietly among the wilds of County Clare and his crimes disappear with him or else he would be caught and spend the rest of his life in prison. Either way they would all be rid of him. Sometimes Diarmit thought that perhaps he wouldn't go to the police after all. What had the police ever done for him? They hadn't even had the common courtesy to come back and tell him how their case against Conal was progressing. Besides, he would have to tell them everything he knew about Conal and that would take hours, take all day, for he knew him as he knew himself, and quite frankly he was getting a bit sick of him, he often thought he'd like to banish him from his mind altogether.

Georgiou had once employed two assistants and a girl part-time but he did so no longer; times were hard and wages high. There were just himself and Diarmit in the shop. The lease came up for renewal in the summer and Georgiou knew his rent was going up, though he did not yet know by how much. 'Sky-high' was what the tenants of the other shops in the row said. Georgiou would not fight it, he said to his wife, he would make the landlords a reasonable offer and if they wouldn't have it, too bad. People talked about the rents going up double, he couldn't pay double, if that happened he'd retire. He was past sixty anyway. No one said any of this to Diarmit. What business was it of his? He was only an employee and if Georgiou retiring meant he had no job, too bad.

Diarmit sat in his window in the evenings and looked across the green at the block of sheltered flats going up next to the hall. Progress had been slow but they were nearly done now. The roof was on. His own mother was dead, God rest her, but Conal's was alive and wouldn't one of those flats be just the thing for her? But Conal would never think of a thing like that, too feckless, too lacking in responsibility.

Sometimes Diarmit gave the room a good clean. The first time he did this he was appalled at the mess Conal had left behind him. Bits of stale food dropped behind things and now coated in mould, a heap of dried-up, mildewed teabags on a newspaper under the bed, dirty clothes in piles, a drawer that had once had biscuits in it now full of mouse droppings.

Once he had cleaned up Conal's mess, he felt really clean in himself and he felt free. Keeping the room and himself that way had become very important to him. Now he would have liked to clean his mind of Conal too, but that was much harder than cleaning a room. Try as he did, he found himself dwelling on Conal when he lay down to sleep, on the way to work, at work and on the way back, when he sat at the window, watching the green and the new flats and the hall where all those cranky people came. He would think of Conal's past and his present, imagining him in the green west and weaving about him long strange fantasies.

And by night he often had a Conal dream in which the other man sometimes appeared bound and gagged and led by a halter, and sometimes, more often, toiling up a hillside, bearing a heavy sack on his shoulders.

Chapter 15

Harold sat in the breakfast room, surrounded by mementoes of Myra, writing his novel. It had come to him some months before, round about the time of Pup's twentieth birthday, that with his surely unrivalled knowledge, it would be a good idea for him to attempt a work of historical fiction. He wrote in longhand on pads of pale blue Basildon Bond. His subject was the unsavoury life of that least exemplary of the sons of George III, Ernest Duke of Cumberland, who was said to have committed incest with his sister and murdered his valet. Harold was treating these allegations as fact. He was in the middle of Chapter Five in which the young prince and the Princess Amelia began their guilty liaison.

He read nothing now but works on and novels about the children of George III. He read them at home and he read them in the shop when the new assistant was attending to customers and Pup wasn't about. Pup was often absent these days, up at the new branch he had opened in Crouch Hill. In an armchair very like the one at home, Harold sat in the storeroom which was now stuffed full of Pup's word processors, and read about the English court in the late eighteenth century. His writing, what he should write next and how the plot should develop, filled his waking thoughts so that he became quieter than ever and apparently morose. This withdrawal into himself was attributed to the loss of Myra and some said that poor Harold was beginning to break up.

He had told no one what he was doing. In the days before he was a writer and had merely been a reader, he had never talked about what he read. He didn't expect others to be interested in what he did; he wasn't interested in them. His children, in these past months, had become rather shadowy to him. He was aware that Dolly was in the house, that meals appeared and housework was done, but he seldom said much to her. She had her own friends, he thought when he thought about it at all.

Ron and Eileen Ridge came round to ask him if he felt like starting bingo again. They would call for him, they would like to. Dolly had admitted them to the house and called out to her father, rather than showing them straightaway into the breakfast room. This gave Harold the chance to hide the Basildon Bond away out of sight and be discovered brooding in his sanctuary.

'You've got to come out of yourself sooner or later, Harold,' said Eileen in a mildly scolding tone. 'You owe it to Myra's memory.'

Harold nodded vaguely.

'I know you'll say you've got your daughter and that's perfectly true.'

'She has her own friends,' said Harold.

Mrs Collins, Wendy Collins, Miss Finlay, Mrs Leebridge. Dolly had never much liked the last two, which was just as well, since she never saw them any more. The Adonai Spiritists had closed their doors to her.

'I couldn't take the responsibility, could I?' said Mrs Collins while Dolly was measuring Wendy for a trouser suit. 'You might have another of your fits and then where should I be?'

'I didn't have a fit.'

'Whatever it was, dear. You can kill a medium like that. Mrs Fitter was under the weather for days. And all because you were privileged to catch a glimpse of young Mrs Yearman.'

Dolly said nothing about its having been more than a glimpse. It was only Pup she had told about hearing the tap of Myra's high heels following her up the path that night and up the steps to the door. Only he knew how she heard Myra's whisper as well as Edith's now. Once or twice, with gooseflesh on her arms, she had felt Myra's hand lift up the curtain of hair and a finger run across the naevus.

Wendy bought the Chinese girl doll with the black pigtail and the dark blue quilted jacket. She wanted it for a present for a friend's child whose birthday wasn't until November. She might as well buy it now, she said, since she didn't expect she would be seeing much of Dolly once the trouser suit was finished. Dolly was left alone with the ballet girl and the Chinese boy who sat together on the mantelpiece staring across the room at Myra's now dead rubber plant and Myra's calendar for the previous year.

Pup did the Rosy Cross ritual to banish Myra. Long ago he had told Dolly that, if you became involved in the serious practice of geomancy, it was likely that the invisible world would begin to intrude on your everyday life. He had told her and then she had read it in one of his books. It might take the form of a series of coincidences or of poltergeist activity or simply of strange sights and sounds. The ritual of the Rosy Cross extended a protection against such things; it placed a barrier or veil between you and them.

As soon as Dolly told him about the voices and the invisible hands, Pup wanted to do the ritual. He said she must have faith in the ritual and then she would be all right. They had gone into the temple together,

Pup had made crosses and circles in the air with an incense stick and had chanted:

> 'Virgo, Isis, Mighty Mother,
> Scorpio, Apophis, Destroyer,
> Sol, Osiris, Slain and Risen,
> Isis, Apophis, Osiris,
> *Ee-ay-oo, el-ewe-ex, lux*, light,
> The Light of the Cross,
> Let the Light descend!'

As Pup and the book had promised, Myra went away after that. But she came back and Edith came back with her. Dolly knew she could have asked Pup to do the ritual again or even attempted it herself and one evening she tried it, chanting the words from the book and making the signs with a sandalwood joss stick. But she had barely finished when she sensed the two women had come into the temple. The lemon scent was so strong it overcame that of the sandalwood. She heard Myra's light brittle laugh.

Edith said: 'That's Pup's job, dear. Better leave that sort of thing to Pup.'

He was away that night and the next and the next on a weekend course in Hertfordshire, learning how to operate the Infra-Hyposonic XH450 word processor. The manufacturers liked retailers as well as prospective customers to be conversant with the intricacies of their equipment. The course was in a country house called West Lawn near Puckeridge. Pup was not the only man there but he was the only one under forty. Most of the girls were young and pretty. It was more like a model school seminar than instruction in working a glorified typewriter.

Apart from the obvious one, Pup recognized an immediate affinity between himself and the prettiest girl. She lived in Islington, a mile or so from his own home. After the Saturday lesson and the lecture on advanced techniques, he drove her down into the village for drinks and chicken and chips at The Green Man.

'Have you got a girl friend, Peter?'

'She just got engaged to someone else,' said Pup with perfect truth. Suzanne, having found out about Philippa and an occasional pal of Pup's called Terri, had declared on the rebound her intention of marrying the brother of one of the students. 'Rather sad but I suppose that's life. I'll survive.'

In the van she sat close up to him. She had a bottle of wine in her room, she said, and if he didn't mind its not being iced . . .

'The sadness isn't so bad,' said Caroline. 'It's the frustration I mind, it's so – well, kind of degrading.'

'Here, let me,' said Pup, taking the corkscrew from her. He gave her his other-worldly look. 'I wouldn't know about that, never yet having succumbed. That may have been part of the trouble with Suzanne. But I mustn't bore you with my problems. Cheers.'

'Cheers. Do you mean what I think you mean?'

Pup nodded. 'I had this idea of saving myself for the perfect girl, Caroline.' He took her hand. 'A kind of crazy idealism, I suppose you'll say.'

'It's the most romantic thing I ever heard!'

He got home to hear that the estate agents had found a buyer for Mrs Brewer's flat. Harold seemed to have lost interest, so Pup had quietly taken the matter over himself. Thirty-one thousand pounds to be paid over a month after exchange of contracts which would be the following week. Caroline had told him that her friend's sister was secretary to a man who was managing director of a company taking a lease for two floors of the new tower block. It was a new company, starting from scratch, and

Caroline not only got hold of its name for him but also the private phone number of this guy her friend's sister was secretary to.

What with that and opening the new branch Pup was kept busy. The shop had been a butcher's and delicatessen, so the whole interior had to be re-modelled and re-fitted. Pup felt rather proud of getting it because he could afford a higher rent than Georgiou who had had the place before.

It was time he spent an evening with his sister. It would have been nice to have gone out somewhere, the cinema or for a meal, but one couldn't associate Dolly with those activities. Dolly wasn't normal. He faced that now and accepted it, though he worried. The amount of wine she drank worried him, and the voices and the isolation she lived in. But what could he do about it? He couldn't stay at home every night or lock up her wine or get introductions for her through a marriage bureau. She would never marry. She would never have a job or lead a normal life and he saw that he would have the burden of her for the rest of their lives. He could never leave her, never even contemplate living apart from her.

These thoughts depressed him, and when he reached home, it was as if they had lifted a veil from his eyes so that for the first time in years he looked at Dolly with no comforting glaze between them. He saw the lines that were beginning to mark her face, particularly the deep lines that ran from nostrils to chin, the curious absent look in her eyes and the way her eyes wandered, no longer coordinated but with the beginning of a strabismus. The great blotch of the naevus was a dark, uncompromising crimson. He noticed how carefully dressed she was, just for an evening alone with him, in a new black-and-red striped dress and with the talisman worn ostenta-tiously on a bright red ribbon. With a sinking of the heart he thought how an evening alone with him was a highspot of her life.

It was useless to talk of going out. He ate his supper and tried not to let her see him looking at her as she finished one bottle of wine and started on the second. Inevitably, they would end up in the temple. He had a constricted feeling in his throat, a sensation of a kind of distasteful embarrassment, when he asked her if she would like him to do another Rosy Cross banishing ritual. Several times he had noticed her seeming to listen or holding herself still and staring the way he had sometimes seen Gingie do, alone on the fence or walking on the garden path.

She shook her head. The voices, at any rate, were company.

'You ought to do something for Dad,' she said. 'You ought to do a ritual for happiness and peace for him.' Even as she spoke she could hear Myra whispering. 'He's only had two books out of the library this week,' she said.

Pup was relieved. Still she hadn't asked the question, made the request he dreaded to hear. Perhaps she never would now, perhaps she was losing her faith in him, and gradually the temple and its contents might be allowed to fall into disuse. There was no sign of that happening, though, in Dolly's manner as they went into the temple and she, with more knowledge than he now retained, outlined to him the kind of Hexagram ritual he should perform.

It was high summer and from the open window the old railway line could be seen like a bit of countryside lying in sunshine, like a piece out of a Constable painting inexplicably surrounded by buildings. The buddleias made drifts of purple on the green, the poplar leaves trembled in the breeze and showed their silver undersides. Pup closed the window and unhooked his robe from the back of the door. But in doing so he caught it on the hook and tore a rent in the neck opening.

'It's all right,' Dolly said, 'it's only the facing. I'll mend it for you tomorrow.'

'Thanks, dear.'

The long tedious ritual was gone through. Pup did his best to make Dolly believe he had generated a solar hexagram. He forgot the names of the Supernal Triad of the Sephiroth, he forgot most of the names of the angels and planetary spirits. Most of what he intoned he made up as he went along. Dolly was enthralled. She had forgotten to bring the rest of her wine with her and it occurred wryly to Pup as he raised the cup and waved the wand that doing this every evening would be a way of curing her addiction.

She gazed raptly at him. He went on for an hour or more, remembering just before he finished to ask whoever or whatever it was he had invoked to call down blessings and riches on Harold, their father.

Pup replaced his weapons on the altar. It had been several weeks since he had handled them, as long since he had worn the robe, and now as he looked down at the hem of it he fancied that it had shrunk. Of course there was another possibility . . . When he was over twenty?

While Dolly, carrying the robe for mending, went downstairs to make their hot chocolate, he slipped into the bedroom that had formerly been his and after Myra's death had become his again. Very faint but still discernible on the wall were the measuring marks he had made when he was fifteen. He stood close up against them and made a new mark with a pencil. Yes, it was as he had thought, he had grown another inch. At twenty he had grown another inch and attained five feet eight. Pup laughed for joy but softly. He ran downstairs. Dolly was in the kitchen, standing over the stove, listening to a voice that spoke to her from invisible lips, her hand behind her ear the better to hear it.

The next day, when the doorbell rang, Dolly thought it was Wendy Collins come for a fitting, though she had said she couldn't come before Friday. But while she had been sitting with her back to the window, sorting through her cotton reels for one of golden thread to mend Pup's robe, she had heard a car draw up. One glance told her it wasn't Wendy's; even if Wendy had changed her car, she would not have done so for a long, green, expensive-looking sports model.

The bell rang again. Dolly did what she always did when she wasn't expecting a caller and there was someone at the door. She pulled down the curtain of hair so that the edge of it came a little way further than halfway along her eyebrow and about an inch out from her nostril. This was her only preparation, the rest of her she knew was all right.

The girl on the doorstep was of the kind she most disliked and resented – on sight. They filled her with a resentful misery for which there was no compensation. She did not particularly take against the Myras or Wendy Collinses of this world, the buck-toothed Eileen Ridges or the dried-up Miss Finlays. But those, like this one, who looked as if they belonged to a different, or to a new and glorious, species made her want to turn her back and close her eyes and shut herself up somewhere in the dark.

The voice was not a girl's or a woman's but a shy child's, a piping voice yet not shrill. 'I do hope I'm not disturbing you. I don't think we've ever met. I'm Yvonne Colefax.' She looked and sounded embarrassed.

Dolly didn't help her much. 'Yes? Was it something to do with Myra?' She had noticed her visitor was holding a largish flat brown paper parcel under one arm.

'Well, no, I . . . I mean, I know about you through poor Myra. It was really – well, I'm looking for a dressmaker!'

Dolly had lost a lot of custom through her alienation from the Spiritists and she felt she could not afford to turn business away, however much she might want to shut her eyes and hide. 'You'd better come in,' she said.

Yvonne had been aghast at the sight of Dolly. Things like that always upset her, any deformity or scar or that kind of thing. She had got it from her father who had been married to two beautiful women and who taught his daughter that to be beautiful was all she need be and that anything ugly to look at was somehow bad and wrong as well. Not that she felt like that about Dolly; that was a feeling that had long been pushed deep down in Yvonne's unconscious mind. What she felt was revulsion, pity and a wish she had not come. How terrible it must be to go through life with a disability like that! For a moment it made Yvonne's own predicament seem light and trivial. But only for a moment. She put the parcel down on the arm of a pine-framed brown-and-white check settee and looked about this room into which she had been once before.

Dolly was very conscious of what other women wore. She could price their clothes, gauge pretty well where they came from. It was seldom that in her own milieu she saw anyone better dressed than herself. Today she was wearing a dress she had made herself out of a blue linen and polyester mixture with drawn thread work on the collar and pockets, blue sandals and around her neck a small blue, pink and green

159

scarf, casually knotted. But this girl made her look dowdy. It was nothing to do with the naevus, nothing to do with that mark of apartness. She would have made most women look dowdy and clumsy and coarse. Everything about her had a delicate ethereal daintiness; she was a puff-of-wind creature with Chinese porcelain skin, thistledown hair, and her bronze silk dress floated here and clung there like a beech leaf – Dolly found herself remembering childhood book illustrations – on a nymph or pixie.

They eyed each other warily in the bright sunshine which streamed through the living-room windows. Yvonne was the first to look aside. In a rush, she began explaining how Myra had said Harold's daughter was a dressmaker, how she had this piece of silk a friend had brought her from Hong Kong, how she just happened to be passing the house. Dolly's eye was caught by the large diamond cluster engagement ring on Yvonne's left hand. She had no illusions about her work. She was a good, average, little-woman-down-the-road dressmaker. But was she good enough for a woman who wore Cacharel dresses and bought her sandals at Kurt Geiger? Yvonne unwrapped the parcel and let unroll a length of rather stiff silk. It was of a brilliant uncompromising pea green, the sort of colour ninety-nine women out of a hundred would have looked terrible in.

'You can wear that colour,' Dolly said grudgingly. Her dislike was evaporating. The fact was that Yvonne seemed altogether too far removed from her, too remote and different, to feel for her such an ordinary human emotion as dislike.

'Well, perhaps.' Yvonne spoke in a serious, concentrated way. She began to talk about colours and textures, about greens and whether you should wear gold or silver with them. Dolly said always gold with that particular colour. And garnets, if you happened to have them. A simple shift dress, didn't Dolly think? Dolly had already thought this. She was very nearly enjoying herself. None of her previous customers had had any real interest in clothes; they simply wanted something to cover them or keep them warm, not to be 'showy', nothing flattering or distinctive or elegant. She hadn't talked clothes like this with anyone since Edith died.

'You'll have to have a pattern. I should have a Vogue pattern, they're the best.'

But Yvonne had never heard of dress patterns. She had never had anything made before. Dolly opened the pattern box, though she had little hope of finding anything in Yvonne's size which was probably a ten or even an eight.

'Couldn't you sort of make it up yourself? What's that?'

Dolly turned round to see Yvonne holding the golden robe which had been hanging over a chair.

'That's my brother's. He's a –' Dolly hesitated. She knew it might sound strange to the uninitiated. Had Aleister Crowley or Israel Regardie had sisters? '– a magician, a geomancer.'

Yvonne didn't look amused or suspicious or even very surprised. 'I've met your brother. Here and at poor Myra's funeral. He told me my – my past. And he got it right, all of it in detail. Wasn't that amazing?'

'He's a genius,' Dolly said simply.

A silence fell. Dolly didn't know why it should have done, for they had seemed to be getting on so well. She said awkwardly, 'I expect I could make the pattern up myself if you just want a straight up-and-down shift. Sleeveless, I expect and with a turtle neck? I don't know why they call them turtle necks but straight across at back and front?'

161

'Because a turtle's neck comes out of his shell like that.' She sounded like a child of seven. And it didn't seem to be affectation, it was real. Myra had said she had had two husbands; she must be twenty-seven or twenty-eight. 'I used to have a tortoise in my garden in Shelley Drive but he ran away and got run over. Well, he walked away, they don't ever run.'

Dolly found herself saying, 'Oh, dear, never mind,' as she might have done once to Pup over some childhood sorrow. 'I'd better measure you, hadn't I? Then I can get it cut out and tacked.'

She drew the curtains against the sunlight and curious eyes. Yvonne stepped out of her Cacharel to reveal art nouveau limbs and Janet Reger underwear. Thirty-two, twenty-two, thirty-three – Dolly had not yet ventured into the metric system.

Yvonne put on her dress. She touched the cheeks of the dolls and smiled at them as if they were real children. She touched the robe again. 'Like a wizard,' she said. 'The wonderful Wizard of Oz.'

'Yes.'

'When shall I come for a fitting?'

They were out in the hall again. 'It's Thursday today. How about next Monday afternoon?' Dolly hesitated. She had an impulse to do something she knew was daring and perhaps reckless, something she had never done before but which now seemed essential. If she let Yvonne go without doing it she knew she would be full of regret. 'Have you got a minute?' she said. 'I'd like to show you something.'

'What sort of something?'

'It's got to do with my brother.'

She led the way upstairs. 'Poor Myra,' Yvonne sighed at the top of the first flight. Dolly heard Myra's heeltaps behind the closed bedroom door but she did not think Yvonne would hear them; Myra appeared to no one but herself. She opened the door to the temple and had the satisfaction of hearing Yvonne gasp.

'What is it?'

'It's the place where he does his magic.' Dolly showed her the elemental weapons. 'He can do anything.'

Yvonne had picked up the pentacle and was holding it rather gingerly between finger and thumb. 'What sort of anything?' She lisped a little when she was excited.

It was on the tip of Dolly's tongue to tell her how he had killed Myra but something stayed her. After all, as Pup himself had said, it was illegal to kill people and it might, for all she knew, be a punishable crime to stick a knife into a rag doll. 'He can make things happen,' she said. 'It's a science, you know, it's not like witchcraft or witch doctors or anything. It's just as much a science as – as being a doctor or working in a lab.' In her enthusiasm she had forgotten to keep her hair over her face and the naevus was exposed to the strong afternoon light. Dolly's voice rose. 'He can do wonderful things, he can do miracles.'

Yvonne's eyes glanced into her face and as quickly darted away again. Dolly blushed. She knew what had passed through the other girl's mind.

'You have to ask him to do it,' she said. 'He's not God.'

Yvonne nodded. 'When he told me about my past, he got it all right, every bit.'

'Last night he did a very special ritual to make our father's life take a turn for the better.'

'Oh, yes, poor man. Poor Myra!'

'You'll see, things will come right for him very soon.'

They went downstairs and Dolly opened the front door. It was plain to her, inexplicably, that Yvonne did not want to go. She wanted to prolong the visit because there was something she wanted to say or ask. But she didn't know how to and Dolly, who was unaccustomed to long periods of social contact with new people, or indeed with any people except perhaps the Collinses, was beginning to feel the strain of it. Yvonne lingered on the doorstep.

'You did say Monday?'

'About two in the afternoon would be best. Goodbye.'

As soon as the door was closed she regretted driving Yvonne away. Not that she was alone. Myra's footsteps came across the hall, the heels clacking as if there were no haircord there but still the old uncarpeted quarry tiles. Dolly pushed past her and went into the breakfast room where Harold kept an *A-Z London Guide* along with the few books of his own he possessed.

'Silly old fool,' said Myra's voice. 'You'd think he'd have the sense to put those paint tins out for the bin men. To be perfectly honest, you ought to do it, Doreen.'

Dolly took no notice. She was looking up Shelley Drive in the index.

'They've got a great big house,' said Myra. 'George's father was a very well-known specialist. He left everything to George. They've got a sauna in their house and a swimming pool in the garden.'

Myra followed her back to the living room. Edith was already there, waiting. The Ivoire that Yvonne had been wearing was drowned in the pungency of lemons.

'You want to pin that silk on to a piece of flannel before you start cutting,' said Edith.

Myra gave one of her laughs. 'Quite candidly, I think it's peculiar her coming here to Doreen. With the money they've got she could go to anyone.'

Dolly sat in the window, stitching the neckline of the golden robe. They did not speak to her again but for a long time she heard them laughing softly and their footsteps as they walked about the room.

Chapter 16

To celebrate the sale of Mrs Brewer's flat, on completion day Pup took Philippa out to lunch at the San Carlo in Highgate High Street. After that they both took the afternoon off, a rare enough lapse for Pup. The people who moved into the flat were a woman and her two teenage daughters. Dolly sat in the window and watched the removal van come. It was raining and the men had to cover the furniture with sheets before making the journey from the van to the front door. The new neighbour was a woman of forty who still dressed in the fashion of her youth – long droopy skirt, scuffed boots, peasant blouse and shawl – for like many of that Beatles generation she had never noticed that the trend had changed. She stood in the rain, getting wet, looking helpless, and presently Mrs Buxton came waddling along under an umbrella with a cup of tea and a plate of biscuits for her on a tin tray.

The Porsche, drawing into the pavement, sent a spray of muddy water from the gutter up on to her fat legs. Mrs Buxton said something to the driver. Dolly couldn't hear what it was but it looked rude, and when Yvonne got out her expression was nervous, even distressed, though by then Mrs Buxton, with Gingie under one arm, had gone off into her own home.

Yvonne made no reference to the incident. She was wearing a raincoat today, though one that was as elegant as and indeed very like a cocktail dress, being of black proofed silk, and with it a wide black patent belt and high narrow black patent boots. A shimmering of raindrops clung to her fine silver-gilt hair. She almost ran into the house.

'What a horrid day! I hate summer days like this, don't you? Oh, look, it's half done! I'm going to love it!'

Dolly didn't want her making water spots on the silk. 'Let me take your coat and hang it up.'

Yvonne's manner seemed unnaturally bright today, almost hysterical. She tore off the coat like someone stripping off after waiting the whole of a long hot day to get to the water's edge. And the pink-and-black striped dress she wore was going the same way. Dolly drew the curtains just in time to stop the removal men getting an eyeful of Yvonne in orchid bra and bikini briefs.

The bright green was right on her. Her white neck rose from it like a madonna lily from its sepals. She looked at herself in Edith's pier glass.

'We can have the curtains back now,' Dolly said.

'No . . .'

'Well, the lights on, if you like.'

'I can see, I can see well enough.' She stood there, gazing at her own reflection. Something in Dolly – or perhaps one of the voices – warned her of impending trouble. Yvonne was so still, gazing at herself, but gazing as if she saw nothing, as trance-like as Mrs Fitter. 'I don't want light,' she said, her voice growing more childlike. 'It's easier when it's a bit dark.' She turned round slowly. 'Can I take this off?'

'Let me. Mind the pins. You're happy with it, are you?'

'Happy?' Yvonne gave a little light laugh. 'Oh, yes, it's fine, it's fine.' She stepped into her own dress.

'About not pulling back the curtains – I meant it's less embarrassing like this. Do you mind?'

Again Dolly sensed trouble coming. Her apprehensiveness sharpened into fear. She shrugged and laid the green slip down.

In a breathless rapid way Yvonne said, 'I've been thinking about what you said about your brother. All over the weekend I've been thinking about it, about how you said he could do anything. You said it was a science, a scientific thing, not like – well, clairvoyants and faith healers and that sort of thing.'

Enormous relief flooded Dolly. What had she been afraid of? Something to do with the naevus perhaps. That Yvonne, like Myra, had been going to give her advice about the naevus. But it was Pup she wanted to talk about. Dolly loved talking about Pup, she couldn't have enough of that.

'You see, I've tried everyone. I even went to this fortune teller. I had my horoscope cast. I've been to my doctor and to a psychiatrist, I've talked to my solicitor and they don't do a thing to help me, not a thing. They don't *understand*. One night I phoned up the Samaritans, I felt so bad. Can I call you Doreen?'

Dolly shook her head. She found herself saying, rather to her own astonishment, 'I'd rather you said Dolly.'

'Dolly. All right. You don't mind me talking to you like this, do you, Dolly? You see, you're my last chance. Well, your brother's my last chance. I think your brother's absolutely amazing, I really do. All my life I shall remember the way he told me about my past life, he was marvellous. So you don't mind me talking, do you?'

No one had confided in Dolly before. It was a new experience. You couldn't count Pup describing what happened at meetings of the Golden Dawn. Her friendless existence had contained no sessions of girlish outpourings. No torch-carrying man had opened his heart to her, no elderly person complained of the neglect of children and the exigencies of living on a pension, no girl confessed sexual adventures. Her brother, she suddenly realized with a pang, was self-sufficient and perhaps always had been. Because of her lack of experience she had no idea of the prompting words required, the 'do you want to tell me about it?' and the reiterated 'go on'. She simply shook her head, unaware that a look of wonder had spread itself across her usually expressionless face.

'Well,' said Yvonne, and she looked away from Dolly. She looked at the ballet girl and the Chinese boy on the mantelpiece and then at the big old black and gilt Singer sewing machine. 'Well, it's George, my husband. He's in love with someone and I don't know what to do.'

This was mystifying. That anyone who had someone as beautiful as Yvonne could conceivably want anyone else was, for a moment, beyond Dolly's imaginings. But intuitively now, she understood that she had to make some sort of reply.

'She must be,' she began awkwardly, 'I mean she must be – well, amazing if she's prettier than you . . .'

Her voice faltered and the blood tore into her face. The words had been terrible to say, they had been wrenched out of her, but now, for some reason, she was tiredly glad she had said them. Impulsively, Yvonne put out her hand and laid it briefly over Dolly's. 'You are nice, you're a dear.' She paused, then gave Dolly a sideways look. 'It's not a she.'

'But you said . . .'

'He says he's in love with a – a beautiful boy!' said Yvonne and with a little preliminary shriek she burst into tears.

*

169

Dolly gave a nervous giggle. Yvonne, drying her eyes, had repeated what she said and Dolly found herself without words. It was quite dark in the room now, the rain pounding on the windows, and inside the atmosphere had become very awkward and strained. It was the kind of atmosphere Edith used to say you could cut with a knife. Edith and Myra were not there now, they had fled. Yvonne turned her face, impervious to tear stains, unmarked by the redness or puffiness of tears, towards Dolly and dabbed at her eyes with a lacy Y-initialled handkerchief.

'I don't know what you want me to say,' Dolly said clumsily.

The delicate, thin shoulders shrugged. 'What can anyone say?'

The only source of Dolly's experience in such matters was the advice columns and answers to readers' letters in the magazines she read, her only mentor the woman journalist who had advised her to go out and meet people and forget about her birthmark. But she did not draw directly from them.

'It's not as if he wanted a divorce to marry this – this person,' she said.

'He would if he could! He says gay people ought to be able to marry each other, he says you can find actual ministers who'll marry them, and if he can find one who'll do it, he'll marry Ashley Clare.'

'A form of marriage,' said Dolly vaguely. She had read this expression somewhere. Yvonne was looking at her eagerly, nodding her head. Evidently, Yvonne expected much from her and suddenly Dolly felt excited, she felt she was enjoying herself. The constraint had gone. The whole experience was so novel, so different. She felt she must enhance it. But how? 'Would you like something to drink?' she said, uncertain of the proper form of words to use.

'Tea, do you mean?'

Dolly shook her head. Until the advent (and the demise) of her father's second wife, Dolly had never had anywhere to chill her wine. She now opened Myra's big Electrolux and got out a bottle of Blue Nun.

'How lovely! What a lovely thought! You are kind.' Yvonne actually clapped her hands at the sight of the tray with the bottle on it and two of Myra's best wineglasses. 'It's just what I need!'

Dolly nodded happily. It was what she needed too. They did not raise their glasses in a toast. Yvonne could think of nothing to toast and Dolly was too used to drinking alone for such a thing to cross her mind.

'Did you know he was –' Never before had she pronounced the word in this context '– gay when you got married?'

'I ought to have known. He was thirty-five and he'd never been married and that's a bad sign.' The utterance of this sophisticated lore sounded strange in Yvonne's baby voice. 'Besides, he was so – well, old-fashioned and gentlemanly to me. Real men aren't like that, are they?'

Dolly had very little idea what real men were or were not like. She re-filled their glasses.

'I'd just lost my first husband. He died of leukaemia, he was only twenty-two. I've had a sad life really, haven't I?' Dolly nodded sympathetically, though to her it seemed a wonderfully eventful one. Once more the tears gathered in Yvonne's eyes. 'I was only twenty-one. We were babies when we got married. I felt terrible when he died and I met George and he was so kind to me and said he'd look after me. And you know, Dolly, I hadn't got any money and George had this huge private practice apart from what his dad left him. He said he'd buy me a house anywhere I liked and he'd give me a car for a wedding present.' When Dolly's eyes went involuntarily to the curtained, rain-lashed window, she said quickly, 'Oh, not that one, I've had two since then.'

'He married you to try and cure himself,' said Dolly, sagely quoting her columnist.

'I suppose so. Of course, Dolly, it never worked.' Yvonne drew a squiggle pattern in the condensation on her wineglass. 'I always knew there was something wrong. You see, I'd had a very passionate relationship with my first husband.'

Dolly didn't want to hear about that. 'What about this Ashley person?'

'I've never seen him, I don't know anything about him except that George says he's a beautiful boy and he met him in a gay club in Earl's Court called The Ganymede.' Yvonne's voice gathered speed and the words rattled out, rather like a toy train charging downhill. 'And he's madly in love with him and he wants to leave me and go and live with him all the time. He wants to sell our house and buy me a flat with some of the money and go and live with Ashley Clare.' On the long vowel of the surname her voice rose on a melancholy wail.

'Don't cry,' said Dolly awkwardly. She put out her hand as she might have done to Pup.

Yvonne clutched it. She would have liked to throw herself into Dolly's arms but the naevus repelled her. The naevus usually had exactly the effect on people that Dolly expected it to have. But Yvonne held on to her hand. 'So – you see – your brother – he's so clever – I thought –'

'That he could do something for you?'

'That he could make it stop!'

'But do you want a – a husband like that?' Dolly asked.

'I want my house! I want to be Mrs George

Colefax. I don't want to be divorced and dropped and just thrown away for a – a beautiful boy! I just want your brother to make it stop. I can pay for it. He's so clever, he can name his price, I know that, Dolly. I shouldn't mind what I paid, I'm so miserable.'

Dolly said almost scornfully, 'He wouldn't want paying.' She poured the last of the wine. The rain had stopped. She drew the curtains apart a few inches and a shaft of watery sunshine came through the crack between. 'Tell me what he looks like, this Ashley. Could you get a photo?'

Yvonne said she would try. She would borrow or steal a photograph from George and get it to Dolly. Relaxed by the wine, she talked about where Ashley Clare lived, what he did for a living and, as far as she knew, what he looked like. Once or twice she called Dolly darling. It had been an eventful and exciting, even exhausting afternoon, and Dolly, watching the Porsche depart up Manningtree Grove, felt so strung up by it that she had to open a fresh bottle of wine a full hour before Pup was due home.

For that evening he intended to spend at home. He had a date with Caroline's friend's sister's boss at his house in Finchley at 6.00 and he was nervous. But he showed none of this nervousness to Philippa, and in spite of it, he did not leave her flat in Muswell Hill until five to.

Half an hour later he came away jubilant. He drove through Hampstead Garden Suburb in the Hodge and Yearman van, forcing himself to drive slowly and carefully, for his instinct was to be reckless. The sun was shining now and it was as if the rain had never been except that but for the rain the lawns would not have been so green or the flowers so fresh or the leaves so sparkling in the bright soft light. The large beautiful houses seemed to look graciously upon him.

Dolly was a little drunk by the time he came in. She was steady on her feet still but her speech was becoming slurred. Pup looked at her flushed face and at the empty Blue Nun bottle and the nearly empty bottle of Yugoslav Riesling but he made no comment. He didn't want to antagonize her, he wanted to tell her what he had achieved that day. He had to tell someone. Harold would only caution him to hold his horses. Philippa was less interested even than Dolly and Caroline was a gold digger. He could have told his friend Dilip Raj but Dilip had gone to his grandmother in Calcutta for a holiday.

'I've had the most wonderful thing happen,' he said, coming across the room to kiss her, almost bounding across. 'I've just been to see a man who's going to give us a contract to supply his new offices with everything they need in the way of equipment – word processors, electronic typewriters, the lot – it'll be an enormous contract. And he's given it to me, Dolly.' This time, though she noticed nothing, he said 'me' and not 'us'. 'I'm on top of the world, Dolly, and I tell you what, I'll have a glass of your wine.'

She poured it for him and brought it to where he was sitting on the brown check settee. Pup, for the occasion, had been wearing his grey suit with the pink-and-grey patterned shirt and a slate-blue silk tie. He took off the tie and his jacket and sat there in his shirtsleeves.

'To us!' he said, raising his glass. 'To the continued success of Yearman and Hodge!'

She looked at him. It was the look of a mother whose son is a wealthy rag and bone dealer but who would have preferred him to be a poor professor. 'I should have thought,' she said, 'you'd leave all that kind of thing to Dad.'

It was rare for him but he was suddenly furiously angry. He controlled himself. 'He's not a business-man. I think I am. I think I'm lucky enough to have a flair for it.'

She said quietly and dolefully, 'I thought you had a flair for – you know what I thought.'

The only thing to do with that was ignore it. 'Come on,' he said, 'we'll celebrate. I'll take you out to dinner.'

She shook her head. 'I'm tired. You know I don't like going out to eat in those places.' He saw what she meant and he was powerless. 'Besides, I've got your meal here.'

Salami, rolled turkey breast sliced thin as paper, cole slaw, potato crisps, chocolate Swiss roll, tinned peaches and tinned custard. He felt disloyal but he was growing out of that kind of food, the child's dream of a feast. Harold was already seated at the kitchen table, *The Daughters of George III* propped up in front of him between his plate and the milk jug.

'Hallo, Dad,' said Pup who hadn't seen him since the morning. 'Had a good day?'

'I don't know about good. I know I'm worn out.'

And this time he was. That afternoon at 5.00, sitting in the room behind the Crouch End Broadway shop, operating one of the new Olympia ES100s, he had finished typing his novel. He was reading *The Daughters of George III* less from need than habit.

Dolly poured out two cups of tea. She sensed it would be unwise that evening to tell Pup about Yvonne Colefax and her trouble. Wait a day or two, wait until next time he was home in the evening. She had had too much wine to feel like eating but she took a piece of bread and buttered it and made herself a sandwich with the sliced turkey. It was rare for Pup to be home two evenings in succession. She almost trembled when she thought of what that might mean, that he was growing tired of the Golden Dawn.

The ins and outs of why Georgiou came to lose the shop Diarmit never fully comprehended. Not that Georgiou, hitherto taciturn, had not talked of it all day long, grumbling in his thick harsh accent about landlords and rent acts and the iniquity to be found everywhere in the United Kingdom. Not that he had not attempted to explain, his voice snapping and crackling as he stumbled over difficult words.

'That place that sells the typing machines, they are after my shop.' Georgiou threw back his head and lifted up his hands. 'Oh, nobody is saying but I have ways of knowing. Expansion is the word, expand, expand, that is all – everything – nowaday. Typing machines, photomachines, this is what people like today. Good food they don't like, they don't care.'

Diarmit smiled uneasily at him, mystified.

'So if that's what people like,' said Georgiou, 'let these typers and photoers pay the rent. Me, I don't care, I retire. I leave this rat race for good.'

Once more Diarmit was on the dole. He had all the time in the world on his hands and no purpose to put it to. He was ashamed of being without work and even more ashamed to be seen to be without it by the other tenants of the house. They would think him no better than Conal, they would think that birds of a feather flocked together.

Of necessity he now spent hours in his room. If he went out it was never for more than an hour or so. He spent all night and most of the day in that room. The fact that Conal's things were in it, were still taking up space in it, began to anger him. He put Conal's clothes and the knives in the Harrods bag in the middle of the room in a pile. Whenever he moved about, he had to step over them or walk round them but he felt that at any rate he had made a gesture, he had made it plain to whomever might call or look in the window or somehow observe the interior of the room that those things were not his and had nothing to do with him. He stopped wearing Conal's red clothes and went back to the denim jeans he had had on when first he came to take over the room.

Then it occurred to him that Conal's sister Kathleen was a more suitable person to give her brother's things house room than he was. He made them all into a parcel which he wrapped in newspaper and bound with adhesive tape. It took him nearly all of one day to pack and wrap that parcel, and on the next, a hot day in August, he took it over to Kilburn on the train from Crouch Hill.

A man opened the door to him. He said he was Kathleen's husband and Kathleen was out at her work.

'She's lucky then, lucky to have work,' Diarmit said politely. 'I could do with work myself.' He had heard the man's voice before, he remembered now, when he had made that phone call on Conal's behalf. Cowardly Conal had got him to phone them because he was scared to. 'These are her brother Conal's things now that I've brought all the way over on the train. I've no use for them, you see, so you'd best take care of them till he comes.'

The man stared. 'She hasn't got a brother called Conal.'

So that was the way the wind blew. They meant to disown him entirely. Diarmit could not blame them but he persisted. 'Moore's the name, same as her maiden name. Conal Moore.'

'My wife's maiden name was Bawne.'

Diarmit laughed. He couldn't help it. The effrontery of it, the sheer nerve of skiving off out of your responsibilities by pretending to be a member of *his* own family! Bawne, indeed. He laughed humourlessly, tossing back his head, and he tried to thrust the parcel into the man's arms, but before he could do so, the door was shut in his face.

Why had the man refused even to admit Conal was his brother-in-law? That he and his wife might want nothing to do with Conal, Diarmit could readily understand. But why deny the relationship and refuse to take in a parcel of Conal's property? It must be because they had had word that Conal was coming back and they were scared of any involvement with him.

He was coming back . . . It was a year now since he had murdered that girl and cut her head off, since they had called him The Headsman and written about him in the papers. He was coming back because it had all blown over and he was safe. Diarmit climbed the stairs to his room. He unpacked the parcel and laid the red clothes out carefully on the end of the bed and over the backs of chairs. The knives and the cleaver were clean but he washed them at the sink and dried them and replaced them in the bag. Conal was coming back and might be back any day . . .

The letter was in a brown envelope addressed to Ms Doreen Yearman and it was such as Dolly had hardly ever received in her life before, for it began 'Dear Dolly' and ended 'Love from Yvonne'. With it was a photograph of two men in a living room sitting at either end of a velvet sofa. It had been taken with a flash and both were blank-faced and stary-eyed. George Colefax was smoking a cigar but the other man sat with his hands rather girlishly folded in his lap. A beautiful boy, perhaps, though that surely had been rather a long time ago. His black hair, swept back Byronically, had silver wings at the temples and although the flash had obliterated lines on the forehead and under the eyes, you felt that they were there.

Dolly put the photograph and the letter in her handbag. Something impelled her to keep taking the letter out and re-reading that 'Dear Dolly' and 'Love from Yvonne'. She was going shopping in the Holloway Road, walking part of the way there along the old railway line. It was a warm hazy day with the promise of great heat by noon and the grass was flushed pink where the rosebay willow herb was in bloom. You could hear the hum of insects in the flowers above the hum of traffic.

As she stepped inside the comparative coolness and darkness of the Mistley tunnel, it occurred to Dolly that it must be a year since The Headsman's murder. It had been a Wednesday, she recalled, the day before Myra's dinner party at which Pup had accurately told Yvonne the events of her past life. She, Dolly, had been out, making her first visit to a seance of the Adonai Spiritists. Because of that she could remember the dates, Wednesday, 12 August, Thursday, 13 August. And today was Wednesday, 11 August. A year had passed, exactly a year, today was the anniversary.

Dolly quickened her step through the tunnel and felt a certain relief at coming out at the other end into the soft warm light. A black and red butterfly flew across, an inch or so from her eyes, and settled on a spray of buddleia. She walked along the old station platform. Approaching her, in the distance, was the woman with the white Pyrennean mountain dog, the animal ambling indifferently as if a year ago it had never nosed out a corpse and then a human head.

Chapter 17

The man in the photograph appeared to have an olive skin, so Dolly made the doll's body from the kind of coarse unbleached linen that is called crash. There was a piece left over from Edith's tapestry work. Dolly embroidered Ashley Clare's face, the curved black eyebrows, the almond eyes, the red sensuous mouth. She sewed a headful of black hair on him but she used silk, not wool, and at the temples she stitched in fine threads of silver. Almost by chance she seemed to have caught the man's expression. The face, she felt, would be instantly recognizable.

In the photograph he was wearing velvet cord jeans, a shirt open at the neck and a zipper jacket but Dolly wanted to see him more formally dressed as he must surely be for his daily work, whatever that might be. She made him a suit from grey polyester that had been left over from a skirt of Wendy Collins's, a shirt from one of Edith's lawn handkerchiefs and a red silk tie from the lining of her own velvet coat. She painted his cardboard shoes with Woolworth's Chinese lacquer. Complete, he was the perfect man doll, the best doll she had ever made.

Even Myra admired him. Myra and Edith had been there with her, watching her work.

'I must say, Doreen, it's a perfect likeness. I saw him once when he came into the surgery. You've got him to a T.'

'You've made a very nice job of that, dear, but isn't he a bit cross-eyed?'

It was rare for them to speak to each other but sometimes they did. 'To be honest with you, Edith,' Myra said, 'he *is* a bit cross-eyed.'

Dolly put him on the mantelpiece between the Chinese boy and the ballet girl. Making the doll had taken up all her time and she had done nothing more to the green silk dress. While she was stitching in the facings at neck and armholes there was a ring at the door and she was sure it must be Yvonne calling unexpectedly. But it was only one of the girls from next door with a pair of denims over her arm to say that Mrs Buxton had told her mother that Dolly did dressmaking, so could she find time to turn her jeans up four inches? She saw the doll, said it looked like Robert de Niro and giggled. Dolly took the jeans and said she would have to charge four pounds and would that be all right? She could see the girl trying not to look at her right cheek.

Since the letter, read and re-read, especially the opening and concluding words, there had been no sign at all from Yvonne. Dolly had never before known what it is to sit by a telephone waiting for it to ring, longing for it to ring. She tacked the green silk hem and began sewing it with fine slip stitches.

'Once you've finished that dress,' Myra said, 'she'll be off like lightning. You know that, don't you, Doreen? She won't bother with you. I mean, frankly, give me one good reason why she should.'

'It's a difficult shade to match the Sylko to,' said Edith. 'That jade is a difficult shade to match and a difficult shade to wear.'

'Her father was a professional man and her husband's a professional man. It's a question of class really. Well, isn't it always?'

Pup was coming home for a meal. He was

wondering – it occupied his mind a great deal these days – how he could get his father to retire. For a long while Harold had been useless in the shop but now he was becoming worse than useless, impeding Pup like an iron on his leg. He mooned about, replying to customers with the vague near-incomprehension of someone who has been addressed in a forgotten foreign language. He was always to be seen stooped over the Xerox or lugging brown paper parcels of the kind that contain a ream of paper.

Pup, however, had a horror of hurting people's feelings, of causing pain. It would be unthinkable to make Harold feel unwanted, he must instead be made to wish to go of his own accord. Perform a Pentagram ritual, Dolly would no doubt advise, but he had lost all belief in the efficacy of that. In the days when he had bargained and cajoled for height, he had had faith – or perhaps the simple answer was that all along five feet eight had been written in his genes.

The first thing he saw when he walked in was the doll. He gave an exclamation which sounded like pure astonishment but was really dismay. Any of these items of evidence that his sister was unlike other women, was growing more and more strange, filled him with foreboding. But he said nothing. Dolly had already begun on her bottle of wine and he started his supper. At the last meal he had eaten at home he had mentioned over the tinned tongue and defrosted sausage rolls that he liked seafood, though knowing as he spoke of it that this would lead to his being served prefabricated prawn cocktail twice a week for years. The first of the series was before him, all the ingredients fresh from a freezer pack and topped with a dollop of bottled sauce.

Dolly was glad to have given him something

different, something he would really enjoy. It distracted her from her preoccupation with Yvonne, though only for a while. They were back in the living room and she three-quarters through her Chianti Classico when she made up her mind. She picked up the receiver and dialled, resolving to put it down again if George Colefax answered.

Yvonne's little girl voice said like a receptionist:

'Dr Colefax's residence.'

'It's Dolly. Your dress is finished.'

'Dolly, did you get my letter? I was expecting you to phone before.'

So it was she, not Yvonne, who had been at fault, she who had committed the breach of conduct. She gave a sigh of relief which made Pup look up from his evening paper.

'Would you – would you like to come over? Would you come over tomorrow?'

But Yvonne said why shouldn't Dolly come to her? She would like to return Dolly's hospitality. Say Monday or Tuesday? It wouldn't occur to her of course, Dolly thought with a flicker of resentment, it never did occur to people with cars, what a difficult and time-consuming journey it would be, getting from Manningtree Grove to the Bishop's Avenue by public transport. But she was too gratified by Yvonne's invitation to demur.

'I'll pick you up on my way home if you like,' Pup said. She had a friend, a young, suitable, normal friend at last. The relief was great. He remembered Yvonne Colefax, he remembered the scent of her and the feel of that slim thigh against his leg. And at Myra's funeral . . . He took his eyes from the olive-skinned, red-lipped doll on the mantelpiece. 'Ask her what time.'

As happy now as she had been tense and fearful before, Dolly sat on the settee beside him and told

183

him of the love affair between Ashley Clare and George Colefax.

'And he's married to that lovely Yvonne?'

'We'll have to do something about it.'

'What can I do?' said Pup absently and he returned to his paper.

When he had first come to London, he had put himself into Conal's hands and Conal had had to look after him. Not that he had made a very good job of it. True, he had provided him with a roof over his head but the job had never come to anything and there was no doubt Conal had simply made use of him as someone on whom to unload all his dreads and terrors. Thanks to Conal, he might even have been suspected of the murder and decapitation of that girl, for Conal had had no qualms about returning here with the knives and his bloodstained clothes. But this time, once Conal had returned and they were together again, Diarmit knew it would be him who must look after the other man. It filled him with anxiety.

The knives in the Harrods bag and the heap of clothes still lay in the middle of the floor. Diarmit cursed them, for every time he crossed from his bed to the sink or from the cupboard to the window he had to step over them and once or twice he stumbled and fell headlong. Dressed in blue jeans, a grey shirt and a grey sweater, he went to the Job Centre but still they had nothing for him. He dreaded having to confess to the feckless criminal Conal Moore that he was out of work, that he was on the dole.

The two dogs scavenged from the litter bins on Mount Pleasant Green, the Dalmatian and the mongrel collie, dissecting the wrappings of takeaway food, running on the grass like a pair of jackals. The old people had moved into the sheltered housing and a woman of seventy or so could be seen in the window of the communal room, arranging flowers in a vase. A lawn had been started in the garden and little evergreen trees planted. The workmen had long been gone. That would worry Conal, Diarmit thought, he would wonder where they were and expect them to come demolishing this house. He would be afraid to stay in in the daytime, it would all begin again.

Sitting at the window, looking across the green in the direction of Crouch Hill station which was the way Conal would come, Diarmit told himself that to avoid Conal he had only to run away. He had only to leave and go back to Liverpool. But it was not realistic thinking, for he knew he would never so shirk his responsibilities, and besides he had no family in Liverpool, they were all dead and only Conal's relations lived there. He could go down on the old railway line and hide out in the Mistley tunnel, taking provisions with him and sleeping on the feather mattress. But that would be no good when the fine weather broke and the autumn came. Diarmit shivered, resigning himself to his doom, waiting for his doom to come across the green from Crouch Hill station.

As it happened, though, when Conal came Diarmit did not see him come. He must have slipped into the room during the night. For when Diarmit awoke he was there, wearing dark red clothes and taking his knives out of the Harrods bag, examining them closely, to check no doubt that Diarmit had taken care of them in his absence. Conal the murderer, Conal the criminal, Conal the outcast. Jobless, friendless, hated, mad Conal.

Because he knew what would happen if he left the house, because he dared not go out yet must have exercise, he began pacing the room. Up and down, he paced the small cluttered room with a heavy dogged tread that after a while grew weary, but he paced on.

He did not speak. There was no one to speak to, for Diarmit had gone.

It was the girl's first day in the Unisex salon in Tottenham Lane and Pup's first visit. They closed at lunchtime on Mondays and he was her last client. His was also the nicest hair she had handled that morning, fair and wavy, more like a girl's than a man's.

'You could do anything with your hair,' she said.

'Like what? Knit it? Grow it up a beanstalk?'

She giggled. 'I mean have it in any style. You know what I mean.'

'Okay, stop that cutting and I'll have dreadlocks. They said your name but I didn't catch it. Anthea?'

'Andrea. I'm going to start the blow-drying now.'

'Wait a minute. The racket it makes kills me. Look, Andrea, I don't know how I'll get through the day if you won't say you'll come out with me tonight.'

'I don't even know your name,' said Andrea.

'You've only got to ask. It's Peter. And you like my hair, don't you? That's a start. We can go to the new disco in the Broadway . . .'

Pup had to pick up Dolly first. He got to Shelley Drive at two minutes past six. Because he was going dancing, he was wearing his tightest jeans but, changing quickly on his return home from work, an idea had come to him that for Dolly's sake he should impress Yvonne Colefax with some sort of weird or magicianly air. Dolly had told him how she and Yvonne had been up to the temple together and how Yvonne remembered him as a clairvoyant. So he put on a plain black velvet sweat shirt and hung round his neck on a long thong the solar talisman – gold letters on black painted metal – he had made for himself when he was sixteen. It was a costume equally appropriate for the disco. Perhaps this thought rather summed up the attitude Pup had come to take towards the practice of magic arts.

The Colefax home was a white-walled, green-roofed hacienda whose architecture also owed something to art deco and Moroccan influence and had in its pillared porch a hint of Palladio. It was not the largest house but among the larger houses in quiet, luxurious, bosky Shelley Drive and its grounds ranged extensively. Those in the front were an intricate layout of little rockeries, cypress trees, gravel walks and geometric flowerbeds, while on the far side at the back a red lacquer Chinese bridge, such as one associates with the Summer Palace of Peking, could be glimpsed. The lawns, as smoothly green as the jade silk dress Pup had seen Dolly making for Yvonne, obviously required the at least twice-weekly attentions of the old age pensioner who was at present steering round the turf with an electric lawn mower. Yvonne came down the steps when she heard the van's tyres crunch on the gravel. She was in a candy-pink lawn dress and she looked very young and fragile.

'It's lovely to see you again. Come in and have a drink. Do you know, I always think of you as some sort of supernatural being, a kind of guru perhaps.'

Pup smiled. They walked across expanses of oak parquet on which pink and yellow Kashmiri rugs were artlessly spread, to where Dolly sat on a terrace in a white cane chair. There was an empty wine bottle on the white wrought-iron table and another bottle which Dolly was rapidly emptying. Pup said he would have a glass of sherry. From the terrace you could see no other houses, only lawns and shrubberies and, surrounding it all, an apparent woodland whose foliage doubtless concealed other scattered palaces. The Chinese bridge spanned a little lake in which swam fish as vermilion as its lacquer. Dolly said the swimming pool was behind that hedge over there.

Yvonne came back with sherry and dry roasted peanuts in a glass dish. She sat in the swing seat and her wispy pink skirt rode up a little to show off her legs that the sun had tanned to a very light biscuit colour.

'I was reading something in a magazine the other day. About ESP and harnessing energy and making use of powers we don't know we have. It said that, in the future, we'd take it for granted these powers existed, we'd accept telepathy as a fact like – like electricity. It said there was about ninety per cent of our brains never got used but still there was this enormous – well, potential in them. That's the kind of thing you do, isn't it?'

She spoke as if she had learned it all off by heart for him, like a little girl reciting a poem she barely understands for a teacher she admires. He was curiously touched. He nodded.

'The power of your mind could alter the way another person's mind thinks and feels?'

'That would be the theory.'

She turned away. 'I shall be all alone after you've gone. I haven't seen George since Saturday morning. I don't suppose he'll bother to come home tonight.'

Dolly said, 'I could stay for the evening. My brother won't mind coming back for me, will you, Pup?'

'Pup?' said Yvonne.

'A pet name,' Pup said imperturbably. 'And I'm afraid I would mind. I've an appointment, I'm going out.'

Dolly looked disappointed but proud. 'He goes to

this society,' she explained to Yvonne. 'It's a kind of sacred order, like – well, Templars or Freemasons, but they learn to be adepts in the occult.'

She was quoting directly from some book, Pup thought, but he didn't deny that the meeting place of the Golden Dawn was his destination that evening. He finished his sherry and got up.

Not much more than an hour later he was gyrating with Andrea under the orange, viridian and purple rippling lights of the Damaria Disco and Wine Bar.

She said nothing to him of the small adventure which had befallen her during the afternoon. She did not yet know him well enough for that. She had gone home to the room she rented in a house at Mount Pleasant Green, expecting the house to be empty at that hour, expecting to have a quiet afternoon setting the room to her liking and arranging her things. On the way there she had bought three small house-plants from a florist: a Christmas cactus, a croton and a fern.

It was like the continuous low rumble of thunder overhead. But a noise which is, so to speak, an act of God is much easier to put up with than that made, and deliberately or thoughtlessly made, by man. The sound was immediately above her, coming from the room over hers, at the back and on the top floor. There were only two rooms on the top because of the way the roof sloped. Andrea went down to the front door and went outside and read under the topmost bell the name 'Diarmit Bawne', printed in a hand that seemed unused to handling a pen.

She had suffered from the noise for more than two hours. Suppose it went on at night too? She would have to move out and she had only just moved in. It took nerve to go up there but she screwed herself to it and went. She knocked timidly on the door and then had to knock again.

It was a young man who opened the door. He was in his middle twenties but she would have described him as a boy, a nondescript boy, neither tall nor short, with dusty-looking brown hair – that his hair was dirty she particularly noticed – and features that looked as if roughly shaped out of putty, grey eyes that stared. She spoke in a rush.

'Excuse me, but would you mind not pacing all the time? You've been pacing up and down for nearly three hours, I timed you. I've got the room below you and the noise is really awful. I don't like complaining but I just don't think I can stand any more of it.'

She wondered why he was looking at her so strangely. Not with antagonism or resentment, it wasn't that, but almost as if he were surprised she existed and could speak at all.

'I mean,' she said in her nervousness, 'if it's the exercise you need, couldn't you go out for a walk? Or is it –' She had read in a novel about someone pacing up and down like a caged lion '– that you're worried about something?'

'I can't go out.' He spoke hoarsely, in a thick salivary Irish brogue. 'I'm allergic, you see.'

Allergic to what? Air? Light? She did not feel she could ask. The window was closed and the room had a fetid, sweetish, sweaty smell. The dark red clothes he wore looked as if they had never been washed or cleaned.

'Well, if you could just try not to walk up and down so much.' She said it awkwardly, confronted by those curious opaque eyes. 'Can't they do anything for your allergy?'

He shook his head. 'Nobody can do a thing.'

She felt a rush of pity for him. She thought she should speak his name before she went but she didn't know how to pronounce his Christian name. It was a strange way to address someone only a year or so her senior but, 'It is Mr Bawne, isn't it?'

'It is not.' He sounded angry and Andrea took a step back. 'Conal's the name,' he said, 'Conal Moore.'

Chapter 18

The flat was in a block at the top of East Heath Road. It was one of those Hampstead blocks that from the outside look more like a Georgian country house. Ashley Clare lived at No. 24. Yvonne had told Dolly that he worked in the West End, he was a designer, something to do with stage design, so Dolly knew that if she wanted to see him she would need to be outside Arrowsmith Court quite early in the morning.

She was torn between her desire to see Ashley Clare and her sense of duty that she must be at home to give Pup his breakfast. She got up very early. Pup's bedroom door was ajar and she could see his bed had not been slept in. Dolly no longer worried herself half to death that Pup might have been mugged or run over but these fears had been replaced by another.

Myra's heels clattered across the landing and Myra's voice said: 'You know very well he had that girl friend, Doreen. I mean, she went away somewhere but that doesn't mean he's never going to have another, does it?'

Edith whispered in Dolly's ear. 'I shouldn't object if he found himself a nice ladylike girl. He'll be wanting to get married one of these days.'

'To be perfectly honest with you, Doreen, a nice-looking boy like that who's earning good money isn't going to live like a monk, is he?'

Dolly, tormented, made a striking motion at them over her shoulder. She swatted them away like flies. Harold's snores could be heard, rising and falling, though it was broad daylight. Dolly dressed herself in her blue plaid dress with the plain blue collar, and she put on navy blue tights and her cream sandals. Yvonne was making her more clothes conscious. There must come a point, surely, when you dressed so well, you looked so smart and elegant, that no one noticed your face. Or would they notice it *more*? Hair that was flat on top and frizzed out at the sides had got very fashionable. Suppose she were to have that done, the frizz part covering up her cheeks? Dolly shook her head at her own image. She had never in her life been to a hairdresser. Her mother had cut her hair, and after her mother died, she had done it herself with the dressmaking scissors and a razor comb. She knew she would never dare go to a place like the Unisex salon Pup went to and put her blemished head into a stylist's hands.

She walked to the bus stop and got the No. 210 bus. Hampstead Heath lay mysteriously veiled in the first mist of autumn. Dolly was not entirely sure why she was there or what she intended to do. Principally, of course, to have a sight of Ashley Clare. She began imagining a future in which George returned to Yvonne and she and Pup became their best friends. They would visit each other's homes in the evening and drink wine. Perhaps they would even go away on holiday together. Dolly had not been on a holiday since she was a child when sometimes the whole family went to the Isle of Wight and sometimes to Newquay. She thought she might enjoy a holiday if she had Pup and Yvonne there to cushion her from the world, and George, that unknown quantity, who was a doctor as well as a dentist and who might . . .

By then Pup would have learned all there was to learn about the science of magic. He would be a master. He might still go to the Golden Dawn sometimes – once a month, say – but for the rest of the time he would stay at home, working in the temple. It would be more a laboratory than a temple really, a place where he could make dreams come true for the four of them. Dolly touched her face where the wind had blown her hair aside.

She was outside Arrowsmith Court now. The glass entrance doors were open and two or three people came out, bound for work. A man got into one of the parked cars and drove off down East Heath Road. Dolly worried in case, early though it was, not yet 8.30, she had already missed Ashley Clare. But as she was beginning to feel awkward hanging about there, to feel that soon one of those departing commuters would come over and ask her what she wanted, the glass doors swung open and the man in the photograph came out.

He looked older. That was only to be expected. Photography done with a flash rejuvenates in a way that early morning light does not. He looked thinner, his face was a little worn, and he was formally dressed in a dark grey suit. But he was unmistakably the man George Colefax had called a beautiful boy. Dolly walked along behind him. She followed him down Heath Street. He was carrying a briefcase and, over his left arm, a folded, cream-coloured raincoat.

Dolly was sure he must be heading for Hampstead tube station, and as she walked, she got her tenpence pieces ready for the ticket machine. Ashley Clare went through into the lift with his season ticket. She followed him in just before the doors closed. From the raincoat pocket he took a copy of *The Times* – it had presumably been delivered to his door – and folding it as small as it would go, began doing the crossword puzzle.

Sex had played very little part in Dolly's life. She tried never to think of it in relation to herself. And she seemed to have known few people to whom sex was important, though the memory of what she had discovered of Myra and her father sometimes still brought her a small shudder. That Pup was uninterested in sex she was certain – hadn't he told her in innocent confession that he was a virgin? This statement may be perfectly true one day and false the next but that never crossed Dolly's mind. She had never, as far as she was aware, known a homosexual. She was no reader and her social life was sparse. But nevertheless, though near the perimeter of it and in the shadows, she lived in her world and its culture. She had an image of a homosexual, a queer, as a mincing creature with scented after-shave and blusher on his face, one who would give you sidelong looks and call you 'my dear'. Ashley Clare, though undeniably very handsome, looked like any normal man, smelled of nothing at all and when he encountered an acquaintance on the platform, lifted his head from the crossword and said a laconic "morning."

The train came in and Dolly followed him into a non-smoker. Ashley Clare sat next to the window in one of the double seats facing the front of the train and Dolly managed to seat herself at right angles to it and immediately behind him. At Belsize Park, the next stop, the train filled up. People were crammed in and standing all down the aisle. That made it hard for anyone to look at anyone else. Dolly knew, anyway, that no one would do more than glance at her and look away. The naevus embarrassed people and made them feel guilty, so no one ever looked at her for long.

Ashley Clare's head and about six inches of his shoulders and back projected above the back of the seat. He was printing in the solutions to his puzzle. Dolly began picking black and silver hairs, mostly black ones, off the collar of his suit jacket. If anyone did happen to see her doing this, they would suppose him to be her husband. They would think them husband and wife who had been unable to get seats side by side and now she was performing a belated grooming on him before they separated to go to their jobs.

He felt nothing. He didn't even twitch his shoulders. She got eight hairs and slipped them into her purse between two pound notes. It was a Bank train, heading for the City, and at Camden Town he left it, presumably to change for Tottenham Court Road or Leicester Square. Dolly also got out and went through the passages to where she could get a northbound train for the Archway. There she stood on the platform, waiting for the train to come and remembering how, on this very spot or close by, she had come within a centimetre and a second of pushing the woman in green over, believing her to be Myra.

But there was no need for such calculated violence when Pup could kindle or destroy with words and water.

Harold sat at the kitchen table, unable to eat. The food was the kind he liked, processed, packaged junk food that Edith and more recently Dolly had always given him, but he pushed it about his plate, staring disconsolately around him.

It was twenty years since he had eaten a meal without reading a book at the same time. When the children were little and Edith busy with them, he had begun to take a book to the table with him and no one had minded or even noticed. It had become a habit. Now he could no longer read, writing had inhibited or exorcised reading for him, and therefore he could not eat. It seemed to him that during the months he had spent writing *Her Highness My Sister*, the library had got in a more than usually rich collection of royal, archducal and aristocratic biographies. They waited temptingly for him when his task was done and the typescript out of his hands, and once he had posted the parcel, off he had gone to the Haringey central library and taken out a wonderful 600-page-long life of Queen Louise of Prussia. He could not read it. The print danced, the sense of the words registered hardly at all, the impetus was gone. The substance of his own novel, which he knew practically by heart, interposed itself between his eyes and Queen Louise and he was forced to lay the book aside in mounting panic.

It made him feel ill. He had hunger pains like a stitch in his side that for a while he thought was the onset of a heart attack and that he might be going to fall down dead like Myra's mother or poor Ronald Ridge. Of course he did not give up at once. He tried a biography of Stanislas II, the collected letters of the Albanian royal family and fictionalized memoirs of Madame de Montespan, all, however, to no avail. Just as working in a sweet factory is said to put one off chocolate, so the manufacture of history had made the finished product revolting to him. It had been a kind of aversion therapy.

'You're not eating, Dad,' Dolly said. 'If you don't want your pie, have a piece of Battenberg cake. Go on. You must eat.'

He shook his head. He was losing weight and he had never had much flesh on him to start with. The next day was Ronald Ridge's funeral, same time,

197

same place, and by the look of the sky it would be raining again.

'Have you got your black tie?'

Harold nodded. He shambled off to the breakfast room and sat in the armchair where, surrounded by mementoes of Myra, he had passed so many happy hours lost in the bypaths of the romantic past. He stared at the rectangle of window, the grey sky beyond, the first drops of rain splashing against the glass.

That day Pup, with mock solicitude (Harold thought), had inquired more persistently than usual after his health, suggesting, though not putting it into actual words, that he might think of early retirement. He had been incensed. He was only fifty-five.

'I'm not getting out for a little whippersnapper like you.'

'I beg your pardon,' Pup said in his courteous way. 'I'm sorry. You'll do as you like of course. Only you don't seem to be getting much fun out of it.'

'Work's not supposed to be fun,' said Harold but his mind harked back to when he had been writing his novel. That had been fun, the best fun he had ever known. A gust of anger shook him. 'All these big ideas you've got, you'll ruin the business I built up and you not yet twenty-one.'

Pup said no more. He watched Harold shamble off the premises, no library book under his arm or in a carrier these days. It would all work out one day, he supposed. Tonight was not one of those times he was obliged to be in. He locked up, got into the van and drove round to Andrea's at Mount Pleasant Green. She had to work Saturdays but Thursday was her day off, the salon closed on Thursdays. She was the most domesticated of his girls, the only one who was

198

houseproud, who could cook. When she came down to let him in, she was wearing an apron.

Halfway up the stairs she paused and listened. All seemed quiet.

'It worries me when he paces up and down like that,' said Andrea. 'Like a caged lion.'

The room was neat and warm, flowers in a vase, hyacinth bulbs poking through the loam in a pot, a Christmas cactus showing buds. Andrea did her level best to make the bed look as little like a bed as possible with cushions and a stripy cover. This evening there was even a tray on it. She had not yet allowed him into it, the stripy cover was never more than rumpled. On top of the little Belling stove were vegetables steaming in a wok and inside it something emitting delicious smells.

'I've made two chicken pies, one for us and one for the boy upstairs.'

'What a kind girl you are!'

'Do you really think so? I like to do what I can. He's really rather pathetic.'

'I'd better go up the road and get us some wine.'

'No need, I've got it. It's in the sink cooling.' She beamed on him, the perfect manager, the future helpmeet, the prize candidate in the fiancée stakes. She came and sat next to him on the bed. 'Peter?'

'Mmm?'

'The boy upstairs, when I asked him his name he said Conal Moore but that isn't his name, his name's Di-ar-mit Bawne, I asked some people downstairs. Someone called Conal Moore used to live there but he went away ages ago, last year, and this boy came. Don't you think it's peculiar?'

'This is a peculiar place,' said Pup. 'It's a rough area. Not the best place for a girl on her own. Can't you find somewhere better?'

'It's only temporary.' She looked into his eyes. 'Do

you think I ought to ask this Di-ar-mit why he says he's someone who went away a year ago?'

'I don't think you ought to have anything to do with him. I think you should keep out of it, Andrea. It's nothing to do with you anyway.'

'I read somewhere,' said Andrea sententiously, 'that no man is an island.'

'I am,' said Pup. 'I'm one of those privately owned islands in the Aegean and I'm very fussy about who comes ashore.'

'I'm not sure I know what that means.'

'It means to keep clear of unemployed Irish riff-raff,' said Pup.

Dolly was making Yvonne a tweed skirt. She knew it was only to be an ordinary everyday skirt to be worn for shopping in the Market Place or a little light gardening. For anything requiring a higher sartorial standard, Yvonne would have gone to Brown's or at any rate Jaeger. The Ashley Clare doll, its legs straddled on the mantelpiece, watched her as she plied the Singer. After she had put the zip in and tacked the waistband in place there was nothing more she could do until Yvonne had had another fitting. She opened the lid of the remnants box and looked at the figure which, wrapped in a sheet of white tissue paper, lay on top of the pieces of material.

The wax from four white candles had gone to shape it. Dolly took off the paper. Her skill was with cloth and a needle, not in moulding wax, and the figure appeared wretched compared to the doll, a sausage-shaped mannikin covered in dirty finger-prints with a tuft of stolen hairs on its golf-ball head. There was something intensely unpleasant about it, something obscene. Dolly, holding it up, could recognize that without knowing why. After all, it was only wax and dust that had somehow got on her hands and hairs from a man's coat collar. She wouldn't have had to make it if Pup had not been so difficult about the doll. He had been home last night and she had carefully prepared the way for asking him. She had watched his face grow wary as she worked up to her question, then harden as the harsh refusal came.

'I'm not making a fool of myself with that, Dolly.'

'You didn't make a fool of yourself when you killed Myra.'

'For the thousandth time, I did not kill Myra!'

'Well, of course he did, Doreen,' Myra said into Dolly's ear. 'On the Other Side we know everything and I can tell you for a categorical fact that healthy girls don't drop dead from giving themselves an ordinary douche.'

Dolly swatted her away. 'You're not going to tell me you're giving up magic?'

He shrugged. Then he looked at her. 'No. No, of course not, not white magic. But I won't play at killing people. Right?'

For the wax doll she cut out and sewed up a piece of the tweed for trousers, a scrap of lawn for a shirt. It took her less than an hour. A long loneliness stretched before her, encompassing half the evening and the whole night and all the next day until Pup was home again. Now she half wished that this evening she had done what she had been doing every evening lately when Pup was out, going to Hampstead to watch Ashley Clare.

She hardly knew why. Simply for something to do? Something to break the loneliness? Or because she thought genuine advantage might be derived from it? Since the morning she had secured the hairs, she had twice seen him come out of Arrowsmith Court and make his way down Heath Street to the station. Once in the evening she had witnessed his return home, at twenty to six, and once he and George Colefax had come home together, Colefax dressed very much as he had been in the photograph, so she had had no trouble recognizing him.

After that, she had stood for a long while outside the flats and had been rewarded by the sight of a light coming on and George Colefax appearing for a moment at the window. He did not draw the curtains. With a lubriciousness or voyeurism unusual in her, Dolly stood there waiting, hoping to see the two of them embracing behind the window, in the yellow light. She did not herself want to be seen even by the porter of the flats, but Hampstead is full of trees and creeper-hung walls and leafy shrubs and one of these hung low over the little wall where she sat, where after a while Myra and Edith came to join her, one sitting on either side.

'You'd think a woman'd have more sense than marry a man who's that way inclined,' said Myra. 'It's not as if she hadn't been married before.'

Edith whispered confidingly, 'When I was young, things like that weren't talked about in public. The expression "homo" meant nothing to me. I still don't know what they do and I don't want to.'

'To be perfectly frank, it's the mothers make them that way. I read that in an article. They're not born like it.'

'Put the blame on the poor parents,' said Edith, 'that's always the way these days.'

George Colefax and Ashley Clare did not embrace, or not where they could be seen from the window, and they came out again at 7.00. George was dressed as he had been when he came off the train, Ashley now in brown sweater and trousers of a fine khaki-and-white check pattern. Perhaps they were going out to eat. Dolly followed them as far as the

Hollybush but no further. She had never in her life been in a pub.

The next morning – this morning – she was outside the flats early. What was the point in staying at home? Pup wasn't there and Harold ate nothing. It was cold and damp, not clear and not foggy either, the kind of day that makes everything look dirty.

Ashley Clare did not appear at all, though George did, very casually dressed for a dentist, Dolly thought, in a kind of anorak and Ashley's check trousers. Or perhaps they were *his* trousers and it was Ashley who had borrowed them last night, not George this morning. It made her feel rather uncomfortable. Nothing so far had shown her the intimate relation in which they stood to each other, but this did. Like sisters or heterosexual lovers, they wore each other's clothes. Poor Yvonne! Dolly felt certain now that the bond between them was unbreakable except through Ashley Clare's death.

She caught the No. 210 bus to Highgate, replenished her wine stocks from her favourite shop and walked home along the old railway line. The leaves were falling but the buddleias were still in flower. A butterfly lay dead on the path, its tiger's-eye wings spread wide. She climbed up out of the damp grassy gully, shoo-ing Gingie who hunted unknown things among the long stalks and seedling trees.

She put the doll back in the box, picked up the phone and dialled. A man's voice answered and she replaced the receiver. George went home sometimes, once a week maybe, Yvonne had said. Dolly had finished the day's bottle of St Nicholas and after a moment's hesitation she opened one of those she had bought that morning.

Presently, from the temple, she fetched some of Pup's books. For the ceremony of the destruction of Ashley Clare, she had decided to ask Pup to evoke a god. Evocations of that kind, all the books said, should only be attempted by a proficient and experienced magician – but what was he if not that after that long training with the Golden Dawn?

The god she fixed on was Anubis, the jackal-headed. There were lists and lists of gods in those books of his. She might have had Enlil or Marduk, the Dagda or Balder, Khol, Sin, Ruda, Wadd, Apollo, Teteshapi or a host of others, but there was a picture of Anubis, a man whose height and thinness somehow reminded her of Ashley Clare himself and whose dog face was not unlike that of the dog who had found the girl's body and her head. But more than that, Anubis was a god of death. The ancient Egyptians called him the Lord of the Mummy Wrappings. It was he who opened for the dead the roads to the Other Side.

Dolly took the books and the rest of the wine to bed with her. Muzzy by now, her head singing, she gazed at the picture of dog-headed Anubis, fearful of what she had to do but unable to see any other way. Pup came home at twelve. She heard him moving about with deliberate care, tip-toeing and closing doors gingerly so as not to wake her or Harold. Myra was sitting on the end of her bed and Edith under the centre light, sewing. She could just see them, but when she tried to look more closely, they, though not their voices, were gone.

'If you want the honest truth, Doreen, you're turning into a real alcoholic, a wino.'

'She's got to have some consolation, poor thing, with that disability of hers. We did everything we could, took her to specialists. Nothing to be done, they all said that.'

'Don't think I'm blaming you, Edith,' Myra said. 'All I'm saying is, we all have our troubles and we have to learn to live with them.'

'That's true, that's very true.'

They began talking to each other as if she wasn't there.

'Get out, the pair of you!' Dolly shouted. 'Get out of my room!'

Pup, coming out of the bathroom, heard her and stared. He went cold down his spine as if someone had put an ice cube down the back of his neck. But he didn't go into her room or even knock on the door. He told himself she had been calling out in a dream.

Chapter 19

Once Diarmit Bawne had gone, Conal felt grand. That was how he put it to himself.

'I feel grand, boy, grand!'

Like a schoolmaster, Diarmit had watched over him and ruled him and told him how to be. But in the end, Conal had been too much for him, refusing to wash or clean the place or go to bed at a regular hour, and he had the law on his side too. It was his room, he was the tenant, not Diarmit. If he said to get the hell out of here, Diarmit had to get the hell out.

'And take your rubbish with you!'

Diarmit had not done that, so one evening when it was too late for anyone to come and start demolishing the building, Conal had taken all the clothes that were not dark red and four plates and some cutlery and a teapot and a mug and stuffed them in one of the litter bins on the far side of the green. That would be a disappointment for the Dalmatian and the collie when they came scavenging in the morning, he thought, laughing. He laughed all the way back to the room.

And now Diarmit was really gone. Conal need not be conscientious or steady or a good citizen any more. Diarmit had kept on at him about getting a job and that was something else he could forget now. He could forget about getting up early and going out into the cold and worrying about his duty and the future. He was Conal Moore who was wanted by the police for robbery and for murder.

These afternoons it began to get dark at four. Once it became dusk he felt safe. He went out and bought himself an electric knife sharpener. He sat on the floor in the middle of the room, sharpening his knives with the knife sharpener and testing the edges on his left hand. After a while the pads of his thumb and fingers were criss-crossed with cuts. He wiped the blood off on his trousers or the tail of his shirt which, being dark red, showed no marks.

Once or twice Diarmit tried to come back. He didn't knock on the door or call out but scrabbled with his nails on the linoleum outside which was how Conal knew it was him. Like a mouse, so who else could it be?

Pup knew very little about Anubis, he had heard of him and that was all. But he mugged it up. He read up about evocation ceremonies and realized it was hopeless trying to get that lot by heart. Presumably, if he had really done two or three nights a week training he would be able to recite evocations from memory in much the same way as a clergyman can recite the marriage service.

Dolly wanted it done for her birthday. She wanted a god evoked. Pup thought of someone – Dilip, say, or Andrea – asking him what was he going to give his sister for her birthday and his saying a god. Putting it like that made him see just how badly disturbed Dolly had become. She must have alcoholic poisoning, he thought vaguely with the hazy notions of someone who on the whole prefers a cup of tea to a double Scotch.

He had asked her if she'd like to go out or have a piece of jewellery or something to wear. At the time she had been wearing that red and green painted bit of tin which, each time he saw it on her, made him wince. She had said no, she'd like them to do something in the temple, she'd like him to evoke Anubis for her.

It was going to be the last time, he was resolved on that. Afterwards, without telling her he would quietly take the temple apart, so that the next time she went up there, she would find an ordinary, shabby, empty bedroom. And his alibis? He would think of something. The time might even be coming when he must tell the truth and let her make the best of it. She could hardly be worse than she was now, could she?

Yvonne had sent Dolly a card. She had happened to mention her birthday was coming and Yvonne had remembered and sent her a card. There was one from Pup and one from Harold with 'Dad' on it in Pup's writing. Dolly bought a Tunis cake for herself and set it out on the tea table.

She had dressed with care. No one was coming and they were not going out but she dressed with greater care than usual in her new plum-coloured velvet skirt and top with the plum and lilac blouse. There was a tradition among the women of the Yearman family that you dressed up on Christmas Day and for your own birthday. All the time she was getting ready, she could hear Edith telling Myra about it.

'No matter how busy I was, I could be up to my neck in it, I'd always find time to run upstairs and change into something nice.'

'To be perfectly honest with you, I'd say life was too short for that kind of carry-on.'

'It was short for us, wasn't it, dear?' said Edith.

Pup blew the dust off the elemental weapons. The cup was the one that would chiefly be used. He wondered to which Sephirah of the Tree of Life

Anubis was attributed. Might as well say the fourth. He drew a circle on the floor with a four-sided figure inside it and hung up over the window a length of sky-blue material which Dolly had given him. On the altar he displayed the four fours of the tarot. He tied round his waist, over the golden robe, a sky-blue sash.

All the time he was doing these things he felt he was behaving in an insane way. He felt this more than he had ever done in the past and it affected him so strongly that from time to time he paused in his preparations and said aloud: 'Are you mad? Are you quite crazy?'

He was glad he couldn't see himself, that there was no mirror in the temple. It was bad enough seeing Dolly, her face flushed as it usually was these days, her eyes bloodshot, yet dressed up as if for a party. He wondered how many bottles of wine she was getting through a week now, he wondered – as often, as daily – what he ought to do. Tell their father, get their father's help? That was a laugh. She was holding something in her hand, wrapped in tissue paper, and he supposed it was the present he had given her. It would be like Dolly to carry about with her wherever she went anything he had given her, though she had not seemed much to like the Hand of Fatima on a silver chain and he doubted if she would replace the tin talisman with it.

He lit the two blue candles on the altar and filled the cup with wine Dolly had brought him in a glass. Before evoking a god the magician should cleanse his temple with a Banishing ritual and Pup had told Dolly this had been done, though in fact he had done nothing, he knew himself incapable now of getting up to any of this mumbo-jumbo while alone.

He turned towards Dolly, who was sitting on a floor cushion, and began the evocation, holding in

his hands the cup of wine. The words he used would
have shocked Crowley or Abremalin the Mage, for
they were a hotchpotch and a mingling of every
conjuring recipe, diabolic litany and summoning
prescription Pup had ever absorbed into his consciousness. From lost mythologies he dredged up
names and titles the world has long forgotten. His
language was that of Dr Dee, of Jacobean sorcery.

'I evoke thee, the Bornless One,
The terrible who dwellest in the Void Places,
Anubis, son of Nephthys,
Of the race of Asar-Un-Nefer, the resurrected Osiris,
Jackal-headed, Lord of the Mummy Wrappings,
Anubis Osirides, Lucifuge, Thanatopher,
Thou who walkest in the Deeps,
And hath sight in thy feet,
O, Adonai, Gnomus, Salamandrae,
Begetter of Light and Transcender of Mortality . . .'

And so on.
Dolly watched and listened, rapt. She had drunk a
whole bottle of Valpolicella before the ceremony
began. Her head was throbbing and she had a feeling
of breathlessness and tension. Now she wished she
had not drunk quite so much. She had selected
Anubis from a book of Pup's called *Interpretations of
the Book of the Dead* because of his attribute of
conducting souls to the Other Side but now she
asked herself if perhaps she had also chosen him
because of his freakishness, his dog's head. She and
the god had something in common, they were both
different, both bearing a disfigurement that could not
be concealed.
She put up her hand to touch the naevus but
Myra's hand brushed it before hers could. They had
come to join her in the temple, she could hear them

whispering to each other, though she could not decipher the words. And she was reminded of Mrs Fitter's seances. There was the same feeling, as of impending excitement, of suspense. Pup, restoring the cup to the altar was setting light to the contents of a small bowl filled with pieces of incense sticks. A powerful scent of burning patchouli and sandalwood arose from it. He blew out one of the candles. The burning bowl glowed red and a little thin smoke came off it. It was dark in the black-walled room now and dark with the darkness of a winter's night at nine o'clock out there beyond the blue blind.

The candle cast a soft beam on Pup in his golden robe but his face was in shadow. In the far corner to the left side of the window, Dolly could make out the dim forms of Myra and Edith, their white robes falling about them like the drapery on Greek statues. Pup entered the chalk circle, closing it where he had stepped in with the point of the elemental wand. He laid the wand across his feet and lifted the glowing bowl up high.

It was silent in the house. The two women had ceased to whisper. The traffic seemed to have stopped, though you could never hear much of it in the back here with nothing much behind but the old railway line.

'I adjure thee, Anubis, Osiris' son or haply son of Ra, come forth! Appear instanter, *venite, venite*, Lucifuge! Come forth and show thyself in thy immortal shape . . . !'

An absolute silence but for his voice. It had grown cold in the temple, nearly as cold as in the hall when Edith had been conjured. Gooseflesh was coming up on Dolly's arms and shoulders.

'Appear, Osirides, Lord of the Lower World, Guide of Souls, Bearer of the Caduceus and Palms . . .'

Dolly had begun to tremble. 'Pup . . .'

He did not hear her. At this stage he always enjoyed himself, he enjoyed the acting. You could understand what those old dabblers in the occult had got out of it, the names and the archaic language alone.

'Arise, appear, I command thee, incarnate Anubis, Conductor of the Dead, Funerary Prince, *fundador sepulcrorum*, come forth . . .'

The yellow fumes which had begun to rise from the square inside the circle now swelled towards the ceiling, hiding Pup from Dolly's sight, hiding the candle and the bowl of smouldering incense. It was the first uncoiling of this smoke which had made her cry out to him. But he was obscured now in thick acrid yellow, a fog that smelled of fire, and his words dwindled as if he were far distant from her.

And now a shape was forming in the dark smoke, rising up, standing there ceiling-tall, its tower of head-dress wreathed in rings of yellow fume. The body was naked and glistening as if made from bronze and the face which thrust itself forward with elevated snout was the face of a dog.

Dolly screamed with all her might. She screamed as she had screamed at the seance when Myra appeared. She leapt to her feet, knocking over with a sweep of her arm the candle on the altar and hurling the little wax effigy into the square at the feet of the god. For a second she stood there, arms out, and then she plunged forward in a faint.

Pup had finished, had run out of epithets and titles when Dolly screamed. He had turned his back and set down the smoky basin and within a moment would have crossed to the door and switched the light on. He spun round when Dolly screamed but he wasn't quick enough to catch her as she fell.

The candle had got knocked over and gone out but in its fall had set light to whatever it was Dolly had had in her hands, something of cloth and wax that burned fiercely on the bare boards. He put the light on. With the help of the dagger he picked the burning object up and dropped it into the bowl.

Dolly opened her eyes. He knelt down beside her. 'Are you okay? What made you do that?'

She stared. She raised herself up and looked at what was in the bowl, still burning.

'You saw him?'

A cold finger seemed to touch his spine. 'I saw nothing. There was nothing to see. I'm sorry, I shouldn't have done it, I'm a fool. I went too far.'

She got up, casting looks about her. The light turned the temple back into a boxroom with unaccountably black walls and a blue rag pinned up at the window.

'Where is he now?'

'Come downstairs,' he said gently. 'I'll make you a hot drink. Are you all right? Shall I carry you? I bet I could.'

She put out her hand and touched the bowl. 'Good, that's good. Are you sure he's gone?'

It was useless to argue with her. 'He's gone. I banished him. I promise you he's gone.'

Pup was almost hysterical with self-disgust. He bundled Dolly out and banged the door. Downstairs he made tea for them both, hot strong Indian tea. Dolly sat silent, drinking it, both hands clasped round the cup. He thought of the beginning of it, the start of her trouble that was a good deal more now than mere strangeness. Surely that had been when, in adolescent folly, he had carried out that soul-selling ceremony on the old railway line. She had been normal before, or as normal as any woman could be with a thing like that on her face. But once he had

213

introduced her to the occult, the blight had begun, the gnawing into her mind of evil. Was that then what the books really meant when they spoke of an invisible world entering the real world of a practitioner or follower of magic, an addict of magic? Was that what one must infer from the ancient writers when they talked of demons conjured up that afterwards could not be banished? Did they really mean a mind split off from reality – schizophrenia? These days Dolly seemed always to be accompanied by invisible companions; she saw things and heard voices. What had she seen just now in that room?

She must see a psychiatrist, she must have treatment. He took her to her bedroom. While she undressed he fetched from the bathroom cabinet a sleeping pill from a bottle that had been Myra's. He sat on the bed beside her and took her hand. He had this piece of business to get done and get done perfectly, he had to find someone he could trust to be left in charge of the new branch – when all that was over he'd find her a psychiatrist. And meanwhile he'd look after her, he wouldn't leave her alone too much, he'd stay in more in the evenings and he'd never have anything more to do with the occult.

The Seconal sledge-hammered her into eight hours' heavy sleep and when she awoke it was to an immediate recollection of how utterly the Ashley Clare effigy had been destroyed. If in the process of that destruction she had been vouchsafed a sight of the dread god, that was the price she must pay. It was proof, too, of Pup's marvellous magicianly powers.

Yvonne was coming in the afternoon. It would be the first time she had ever come without a reason – that is, a reason apart from just wanting to see Dolly. This time there was no green dress to be fitted or skirt hem turned up. Dolly went up to the temple and unpinned the blue blind from the window. She picked up the candle and put it back in the candlestick and she took hold of the bowl and examined its contents. The tweed and cotton and the hairs had been entirely consumed in the burning and the body had melted, so that all that now remained in the bowl was a twisted lump of grey wax with bits of joss stick embedded in it.

The doll she put away in the remnants box. She didn't want Yvonne to see it. When she had dusted the room and put a bottle of Asti in the fridge, she went upstairs and dressed herself very carefully for Yvonne, the soft dressmaker suit in blue-and-grey check Viyella, fuchsia-pink polyester blouse with the Princess of Wales stand-up neckline and bow tie, navy belt and navy pumps, grey ribbed tights. Her hair was longer than it had ever been, grown long because Yvonne's was. She looped it carefully across three-quarters of the naevus and fastened it above her ear with a pink slide. Myra and Edith whispered together in a corner of the bedroom. It was as if they had a secret, for they kept breaking off to look at her, and sometimes they giggled. She had never known them to giggle before.

Pup intended to get home early. He was going to stay in that night and the next and the next, until he was sure Dolly was better. Andrea cut his hair at 4.30, blew it dry, pouted when he said he had to get home to his sister. He drove her back to Mount Pleasant Gardens and saw for the first time Diarmit Bawne who had come out of the house, down the steps, carrying a green and gold Harrods bag.

For a moment, as he parked the van, he thought Yvonne hadn't come. There was no green Porsche parked outside. But as he entered the hall there came to him a delicate floating nuance of musk and flowers. The relief was enormous, disproportionate somehow. But he told himself he wanted her friend to be there, he wanted her to have a friend.

They were sitting on the sofa, drinking Asti, Yvonne, naturally, on Dolly's left side. He was seized with a pang of compassion for his sister, so dowdy in her homemade clothes, the silly blouse that showed up her florid skin. Of course it was the contrast with Yvonne that highlighted it, Yvonne who was a sprite, a pixie, a naiad, in a dress that was of wool yet filmy and lacy, pale as ivory, with a malachite necklace and thin silver bangles on her white arms.

> *Nymph, nymph, what are your beads?*
> *Green glass, goblin, why do you stare at them?*
> *Give them me – No.*

What had made him recall that from some old school anthology? He asked her how she was, sat down and accepted a glass of their wine.

'My car's being serviced and I won't have it till tomorrow. Dolly says you'll be awfully kind and take me home. But you don't have to, really you don't, I can phone for a taxi.'

'Of course I'll take you home.'

'We'll have another bottle of wine,' Dolly said.

She didn't see the quick glance that passed between Pup and Yvonne. Pup shrugged.

'I'd rather have something to eat.'

Dolly said rather huffily, 'It's all ready for you on the kitchen table. Don't I always have your meal ready for you?'

He fetched a trayful of it into the living room: cold Tandoori chicken wings, bridge rolls, potato crisps, pickled gherkins, lemon curd tarts and pineapple-flavoured yoghurt. Yvonne accepted a potato crisp or two and then she ate a tart and all the yoghurt. Dolly opened a second bottle of Asti. She did it quickly, she hurried. For some reason she didn't like being out there alone in the big old kitchen after dark.

It was nearly 10.00 before Yvonne said she ought to go. She said to Dolly on the doorstep: 'George was going to be home for the weekend but he phoned and said he couldn't make it. He's going to stay at that flat and look after Ashley Clare.'

'Look after him?'

'Didn't I tell you? He's ill. He's got a mysterious virus, he's quite ill.'

Chapter 20

Venus (or possibly Psyche or Helen) reclined on cushions, naked but for the obligatory wisp, and contemplated her beauty in a gilt-backed hand-mirror while a wrinkled crone – her face providing a contrast and, to non-immortals, a foreboding – crouched on the far side of the bed, holding in her outstretched hands a necklace of pearls. The painting was large, executed but for the flesh of the young beauty in rather dark oils. Its gilt frame sat opulently on the ivory watered silk with which the walls of Yvonne's bedroom were covered.

'George never liked it,' Yvonne said.

'Well, he wouldn't, would he?' Pup sat up, bent over her and smoothed the thistledown hair back from her forehead. 'She's too fat for modern taste, though. She's not half as beautiful as you.'

'No one's ever said I was beautiful since my first husband died.'

'We don't have to talk about him, do we? Or George. One's dead, poor chap, and the other one's no good to you, so let's forget them and talk about us. I think we ought to get up now and get dressed and then I ought to take you out to dinner.'

Yvonne looked at her diamond watch on the bedside table and gave a little shriek. 'Oh, look at the time! D'you know we've been in bed for seven hours!'

'And on a Sunday too.'

'Peter, I want you to know I was never unfaithful before, not to either of my husbands. I promise you I won't mention them again but I just wanted you to know. I mean that I don't make a habit of this sort of thing. It really has to mean something to me. I won't say I was attracted to you that first time we met when poor Myra was alive, it was more like a huge emotional upheaval I felt. And that combined with your powers, Peter, like some kind of god or guru . . .'

'I'd like you to call me Pup, please,' said Pup, getting out of bed. 'And I've never asked anyone that before.' He began putting his clothes on. 'But you'd better forget that god and guru stuff, it never was and it never will be. It's all in Dolly's head. Whatever she says, there's nothing I can do to split up George and this Ashley chap. Why bother anyway? You don't need George now.'

She looked at him doubtfully and then she smiled.

George had not spent a night in his own home for a fortnight. Ashley Clare was a heavy smoker and the virus had affected his chest. Yvonne told Dolly this on the phone when she made an excuse for not coming to Manningtree Grove as she had promised. He lay in bed, too weak to move, his temperature rising each evening so that the doctor talked of having him in hospital for tests. All the time he was not at his dental practice, George was at his bedside.

Dolly was not surprised but still she felt a kind of awe. This had been done by Pup who had not even known he was doing it. Pup had conjured up the god and the god had consumed Ashley Clare in his fire. His was not to be a quick death like Myra's but long-drawn-out, yet ultimately he would die. Just as they had said Myra had died of an air embolus so they would say his death was due to heart failure or an allergy to antibiotics. Only she would ever know Pup had brought it about by magic.

She was impatient for news but Yvonne no longer came or even rang up. Dolly knew perfectly well why this was. It was because she was tired of waiting. She had no real faith in Dolly or Pup; perhaps she even thought Dolly had never mentioned the matter to Pup and had done nothing about it. Instead of coming back to her, she saw that George was more devoted to Ashley Clare than ever.

Well, it was only a matter of time. Dolly missed Yvonne but she could understand how Yvonne felt, disillusioned, bitter perhaps. Once Ashley Clare was dead, she would come back, she would be grateful. George would return to her and the two of them with her and Pup would become eternal fast friends. She thought of them all going out together, in the Porsche perhaps or in George's Mercedes. They would go to restaurants in Hampstead. People would take her and Pup for husband and wife. Dolly went through Edith's things and found her wedding ring. It fitted the third finger of her left hand as neatly as it had fitted her mother's.

Seeing the ring, Edith said to Myra, 'I'm glad to see her wearing that. It was hurtful to me her not wearing my ring. I always wore my mother's wedding ring, on my right hand of course.'

Dolly switched the ring over to her right hand. She sat at the sewing machine, stitching the long seams in the green cord dungarees she was making for Yvonne. Yvonne hadn't asked for them. She was making them on spec, for a surprise, but she knew Yvonne would be pleased. The two voices were whispering over in the corner by the remnants box, whisper, whisper, they had become close friends. They never spoke directly to Dolly any more.

'Candidly, Edith, no one in their senses would actually take Doreen for your son's wife.'

'No, dear, I know.'

'That disfigurement of hers really puts that kind of thing out of court, if I may be honest.'

Dolly treadled furiously, trying to silence them with the sound of the machine. It was raining, dark outside at 4.30 as the winter solstice approached. The seam came to an end and she had to stop. Whisper, whisper. How was it they could read her thoughts? And read, too, the thoughts she had but never expressed on the exposed surfaces of her mind?

Myra said confidingly, 'Peter's very clever, of course, I grant you that. It's not impossible he could do something for her.'

'We did everything in our power. We took her to specialists, they all shook their heads, they all said there was nothing to be done.'

'Not by medical science maybe, that's a different thing altogether. Why doesn't she ask him to use his powers to take away that birthmark?'

Dolly jumped up. She threw a cotton reel at them and they vanished. It had made her tremble a little, what Myra had said. She went out to the kitchen to fetch her Frascati from the fridge. Nothing happened when she tried to switch the light on; the bulb had gone. The kitchen was dim, lit only by the blue gas pilot on top of the oven.

He was standing between the back door and the fridge, tall and glistening, his crested head-dress reaching to the ceiling, his furred snout twitching and his muzzle bared in a snarl. Lord of the Cemetery, Anubis, jackal scavenger, bearing in his hands the caduceus and the palms. Dolly screamed. There was no one to hear her. She screamed and slammed the door on him and fled back to the living room where she lay screaming and beating the floor with her fists.

The footsteps sounded heavily above them, pacing up and down. It was unpleasant, inescapable, it made the room vibrate.

'It's worrying me,' Andrea said. 'I'm worried sick.'

'You'll have to move,' Pup said. 'What else can you do? You've been up and asked him to stop and I've been up. I'll do anything you want but I don't know what to suggest.'

Andrea looked at him. They were sitting on her neat bed eating Eggs Benedict which she had gone to infinite trouble to make for him.

'There is one thing you could do. Come with me to a doctor and tell him we think the boy upstairs is having a – well, a mental breakdown, and ask him to do something. He ought to be in a mental hospital, Peter, he ought to be having treatment.'

'I don't think I could do that,' Pup said slowly. He told himself that he had trouble enough of that kind at home without looking for it outside. 'It's nothing to do with me.'

'Who is it to do with, then? He's all on his own, he doesn't seem to have any family. I said mental breakdown but it's more than that, he's not sane, I'm sure of it, he's crazy. He thinks if he goes out in the daytime, workmen are going to come and demolish the house, he told me so, he believes it. And he says his name's Conal Moore. Three people in this house have told me Conal Moore was a big, tall, fair fellow who moved out last July twelvemonth and hasn't been back since.'

'You want me to go with you and tell a doctor that? What doctor anyway?'

'I haven't got a doctor here yet but you must have. You must have a GP.'

'You mean you want to have the poor guy – what do they call it – committed? You want him committed to a mental hospital?'

'It would be for his own good, Peter.'

'You go to a doctor if you must,' said Pup, 'but you can count me out. If I were you, though, I'd find another place to live. It would be simpler.'

She looked at him as if she wanted to say something but did not quite dare. He raised an eyebrow but the moment was past and she shook her head. She took their plates and began to de-mould a *crème brûlée*. Above them the footsteps marched wearily back and forth across the twelve-foot-square floor space.

Later, when he got home, Dolly asked him to put a new bulb in the kitchen light. He noticed she wouldn't go out there until the new bulb was in and the light switched on. She smelled of brandy this evening, not wine. There had been some brandy in the sideboard, he remembered, left over from the days of Myra.

Charity begins at home. Before he did anything about Diarmit Bawne he must do something about his own sister. He watched her creep fearfully into the brightly lit kitchen and look wide-eyed about her. Without thinking of the implications, wanting only to bring her back to normalcy, he said: 'By the way, George Colefax's friend has been taken into the Royal Free.'

'Into hospital?'

He nodded. 'He's got congestion of the lungs. He's quite seriously ill.'

'How do you know?' she said sharply.

Which of them was she jealous of? Him or Yvonne? He lied smoothly, 'I was doing a servicing job in the Suburb and I ran into Yvonne.'

Her eyes and her very slightly trembling mouth

223

were full of suspicion. He saw her keep glancing at him. At breakfast next morning she began on the subject again.

'I don't know any more,' he said, an edge now to his usually gentle voice. 'Only that he's in this hospital and they're not happy with the electrocardiograph they did. They say he has a heart murmur.'

She gave a sort of grunt, staring intently at him like one of those mothers who say they can tell their child's deceit by the way his eyes shine. Harold came to the table in his best suit but tieless. He accepted a cup of tea and scattered dry rustling cornflakes into his bowl, though making no attempt at first to eat them. The suit hung in folds on his small, now emaciated frame.

'Not another funeral, surely?' said Pup.

Harold shook his head. 'Can you let me have a loan of a tie? Mine aren't up to much. Nothing flashy, mind.'

Pup went upstairs and brought him down three ties, a navy patterned with white daisies, a dark grey with tiny fawn and pink squares, a cream and silver stripe with a brown chevron cutting across the centre. Being Pup's, they were all of silk. Harold chose the dark grey.

'I shan't be in the shop today. I'm going up to town.'

'Christmas shopping?' said Pup.

Harold, who had not smiled for weeks, now burst into a high-pitched cackle of laughter. The idea of him going Christmas shopping!

'I don't know about that, I don't know about that at all.' Mirth shook him. As if his laughter had effected some kind of catharsis or liberation, he suddenly grabbed the sugar basin, sugared his cornflakes, poured milk on them and began voraciously to eat. Pup said no more. He could tell his

224

father didn't want to say where he was going or why. Probably, whatever it might be, it had something to do with the typewritten letter which had arrived for him two days before and which had thrown him, also at breakfast, into a minor excited panic.

After they had gone, Dolly phoned the Royal Free Hospital. It took her a while to find out which ward Ashley Clare was in. When they put her on to the staff nurse on duty, she said she was his sister.

'There's no change,' the nurse said. 'He's as well as can be expected.'

Dolly had to be content with that. She tried to phone Yvonne but there was no reply. Since that evening in the kitchen she had not directly seen Anubis, not face to face, but she had glimpsed him out of the corner of her eye, the glitter of his head-dress, the snakelike skin, or his dog's face had looked at her suddenly out of a darkening recess of the room. She could bear it, she set her teeth against the fear. He would stay until his work was done, she thought, but when Ashley Clare was dead he would depart.

She finished the green cord dungarees. The idea came to her of making a doll for Yvonne, a doll to match her white and gold bedroom, to sit on her bed and conceal a nightdress under its skirts. That night she dreamed of Anubis for the first time. He was performing his function of conducting the dead along the path to the underworld or Other Side. Edith and Myra followed him and Ronald Ridge and Mrs Brewer with Fluffy in her arms, but ahead of them all, at the god's side, was Ashley Clare. And the path they walked along, leading into the Mistley tunnel, was the old railway line.

Pup came home at about eight in the evening. He kissed her cheek and she smelled Balmain's Ivoire on him. She heard Myra and Edith whispering and she jumped away from Pup as if, instead of French perfume, she had smelt a foul stench. He didn't seem to notice.

'I've got something interesting to tell you,' he said.

She was instantly suspicious. 'What sort of something?'

'Dad's written a book. It's a historical novel and it's going to be published. That's where he was going the other day, to see these publishers. They wrote to him to say they like the book, they want him to make some changes but they like it and they want him to do a sequel. How about that? He's going to retire and leave me a clear field.'

'Oh,' she said, thinking.

'He's over the moon. I left him in the pub, having a drink with Eileen Ridge to celebrate.'

'So he's happy and successful,' she said in a strange concentrated tone. 'He's got what he wanted. Everything has come right for him.'

'You could put it that way, yes.'

She was silent. He suddenly felt, without knowing why, extremely uncomfortable. She was staring at him, her eyes slightly out of alignment, so that the left one seemed to be looking at something beyond or behind him. It made him turn round and look. She had been making a doll that looked exactly like Yvonne, with beige-blonde nylon hair and dressed all in bridal white. Why? he asked himself, what for?

She said, 'Pup?'

'Yes, dear?'

'Could we go up to the temple?'

He shrugged. He was tired and he had a lot to think about. The colour had come up into her face, a dark ugly flush.

'You can do anything,' she said. 'I know that now. You've got power, more than a doctor, more than anyone . . . So will you – will you . . .' Her hand went trembling up to her cheek. 'Will you take this away?'

He was speechless. She held her hand there, covering the naevus.

'You could do a Pentagram ritual,' she said. 'Or an invocation. You could do it by degrees, it doesn't have to be all at once, you could . . .'

He shouted at her when of all times he should have been gentle. 'I can't! You know I can't!'

She nodded, said in perfect faith, 'You can do anything.'

'Dolly, I can't. Listen to me.' He came and sat beside her, taking her by the shoulders. 'I'm sorry I shouted at you, I shouldn't have done that. I can't take away your birthmark, do you understand? I can't, it's impossible.'

'You mean you won't.'

'No, I don't mean that. Listen to me, I'd give everything I've got, I'd give years of my life to take it away if I could.' He believed he was speaking the truth. 'I'd do anything in the world for you but it's not in my power to do that.'

She said slowly, heavily, 'You killed Myra, you made yourself pass your driving test, you brought Dad happiness and success, you've got the business for your own, so why can't you do that for me?'

'I did not do those things. They happened. Don't you see? Myra dying was a coincidence. I passed my driving test because – well, because I can drive. Dad wrote his book himself, didn't he? How could magic make him a writer?'

'I don't understand what you're saying.'

Desperately, forgetting the consequences, he said, 'There's no such thing as magic, Dolly. There never was and there never will be. They were all crooks or mad or superstitious fools who wrote those books. It's all rubbish. You can't reverse the laws of nature

227

with water and incense and stupid words, you can only deceive people. If I've deceived you, I'm sorry, I'm desperately sorry, but you've got to know sometime, it may as well be now. I was just a kid dressing up and pretending, don't you see?'

She didn't. He saw, to his horror, disbelief in her face and pain and resentment.

'Why did you keep on with it then? Why do you go to the Golden Dawn?'

'I was wrong,' he said bitterly. 'I was wrong and I'm sorry. I'll never do it again, though, that I can promise you. I'm going to see to it I never can do it again.' He jumped up and went swiftly out of the room, closing the door behind him.

She sat there quite still. She could see herself in the small mirror that Myra had hung on the opposite wall and she turned her face aside. Pup's footsteps running up the stairs made a soft pounding through the house. The front door opened, closed, and she heard Harold cross the hall and go into the breakfast room.

'He doesn't mean it,' Edith's voice said. 'He'll calm down in a day or two.'

Myra laughed. 'The fact is, Edith, he's been seeing Yvonne Colefax, he's been in her house with her, I could smell that perfume she uses all over him. Well, she was bound to prefer him over Doreen, wasn't she? It stands to reason.'

'He's upstairs now looking through his books to see what he can do for poor Dolly.'

'Mind you,' said Myra, 'once that fellow is dead and George goes back to her, he'll put a stop to that. He won't want Peter there and Yvonne won't want Peter either. The sooner that happens the better for all concerned, I'd say.'

'He's upstairs making holy water and studying high magic,' Edith whispered.

At 9.30 Dolly picked up the phone. Yvonne answered after the second double ring. This time she did not say it was Dr Colefax's residence but uttered a timid, 'Hallo?'

'It's Dolly.'

'Oh, Dolly, how are you?'

'I'm all right. I've made you something for a surprise. Well, two things. Something to wear and something else. Would you like to come and fetch them sometime?'

Yvonne did not reply immediately. Her voice sounded strained and awkward.

'I'm a bit busy at the moment actually, Dolly.'

'I could come to you.'

'Just let's leave it a bit, shall we? I mean, unless you think your brother would run them up to me sometime in the van. I tell you what, I'll ring you.'

Dolly felt cold. She needed a glass of wine. As soon as she had rung off, she would brave the passage and the kitchen and fetch herself a fresh bottle of wine. But first . . .

'How is Ashley Clare? Is he – is he dead?'

'Dead?' echoed Yvonne shrilly. 'No, of course he isn't dead. He's much better. He's coming out of hospital for Christmas and George is taking him to Morocco for a week to convalesce.'

Dolly put the receiver back and left the room. There were no voices now, no shapes in the dark corners, nothing but herself alone, walking towards the kitchen and her wine. She had failed Yvonne and because of that Yvonne would never want to see her again.

Chapter 21

The girl downstairs was a policewoman. Either that or a spy set on him by the builders. He was not sure which or she might be both, it hardly mattered. What was important was not to have too much to do with her. He must never allow himself to forget that he was wanted for murder, the police wanted him for murder, only as things stood they couldn't quite pin it on him.

The girl downstairs called him Diarmit, pronouncing it incorrectly. He supposed she did that because the name Diarmit Bawne was still under his bell at the front door. He had left it there deliberately to keep the police from knowing Conal Moore had come back. That she called him Diarmit proved she didn't know. She said she was called Andrea, an obvious invention, laughable when you thought about it.

'You ever go down on the old railway line?' he had asked her.

She shook her head. She said she had never heard of it, she didn't know there was an old railway line.

'There was a girl murdered down there a year and a half back,' he said. 'You want to be careful. He might strike again.'

'I don't go there,' she said. 'I told you, I don't even know where it is.' And he saw that he had frightened her.

But he must be careful to give her a wider berth

now, not to get talking with her, he might say dangerous things. Before he said that about the girl being murdered, she had tried to persuade him that there was no fear of the house being pulled down. As if she would know! Sometimes he thought she was a bit mentally unbalanced. At Christmas, before she went off somewhere for the four days, she brought him a piece of cold roast turkey and four mince pies. He didn't eat them, though, he knew for a fact they had a truth drug in them which would make him reveal everything next time he saw her. He took them across the road by night and left them on the green for the Dalmatian and the collie to find in the morning. Truth drugs were harmless to dogs who couldn't talk anyway.

The New Year was two days old when the builders came back and started pulling down a row of shops with mansion flats over them on the west side of the green. The shops had been boarded up for months. He felt very relieved to see the men so fully occupied over there because it meant they couldn't start here yet. For the first time in months he went out in daylight and the place he went to revisit was the old railway line and the Mistley tunnel, scene of Conal Moore's crime.

Coming home, he met Andrea in the hall and with her that police colleague of hers, the fair-haired cop who drove a van camouflaged to look like it came from a typewriter firm. He looked through them, he ignored them, not speaking a word, it was the only way.

'You see?' said Andrea. 'Now don't you think we ought to do something?'

'He's harmless,' said Pup. 'It's no business of yours.'

'Yours', not 'ours'. She noticed that. They went upstairs and Andrea unlocked the door of her room.

Knowing he was coming home with her, she had left the room spick and span before she went out in the morning. The steel of the draining board, glimpsed through the canework of her new room divider, shone like a mirror. On the coffee table lay a large and glossy Haringey Public Library book of Audubon prints, open at a printing of Columbian humming birds. He felt uncomfortable and sad.

She began making coffee. Overhead the pacing had started. 'I still think I ought to do something,' she said. 'I', he noticed, not 'we'. She looked at him. 'Peter?'

'Mmm?'

'Mr Manfred's opening a new salon in St Alban's. He says if I'll go there he'll let me have one of the flats.'

As the footsteps pounded, 'That might be the answer,' he said.

'Oh,' she said. 'It was just that I thought ... Oh, well.'

He knew what she thought. That there was a chance he might ask her to stay, to tell her they'd start going steady, get engaged.

'It wouldn't work out,' he said gently. 'Really. We've had a nice time but it wouldn't work.'

She glanced at the bed where the cushions were arranged with perfect symmetry, as smooth and shiny as mint humbugs. 'Is it because I wouldn't – you know?'

'Oh, no.'

'My mother says that, if you do, a boy doesn't want you afterwards but my girl friend at the salon says they only want you if you do. It's hard to know.'

'It wouldn't have made any difference. Really.'

Andrea poured two cups of coffee. 'I'll tell Mr Manfred in the morning that I'll go to St Alban's. I think it could be quite soon.'

'It'll be the best thing, you know,' said Pup. 'No more of that racket going on and you won't have to do anything about him.'

'I wouldn't have anyway. Not on my own.' She looked out of the window. It was snowing lightly, flakes melting on the glass and running down. She drew the curtains. 'Is there someone else, Peter?'

'Yes,' he said. 'Yes, there is.' He was tired of telling lies, he thought he might try never to tell any more.

Andrea looked as if she was waiting for him to go so that she could have a good cry. What could he do about that? He had never made her any promises or led her to believe that he felt any more for her than liking sometimes to be with her. She stood up and looked wanly at him. He hugged her and said goodbye and went downstairs out into the snowy evening. They were all gone now, Suzanne married, Philippa in Australia, Terri with a new boy friend. Caroline had never been more than a flash in the pan.

Fidelity now seemed extraordinarily attractive to him. He wondered if he could ever again fancy a girl who was not blonde, whose eyes were any shade but aquamarine or who weighed more than a feather-light seven stone. He got into the van, switched on the wipers and drove carefully through the driving sleet up to the Bishop's Avenue.

It took Dolly a while to believe, fully to realize. Like a trustful cripple she had gone to her Lourdes and the miracle she knew must happen had not happened. There had been no surprise in hearing from Yvonne, the day after the conjuring of Anubis, that Ashley Clare was ill. She had expected that, known it already. And later on she had known he would die, it was simply a matter of time. That he was recovering,

233

that he was better and would get well, was not only dismaying – for a while it was incredible.

She could not believe that Pup had failed. If the evocation had not worked, it was because he had not known what its purpose was or even of the existence of the little wax figure. It was she who had done it wrong, it was her fault. Gradually she was coming to understand that the evocation had not succeeded, that Ashley Clare was in truth recovering and that this was because she had made a mess of things.

Yvonne had promised to phone and Dolly waited almost hourly for that phone call. She disliked going out in case Yvonne phoned while she was out. The green cord dungarees hung on a hanger from the picture rail in the living room and the blonde doll in the white diaphanous dress sat on the mantelpiece between the ballet girl and Ashley Clare.

Dilip Raj phoned for Pup. Someone who said she was a friend of Caroline's sister phoned for Pup. Wendy Collins phoned. She didn't say what she wanted apart from asking Dolly how she was. A bit later on she came to the house and behaved in an abstracted way as if she were listening or looking for someone who wasn't there. Dolly thought she had put on weight. She had never before seen Wendy's hair in such stiff curls; it looked like a wig.

'I love your sweet dolls,' she said. 'I've always liked dolls since I was a wee thing. I never had any time for other toys, only dolls.'

'Pity you never had any children of your own,' said Dolly.

Wendy tossed her head. 'I've got plenty of time yet. Would you make me some of those?' She pointed at the dungarees.

It was the first time Dolly had felt like laughing for ages. But it wasn't for her to comment on what was suitable or unsuitable for potential customers.

'If you like.'

Dolly wondered why she lingered for a good five minutes in the hall before leaving. The phone rang. It was Christopher Theofanou for Pup. Each time the phone rang, every single time, Dolly thought it must be Yvonne. Yet she was never really surprised, for in her heart she knew why Yvonne didn't phone, why she wanted no more to do with her. She recalled that breath of perfume she had smelt on Pup. Yvonne liked Pup better than her. Now that she knew him personally, she had probably asked him herself to break up the friendship between her husband and Ashley Clare.

He might do it for her, Dolly thought, though he would do nothing for his own sister who loved him like a mother.

'To be perfectly honest,' Myra said to Edith, 'he was just having Doreen on when he said he didn't believe in magic. Of course he believes in it, it's his life. He's still going to those meetings of his, isn't he?'

Edith said something Dolly couldn't catch.

'He's at the Golden Dawn now,' said Myra. 'It stands to reason he wouldn't waste all those years of study.'

Pup didn't want to *kill*, that was the trouble. It had upset him, killing Myra, he really only wanted to do white magic. Not even to please Yvonne, not even to bring her husband back to her would he kill Ashley Clare. That, Dolly thought, must have been why Ashley Clare hadn't died, because Pup hadn't willed it. She sat by the living-room window, her first glass of wine from the second bottle of the evening in her hand. It was snowing lightly. She heard Harold let himself out of the house. He walked along the pavement under the bare branches of the ginkgo tree without looking up at the lighted window. Since becoming an author, he had taken to wearing a brown tweed hat.

He was never much comfort to her, yet she felt more alone when he had gone out. If Ashley Clare didn't die, she would never see Yvonne again. She knew that for certain, she knew it as positively as she believed in Pup's spells. For promising to get her husband back and then failing, Yvonne would hate her for ever.

During the night there was a frost and icicles hung in fringes from the eaves of houses in Manningtree Grove. In spite of the cold, Dolly got up very early and walked to the Archway and caught the No. 210 bus. She wore her old thick winter coat, one of the few garments she had that she had not made herself, and knee boots and a scarf round her head. She noticed people who had wrapped scarves yashmak-wise round their faces, and while she waited for the bus, she did the same with her scarf. Afterwards she felt just like anyone else, unscarred, unmarked, not set apart, and holding her head high, she looked others in the eye.

It was George Colefax she hoped to see emerge from the entrance to Arrowsmith Court, not Ashley Clare. She wanted only to check that they had returned from Morocco. Ashley Clare would still be convalescent, would hardly yet venture out early on an icy morning like this one.

She paced up and down the pavement, rubbing her hands together in their woollen gloves. People were knocking snow off the roofs and bonnets of cars. There was a silvery icing of hoar frost on the branches of trees. The low sun had come just above the horizon, reminding Dolly of that lovely morning – years ago, it now seemed – when she and Pup had walked along the old railway line to cut the flowering hazel branch at sunrise.

Out of the swing doors at the entrance came Ashley Clare. Dolly was surprised. He was going to work, she was sure of that; so soon after his illness he was back at work and walking briskly down the hill towards the station. He wore a coat of white or natural-coloured sheepskin, full-length and belted, a grey fur hat, and around his mouth and nose a scarf was tied just as she had tied hers. She followed him for a little way, then turned back and made for the bus stop at Jack Straw's. It seemed that he had made a complete recovery, was more fully restored to health than she had expected. She felt depressed and afraid. It was as if she was having to learn all over again that the magic had failed.

Because the sun had come up and the sky was blue, she walked home from Highgate along the old railway line. Until she walked there, it had been a white avenue of virgin snow, undisturbed, unprinted. Gingie, stalking hungry birds, showed up on the snow like a spoonful of marmalade on a white plate, and from the Mistley tunnel, feathers, discoloured grey, still blew out from the inexhaustible mattress. Dolly had to go up the steps. She couldn't manage the slippery, snow-covered embankment.

As she let herself into the house she fancied she heard a woman's voice, and not Myra's or Edith's. The breakfast room door had been open when she went out but now it was shut. Eileen Ridge, she thought, and she seemed to know what she was about to hear.

'It's for the companionship, isn't it?' Edith's voice said.

'You could see that coming a mile off, to be frank,' said Myra. 'You could see that coming from the day of poor Ronald's funeral.'

'She could do worse when all's said and done,' said Edith.

Dolly hesitated and then opened the door. Myra's paints and brushes and dust sheets were gone. The two of them were sitting at the gateleg table, reading together some sheets of manuscript. The woman was Wendy Collins and she was wearing the trouser suit Dolly had made her.

'Here's Dolly at last,' she said. 'We can tell her our news, Harry.'

Dolly minded much less than she had about Myra. What it would mean for the future did not trouble her.

'If there's anything could put Doreen's nose out of joint, this will,' Myra said and yet she was wrong. It had hardly touched her.

If Pup would be what he had once been, if Yvonne would come back and be her friend, nothing else was important. If that would happen she even felt Edith and Myra might go away and not come back. As she put the wine that she had bought into the fridge, she thought she saw the dog-faced god looking in through the window at her, but she stared hard and bravely at him and he vanished, he melted away with the snow and the icicles that the sun was now melting.

Suppose she were to try and do magic herself? In the past, she had felt too humble to attempt it. It had been Pup's province, the province of the male magus. Yet women could become adepts as well as men. If you believed, surely, if you had faith, and did all the right things, drew the circles and the penta-grams correctly, made the holy water, learned the words without mistakes ... And there was some-thing psychic about her, something of the invisible world. Her ghosts, raised by Mrs Fitter, had stayed with her and not departed as those others had. The god she picked out had come and still remained, waiting like a genie. There was more affinity with the occult in her than there was in Pup, the geomancer.

The books would instruct her as they had instructed him. She could work in the temple, wear the robe and use the elemental weapons. She went up the stairs. At about lunchtime Harold had gone out and Wendy with him and they had not come back. The phone had not rung once all day. It was four in the afternoon, not dark yet, not quite dusk, but on the point of twilight, the sky and air dark blue, lights coming on everywhere and the streets glistening with yellow light that gleamed on the half-melted snow. A bluish glimmer, reflected off the snow, filled the house.

At the foot of the top flight she switched a light on. It seemed to fill a little space and leave dark corners everywhere. Yet she was alone, there were no voices whispering and no half-glimpsed shapes. She crossed the landing and opened the temple door. A feeling of faintness came over her and she gasped, for the temple was gone and as if it had never been.

It was just a shabby little back bedroom. The walls were white, or whitish, and patchy, the floor was bare, and in the middle of the floor stood a rickety bamboo card table. The whole room rocked as she looked at it. She steadied herself, holding on to the doorknob, a singing in her head. For a moment she had a dreadful thought that she had imagined it all, the years of its existence and everything that had happened and been made to happen in it. Then she switched the light on.

The uncurtained window became a blue rectangle, patterned with a trellis of black branches. She saw what the bamboo table was. Once it had been the altar on which the elemental weapons had lain. Now the weapons were gone and the robe was gone from behind the door and the *tattwas* had disappeared from the walls. But its existence had not been in her imagination only. The black could still be seen through the rough whitewashing of the walls. There was a burn mark still on the floorboards where the wax image had caught fire in the bowl.

Pup had done it. He had meant what he said. On that very night when he had told her magic was nonsense, he had done it, on other nights too perhaps, when she thought he was out or asleep. He had fetched Myra's paints from the breakfast room and painted over the black of the walls. He had stripped the cloth covering from the altar and taken away the weapons to destroy them. Suddenly she remembered the books. What had he done with the books?

She ran from room to room, looking for them. They were nowhere on this top attic floor. She went down to his bedroom and searched it. Without qualms, without caring for his privacy, she threw open cupboard doors, rifled drawers, looked under the bed, even under the mattress.

They were nowhere. They were not in the house. He had burned them or sold them. She trailed away, down to the kitchen, down to her wine. She opened the bottle, poured the first glassful, with hands that shook. What use would they have been anyway? What use was anything with the temple itself gone?

She understood now that the days of magic and all that magic could do were over.

Chapter 22

Pup was very gentle with her and very kind. He came home every evening, though sometimes very late. She made a point of not asking him where he had been; she told herself that perhaps he still had to go to the Golden Dawn to complete a course or some such thing. She hardly saw Harold, and after that day when she had surprised them together, she never saw Wendy. Once she happened to overhear Mrs Collins say: 'Poor Dolly's gone down hill a lot, hasn't she? Miss Finlay saw her out shopping the other day talking to herself.'

And Wendy who was out in the hall with her laughed. 'The first sign of insanity, they used to say.'

It was Pup who told her Wendy and their father intended to live in one of the flats over the new shop.

'Then there'll just be you and me here?'

He nodded. 'That's right.'

A house of their own, a house to themselves . . . 'You could have one of the bigger rooms for a temple. You could start all over again.'

'No, I couldn't, dear. I shall never start it again, I told you. It's nonsense, Dolly, ask any rational person.'

She knew no rational people, she knew no one. 'Did you burn the books?'

'I sold the lot for a pound to a dealer on Highgate Hill.'

'What are people going to think?' she heard Edith

whisper to Myra over by the sewing machine. 'I feel quite awkward about it.'

'What are people going to think of you?' Dolly said. 'All those Golden Dawn people?' She brought the name out with a bitter edge. 'What's Yvonne going to think?'

'I shan't tell people,' he said lightly. 'Why should I?'

Yvonne didn't know, then. Yvonne still waited, expecting Dolly – or Pup through Dolly – to get her husband back.

'Hope deferred,' said Edith sententiously, 'maketh the heart sick.'

Yvonne's heart was sick and sore and therefore she kept away from Dolly, hating her for her failure. Dolly came to a decision. The doll she would keep in reserve but the dungarees should be sent to Yvonne by the means she herself had suggested. She bought dark green tissue paper and wrapping paper patterned all over with ivy leaves and wrapped up the dungarees and asked Pup to take them to Shelley Drive.

'If you're up that way,' she said, kissing him goodbye.

'I expect I shall be,' he said.

It was very late when he got home that night but Dolly was still up, drinking Yugoslav Riesling. He brought her a note from Yvonne. 'Dolly', it began, the name written diagonally across the top and underlined, 'the dungarees are super, a perfect fit, and I am thrilled. Thank you so much. You must let me know what I owe you, at least for the material. Yours, Yvonne.'

Nothing about when she would see her, nothing about getting in touch. That bit about paying for the material hurt. Dolly thought Yvonne had meant it to hurt. Had she only mentioned payment to remind

Dolly of that much greater service she had offered to pay for but which had never been performed? But what most pained Dolly was the way the letter opened and the way it ended, cold as ice and standoffish, no 'dear' and 'love' this time.

Once more there clung to Pup the scent of Ivoire. Of course, she knew he had been up to Yvonne's, she had asked him to go there, of course he had very likely shaken hands with Yvonne, and yet her imagination and her reasoning told her that secretly Pup and Yvonne had become friends. Lonely without her husband, Yvonne had turned to Pup and unless George went back to her . . .

'To be perfectly honest, Edith,' Myra whispered, using the same phrases she had once used to Dolly in life, 'to be perfectly honest, I can't say it doesn't look as if they've got a serious thing going because, frankly, it does.'

Back in the summer, when the subject had first been raised, Dolly had wanted the world rid of Ashley Clare for Yvonne's sake. Now she wanted it for her own. Remembering the heart murmur Pup said he had, she worked in quite a precise and scientific way on the doll next morning, plunging not pins but two long tapestry needles into the region where its heart might be supposed to be. It seemed impossible to her that such vehemence of will and such concentrated malice could be expended without result, yet she had achieved nothing. Because she dared not ask Pup and could not ask Yvonne, she went over to Arrowsmith Court herself on the bus and waited outside for hours and in vain. It was only on her third visit that she saw Ashley Clare. At 9.00 in the evening he came out of the flats and got into George Colefax's Mercedes.

On the way back, perhaps because a woman sitting behind her mentioned to her companion that she lived in Camden Town, Dolly remembered those minutes on the platform when she had put up her hands and been prepared to push a woman over the edge and out of life.

'I used to wear that emerald shade a lot,' said Myra, coming to sit beside her while Edith squeezed up on the edge of the seat.

'It's a difficult colour to match and a difficult colour to wear,' Edith said.

Dolly swatted them away but they were waiting for her at the bus stop. 'You don't know everything,' she said to them. 'You said Pup was doing magic when he wasn't, he was breaking up the temple.' She shouted out, 'You said Ashley Clare would die!'

A man coming down the hill said, 'Here, steady on, love. Real little piss artist you are.'

Under the light he saw her face, her cheek, and she saw him look away embarrassed. He thought she was drunk. The funny thing was it was the first evening she could remember when she hadn't had a drink. Her body craved it. She went up the steps on to the Archway bridge and Hornsey Lane. Standing on the bridge, close by one of the yellow-painted, concrete lamp standards, Anubis pointed his dog snout at the smoky purple sky. She looked away and looked again and he was gone, melted into the ironwork. In Manningtree Grove she met Miss Finlay, scuttling home from the Adonai Spiritists, but she did not acknowledge Miss Finlay's timid greeting. She passed on, her head averted, scolding Myra who kept touching her and whispering. The wine, after the first tumblerful, drove Myra and Edith temporarily away.

'I'm leaving,' the policewoman said. 'I'm moving out.' He saw her give him a cunning look, seeing how he would take it. 'I've come up to say goodbye.'

He wondered whether to believe her. You could never really trust those people.

'I'm moving to St Alban's,' she said. 'I've got a flat there.'

An unlikely story. 'Who'll be moving in then?'

She said she didn't know. She was going in an hour or so and she had all this stuff left over, tins of food and jam and some potatoes, scouring powder and washing-up liquid, and she wondered if he'd like to have it. It seemed a pity to throw it away.

'You can leave it with me,' he said and he smiled, pulling the wool over her eyes. They still thought they could drug him. If you looked closely at those tins you'd see minute pin holes they'd pushed the hypodermic through. The potatoes too. They must think him daft if they reckoned on him eating that jam.

'Well, I'll say goodbye then, Diarmit.'

That angered him and told him a lot. 'My name's Conal Moore, I'll thank you to call me by my name.'

She shrugged. 'Goodbye.'

After she had gone and it got dark he took the tins and the potatoes and the jam across the street to the green and divided them among the three litter bins. Someone had been up and searched the room in his absence, he was sure of it. The Harrods bag containing the knives was lying a little further from the bed than it had been. He could smell that girl in the room. Cautiously he sniffed the scouring powder, the washing-up liquid, then the scouring powder again. It made him sneeze. He sneezed twenty times or more and his nose started to run. They were trying to poison him now. He opened the window and put his head out into the frosty February night.

After a time his head cleared a little and he began to understand what they were doing. They had tried to make him say he was Diarmit Bawne, for Diarmit

245

Bawne was a witness and could tell the whole truth about Conal Moore. Hadn't he helped the police before? That responsible hardworking citizen had helped the police before, had them here in Conal's room, talked to them, asked them to keep in touch. They'd tried that on with persuasion and drugs, sending that woman to disarm him, but they had failed. No one should make him say he was who he was not. But he would have to get out of here, he was in grave danger here.

He must get out before the new policeman moved in downstairs. Carefully he scattered scouring powder, a very thin, almost invisible, film of it, on to the surface of the Harrods bag, on to the heap of red clothes, on to the draining board and around the knob on the cupboard door. Then he put out the light and crept downstairs with the tin of powder and the plastic container of liquid. These he deposited in one of the house dustbins in the side entrance. Returning, he removed from under his bell by the front door the piece of card with 'Diarmit Bawne' on it to reveal the old one that said 'C. Moore'.

Slowly he went back upstairs, allowing them plenty of time for their searching. But when he came into the room he found everything undisturbed and the scattered powder lying as he had left it, like a slight fall of virgin snow.

Pup and Yvonne stood on the Chinese bridge, looking down at the red fish in the dark water. It was one of those mild days that sometimes occur at the start of Lent and it was the eve of Pup's twenty-first birthday.

'So it looks,' said Yvonne in the voice that had never grown up, 'it looks as if he won't live very long. Poor Ashley! I never thought the time would come when I'd say poor Ashley.'

'What is it exactly that's wrong with him?'

'Something with his heart. He can't work any more, he's had to give that up. He could just drop down dead in the street, George said. I've never seen George so depressed.'

'And if he dies,' Pup said in a low voice, 'George will come back here? Come back for good?'

'I don't know. I suppose. Let's go in, I'm getting cold.'

Pup put his arm round her and they walked back to the house. He was very much in love; he was, as he had never been before, ill with love. With Yvonne, primarily and absolutely with Yvonne, but also with everything she represented and everything that formed the matrix of her, with Ivoire perfume and Cacharel clothes, red lacquer bridge and swimming pool, house and car and breath of affluence. For wasn't Yvonne herself those things and weren't those things Yvonne?

They sat on the white fur rug in front of the log fire that Yvonne's cleaner had built and lit and maintained. Yvonne's fingernails were painted a pearl colour and she wore a pearl ring. Pup kissed her hand and her wrist.

'I love you. I don't want to lose you to George.'

'Ashley might live for years,' she said. 'Isn't it funny? It's not very long since I asked Dolly to get you to split them up. And now I only want them kept together. Could you have?'

'Split them up? Of course not. Yvonne?'

'Yes, darling?'

'I wish you still saw Dolly.'

'It's a bit embarrassing, isn't it? You know, you and me. After what I told her about George. And besides – you mustn't be hurt.'

'I won't be hurt.'

'She's so strange. I'm afraid of her.'

'She's harmless,' said Pup. 'She loves us – I mean us two – more than anyone in the world. She'd do anything to make us happy. At least give her a ring sometime, would you? To please me?'

'Shall I tell her about us?'

He looked into her eyes. They were the only eyes he had ever seen that actually reminded him of jewels, large, uncut, water-washed gems. 'There isn't much to tell, is there? Only that I love you and you say you love me – and your husband's coming back.'

Yvonne, having rehearsed what she would say, tried to phone Dolly next morning. Dolly was out, buying her wine. She tried again in the evening and Dolly, machining the seams of a dress for herself, heard the phone but let it ring. She thought it was Wendy Collins who had already phoned twice that day. Yvonne gave up, postponing her call until the next day.

She could only have been in time, she could only have talked to Dolly in time, if she had phoned before 7.30 and no one does that.

The Yvonne doll and the Ashley Clare doll sat side by side sedately on the mantelpiece. Dolly looked at them with a constriction in her throat. What she had to do frightened her and if there had been another way she would have taken it. There was no other way, she had tried the other possible means and this was all that remained.

It was a blue morning, bright and with a tearing wind. She wrapped up warm, once more tying the scarf to hide half her face. The confidence this gave her she needed. Myra and Edith meant to go with her, there was no escaping them. Myra's greenness awaited her in the hall by the front door, a misty mass of emerald green, and as she approached it to open the door, her hands held out in front of her, she recalled another occasion when her hands had reached towards greenness. She seemed to see that shocked face looking at her, the aghast eyes, full comprehension of what she had been about to do distorting a pleasant, kindly face into a mask of shock.

The green mist melted away and for a while there was no whispering. Dolly walked along through the driving wind to the bus stop down below the Archway. It was more than likely, of course, that she would not see him. She was rather late. Perhaps she should postpone it till tomorrow. But what was the point of putting off and putting off while Yvonne's disappointment in her grew and Yvonne began more and more to hate her? The bus came and still, as it drew to a stop, she considered postponement, going home, leaving it for a day or a week even. But she got on the bus and paid her fare to the driver and found herself a seat where she could sit with her right cheek against the glass.

Edith and Myra had got on the bus with her and they chattered to each other in a fretful, scared kind of way. The bus was going down Hampstead Lane, already under the overhanging trees of Kenwood, before she could make out what they were saying. They wanted her to stop, they wanted her to stop now and go back.

'I'm on the bus, I can't go back,' she said to them.

A man sitting in front of her looked round and at the empty seat beside her. Dolly was embarrassed because the man was not psychic and couldn't hear them. She held her hand over her mouth. While she was dressing she had put on Pup's talisman, put it on over her dress which was rust red and matched it, but now, to feel the comfort of it closer to her, she undid the top button and slipped the talisman in against her skin. The whispering had not stopped but it had become very faint. No one, whatever they might say about magic, whatever Pup might say, was going to convince her the talisman was not fraught with power and charged with protection.

The wind caught her as she stepped off the bus. It caught one passenger after another, tore them off the bus and sent them half-running, holding on to hats and scarves. A regatta of tiny clouds was racing across the blue sky. London lay down there in the bowl beneath the heights, all bright and glittering in the smokeless, fogless, clear air.

It had been precisely 8.30 when he had come out last time, just after 8.30 that morning when she had followed him into the train and plucked the hairs from his coat collar. The time now was twenty-five past. She had no clear idea yet of what she would do when she saw him, how she would act, certain only of one thing, that she would follow him and stick to him, all day if necessary, for the rest of her life if necessary, until she had done what had to be done. After all, what else was there for her to do?

George Colefax's Mercedes stood in the car park, the nearest vehicle to the flats' entrance. A girl came out of the swing doors, then a couple, then, walking languidly in spite of the cold, a man in a long white sheepskin coat. It was Ashley Clare.

He glanced into the car as he passed it. He turned up the collar of his coat and pushed his hands into his pockets. She saw his face closer to and more clearly than she had ever done. It looked dark and drawn with deep lines running from the nostrils to the corners of the mouth, it looked very middle-aged. There was a sallow pallor about that face as if there were no blood under the skin to give it colour.

He passed within a yard of Dolly. She let him get a little ahead and then she followed him down the hill, down steep, winding Heath Street where the ramparts of walls and tall houses did something to shelter the narrow defile from the wind. He walked with his shoulders hunched and his head dipped as if the cold pained him. At the bookstall outside Hampstead tube station she expected him to stop and buy a paper so that he could do the crossword as he had before, but instead he went straight into the station and, holding out his season ticket, turned left for the lift. Neither of the ticket machines was working. Dolly had to join the queue to buy a ticket, but Ashley Clare had not gone down. The green metal doors had already closed before he reached the lift which must have contained its requisite maximum of thirty passengers.

The station was crowded this morning. Unlike last time there was for some reason a great crush of people. Ashley Clare and Dolly were among the first to get into the lift and Myra and Edith got in with them. Dolly couldn't see the greenness or smell the lemony scent, nor could she decipher their words but their whispering had become intense and shrill.

In the passage at the bottom of the lift a gale was blowing as strongly as above ground, only here the wind was warm and with a metallic smell. The crowd went hard along the passage and over the bridge above the line like a herd of animals starting to stampede. Once or twice Dolly lost sight of the white sheepskin coat ahead of her and then, as they went down the steps, it was gone altogether.

It was a train northward bound for Golders Green that was making the hot wind. Dolly and almost everyone else took the left-hand turn for the line that went down into the centre of London. It was a nasty moment for Dolly when she thought she saw the bun-faced woman in the brown coat who, that evening at Camden Town, had seen her hands flexed to push. She was standing reading a poster for a new film. Dolly gazed. The woman turned and looked at her and of course it was not the same one at all, not in the least like, only the coat was similar.

Dolly walked along the platform, looking for Ashley Clare. Last time she had made a mistake, she had picked the wrong person, which in the circumstances had hardly mattered. But what if her hands had not drawn back? What if she had pushed? There would be no other man here wearing white sheepskin, she thought, and then she looked up and saw him. He too had been reading a film poster and now he was looking at her, studying her so intently, that she wondered for a moment if, once upon a time, Myra had told George and George had told him of her stepdaughter with the birthmark or if Yvonne had told George . . . But it was more likely that with the arrogance of the handsome unblemished he was merely staring at the naevus itself. She returned the look so savagely, hating him with a personal hatred now, that he moved his eyes, turned his head and, with his hands still in his pockets, walked towards the edge of the platform.

Once more the waiting passengers had formed themselves into huddled groups at points where they guessed the doors would be. Instead of doing the same, Ashley Clare had stationed himself between two such groups and he stood there with his head bowed, very close to the edge. But a fresh surge of people had come on to the platform from the next lift and he was joined by a man on one side of him and a woman on the other. Dolly moved herself in behind him. She looked up at his hair above the coat collar and thought it seemed greyer than before. Edith and Myra were chattering away urgently now, they sounded nearly hysterical.

The train would come in from the left. Already the

warm wind had begun to blow. There were two people standing very close behind Dolly now and they seemed very tall people. She was surrounded by tall people, a man at least six feet two on her left, a girl stilted up on immense heels on her right. She felt small, hidden, squashed. She heard someone say over her head that there had been a breakdown and a train left out, that was why there was such a crowd, the whole platform packed. Hemmed in, towered over – or so it felt – she moved her hands. The cream woolly gloves she wore were almost exactly the same colour as the sheepskin. One of his hairs, a dark one, such as she had used in the making of the useless wax image, fell from the back of his head to alight on the pale knitted back of her glove. She looked at it, clinging there, and Myra and Edith's frenzied shouting roared around her.

The train came out of the tunnel and through a gap between sheepskin and the tall man's herringbone tweed she could see the driver's face, young and pink. Before he was lost to view she saw his mouth open and screaming, for by then she had pushed.

He might have given a cry as he went over. How could she tell when, as the crowd went back like a wave, a sound rose from it that was a mingling of screams and gasps and dreadful moans? She cried out with them and the wave drew her back with it. An impersonal, inhuman voice arrested movement and made temporary silence.

'There has been an accident. I repeat, there has been an accident. Please keep calm and don't panic . . .'

A woman standing beside Dolly, a stranger, began to weep.

Chapter 23

The man who had moved in downstairs came under immediate suspicion. Conal had seen him only in the distance, the dark hair, the blank meaningless face, the blue jeans. He heard his voice too, with the false English accent they had taught him while he was away training to be a police spy. Could he be Diarmit Bawne? For a moment the fog cleared and Conal knew he was himself Diarmit, it was his mind that had done this to him. But it was only for a moment. The fog rolled back and he was Conal again. That evening, he thought, the man downstairs would come up and knock on the door, introduce himself by some outlandish name and offer Conal food or ask him to make less noise. Conal was very careful to make no noise and at 7.00, when Diarmit had not appeared, he went out.

He had no doubt the room would be searched in his absence. Diarmit had a key and would have no need to pick the lock as the so-called Andrea had done. This time he had not scattered any scouring powder. What was the point? He knew they would search and he was tired, he hardly cared any more. Most of the energy and high spirits essential to Conal Moore had subsided and he felt himself becoming as slow and steady and *dead* as Diarmit had been. He tramped the silent streets with nothing to do and nowhere to go, half afraid to go back.

But at last he had to. He fully expected the man

who was to be inside the room, waiting there to speak to him and urge him to give himself up. Find a priest to confess to, tell it all to Kathleen, then go to the police. But it was worse than that, more sinister than that, for the room was empty and reeking of Diarmit and the girl, her perfume and Diarmit's stinking clothes.

They had taken the knives. He couldn't see the Harrods bag anywhere. In a burst of panic that renewed his strength, he threw open doors and drawers, pulled the pile of red clothes apart, scrabbled under the bed, pulling out papers, old carriers and, at last, *the* carrier. He fell asleep on the bed from the exhaustion of it.

When he awoke in the deep middle of the night, he saw chaos around him. They had searched without caution, without caring if he knew. Drawers were tumbled on to the floor, their contents scattered, clothes lay everywhere and in the middle of the room, as a signal to him, he supposed, that all was now known, on top of a pile of newspapers and carrier bags lay the cleaver and the two knives.

It was then that he knew he must get out and defend himself against them. Once the morning came he must get out, taking his property with him, to find himself a refuge. The electric knife sharpener made scarcely any sound. He sat cross-legged on the floor, sharpening the knives and testing them on his left hand until the fingertips were all scored across and bloody. If Diarmit heard the faint noise and came up, he would be ready for him, but Diarmit did not come.

It was in a state very like a trance that Dolly walked back up the steep hill. And for almost the first time since Myra died she found herself in silence. Myra and Edith had whispered together, making a sound like the shrill twittering of frightened birds, then sighed, then gasped, then gone. She knew she would never hear them again or smell the lemon of her mother or see the green that was Myra. They had gone and left her in utter silence.

She hardly noticed the wind. The bus came after she had waited twenty minutes for it. For a stupid moment she thought the bus driver had a dog's face but she closed her eyes and opened them and saw a brown man, an Indian, with an aquiline nose. A deadly silence enclosed her on the bus. She put up her hand and felt the hard edges of the talisman through her dress and it made her easier, it brought her a little life.

There was no need to hurry home. She could not have hurried if she had wanted to. The news would not reach Yvonne until the evening or perhaps even tomorrow if she saw no paper and had to wait for George to tell her. Dolly got off the bus in Highgate village and walked slowly, buffeted by the wind, down the hill to Holmesdale Road where she made her way on to the old railway line.

Spring catkins were appearing on the birch trees and the willows. By the time the summer came, she and Pup would be on their own in their own house and George and Yvonne happy again in their own house. Tomorrow, if she hadn't heard from Yvonne, she would send her the blonde bridal doll by Pup. It was wonderfully peaceful without Myra and Edith. Dolly thought she would drink a bottle of wine when she got home, though it was so early. Enough wine would kill the day for her until Yvonne phoned.

She touched the talisman. Feathers were flying out of the mouth of the Mistley tunnel like snow blown from a drift. Dolly walked through the tunnel and went up the steps on the other side.

Harold was at home. She could hear the clatter of

his typewriter from the breakfast room. In the kitchen she opened a bottle of burgundy and drank a glassful down at a gulp. She took the bottle with her into the living room and began drinking the wine steadily, not bothering to make it last. There was another bottle where that one had come from; in the wineshops there was an infinite number of bottles waiting for her to come and buy. The typewriter rattled away on the other side of the wall. She missed Edith and Myra. Often she had hated them and tried to drive them away, but now that they had gone back to their abode on the Other Side, she wanted their voices back again, their comments on what she had done, their judgement.

She fetched the other bottle and drew the cork. Her hands were shaking. She realized that tremors had been passing through her whole body ever since she came back into the house. It was a strange thing to happen because she was happy, now Ashley Clare was dead she was as content with her life as she ever could be.

Wendy Collins arrived in her car to take Harold out somewhere. Dolly thought of when she and Pup would be alone, of turning the dining room into a temple, of George and Yvonne coming. Her thoughts buzzed in her head like a skep full of bees. Harold and Wendy went arm in arm down the path and got into Wendy's car. Dolly thought she might sleep, it was many nights since she had slept well. The dolls on the mantelpiece seemed to be watching her, their eyes following her, swivelling in their padded rag faces.

She sat down at the sewing machine but her hands were too unsteady to hold her work. Half the bottle of burgundy remained. She slopped some of it into the glass, spilling red drops, a little red pond of it, on to Myra's haircord. The dolls put their heads on one side and stared, Ashley Clare and Yvonne began to shake their heads and roll their embroidered eyes. Dolly finished the wine and got up, holding on to the furniture to help her across the room. She saw her face and the masking red naevus in Myra's mirror and as she looked at it with misted, distorting eyes, she saw another face appear behind her, its dog snout peer over her left shoulder.

She closed the door and turned the key in the lock, shutting Anubis in with the dolls. It was impossible to walk upstairs, so she crawled from tread to tread, crawled across the landing, climbed on to her bed and slept.

The winestains on the carpet looked like spots of spilled blood. Dolly moved the sewing machine table a foot or two to hide them. She had slept for ten hours, turning day into night, and now, primed with aspirin – she had taken six – she felt weak and shaky and somehow disembodied. Harold was still out or had gone out again, Pup had neither come nor phoned. Or she supposed he had not phoned. She had been dead to sound or any change or disturbance of her surroundings.

She could feel the presence of the dog-faced god but she could not see him. She walked about the house, turning the light on as she entered a room and off as she left it. It was as if she were getting her bearings, taking a view of the new life that was opening ahead of her. All the time as she walked she could hear, or perhaps only feel by means of soft vibrations, some creature always padding a little way behind her. When she looked to see, there was nothing there. It was a couple of days since she had eaten anything more than a biscuit or two but she did not feel like eating now. She took a bottle of white wine, Sauterne, out of the fridge, drew the cork and sipped it slowly straight from the bottle. It made her feel queasy and weak-kneed but she went on drinking it.

Still Pup did not come. Once she would have believed him to be at the Golden Dawn but she could hardly think that now. Once, before the Golden Dawn days, she would have worried, imagining him mugged or run over. He had grown too self-sufficient, indeed too great and powerful, for her to feel those things now.

Harold was back. She heard Wendy leave him and the smack of their good-night kiss. Night had become day for her. She would sit up through it, sit in the living room with her last bottle of wine, waiting for Pup to come.

Very early in the morning, Saturday morning, Conal began moving his stuff out. He started before it was light. There was a lot of stuff belonging to Diarmit Bawne: a grey duffel coat, a raincoat, blue jeans and light shirts that had to be washed and ironed. There were tins of food and bottles of sauce, a coloured blanket that looked as if it had been made out of wool by some woman, an ashtray with a shamrock leaf painted on it. All this he left behind for its rightful owner. Into the place where he would withstand their siege he took his red clothes and the knife sharpener and the Harrods bag with the knives and the cleaver in it. He walked through the cold dark morning, carrying his possessions, down the muddy steps to the platform of the old station.

He had to make three journeys. When he had got everything that was Conal Moore's and left everything that was Diarmit Bawne's, he opened the room door and left it propped wide open with one of Diarmit's cans of Campbell's soup. Diarmit would not have been capable of writing them a note, he could write his own name and that was about all. Conal could write, he was an educated man, but he did not choose to do so. Why bother with them? Why make their job easier for them?

They would guess where he was anyway. When they came he would be ready for them. The dawn had come, it was almost sunrise, the sun was showing in pale yellow bars above a ridge of black roofs and the black featheriness of tree branches. He humped his stuff along the platform and into the tunnel. The mattress had dwindled in the eighteen months that had passed but it was still a mattress and it was still possible to stand it up on its side and curve it round into a windbreak or defensive barrier. He had brought a blanket from the bed and the dark red anorak that Conal had bought third or fourth hand in the Mind shop. The knives and the cleaver were what were important, his weapons. The sight of them, sharp and shining, laid out carefully, each parallel to the others, on a thick pad of damp newspaper, comforted him and made him feel safer. Any policeman or woman, any spy, who came near him had better look out, that was all.

Conal Moore had always been a brave boy, a daredevil, a wild fellow. He sat down behind the barricade on a mound of wet newspaper, the blanket tented round him, ready for anything.

At 9.00 in the morning Pup came home. Dolly, waking up on the living-room sofa, heard him go straight upstairs. She just had time to put her shoes on, run her fingers through her hair, stretch, before he came running down again and was in the room with her.

She hoped to avoid having to explain, she hoped he would simply think she was up and dressed early for a Saturday. But he was not even looking at her. He was looking at the dolls on the mantelpiece.

'Don't you think we'd better put them away now?' he said gently. 'Well, the – the man, anyway. Not in very good taste.' He hesitated. 'You do – know?' She remained still, saying nothing. He picked the dolls off the shelf. 'I tried to phone you a good many times yesterday.'

She said indifferently, 'I was out a lot yesterday,' and with a show of insouciance, 'What should I know?'

'You didn't see an evening paper?'

She shook her head, waiting for the pleasant news that was no news to be broken.

He opened the lid of the remnants box and slipped the dolls inside. She thought he looked suddenly much older, far older than his years, and content in a strained kind of way. He must be happy for Yvonne, relieved for Yvonne getting her husband back. She laid her hand on his sleeve.

'It's been quite a shock,' he said. 'Yesterday morning – well, twenty-four hours ago now, George Colefax fell on to the line at Hampstead in front of the incoming train.'

Chapter 24

After he had gone, she found the photograph
Yvonne had sent her and looked at it. For some
reason – because George Colefax had spoken of
Ashley Clare as a beautiful boy? – she had taken the
man smoking the cigar for George and the slimmer
handsomer one for Ashley Clare. She had been
wrong, just as she had been wrong that evening on
the platform at Camden Town, only then it hadn't
mattered, it hadn't been too late and beyond remedy.

Yvonne's husband was dead. She had murdered
him. Since Pup told her, her head had been full of a
rushing, roaring sound and full, too, of thick mist.
She sat where he had left her, quite still, staring,
afraid to move lest any movement she might make
should bring down fresh disaster on them all.

The thought came to her that she would never see
anyone again, no one would ever again see her or
speak to her. There was even no sound of Harold in
the house this morning. Pup had gone without
saying when he would come back. Yvonne hated her.
She was left alone for the rest of her life – or alone
but for a single companion and even he had deserted
her since, just before Pup came, she had for a
moment seen the shadow of his dog's head appear
on the wall.

It was more than twenty-four hours, much more,
since she had taken her clothes off. The rust-red
dress was crumpled and it seemed to her that it

smelled of sweat and pain. Without getting up, without drawing the curtains, she began unbuttoning it. But before she had reached the waist she was aware of loss, of something – more than everything else – being wrong, of a terrible lack. Both her hands went to her neck, her breasts, searching.

The talisman was gone.

She cried out, a useless cry, since there was no one to hear her and no one to come. Was it because she and the talisman had been parted that this horror had happened? But no, it had been with her then, she had felt it against her skin. If she were not to lose everything, to lose her own self as well, she must find the talisman, she must not permit it to be lost, to wander the world ownerless.

Feverishly she began to search the house.

'I suppose,' Yvonne said, holding on to Pup very tight, her head on his shoulder, 'I suppose what happened to poor George was like they say in the papers, the balance of his mind was disturbed. The policeman said to me it would just be made out to be accidental at the inquest but what I think is he meant to do it, don't you?'

'It seems an odd way to do it,' said Pup, 'and an odd place to choose.'

Yvonne shivered. 'If your mind's unbalanced you don't think of things like that. It was quick. You see, he told me he couldn't live without Ashley and the chances were Ashley'd be dead in a year. I think he must have been feeling very sort of low and he got down on that platform and despair came over him and he jumped. But we don't have to tell them that at the inquest, do we?'

'Of course we don't.'

'Poor George. I was very fond of him once, you

know. I do feel quite upset. It's awful to have been a widow twice when you're only twenty-five.'

'Twenty-seven,' said Pup gently. 'I think you and I should get married quite soon, don't you?'

'Oh, yes, please,' said Yvonne, putting up her lips for a kiss.

Pup saw no reason why they shouldn't be very happy. He wanted a large family. George hadn't made a will but that was of no consequence since Yvonne was his sole heir. Above her downy golden head, Pup surveyed what he could see of the house that would soon be his and took in a corner of Kashmiri rug, a segment of Chippendale cabinet, a scarlet shimmer of Chinese bridge beyond the window in the green grounds. Sometime or other he had promised to go down to Arrowsmith Court and fetch home the Mercedes. It wasn't bad, he thought, to have got everything you wanted by the time you were twenty-one, a flourishing business, a successful career, an apparently attractive appearance, a beautiful wife and a million pounds' worth of house just off the Bishop's Avenue.

Dolly would say he had got it through selling his soul to the devil. In which case, like poor old Faustus, he would presumably be expected to pay some sort of awful price for it. Pup couldn't think of any awful price that might be exacted from him and he laughed aloud, it was all such nonsense.

'I know,' said Yvonne, snuggling up. 'I feel happy too. Aren't we awful?'

Dolly could have the Manningtree Grove house. And laser treatment for the naevus, there would be money for that, whatever it cost. Pup kissed Yvonne and dismissed Dolly from his mind.

Amid the rushing in her brain and the swirling mists, Dolly's memory was clear. She could remember she was still wearing the talisman when she left the station, still wearing it on the bus and when she walked down Southwood Lane, across the Archway Road and up on to the old railway line. She thought she had still been wearing it when she passed over the bridge at Stanhope Road and came down into the valley, but that she could not quite remember.

It was a bland day, white-skied and colourless. She put on her coat, and as she came to the front door, she saw the shadow of Anubis on Myra's biscuit-coloured wall and now his face was neither friendly nor indifferent but twisted into a snarl. She wouldn't look. She thought she would forever be afraid to look behind her. Out in the air it was better. She shook her hair down to cover her cheek. There were a few people about going Saturday morning shopping and they all had the heads of dogs set on the shoulders of their coats or sweaters. Sometimes if she looked away and looked back quickly they became people again, staring back with hostility. She walked back as far as the bridge at Stanhope Road. She was sure she had still had the talisman before she reached there.

Perhaps because it was so wet underfoot and the tree branches dripped dampness, there was no one else on the old railway line. If no one had been along, or no observant person, since she had, the talisman might still be there. She walked slowly, her head bent and her eyes down, and presently she picked herself a long thin wand of poplar with which to probe the grass. With a wand very like this, cut from a tree very near here, Pup had done so many wonderful magical things. The talisman was all that was left from that time and she must find it.

In the wider valley, searching was slower. She could not remember exactly where she had walked the day before. Against the grass the green of it would not show and the red part was very small. She peered from side to side, her head moving rhythmically. A feather, borne on a light breath of breeze, fluttered down and fell at her feet, and suddenly the memory came back to her, the feather recalling it, how on the morning before she had felt the talisman on her skin as she entered the Mistley tunnel.

So she had lost it somewhere between here and home. It was darkish inside the tunnel but no grass grew there, the ground was bare, dark and damp. A feather touched her face as lightly as Myra's spirit fingers used to touch it.

Someone had heaved the mattress up on to its side. Dolly did not think it had been like that yesterday. Was it possible that she could remember just at this point a slippery touch as the thong of the talisman had come unfastened and slid down through her clothes? In the twilight of the tunnel, mud and feathers underfoot, she moved towards the mattress, the wand in her hands like a diviner's rod.

And then she saw him, just the shape of him in the gloom, not his dog's head nor his glistening body, and in his outstretched hands not the caduceus and the palms but two bright knives that caught what little light there was.

He had waited for her, knowing she was bound to come. She had known she must be caught by him sooner or later. Everything that had happened to them had inexorably led to this end, and as they closed together with the knives between them, each gave an equal cry of fear.

Live Flesh

1

The gun was a replica. Spenser told Fleetwood he was ninety-nine per cent sure of that. Fleetwood knew what that meant, that he was really about forty-nine per cent sure, but he didn't attach much weight to what Spenser said anyway. For his own part he didn't believe the gun was real. Rapists don't have real guns. A replica does just as well as a means of frightening.

The window that the girl had broken was a square empty hole. Once since Fleetwood arrived had the man with the gun appeared at it. He had come in answer to Fleetwood's summons but had said nothing, only standing there for perhaps thirty seconds, holding the gun in both hands. He was young, about Fleetwood's own age, with long dark hair, really long, down on his shoulders, as was the prevailing fashion. He wore dark glasses. For half a minute he stood there and then he turned abruptly round and disappeared into the shadows of the room. The girl Fleetwood hadn't seen, and for all he knew she might be dead.

He sat on a garden wall on the opposite side of the street, looking up at the house. His own car and the police van were parked at the kerb. Two of the uniformed men had succeeded in clearing away the crowd which had gathered and keeping it back with an improvised barrier. Even though it had now begun to rain, dispersing the crowd altogether would have been an impossible task. Front doors stood open all the way down the street with women on the doorsteps, waiting for something to happen. It was one of them who, hearing the window break and the girl scream, had dialled 9-9-9.

A district that was neither Kensal Rise nor West Kilburn nor Brondesbury, a blurred area, on the borders of nowhere in particular. Fleetwood had never really been there before, had only driven through. The street was called Solent Gardens, long and straight and flat, with terraces of two-storey houses facing one another, some Victorian, some much later, from the nineteen twenties and thirties. The house with the broken window, number 62 Solent Gardens, was one of these newer houses, the end of a terrace of eight, red brick and pebble dashing, red pantiles on the roof, black and white paintwork, a pale blue front door. All the houses had gardens at the back and gardens at the front with lonicera or privet hedges and bits of lawn, and most of them had low brick or stone walls in front of the hedges. Fleetwood, sitting on a wall in the rain, began to wonder what he should do next.

None of the rapist's victims had mentioned a gun, so it would seem as if the replica had been recently acquired. Two of them – there had been five, or at any rate five who had come forward – had been able to describe him: tall, slim, twenty-seven or twenty-eight, olive skin, dark longish hair, dark eyes and very black eyebrows. A foreigner? Oriental? Greek? Perhaps, but perhaps just an Englishman with dark-skinned forbears. One of the girls had been badly hurt, for she had fought him, but he had used no weapon on her, only his hands.

Fleetwood got up and walked up to the front door of number 63 opposite to have another talk with Mrs Stead, who had called the police. Mrs Stead had fetched out a kitchen stool to sit on and put on her winter coat. She had already told him that the girl's name was Rosemary Stanley and that she lived with her parents but they were away. It had been at five minutes to eight in the morning, one and a half hours ago, when Rosemary Stanley had broken the window and screamed.

Fleetwood asked if Mrs Stead had seen her.

'He dragged her away before I got the chance.'

'We can't know that,' Fleetwood said. 'I suppose she goes out to work? I mean, when things are normal?'

'Yes, but she never leaves the house before nine. Ten past as often as not. I can tell you what happened, I've worked it all out. He rang the doorbell and she went down in her nightie to answer it and he said he'd come to read the electric meter – they're due for this quarter, he'd know that – and she took him upstairs and he had a go at her, but in the nick of time she bashed the window out and uttered her desperate cry for help. That's the way it's got to be.'

Fleetwood didn't think so. For one thing the electricity meter wouldn't be upstairs. All the houses in this part of the street were the same and Mrs Stead's meter was just inside the front door. Alone in the house on a dark winter morning, Rosemary Stanley would hardly have opened the door to a caller. She would have leaned out of the window to check on him first. Women in this district had been so frightened by tales of the rapist that not one of them would set foot outside after dark, sleep alone in a house if she could help it, or open a front door without a chain on it. A local ironmonger told Fleetwood that there had been a boom in the sale of door chains these past few weeks. Fleetwood thought it more likely the man with the gun had forced an entry into the house and made his way to Rosemary Stanley's bedroom.

'Could you do with a coffee, Inspector?' said Mrs Stead.

'Sergeant,' Fleetwood corrected her. 'No, thanks. Later maybe. Still, we must hope there won't be a later.'

He crossed the road. Behind the barrier the crowd waited patiently, standing in the drizzle, coat collars turned up, hands in pockets. At the end of the street, where it turned off the main road, one of the PCs was having an argument with a driver who seemed to want to bring his lorry down here. Spenser had predicted that the man with the gun would come out and give himself up when he saw Fleetwood and the others; rapists were notorious cowards, that was a well-known fact, and what did he have to gain by holding out? It hadn't been like that, though. Fleetwood thought it might be that the rapist still believed he had a chance of escape. If he was *the* rapist. They couldn't be sure he was, and Fleetwood was a stickler for accuracy, for fairness. A few minutes after the 9–9–9 call a girl called

7

Heather Cole had come into the police station with a man called John Parr, and Heather Cole had said an attack had been made on her in Queens Park half an hour before. She was exercising her dog when a man had seized her from behind, but she had screamed and Mr Parr had come and the man had run off. Had escaped this way, Fleetwood thought, and entered 62 Solent Gardens for refuge from pursuers rather than with the intention of raping Rosemary Stanley because he had been baulked of Heather Cole. Or that was Fleetwood's guess.

Fleetwood came the nearest he had yet been to the Stanley house, opening the small ornate wrought-iron gate, crossing the square of wet bright-green grass, making his way round the side. There was no sound from the interior. The exposed side wall was sheer, without drainpipes or projections, with three small windows only. At the back though, the kitchen had apparently been extended and the roof of this extension, which was no more than eight feet from the ground, could be reached by scaling the wall against which grew a sturdy thornless climber – a wisteria probably, thought Fleetwood, who in his leisure hours was fond of gardening.

Above this low roof a sash window stood open. Fleetwood was proved right. He noted access to the garden from a lane at the back by a path of concrete slabs leading past a concrete garage. If all else failed, he thought, he or someone could always get into the house by climbing up the way the man with the gun had.

As he came round the front again, the voice shouted at him. It was a voice full of fear but it was itself none the less frightening for that. It was unexpected and it made Fleetwood jump. He realized he was nervous, he was afraid, though he hadn't thought of this before. He made himself walk, not run, on to the front path. The man with the gun stood at the broken window, the window from which he had now knocked out all the glass into the flowerbed below, holding the gun in his right hand and the curtain back with his left.

'Are you in charge here?' he said to Fleetwood.

As if he were running some sort of show. Well, perhaps he was, and a successful one to judge from the avidity of the audience, braving rain and cold. At the sound of the voice a noise came from them, a crowd-sigh, a collective murmur, not unlike wind in the treetops.

Fleetwood nodded. 'That's right.'

'So it'd be you I'd have to make terms with?'

'No terms are going to be made.'

The man with the gun now appeared to consider this. He said, 'What's your rank?'

'I'm Detective Sergeant Fleetwood.'

Disappointment was apparent in the thin face, even though the eyes were hidden. The man seemed to think he merited a chief inspector at least. Perhaps I'd better tell Spenser his presence is required, thought Fleetwood. The gun was pointing at him now. Fleetwood wasn't going to put his hands up, of course he wasn't. This was Kensal Rise, not Los Angeles, though what real difference that made he didn't know. He looked into the black hole of the gun's mouth.

'I want a promise I can come out of here and have half an hour to get away in. I'll take the girl with me and when the half-hour's up I'll send her back here in a taxi. OK?'

'You must be joking,' said Fleetwood.

'It'll be no joke to her if you don't give me that promise. You can see the gun, can't you?'

Fleetwood made no reply.

'You can have an hour to decide. Then I'll use the gun on her.'

'That will be murder. The inevitable sentence for murder is life imprisonment.'

The voice, which was deep and low, yet colourless – a voice which gave Fleetwood the impression it wasn't used much or was always used economically – turned cold. It spoke of terrible things with indifference.

'I shan't kill her. I'll shoot her from the back, in the lower spine.'

Fleetwood made no comment on this. What was there to say? It was a threat which could provoke only a moralistic condemnation or shocked reproach. He had turned away, for he noticed out of the corner of his eye a familiar car arriving, but a gasp from the crowd, a kind of concerted indrawing of breath, made him look up at the window once more. The girl, Rosemary Stanley, had been pushed into the empty square from which the glass had gone and was being held there, her stance suggesting a slave pinioned in a market place. Her arms were grasped in other arms behind her back and her head hung forward. A hand took hold of her long hair and with it pulled her head back, the jerking movement causing her to cry out.

Fleetwood expected the crowd to address her or her to speak, but neither of these things happened. She was silent and staring, statue-still with fear. The gun, he thought, was probably pressed into her back, into her lower spine. No doubt she too had heard the man's statement of intent. So intense was the crowd's indignation that Fleetwood fancied he could feel vibrations of it. He knew he ought to say words of reassurance to the girl but he could think of nothing not absolutely false and hypocritical. She was a thin little girl with long fair hair wearing a garment that might have been a dress or a dressing gown. An arm came round her waist, pulled her back, and simultaneously, for the first time, a curtain was drawn across the window. This was in fact a pair of thick-looking lined curtains that drew tightly together.

Spenser was still sitting in the passenger seat of the Rover reading a sheet of paper. He was the kind of man who, when not otherwise occupied, is always to be found perusing some document. It occurred to Fleetwood how subtly he was grooming himself for future commander-hood: his abundant thick hair just silvering, his shave cleaner that ever, the skin curiously tanned for deep midwinter, his shirt ice-cream transmuted into poplin, his raincoat surely a Burberry. Fleetwood got into the back of the car and Spenser turned on him eyes the blue of gas flames.

In Fleetwood's view, his reading had, as always,

informed him of everything that was irrelevant while contributing nothing to the cooling of crisis.

'She's eighteen, left school last summer, works in a typing pool. Parents went to the West Country first thing this morning, left in a taxi around half-seven, a neighbour says. Mrs Stanley's father in Hereford had a coronary. They'll be informed as soon as we can reach them. We don't want them seeing it on TV.'

Fleetwood immediately thought of the girl he was to marry next week. Would Diana find out he was here and worry? But no TV camera crew had appeared, no reporters of any kind yet, as far as he knew. He told Spenser what the man with the gun had said about a promise and getting away and shooting Rosemary Stanley.

'We can be ninety-nine per cent sure it's a replica,' said Spenser. 'How did he get in there? Do we know?'

'By means of a tree growing against the rear wall.' Fleetwood knew Spenser wouldn't know what he was talking about if he said wisteria.

Spenser muttered something and Fleetwood had to ask him to repeat it.

'I said we'll have to go in there, Sergeant.'

Spenser was thirty-seven, nearly ten years his senior. Also he was growing rotund, as perhaps was appropriate for a commander-to-be. Older than Fleetwood, less fit, two grades up in rank, Spenser meant by his 'we' that Fleetwood should go in there, maybe taking one of the young DCs with him.

'By means possibly of the tree you spoke of,' Spenser said.

The window was open, waiting for him. Inside was a man with a real gun or a mock gun – who knew? – and a frightened girl. He, Fleetwood, had no weapon at all except his hands and his feet and his wits, and when he talked to Spenser about being issued with a firearm the Superintendent looked at him as if he'd asked for a nuclear warhead.

The time was a quarter to ten and the man with the gun had made his ultimatum at about nine twenty.

'Are you going to talk to him at all, sir?'

Spenser gave a thin smile. 'Getting cold feet, Sergeant?'

Fleetwood took that in silence. Spenser got out of the car and crossed the road. Hesitating for a moment, Fleetwood followed him. The rain had stopped, and the sky, which had been uniformly grey and smooth, was now broken into grey and white and patches of blue. It seemed colder. The crowd now reached as far as the main road, Chamberlayne Road, that runs over Kensal Rise to meet Ladbroke Grove at the bottom. Fleetwood could see that the traffic in Chamberlayne Road had been halted.

Up at the broken window in the Stanley house the drawn curtains moved about in the light wind. Spenser stepped on to the muddy grass from the comparative cleanness of the concrete path without a pause, without a glance at his well-polished black Italian shoes. He stood in the centre of the grass, legs apart, arms folded, and he called up to the window in the authentic voice of one who had ascended the ladder of rank in the police force, a chill clear tone without regional accent, without pretension to culture, almost uninflected, the note of a sensitively programmed robot: 'This is Detective Superintendent Ronald Spenser. Come to the window. I want to talk to you.'

It seemed as if the curtains fluttered with greater violence but this might only have been the wind blowing coincidentally.

'Can you hear me? Come to the window, please.'

The curtains continued to move but did not part. Fleetwood, on the pavement now with DC Bridges, saw the camera crew elbowing through the crowd – unmistakable newshounds, even if you couldn't see their van parked on the street corner. One of them began setting up a tripod. And then something happened to make all of them jump. Rosemary Stanley screamed.

The scream was a dreadful sound, tearing the air. The crowd acknowledged it with a noise like an echo of that scream coming from a long way off, half gasp, half murmur of distress. Spenser, who had started like the rest of them, stood his ground, digging in his heels, positively sinking into the mud, his shoulders hunched, as if to show his firmness of purpose, his determination not to be moved. But he didn't speak again. Fleetwood thought what everyone thought, what perhaps Spenser himself thought: that his speech had caused the action that had caused the scream.

If the man with the gun had done as he was bidden and come to the window, it would have provided a distraction, under cover of which Fleetwood and Bridges might have climbed up the house and gone in at the open window. No doubt the man too knew that. Fleetwood felt strangely comforted, though. There had been no detonation. Rosemary Stanley hadn't screamed because she had been shot. Spenser, having demonstrated his fearlessness and his phlegm, turned from the house and slowly walked across the soggy grass, the path, opened the gate, came out on to the pavement, gave the crowd a blank dispassionate stare. He said to Fleetwood, 'You'll have to think about going in.'

Fleetwood was conscious of his photograph being taken, a shot of the side of his head and a bit of profile. It was Spenser's face they really wanted a picture of. Suddenly the curtains were flung apart and the man with the gun stood there. It was funny the way it reminded Fleetwood of the pantomime he and Diana had taken her niece to at Christmas: a pair of curtains thrown apart and a man appearing dramatically between them. The villain of the piece. The Demon King. The crowd sighed. A woman in the crowd uttered a high-pitched giggle of hysteria, which was abruptly cut off as if she had laid her hand across her mouth.

'You've got twenty minutes,' said the man with the gun.

'Where did you get the gun, John?' said Spenser.

John? thought Fleetwood. Why John? Because Lesley Allan or Sheila Manners or one of the other girls had said so, or just for Spenser to have the satisfaction of hearing him say, 'My name's not John'?

'These replicas are very good, aren't they?' Spenser said

conversationally. 'It takes experience to tell the difference. I wouldn't say expert knowledge, but experience, yes.'

Fleetwood was part of the crowd now, caught up in it, as was Bridges. They were pushing their way through it towards the main road. How long could Spenser keep him talking? Not long, if all he could do was mock him, take the piss about that gun. From behind him he heard, 'You've got just seventeen minutes.'

'All right, Ted, let's talk.'

That was better, though Fleetwood wished Spenser would stop calling the man with the gun by phony Christian names. He was out of earshot now, out beyond the crowd and in the main road, where the traffic was jammed solid. He and Bridges went down the alley, closed to vehicles by an iron bollard, that became the lane at the back of the houses. The Stanley house was easy to find, distinguished by the ugly concrete garage. By this time the man with the gun might easily have closed that sash window, but he hadn't. Of course, if the window had been closed, it would have made it virtually impossible to get into the house, at any rate to get in silently, so Fleetwood ought to have been pleased, he thought, that John or Ted or whatever his name was hadn't thought to close it. But instead it struck him with a sense of vague cold dismay. Surely if the window hadn't been closed, this was not inadvertent. It had been left open for a purpose.

Now they were once more near enough to hear Spenser's voice and the voice of the man with the gun. Spenser was saying something about letting Rosemary Stanley out of the house before they could begin bargaining. Let her come down the stairs and out of the front door and then they could start making terms and conditions. Fleetwood couldn't hear the man's reply. He put his right foot up on to the wisteria where it bent at almost a right angle, his left foot a yard higher into the fork and then hauled himself on to the extension roof . . . Now all he had to do was swing his leg over the sill. He wished he could still hear the voices but he could hear nothing but the groaning of brakes on the main road, the mindless sporadic hooting of

14

impatient drivers. Bridges started to climb up. It was odd the things you noticed at times of tension and of test. The last thing that mattered now was the colour the windowsill was painted. Yet Fleetwood took note of the colour, Cretan Blue, the same shade as that on the front door of the house he and Diana were buying in Chigwell.

Fleetwood found himself in the bathroom. It had green-tiled walls and on the floor creamy-white tiles. Footprints, made in liquid mud and now dry, crossed it, growing fainter as they reached the door. The man with the gun had come in this way. Bridges was outside the window now, bracing his weight on the sill. Fleetwood had to open the door, though he couldn't think of anything he had ever wanted to do less. He was not brave, he thought, he had too much imagination, and sometimes (though this was no time to think of it) it seemed to him that a more contemplative, scholarly life would have suited him better than police work.

From here the traffic sounds were very faint in the distance. Somewhere in the house a floorboard creaked. Fleetwood could also hear or feel a regular throbbing but this, he knew, was his own heart. He swallowed and opened the door. The landing outside was not at all what he had expected. It had a thick pale cream carpet and at the head of the stairs there was a polished wooden handrail and on the stair wall were little pictures in gilt and silver frames, drawings and engravings of birds and animals, and one of Dürer's *Praying Hands*. This was a house where people were happy and where loving care had been expended on its furnishings and its maintenance. A surge of anger came to Fleetwood because what was happening in the house now was an assault on this quiet contentment, a desecration.

He stood on the landing, holding the handrail. The three bedroom doors were all closed. He looked at the drawing of a hare and the drawing of a bat with a face that was vaguely human, vaguely pig-like, and wondered what there was about rape that made any man want to do it. For his part he couldn't really enjoy sex unless the woman wanted it just as much as he. Those poor girls, he thought. The

15

girl and the man with the gun were behind the door to the left of where Fleetwood now stood – on the right, as far as the observers outside were concerned. The man with the gun knew what he was doing. He wasn't going to be fool enough to leave the front of the house unmanned while investigating what went on at the back.

Fleetwood reasoned: if he shoots me, I can only die, or not die and get well again. His imagination had its limits. Later on he was to remember what he had thought in his innocence. He stood outside the closed door, put his hand to it and said in a bold clear voice, 'This is Detective Sergeant Fleetwood. We are in the house. Please open this door.'

There had not been total silence before. Fleetwood realized this because there was total silence now. He waited and spoke again.

'Your best course is to open this door. Be sensible and give yourself up. Open the door now and come out or let me in.'

It had hardly occurred to him the door might not be locked. He tried the handle and it gave. Fleetwood felt a bit of a fool – which, in a curious way, helped. He opened the door, not flinging it; it flung itself, being the kind of door that always swings open to hit with a crash the piece of furniture immediately to the right of its arc.

The room burst into view before him like a stage set: a single bed with blue covers and blue bedspread thrown back, a bedside cabinet with on it a lamp, a mug, a book, a vase containing a single peacock feather, walls papered in more green and blue peacock feathers, wind blowing through the broken window, lifting high the emerald-green silk curtains. The man with the gun stood with his back to a corner wardrobe, pointing the gun at Fleetwood, the girl in front of him, his free arm round her waist.

He had reached a pitch of dangerous panic. Fleetwood could tell that by the change in his face. It was scarcely the same face as that which had twice appeared at the window, having been overtaken by animal terror and by a regression to instinct. All that mattered to this man now was self-preservation; he had a passion for it, but in this passion there was no wisdom, no prudence, only a need to escape by killing all who hindered him. Yet he had killed no one, thought Fleetwood, and he held a replica gun . . .

'If you put that gun down now,' he said, 'and let Miss Stanley go, let me take Miss Stanley downstairs . . . if you do that, you know the charges brought against you will be minimal compared to what they might be if you injure or threaten anyone else.' And the rapes? he wondered. There was no proof yet that this was the same man. 'You need not drop the gun. Just lower the hand you're holding the gun in. Lift your other arm and let Miss Stanley go.'

The man didn't move. He was holding the girl so tightly that the veins on his hand stood out blue. The expression on his face was intensifying as his frown deepened; the skin around his eyes creased further and the eyes themselves began to burn.

Fleetwood heard sounds at the front of the house. A scuffling and a thud. The sounds were drowned in rain noise as a sudden hard shower lashed the unbroken upper part of the window. The curtains blew in and ballooned. The man with the gun hadn't moved. Fleetwood didn't really expect him to speak and it was a shock when he did. The voice was strangled with panic, not much more than a murmur.

'This gun I have is not a replica. It's for real. You'd better believe me.'

'Where did you get it?' said Fleetwood, in whom nerves affected his stomach rather than his throat. His voice was steady but he was beginning to feel sick.

'Someone I know took it off a dead German in 1945.'

'You saw that on TV,' said Fleetwood. Behind him Bridges was standing in the short passage behind which were the banisters and the stairwell. He could feel Bridges's breath, warm in the cold air. 'Who was "someone"?'

'Why should I tell you?' A very red tongue came out and moistened lips which were the same olive shade as the man's skin. 'It was my uncle.'

A shiver went through Fleetwood because an uncle

17

would be the right sort of age, an uncle would be in his fifties now, twenty-five or thirty years older than this man. 'Let Miss Stanley go,' he said. 'Why not? What have you got to gain by holding on to her? I'm not armed. She's not protecting you.'

The girl didn't move. She was afraid to move. She sagged over the supporting arm that held her so tightly, a small thin girl in a blue cotton nightdress, her bare arms goose-pimpled. Fleetwood knew he must make no promises he wouldn't be permitted to keep.

'Let her go and I can guarantee it will count very much in your favour. I'm not making any promises, mind, but it will count in your favour.'

There was a thudding sound which Fleetwood was pretty sure was someone putting a ladder with padded ends up against the wall of the house. The man with the gun didn't seem to have heard. Fleetwood swallowed and took two steps into the room. Bridges was behind him and now the man with the gun saw Bridges. He lifted the hand which held the gun an inch or two and pointed it up towards Fleetwood's face. At the same time he drew his other arm from round Rosemary Stanley's waist, as if pulling his nails hard across the skin. And indeed the girl did give a shuddering whimper, shrinking her body. He pulled his arm back very sharply and kneed her in the back so that she staggered and fell forwards on to all-fours.

'I don't want her,' he said. 'She's no use to me.'

Fleetwood said quite pleasantly, 'That's very sensible of you.'

'You've got to make me a promise though.'

'Come over here, Miss Stanley, please,' Fleetwood said. 'You'll be quite safe.' Would she? God knew. The girl crawled, pulled herself up, came towards him and held his sleeve with both hands. He repeated it though. 'You're quite safe now.'

The man with the gun also repeated himself. His teeth had begun to chatter and he gobbled his words.

'You've got to make me a promise.'

'What, then?'

Fleetwood looked past him and, as the wind raised the curtains almost to ceiling level, saw the head and shoulders of Detective Constable Irving appear at the window. The DC's body blocked half the light but the man with the gun didn't seem to notice. He said, 'Promise I can go out of here by the bathroom and give me five minutes. That's all – five minutes.'

Irving was about to step over the sash. Fleetwood thought, it's all over, we've beaten him, he'll be quiet as a lamb now. He took the girl in his arms, hugged her for no reason but that she was young and terrified, and thrust her at Bridges, turning his back on the man with the gun, hearing behind him the chattering voice say, 'It's real, I warned you, I told you.'

'Take her downstairs.'

Above the banisters, on the wall down which the staircase ran, hung the reproduction of those praying hands, a steel engraving. Across the front of it came Bridges to hold the girl and take her down. It was one of those eternal moments, infinite yet swift as a flash. Fleetwood saw the hands that prayed for him, for them all, as Bridges, whose body had obscured it, moved down the stairs. Behind him a heavy foot dropped on to the floor, a sash slammed, a chattering voice gave a cry, and something struck Fleetwood in the back. It all happened very slowly and very quickly. The explosion seemed to come from far away, a car backfiring on the main road perhaps. There was no more pain, and no less, than from a punch into the base of the spine.

He saw as he fell forward the loosely clasped beseeching hands, the engraved hands, sweep upwards above his view. Slumping against the banisters, he clutched on to them, slipping down as might a child holding on to the bars of a cot. He was fully conscious and, strangely, there was no more pain from that punch in the back, only an enormous tiredness.

A voice that had once been soft and low he could hear screaming shrilly: 'He asked for it, I told him, I warned

19

him, he wouldn't believe me. Why wouldn't he believe me? He made me do it.'

He made me do – what? Nothing much anyway, Fleetwood thought, and holding on to the bars, he tried to pull himself up. But his body had grown heavy and would not move, heavy as lead, numb, weighed down or pinned or glued to the floor. The red wetness spreading across the carpet surprised him and he said to all the people, 'Whose blood is that?'

2

All his life, for almost as far back as he could remember, Victor had had a phobia. A teacher at college to whom he had been unwise enough to mention it had called it chelonophobia, which he claimed to have made up from the Greek. He made stupid cracks about it whenever the opportunity arose, such as when the Principal's cat wandered into the lecture room one day or when someone was discussing *Alice in Wonderland*. Victor had his phobia quite badly, to the extent of not wanting to hear the creature named or even to name it himself in his thoughts, or to see a picture of it in a book or some toy or ornament made in its image, of which many thousands were in existence.

During the past ten years and a bit he had neither seen it nor heard it spoken of, but sometimes it (or one of its allotropes) had come to him in dreams. That had always happened and presumably always would, but he fancied he was a bit better about the phobia than he had used to be, for he no longer screamed aloud in his sleep. Georgie would have told him if he had. Even when he only moaned a little Georgie made enough fuss about it. One of those dreams had come last night, his final night in there, but he had learned by now how to wake himself up, which he did, whimpering and reaching out with his hands for reality.

The girl came for him in her car. He sat beside her in the front but he didn't look out much, he didn't really want to see the world yet. It was when they stopped at a red light and he turned his head aside that he saw the pet shop, and that reminded him he would be a prey to his phobia once more. Not that there was anything of that sort in the window, no reptiles of any kind, but a white puppy and two kittens playing in a pile of straw. He shivered just the same.

'You all right, Victor?' the girl said.

'Fine,' he said.

It was Acton they were going to – not his favourite place, but they hadn't given him much choice. Somewhere not totally unfamiliar, they had suggested – Acton, say, or Finchley or Golders Green. Well, Golders Green might be on the expensive side. He had said Acton would be all right, he had grown up there, his parents had died there, he had an aunt living there still. He found looking out of the car and seeing the familiar place, the same yet changed, still there, still going on while he had been a decade away, almost unbearably painful. That was something he hadn't expected. He closed his eyes and kept them closed until he felt the car turn and head northwards. Hanger Lane? No, Twyford Avenue. This was motherland and fatherland all right. They weren't going to stick him in the same street, were they? They weren't. Mrs Griffiths's house in Tolleshunt Avenue was three or four streets further west. Victor thought he would have liked to stay sitting in the car for ever but he got out and stood on the pavement, feeling dizzy.

The girl led the way. Victor followed her up the path. She had one of those handbags that are divided into many compartments with zip-up sections and extraneous purses, and from one of these she took a ring with two keys on it, one of gold metal, one of silver. It was the gold one she inserted into the lock, opening the door. She turned and gave him a reassuring smile. All he could see at first was the staircase. Most of the hall was behind it. The girl, whose name was Judy Bratner and who had asked Victor to call her Judy from the start, led the way up the stairs. The room was on the first floor, its door opened by the silver metal key. Victor was surprised to see how small the room was, for Judy had told him what the rent would be, though he would not be paying it, and he stood on the threshold for a moment, letting his eyes travel from the tiny sink and draining board in one corner to the curtainless window with its cotton blind and thence to the beanpole figure of Judy and her earnest well-meaning dedicated face.

The blind was down and Judy's first self-appointed task was to raise it. Some diffident apologetic sunshine came in. Judy stood by the window, smiling more confidently now, as if she had personally caused the sun to shine and had created – by painting it on canvas perhaps – the view. Victor went to the window and stood beside her, looking out. His right shoulder was a good six inches from her left shoulder but nevertheless she flinched a little and moved fractionally to the right. No doubt she couldn't help it, it was a reflex action, for she would know about his past.

Looking down, he could see the street where he had been born and brought up. Which house it was he couldn't be precisely sure from here, but it was one of those in the terrace with the grey slate roofs and the long narrow gardens separated from each other by chestnut paling fences. In one of those houses, for the first time, he had seen it . . .

Judy spoke regretfully and as if she had had to brace herself to do it. 'We haven't been able to come up with any sort of job for you, Victor. And I'm afraid there's no prospect of anything just at this moment in time.'

How they talked! He knew about unemployment, how it had come up like a cloud during the latter part of his lost years and now hung fog-like over the whole country.

'You might go to the Job Centre yourself once you've settled in here. Of course you'd have to be open about your . . .' She sought a word, preferably a euphemistic piece of jargon.

'Antecedents,' he said flatly.

She seemed not to have heard, though her face coloured. 'In the interim,' she said, 'it will take you a while to find your feet here. Things will seem a bit strange at first – externals, I mean. But we've talked about that.'

Not as much, in fact, as Victor had expected. Other prisoners, coming to the end of their terms, had been gradually acclimatised to the outside world, taken out for a day, let out for a weekend. Nothing like that had been done for him and he wondered if there had been new rulings on release techniques for long-term prisoners. Newspapers found their way into the prison and there was no ban on reading them daily, but they were not *serious* newspapers, the kind known as 'quality', and they gave you headlines and pictures rather than information. For instance, after that talk with the governor which had taken place early on, there had hardly been any news about the policeman.

Then, six months before his release was due, his 'rehabilitation programme' began. He was told about this in advance but all that happened was that Judy Bratner or her colleague, a man called Tom Welch, came to talk to him for half an hour once a fortnight. They were voluntary associates of the Probation and After-care Service or some such thing, though emphatically not to be called prison visitors. Exactly what they were and whom they were Victor had never found out, because Judy and Tom, though kind and bent on helping him, treated him as if he were a very stupid illiterate twelve-year-old. He didn't care because he didn't want to know. If they would do as they promised and find him somewhere to live and tell him how to get the Department of Health and Social Security to keep him, that was all he wanted. Now what he wanted was for Judy to go.

'Oh, I almost forgot,' she said. 'I have to show you where the bathroom is.'

It was at the end of the passage, down six steps and round a corner, a small cold room painted the green of tinned peas.

'All you can possibly want, you see.'

She began explaining to him how the room heater could be made to function by the insertion of twenty-pence pieces and the water heater fifty-pence pieces. Victor couldn't recall ever having seen a twenty-pence piece. It was one of those new coins. There was a pound coin now too, he seemed to remember. They walked back along the passage. A strip of beaded wood, which Victor thought was called a chair rail, ran along the wall at waist height, and on the plaster above this rail, in letters no more than half an inch high, someone had written in pencil: *The shit will hit the fan*.

'Now I'm going to leave this number with you, Victor, so that you can give us a call if there's anything bothering you. Well, there are two numbers, just to be on the safe side. We don't want you to feel you're out on your own. We want you to feel there are some supportive people who do genuinely care. Right?'

Victor nodded.

'Of course, needless to say, I or Tom will pop back in a day or two to see how you're making out. Did I tell you the pay phone's on the ground floor, just back of the stairs? You'll need five- and ten-pence pieces for that. Now you're OK for money, aren't you, till your DHSS comes through? I'm afraid Mrs Griffiths, who owns this house, she does *know*. I just thought I'd tell you, but there's no way she couldn't be told.' Judy's face screwed up with the agonizing effort of it. Her working life consisted in recounting horrible unpalatable truths – there is no job, there is no security, comfort, ease, peace, future – and it was beginning to show on her troubled pinched face. 'I mean, we always have to tell them because they'd find out, you know. Actually, Mrs Griffiths has been on our books quite a while.'

What did that mean? That half or all the other tenants were also ex-prisoners? Ex-criminals?

'But she doesn't live on the premises,' Judy said with the air of one telling first the bad news, then the good. She seemed to be searching for a remark with which to take her leave and grabbed at a whole clutch. 'It's really a nice area, not at all rough. This is a quiet street, not a through road. You might think about joining things, making friends. What about an evening class?'

Over the banisters, he watched her go downstairs. The front door closed behind her. He wondered if he were alone in the house. There was no internal sound at all. He listened and heard Judy's car start up, then a heavier vehicle with a diesel engine park further down the street, the shriek of a woman, followed by a ringing laugh. Victor went back into his room and closed the door. Judy or someone had placed on the draining board and the shelf beside it a wrapped loaf, a carton of margarine, long-life milk, canned mince and canned beans, tea bags, instant coffee and granulated sugar. The staples of English working-class diet as seen through the eyes of a social worker.

Victor examined the sink, the taps, the small cylindrical water heater, familiarizing himself with the place. Between sink and window was a cupboard, of triangular shape, formed by constructing a frame with a door in it across this corner of the room. Inside it hung his few clothes, some of which, he saw, were those he had possessed in that far-off time before his imprisonment. Everything he had owned then had gone into his parents' keeping, and both his parents were now dead, his father having died first and his mother a mere six months later. Victor had been told he might be temporarily released to attend his parents' funerals, but he had not wished to do so. It would have been embarrassing.

The bed was a single size, made up with pink nylon sheets, two multicoloured blankets manufactured in the Third (or maybe Fourth or Fifth) World and a cover that had seen better days as a french-window curtain. The tape through which the hooks had been inserted was still attached to it. The only chair in the room was of Korean cane and there was a cane and glass coffee table on the stout frame, on which someone – the graffitist prophet of disaster? – had stubbed out a hundred cigarettes, giving almost but not quite the effect of pokerwork. Upon the slippery linoleum, red-patterned with cream rectangles so that the impression given was of ravioli in tomato sauce, lay two small rugs of green nylon fur.

Victor looked out of the window. The sun had gone in and the roofs of West Acton lay red and grey and terracotta under a pale grey sky across which a large gleaming unidentifiable aircraft was making its way to Heathrow. There was no wind and it was very clear. A main road could be seen along which traffic flowed in a metallic stream. This road was just behind the gardens of the street where his parents' house had been – or, rather, where stood the house his parents had rented for the duration of their married life. He was glad they were dead – not from any conventional or sentimental standpoint, such as shame at having to confront them or fear of giving them pain, but simply because here was one additional trouble and stumbling block out of the way. Yet he had loved his mother deeply, or had told himself he had so often that he believed it.

When he had gone to prison he had supposed he would begin regular sessions with a psychiatrist, for in pronouncing sentence the judge had repeated the jury's recommendation that he should receive psychiatric treatment. But he had never seen a psychiatrist – on account he supposed of shortage of funds or shortage of psychiatrists – and the only time it had been suggested that treatment might be meted out to him for a possible mental instability had been when he was asked, only two years ago, if he would care to volunteer for group therapy as part of an experiment carried out by a visiting sociologist. Victor had refused and no more had been said. But while he had been awaiting the summons to a psychiatrist in those early days he had sometimes turned over in his mind what he would say to this man or woman when the time came. Most of all he had thought about his phobia and the grotesque way it had begun and about the panics and the violent anger. He had asked himself too why the child of happily married middle-class parents, whose childhood had been for the most part uneventful and contented, should have needed to make motiveless unreasoning attacks on women.

A psychiatrist might have come up with some answers. On his own, Victor had not been able to supply any. And he became angry when he thought about his anger, panicky and confused when he tried to examine his panics. Sometimes he thought of them as symptoms of some disease he had caught, for they could not have been inherited nor yet brought into being by ill-usage or neglect when he was young. In prison what he had felt most of the time, more than any other emotion, was self-pity.

27

One day the Governor had sent for him. Victor thought it might be to tell him that his father, who had been unwell, was worse or even dying. But in fact his father was not to die for another five years. A prison officer took him to the Governor's office and sat down in a chair specially provided for such custodians, more or less between Victor and the Governor, who was in any case protected by his large oak desk. The warder sat in the way warders and policemen waiting for something or keeping a watch on people always do sit: upright, legs apart, hands folded in lap, and wearing an expression of blank idiocy.

'Well, Jenner,' the Governor said, 'we thought you might care to have some news of the progress made by Detective-Sergeant Fleetwood. Am I right?'

'Yes, sir,' said Victor. What else could he say? He would have liked to say he didn't care and it was nothing to him. He would have liked to pick up the inkwell from the desk and hurl it at the Governor's head, seeing the ink drip down the Governor's chin like black blood on to his immaculate collar. But he wanted to get the maximum remission. In those days he longed to get out.

'Sergeant Fleetwood has been in Stoke Mandeville Hospital for a year now. That is the orthopaedic hospital, you understand, which means specializing in injuries to the spine and limbs.'

It didn't mean that. It meant correcting deformities. But the Governor was an ignorant bastard who spoke to everybody alike, as if they were all the same illiterate boneheads.

'I'm glad to tell you he has made great strides . . .' The Governor seemed to realize what he had said and, pausing, he cleared his throat. 'Of course he cannot walk without a mechanical aid, but there are hopes he may one day be able to do so. He is in good spirits and will soon be leaving hospital to make a life for himself in his own surroundings.'

'Thank you, sir,' said Victor.

Before the trial, while he was on remand in custody, he had read articles in the newspapers about Sergeant Fleetwood. He had never felt pity for him, only contempt and a kind of exasperation. If Fleetwood had been sensible, had listened to him and believed him, if he had believed him when he said the gun was a real gun, Fleetwood would be a fit vigorous man today, a man leading a normal life and doing his job. But he hadn't listened and Victor had lost his head. It was something he did in times of great stress or pressure; he always had. He lost his head, panicked and did things in that panic. Which was why it had been wrong to charge him with and convict him for attempted murder. He had not *intended* to kill or even maim or hurt Fleetwood. Panic came over him like a kind of electric suit, fitting him as a second skin, prickling him all over, crawling on him, tingling and sending into his hand an impulse that pulled that trigger and fired that gun. That was the only way he could describe what one of his panics was like: an electric suit full of tingling wires.

There had been a sentimental article about Fleetwood in one of the popular tabloid papers. It said that his first name was David and he was twenty-eight (the same age as Victor) and engaged to be married to a girl called Diana Walker. There was a picture of her and him taken at their engagement party. The article made much of the fact that Fleetwood had been due to get married the following week. He hadn't got married but his girlfriend told the paper that they were only waiting for Fleetwood's superficial injuries to heal. She was going to marry him just as soon as she could. Never mind if he couldn't move, couldn't walk and might never walk again, she was only too happy to have him alive. They would win through, the two of them together. It was being together that was important. There was nothing in the article about Victor Jenner. Of course there couldn't be – nothing about what a monster he was and how it was a pity people like him couldn't be flogged within an inch of their lives – because that would be *sub judice*. But there was a great deal about what a wonderful policeman Fleetwood had been. The way they wrote about him, his brilliant brain, sweet nature, invincible courage, unselfishness, powers of judgement and deductive faculties, made you wonder why he wasn't at least a chief superintendent or maybe Attorney General.

Victor saw him as the instrument whereby he had been sent to prison for fourteen years.

After that interview with the Governor, Victor had never been told another word about Fleetwood. He didn't see newspapers every day. Sometimes he didn't see a newspaper for weeks on end. But one day, some two years later, he did read a paragraph about a charity concert at the Albert Hall organized in aid of the dependants of injured policemen, and this concert had been compèred by David Fleetwood. There was no picture but the paragraph mentioned that Fleetwood had introduced the performers from his wheelchair.

Most of what went on in the prison the Governor knew nothing about. Word had got round as to details of Victor's conduct before he shot the policeman; the other men in the prison knew he was the Kensal Rise rapist and they all had a kind of virtuous antipathy towards rapists just as they did towards child molesters. It was all right to beat old ladies over the head in tobacconists' shops and break into the till, it was OK to rob banks; but rape was something else again, beyond the pale.

Victor knew what it was like to be raped now. Four of them raped him one night and Cal, who later became his instructor in the office furniture shop, told him afterwards that maybe that would teach him not to do it again. In pain and bleeding but not on this occasion in a panic, Victor fixed him with a cold stare and managed, though there were tears on his face, a small tight smile. He was staring and smiling at such ineffable ignorance of human nature and life and the way men are.

Did something like that teach you not to do it again? Victor didn't know. His eyes, while he had been dwelling on the past, had been fixed mesmerically on what he thought was the roof of the house he had lived in as a child, a red patch among other reds and greys, the white of streets and the green of gardens. He shook himself and blinked his eyes to break the hypnosis.

It was April. The clocks had gone on three weeks before and the days were long and light. Immediately below this window was a garden of sorts with a shed in it, four dustbins and a rusted filing cabinet. In prison he had worked in the office furniture shop, making filing cabinets like that one and stands for photocopiers and swivel chairs. Of course that couldn't be one of his grown old, for items made by prisoners were not allowed to be sold to the general public. Mrs Griffiths's garden wasn't the kind you sat in or gardened in but the kind you ran out into with a bag of rubbish or to fetch a bucket of coal. A good many similar junk-filled backyards were visible as well as tended gardens, but otherwise it was all backs of houses. Victor wondered if Judy and Tom had purposely arranged it this way to avoid Victor's seeing people walking along when he looked out of his window . . .

What they wouldn't want him to see were women.

Was he crazy to think like this, to attribute such caution to others? As soon as he went out he would see women. They were half the human race. Judy and Tom might not know, he told himself, and Judy might have flinched and drawn away from him for quite some other reason.

It wasn't, after all, for rape that he had gone to prison but for attempted murder.

3

That first night he lay in bed listing in his mind all the things he had to do. He hadn't been able to bring himself to go out, for as soon as he opened the door and stepped on to the landing and heard voices from below and a girl's laugh, the electric suit had begun to fit itself around his body and his limbs, fastening itself at the neck and constricting his throat, prickling his wrists and ankles and squeezing his chest. Into the room he had retreated, gasping for breath. He had covered his head and the upper part of his body with bedclothes and lain on the bed for some half an hour. Then he got up and made himself tea and baked beans on bread, taking strong deep breaths all the time to steady himself. It took a deliberate effort of will and great concentration to make himself think of practical things but at last, after it got dark and he was lying in bed with the blind down and the top light and bedlamp on, he succeeded. The DHSS first, then register with a doctor, go to the bank and find out about his money. Then a telephone call to his aunt in Gunnersbury. Then the Job Centre.

Great changes must have taken place, out there in the outside. Some intimation of this had come to him during the ride home with Judy. He fancied London looked dirtier and the people shabbier, and it all somehow looked *bigger*, though he could have imagined that. And he knew nobody, he had no friends, he was utterly alone. He remembered boasting in the old days that he didn't know what loneliness was, he liked his own company, but now he was less sure. Doubts came to him as to what he meant by his own company, as to exactly what that was.

He had shared a cell for so long in a building full of

people that he found himself afraid of the comparative solitude of this room. But he finally did sleep and his sleep was crowded with dreams. He had always been a great dreamer and had dreamed a lot in prison, especially the dream about the road through life and the houses and, of course, inevitably the phobia dream, but never about the house in Kensal Rise, at 62 Solent Gardens. Now, after more than ten years, he did. He was in that bedroom again, an animal in a den with the hunters coming first by the back way, then by the front. As a hostage the girl was hopeless because he could only kill her and then what could he do? At this point in the dream Victor realized he was dreaming, for things had not actually happened quite like this. He thought he would wake himself out of the dream before it got to the bad part.

Fleetwood opened the door and came in – only it wasn't Fleetwood, it was himself, or his mirror image. Victor heard himself shouting at Fleetwood to send a real policeman, not someone disguised, and Fleetwood, as if he understood, metamorphosed before his eyes, growing taller and thinner and paler. Behind him, on the wall, hung a picture, a line drawing or engraving, whose subject Victor could not make out, but which he feared.

'I'm dreaming,' Victor said, and he closed his eyes and opened them again, willing himself to wake, but the dream refused to go. 'This is a real gun,' he said to Fleetwood. 'I got it from my uncle who was a high-ranking officer in the German army. You'd better believe me.'

'Of course I believe you,' Fleetwood said, and then Victor knew there wasn't going to be a bad part to the dream. 'You can have ten minutes to get away in. I'm not looking, see? I'm looking at this picture.'

Fleetwood turned his back and looked at the picture, leaning on the banisters. It wasn't what Victor thought it might be but a pair of praying hands. With his arm round the girl, Victor went past him into the bathroom; only, when they got there, it wasn't a bathroom but his Aunt Muriel's house in Gunnersbury, and his mother and father were there and his aunt and uncle, having tea. When his mother saw the girl she got up and said, 'Hallo, Pauline, you *are* a stranger.'

Victor woke up. The room was full of sunshine. He reflected on his dream. How many people had to dream of things that happened ten years before and of people who were dead or disappeared because they knew no one new? Of course knowing no one worked both ways. He didn't know them – and they didn't know him. That, however, was something which would rapidly change. It would soon change if he registered with a doctor, made himself known to his fellow tenants and did what Judy had suggested in the way of joining evening classes.

He would have to tell everyone he encountered who he was and where he had been for the past ten years. He would either have to do that or tell elaborate lies. Change his name, for a start, say he had been ill or living abroad. If he was going to do that, he must do it from the start. He mustn't even stay in this house longer than was strictly necessary. First, though, it was absolutely essential to go out. Rather as a man who has been in a motor accident knows he must as soon as possible get into a car and drive it again or he never will, Victor knew he must go outdoors. It had been bad getting into Judy's car and being driven here. Everything had seemed very big and changed and unreal. And that was nothing to how it would feel if he were on foot with no strong capsule of glass and metal to protect him. But go he must, and this morning.

He waited, lying in bed, until the sounds in the house ceased. The night before he had calculated that there were four other occupied rooms in the house, so when he heard the front door slam four times he got up. There might be more people, of course, wives who didn't work or old people, but that was a chance he had to take. As it happened, he met no one on his way to or from the bathroom. He dressed in clothes that had been his before his arrest, a pair of grey worsted trousers and a green velvet cord jacket. The trousers were tight on him and he had to draw in the belt under his belly, for he had put on weight in prison, on account no doubt of the stodgy food.

Getting out wasn't easy. He went back twice, once because he thought he hadn't closed the window, and the second time – by then he was at the foot of the stairs – because he thought he might be cold and need a sweater. The big sunny windy terrible outdoors received him like icy water receives a naked diver. He gasped for air and the air rushed in to fill his lungs. For a while he had to stand still and hold on to the gatepost. This, presumably, was the agoraphobia from which his Auntie Muriel said she suffered. At any rate, his mother used to tell him she hadn't been out of doors for five years. If she felt like this, he could understand it.

Presently he began to walk slowly along the street in the direction of Acton High Road. This led him past the house where he used to live. He walked along fearfully with a powerful sense that he was being followed. Every few seconds he found himself looking round sharply but there was never anyone there. He thought what a lot of cars there were, cars parked everywhere, double, treble the number there had been ten years ago. A woman came out of her front door and slammed it. The sound made him jump and he almost cried out. Outside the gate of his parents' house he stopped and looked at it.

His mother hadn't been a fussy or even very careful housekeeper and in her day, from the outside certainly, the place had had a drab look. There had been curtains of different, and not very attractive, patterns at all the windows. Now every window was festooned with snowy white net, gauzy flounces ruched and looped up like a girl's petticoat. Victor had a strange feeling of breathlessness and an indefinable discomfort when this particular comparison came to him. Girls didn't wear petticoats, did they? Not unless fashions had changed drastically. He relaxed a bit when he remembered that his mother herself had possessed just such a petticoat, white and frilly and stiffened, in the mid-fifties, when such garments enjoyed a vogue.

The stucco surface of the house had been painted white as icing on a Christmas cake and the woodwork a bright emerald green. On either side of the front door were green and white tubs with cypress trees in them. Victor realized that the house looked so well tended because its occupants owned it. You took more interest in the appearance of a house when it was yours. His grandmother, his mother's mother, had been the original tenant, and when his parents got married they went to live with her. That was just after the Second World War. His grandmother died a few months before he was born and his parents continued with the tenancy, the rent being so low and the housing shortage so acute. His mother had been a happy woman who had had the good fortune to fall in love, marry the man she was in love with and remain in love with him for the thirty-five years until he died. Victor had never been in love and couldn't imagine what it would be like. His mother had been only fifty-seven when she died. His father, who was ten years older, had died first. He had had a stroke five years after Victor went to prison and after that could only get about in a wheelchair. Propelling himself along the pavement one summer morning – on this very stretch of pavement, Victor supposed, between here and the corner – he had keeled over and died, running the wheelchair into a brick wall and overturning it. The cause of death was a massive heart attack. What his mother had died of Victor didn't know, though the death certificate which he had been shown gave the cause as coronary disease, which was surprising because she had been a strong woman. She had survived his father by only six months. But perhaps it wasn't so surprising, for her husband had been her whole life, the heart and core of her existence. Victor had sometimes tried to imagine how life had been for his mother on her own, but he had simply been unable to see her without his father.

From babyhood Victor had been used to the society of demonstrative people. His mother was young and pretty and his father was always touching her, putting his arm round her and kissing her. They never sat in chairs but always on the settee, holding hands. When he looked back (as he did when rehearsing what to say to the psychiatrist), he was never able to see his parents singly or recall times when he had been alone with his mother, though these must have been numerous, as for instance after school before his father returned from work. They never quarrelled, as far as he could remember. They were kind, affectionate parents too, and if Victor's mother always seemed to favour her husband over her son, as in the case of serving him first at table or giving him preference when it came to titbits – this was the hungry aftermath of war – Victor would have told the psychiatrist that this was only what he would have expected, his father being older and bigger and more powerful than he.

His parents had few friends and almost the only visitors to the house were relatives. They were all in all to each other, locked in an exclusive relationship of companionability, devotion and sex. Victor's mother answered all his questions about sex carefully and fearlessly so that by the time he was five he knew how babies were made and knew too that parents went on doing that thing that makes babies, the man pushing his willy into the lady's bottom, even when they don't want babies but because it was right and, his father said, what men and women were for. His father drew diagrams for him – well, he didn't exactly draw them, he traced them out of a book, which rather disillusioned Victor – and answered questions his mother couldn't or wouldn't answer, such as what wet dreams were and how it felt to want to do that thing that made (or did not make) babies.

For all that, he never really connected it with his own parents. Once, when he was about six, getting up to go to the bathroom, he had passed their bedroom door and heard his mother groaning: 'Don't, don't – Oh, no, no, no!' and then she gave a low howl like an animal. But she had looked so happy before she went to bed! With that howl still in his ears, he remembered her soft rippling giggle, her sidelong smile at his father, her hand caressing the nape of his neck. Victor wasn't at all afraid of his parents but he was afraid to go into the room. Just the same he screwed up his courage and tried the door handle. The door was locked. Next morning the first thing he heard when he woke was his mother singing. She was singing a pop song of the time called 'Mr Sandman, bring me a dream'. There was a line in it that went 'Tell me that my lonesome nights are over'. She came into Victor's bedroom still laughing at something his father had said and she gave Victor a morning kiss and said it was a beautiful day and swept the curtains back to let the sun in. So he knew it was all right and that she wasn't hurt but happy. He even wondered if he had dreamed what he had heard, if in fact Mr Sandman had brought him this dream like in the song. He still wondered that. Certainly he had never listened outside that door again, which was why he had been utterly flabbergasted when, years later when Victor was in his twenties, he heard his father telling someone what a nuisance he had been when a little boy – 'a pest', his father called him – always wandering about the house at night, and he had once been found fast asleep on the threshold of their bedroom.

The night before his seventh birthday he had seen them doing that thing. Later on, he had read in a magazine – the *Reader's Digest* probably – that this is called in psychiatrist's terms 'the primal scene', and in another article that seven is regarded as the onset of the age of reason; in other words, you know what you're doing after that, you're responsible. It was the night before his birthday, and he knew they had bought him a present and hidden it somewhere and he was unashamedly looking for it. It was the same on Christmas Eve. He went about hunting for his presents, and they knew it, he thought; they knew it and half enjoyed his curiosity, playing up to it and hiding the presents in unlikely places.

He wanted a cat or a dog but didn't think there was much chance of his getting either. As third best he hoped for a rabbit. They had more or less promised a 'pet'. He got out of bed at about half past nine, having been unable to sleep, and came downstairs looking for his present. There was no television in those days, or at least there was, but they didn't have it. His parents had the radio on in the evenings. Soft music was coming from the living room. He opened the door very quietly, to check if they were sufficiently occupied not to be aware he was out of bed. They were sufficiently occupied. His father, with a shirt on but no trousers, was humping up and down on top of his mother, who lay on her back with her skirt up and her blouse undone on the brown velvet settee.

It was not so much the movements they made as the noises, a kind of sucking slurping, his father puffing and gasping, his mother giving long sighs and short squeaks. It was not so much the noises as the movements, the way his mother thrashed from side to side, the way his father bounced and drove. It was both. He need not have worried about disturbing them. A shotgun (he thought years later) let off in that room wouldn't have disturbed them.

He turned round and went away. Into the kitchen. He wanted a sweet or a biscuit, though this was forbidden after teeth-cleaning, he wanted something sweet for comfort. They possessed a small fridge but no sweet things were kept in it. The larder was a walk-in cupboard with a stone floor, a wire-mesh window in the door and an airbrick to the outside. Victor wasn't tall enough to reach the door handle but the door wasn't quite closed and he took hold of the edge of it and pulled it open.

A huge shell. A head reared up from under the rim of it, snake-like but blank and dull-eyed, questing, moving from this side to that, two armoured feet sluggishly waving, the whole of it an inch or two from his face. He screamed. He covered his face and his ears and his eyes and rolled on the floor, screaming. His father and mother had finished, for they heard him and came running, fastening their clothes and calling out to him. His mother picked him up and held him, asking why, why? Afterwards he understood, he accepted explanations. It was his birthday present, kept for the night in a box on the larder floor, but he hadn't seen the box or the straw or the wire netting. Only the tortoise. They gave it away, of course, to the Macphersons down the road.

That was the Macphersons', five houses down. Perhaps they were still alive, though the thing he had named once in his thoughts but wouldn't again couldn't be. Mrs

Macpherson might at this moment be watching him from her window. What had his mother told the neighbours? She would have had no chance of concealment. For days the papers had been full of him and then again at the time of his trial. He wondered if in fact she had cared so very much. It had been he, after all, and not his father who had been taken from her and shut up in prison.

Victor moved away from the gate, for he had been leaning on it. Round the back there, behind the side gate, was a little paved sunny yard where his mother had grown tomatoes in pots, and one of the windows – or in this case a grid – that gave on to the yard opened out of the larder where the – thing had been in its wire-netted box. It occurred to Victor for the first time that only a very slatternly housekeeper would have thought of keeping an animal, a creature like that, in a larder overnight, and for some reason he shivered. His life would have been different if he hadn't opened that larder door, but perhaps not so very different.

Victor gave the house a last look. He hadn't really lived there since he had left school and gone to the polytechnic. It was a pity his parents hadn't bought it so that he rather than the landlord might have had the – what sort of sum did a house like that fetch now? Twelve thousand pounds? Fifteen? He was astounded by what he saw in the estate agent's window when at last, his confidence very gradually increasing, he reached the High Street.

Forty thousand for a house like that! What then was his bus fare going to cost him? Suppose he wanted to take a taxi? Victor was reminded of a joke which had been going the rounds before he went to prison and inflation had begun to take off. Alan that he worked for had told him.

'There was this man who thought he'd take advantage of inflation. He had himself put to sleep and frozen for twenty years. When he woke up the first thing he saw was a letter from his stockbroker, a year old, saying his investments were worth a million pounds. He went down the road to the callbox to phone his stockbroker and as he was feeling in his pockets for some small change he read the instructions on the pay phone and they said: dial the number you require and when you hear the ringing tone insert nine million pounds . . .'

It wasn't apathy or fear that kept him from doing more than make sure of his Social Security payments. He found himself increasingly reluctant to root himself here in Acton. After a week of freedom he had succeeded in avoiding contact with all the other occupants of the house, and he had seen neither his landlady nor her agent. His rent was paid direct. Presumably the DHSS believed – and with justification – that, if they gave the rent money to the tenant, the tenant would keep it for his own use. There would be time enough to register with a doctor when he was ill.

Reading newspapers and magazines daily gave him instruction in current ways and current parlance. There was an expression 'to psych up' which he couldn't remember having heard before. Victor psyched himself up to go to the bank and find how much was in his deposit account – or he was in the process of psyching up, telling himself that once he was in the bank talking to the manager or whoever he wouldn't feel afraid, when something happened to drive him out. He had been almost a week in the room in this house when contact with another human being was forced upon him. There came a tap at his door at ten one morning and when he opened the door, sick and cold with trepidation, he found a woman outside announcing that she was Noreen and that she had come to clean his room.

'I don't want the room cleaned,' he said. 'It doesn't need cleaning. I can't afford to pay for that.'

He hadn't used his voice much in the past week and hadn't resorted to talking to himself, so his speech sounded stilted and strange in his ears. Noreen was not apparently sensitive to these nuances. She walked in, pushing a vacuum cleaner.

'That's all taken care of,' she said. 'It comes in your rent.' She looked round her. 'Doesn't need it! You could have fooled me.'

41

She set to work with furious vigour, yanking the bed away from the wall, piling the cane chair and table and rugs into the middle of the room, the vacuum cleaner already switched on though immobile, as if it needed to warm up. She was a small rather pretty woman of about thirty-five with long greasy curly dark hair. Her body was rather plump and bulgy but her legs were thin with fine slender ankles. She wore a black cotton skirt, mauve tee shirt and Scholl sandals. Victor felt an unexpected shocking violent surge of desire for her.

He edged away and stood between the cupboard and the sink. The electric panic suit began to enclose him. In the past week he had been glad that he felt nothing. Why did this urge grip him now? She was not much to look at, this Noreen, and she smelled of sweat. She wasn't very young. Was it because he was in his own place and feeling reasonably safe while outside he was still afraid and astonished most of the time? He wanted to whimper and bleat like an animal. He wanted to scream.

Noreen shouted above the sound of the vacuum cleaner, 'If you've got anything to go out for, I should go out now. Then you won't be under my feet. I usually get done in half an hour.'

He put on his jacket and edged past her, walking with his hands on the walls. The years in prison hadn't killed it then. Had he ever supposed they would? Outside the door, on the landing, he fell on his knees and crouched forward with his head on the floor. He rocked back and forth. The vacuum cleaner whined and groaned and hiccupped behind the door. Victor banged his forehead on the floor. He lurched to his feet and staggered down the stairs. With his room taken over, there was nowhere for him to hide. He thought of a line he'd read somewhere once, long ago. No doubt he'd come across it in that mixed English–Sociology–Economics course he'd started at the polytechnic. For this is hell, nor am I out of it. He hadn't the least idea who had said that, but this was hell and he was in it up to his neck.

The money his parents had left him was in a deposit

account at the local branch of Lloyds Bank. There had originally been something in the region of a thousand pounds but out of that had had to come the cost of his mother's funeral and payment for the removal of the furniture. Victor forced himself to walk to the bank, teeth gritted, hands stuffed in his pockets. Part of the way he walked almost blind, his eyes half closed, his head bent so that he was looking down at the pavement.

In the bank everything was so easy that he wondered what had stopped him coming days before. He gave his name, which the bank teller didn't recognize, which obviously meant nothing to him, and though he couldn't give the account number, this hardly seemed to matter. They found out everything like that on computers now. Victor, who barely knew what a computer was, felt ignorant and awed.

His account contained only just over three hundred pounds. A slip of paper, folded in half, was passed to him via the little trough under the grille. They were a lot more security-conscious in banks than they had been ten years ago. Cal had been inside for doing a bank, he remembered, and Georgie for holding up a postmaster in some Hertfordshire post office at gunpoint while his mate helped himself to a couple of hundred old-age pensions. Three hundred pounds – and that included the accumulated interest over five or six years.

Victor didn't want to use the phone that was attached to the wall in the area behind the stairs. He might be overheard. It was always impossible to tell whether or not the house was empty. There was a pair of phone boxes outside the Job Centre, both unoccupied. Victor looked at what was on offer in the Job Centre window. The number of jobs going was at variance with what he had been told by Judy but no doubt when you came to apply they would turn out either to be filled or not what they seemed. There was even one that might suit him: 'Skilled or semi-skilled metalworker/cabinet maker wanted for office furniture workshop.' In the days he'd worked for Alan it had been as a driver in Alan's car-hire company. He could drive all right, drive anything, and he could make filing cabinets – but what was he going to tell them when they asked about his previous experience?

He pulled open the door of the first phone box. There were no directories and when he tried to use the phone he found that it was dead. In the next box not only was the phone dead but the receiver had been cut off and laid on its side in the metal box where the directories should have been. Victor couldn't understand it. His face must have expressed his bewilderment for, as he came out of the box, a woman walking past said to him, 'Them two've been vandalized, love. They've been like it for weeks.'

Victor thought it was outrageous that people could go about doing damage like that and getting away with it, going unpunished. He had been going to phone his aunt but now he asked himself what was the point? Whenever he chose to go there, she would be in. She never went out. Noreen might have finished cleaning the ravioli linoleum by now, but very likely she would still be in the house. He wasn't going back while she was still there.

He began walking down Gunnersbury Avenue, for he couldn't get up the courage to take a bus. Traffic on its way to Heathrow pounded past him at rush-hour volume, though it was only eleven in the morning. It made him wonder what it would feel like and how he would feel if he tried driving a car again after ten years. This used to be what his mother had called a 'select area', but Victor had always thought it bizarre, rows and rows of large neo-Tudor houses, every square foot of their surfaces adorned with half-timbering, their roofs steeply pitched and their windows leaded and glazed with stained glass. It might not have been so bad if there had been space enough, if each house had been allotted half an acre of land, but instead they were crammed together. Mostly, the front gardens were rockeries with steps winding up through them to the front door. His aunt's was a corner house with the front door a studded oak medieval imitation and a kind of granite cliff hung with rock plants supporting the porch.

Muriel Faraday had married late. She was older than his mother but Victor was sixteen before she got married. He could remember going to the wedding because it was just after his 'O' Level results had come in and at the reception his father went about telling people his son had eight 'O' Level passes, which had embarrassed Victor. The marriage had been in some registry office, he couldn't remember where, and Muriel had worn high heels and a big hat which had made her look huge beside the stooping elderly man who was her husband. Sydney Faraday was the owner of three prosperous greengrocery shops, a widower with grown-up children. Victor's mother told him that Muriel had stipulated that if she agreed to marry him there was to be no question of her ever serving in one of the shops, not even to help out in an emergency.

Victor and his parents derived no benefit from Muriel's new prosperity, though his mother had had high hopes of fruit out of season and a discount on new potatoes. 'Not so much as a punnet of strawberries,' she used to say. It would have been difficult for such presents to be handed over since his mother invited people to the house or accepted invitations very rarely and his aunt, soon after her wedding, developed a phobia about going out. On only two or three occasions had Victor gone to his aunt and uncle's house, for Christmas dinner twice and one other time, but he remembered perfectly where it was.

Before going up the steps to the front door, Victor walked down the steep ramp to the garage at the bottom. This garage was half timbered and had little diamond-paned windows like a country cottage on a calendar. Victor looked through one of the windows at the furniture inside, all of it covered up with his mother's curtains. On top of the curtains bric-à-brac from his mother's shelves and cupboards lay in heaps – cups and plates and vases and ashtrays and paperweights and candlesticks. Where one of the curtains had slipped, he could see the bedhead from his parents' bed, old gold quilted satin across the padded buttoned surface, from which hung a long thick cobweb.

A concrete staircase, winding and rustically uneven, led

to the front door. All around it loomed artificial outcroppings of stone, hung with trailing plants and partly
obscured by dark fan-shaped growths of horizontal conifers. For as long as Victor could remember – from the
time, that is, when Muriel married Sydney and moved in
here – garden statuary had relieved the gloomy starkness
of these escarpments, creatures cast in concrete: a frog, a
rabbit, an owl with painted yellow eyes, and a tortoise.
Fortunately for Victor, the tortoise was the least obtrusive,
for the stone on which it stood was the one nearest to the
box hedge and half covered by fronds of juniper. Giving it
only a cursory glance, you might have taken it for a stone
itself. Victor, of course, had never approached it nearer
than these steps, had never looked at it except out of the
corner of his eye. Now he noted only that it was still there,
neither more nor less obscured than it had been last time
he was here, more than a decade ago. Either the juniper
had not grown or else it was purposely kept trimmed back
to this level.

The front door looked as if it hadn't been opened for
months or as if it were in fact the entrance to some fortress
and his summons, by means of the bell that must be rung
by pulling a twisted iron rod, would call forth a doorkeeper
in chain mail holding a club. Victor hesitated before pulling
it. He didn't want that furniture, he had nowhere to put
it, and even if he had possessed an empty house waiting to
be furnished, almost anything would have been preferable
to these pieces in which memories and pains and shames
were somehow petrified. But perhaps he hadn't really come
for that at all, perhaps he had come to see Muriel, who
was his only living relative, the only link left in that flesh
and blood chain that anchored him to the past.

She might be dead. They wouldn't have bothered to tell
him that in prison. She might be bedridden or in a home.
The house didn't look lived in. But it hadn't looked lived
in when he had come on Christmas Day with his parents;
there hadn't been a paper chain or a card on display. He
reached for the iron rod and pulled the bell.

All the windows down the street that he could see, all

diamond-paned casements with curly metal handles in wooden mullions, gleamed with a kind of black glitter, but those in his aunt's house seemed to have a grey mist on them, a dusty bloom that had been rained on and then filmed with more dust. He rang the bell again. This time he heard something. Absurdly – because this was his old aunt he was calling on, he reminded himself, a nothing, nobody that mattered – he felt the tingle of panic, electric tremors in his shoulders and down his back. He drew in his belly and put back his shoulders and breathed deeply.

The door came ajar slowly, drawn open with extreme caution, a crack, six inches, a foot. An old face peered out at him, twitching, mouse-like. She had aged so that he would hardly have known her, would not have known her in the almost impossible eventuality of their encountering each other elsewhere. He stared, his throat constricting. She had been a mountainous woman with a big floury-painted puffy face that used to remind him when he was a teenager of some elaborate cake in a patisserie window, powdery white with cherries on it and marzipan, surrounded by a golden frill. The cake had fallen into ruin, dust and cobwebs where the icing had been, a furriness as of mould on the spongy cheeks. The stout body, once tightly corseted, was wasted and bent. Muriel wore a pink net or snood on the wispy grey hair that in former times had been peroxided, a dirty blue wool dressing gown and dirty blue feather mules.

Victor didn't know what to say. He swallowed. He waited for her to say something and then he understood she didn't know him.

'It's Victor,' he said.

She stepped back, putting a hand up to her mouth. He walked into the house and shut the door behind him. She spoke in a hoarse whisper. 'Have you escaped?'

He would have liked to kill her, he could imagine doing that. And then he understood that she was afraid.

'What do you mean, escaped?' he said roughly.

'There's four more years for you to go.'

'Haven't you ever heard of remission for good behaviour?'

Horrified, she stared at him. She looked him up and down, her hands holding her face claw-like. A thin nervous giggle came from her.

'Good behaviour!' she said. 'I like that – good behaviour.'

From distant times he remembered where the living room was. He pushed the door open and went in. She followed him, shuffling.

'I thought you must have got out over the wall.'

He took no notice. The living room was full of newspapers and magazines. Against the wall opposite the fireplace four tower blocks of magazines reached from the floor to the ceiling. The impression was that the building had ceased only because the ceiling was reached. In the embrasure of the bay window, newspapers were piled, broadsheets on the left and tabloids on the right, to a height of about four feet. More magazines filled the area between the refectory table top and the floor beneath, the three bookcases, the alcoves on either side of the fireplace, even the sofa and one of the armchairs. A small space in the centre of the carpet only was free of them, this and the armchair draped with a blanket in which his aunt presumably sat in front of the television.

And she never went out! How did one old woman who never went out assemble this hoard of paper? If you never threw anything away, he thought, if you took one daily paper and two weeklies, say, and two or three monthlies and you never threw anything away . . . Had she always been like this? He couldn't remember. He turned round to her.

'You've got my furniture.'

It occurred to him, immediately he had spoken, that she would probably start in about how generous she'd been, what it would have cost him to have the furniture stored, and so on. But she only said, 'It's in the garage.'

'Could you take me, please?'

She shook her head. 'It's outside,' she told him, as if some people had garages in the centre of their houses. 'You can go through the kitchen and in the back way. There's keys. I'll get you the keys.'

She shuffled along through the house and he followed her. Her husband had been well off and it was a big house, furnished with big expensive over-upholstered furniture from the thirties. The dining room had a lot of magazines in it too, arranged in similar pillar-like stacks. If no one had cleaned the place for several years, there had been nothing much to make it dirty. Pale soft dust was everywhere and a dusty smell. The kitchen looked as if no one had cooked food in it for a long time. His aunt opened a drawer and took out a bunch of keys. She had guarded his property well, for three separate keys were needed to open the garage door. She wasn't a bad old girl really, he thought. Maybe it was natural she'd been frightened when she first knew who he was. He had suspected her of malice and censoriousness but she was only a bit ga-ga. In the ruined face he could see something of his mother, which was odd because his mother had been lovely, but it was deep in the eyes, a something in the shape of the nostrils, the modelling of the temples. This made Victor feel strange, weak, worse in a way than he had when he knew his mother was dead.

He unlocked the garage door, using the three keys. Even then it stuck and he had to put his shoulder to it. No one had been in there for a long time. Victor stood on the threshold, gazing at his past, his childhood, cradled in these beds and mattresses, in these tables and chests and chairs, all of it shrouded in the multicoloured fabric that had covered the windows and kept the outside at bay.

Closing the door behind him, he pushed his way into the depths of it. He moved like someone who finds himself in a thicket or maze composed of trees he must not damage. The furniture smelled of his mother's house, a smell he had not been aware of while he lived with her, but which he at once recognized as personal and unique: his father's tabacco, beeswax, witch hazel, Coty *L'aimant* talcum powder. Victor found himself inhaling it as if taking in gulps of fresh air and he had to stop himself doing this.

49

He closed his eyes, opened them, took hold of the hem of a curtain and tugged at it. Revealed beneath was the settee, upholstered in brown velvet, on which his parents had used to sit holding hands and on which, on the night of the tortoise, he had come upon them making love. Folded on its cushions was a brown check travelling rug. Pressed up against its back was a wheelchair.

This must be the wheelchair his father had been confined to. After his father had suffered that first stroke Victor had never seen him again but his mother had continued to visit the prison, not noticeably cowed or dispirited by the atmosphere or even distressed by her son's being in there. She had been tranquil and talkative as ever, and he didn't think it had been put on for his benefit. Why should she have worried? She had his father, who was all she had ever wanted. He remembered her talking about this wheelchair and how clever he was at managing it, 'whizzing along the pavements'. That was the phrase she had used.

Victor wondered why it had been kept. It should have been handed over to the social services surely, that was obvious. Why hadn't someone written to him about it? The solicitor, for instance, who had been executor of his mother's will, had arranged with his aunt for this storage of the furniture, and neatly abstracted his own fee from Victor's legacy. What persons in their right mind had thought *he* would have a use for a wheelchair?

He covered it up again. All this stuff would have to be sold, that was the only thing to do with it. Walking along Acton High Street, he had passed a junk shop with a notice outside that said: *Flats and houses cleared and good prices paid*.

The door locked once more with the three keys, Victor went back through the house. It was a very quiet house that might have been in the depths of the country rather than in a London suburb on the main route to Heathrow. He called out, 'Auntie Muriel?'

There was no answer. He came to the dining-room door and saw her inside, leaning over the table which was covered with pieces of paper. Victor went into the dining room. He saw that the pieces of paper were cuttings from newspapers and magazines, all neatly clipped out, not torn, as if prepared for a scrapbook. Perhaps they *had* been prepared for a scrapbook, perhaps that was his aunt's design. When he saw what they had in common, he felt a great wave of heat, like a breaker in a warm sea, wash over him, flood up to his face and over his head. He felt sick, not because he cared or was remorseful, but because he thought she must have taken all these magazines, all those papers and periodicals, just for this, to this end. He held on to the edge of the table and gritted his teeth. That was nonsense, of course, no one would do that, and yet . . .

He swung round and took hold of her by the shoulders. She made a little gibbering noise and cringed. He had meant to shake the life out of her, but he let her go, though roughly enough to send her staggering so that she almost fell.

The cuttings on the table were all accounts, stories, photographs of David Fleetwood and the life he had led since Victor shot him ten years before.

51

4

Having only two topics of conversation, the Second World War and the greengrocery trade, Sydney Faraday had talked exhaustively about battles and beetroot, the former slightly dominating. He had been a sergeant with a tank regiment, part of Montgomery's Second Army that swept across northern Germany in the spring of 1945. One of his favourite stories was how he and a corporal and a private had gone into a farmhouse kitchen near the Weser, found the occupants gone, nothing to eat but a sucking pig roasting, in fact ready to eat at that moment, in the oven. Another was the one about the gun. Outside Bremen Sydney had found a dead German officer lying in a ditch. He was still holding a gun in his hand which led Sydney to believe (on no other evidence) that he had shot himself out of despair at the way the war was going. On the altruistic grounds of not wanting the man branded a suicide, Sydney took the gun and kept it. It was a Luger.

'A German military small-bore automatic pistol,' Sydney would explain to the company, rather in the manner of an encyclopedia.

The first time Victor heard this story had been after Christmas dinner. He was only seventeen and still going about with his parents. He heard it again ten years later when his mother said she never saw him these days and then nagged him into going with them to Muriel's on Christmas Day. Things were just the same: the same undercooked defrosted turkey, this time with canned potatoes, for there had been technological progress during the intervening decade, and greens that were perhaps sub-standard for the shop. While they ate the shop-bought, home-boiled pudding and drank the only pleasing constituent of the meal, Sydney's port, Sydney told the story of the German officer and the gun once more. Victor's mother murmured, though to no avail, that she had heard it before. Muriel, who had no doubt heard it many many times, interjected mechanically with 'My goodness!' and 'I say!', uttered expressionlessly as if she was learning these exclamations as part of a minor role in a play. She had grown fat, and the more fat she became the more withdrawn. It was as if whatever spirit she had ever had was being steadily suppressed, muffled and smothered under layers of flesh.

At the time Victor couldn't precisely remember from ten years before the exact words Sydney had used in telling the story of the dead German officer, but he didn't think they varied much from the present version. Perhaps the narrative had filled out a bit.

'So I thought, poor old devil, he must have been at the end of his tether. No future, I thought, nothing to look forward to. I reckoned on him being found and his wife and kids back home getting told he wasn't a hero, he wasn't killed on active service. Oh, no, he done himself in. You know how you get arguing with yourself on what's right and what's wrong. I thought to myself, Sydney, the only good German's a dead German, you know that.'

'My goodness!' said Muriel, deadpan.

'But somehow, I suppose the truth is we've all got the quality of mercy in us somewhere, somehow I couldn't leave him there to be branded a rotten coward. I picked up his dead stiff hand, cold as ice it was, I remember like it was yesterday, and took that Luger and stuck it in my pocket and never said a word to no one. That was a little secret between me and the dead, my own private mark of respect.'

'Can I have some more port?' said Victor.

Sydney pushed the bottle at him. 'And you won't believe this but I've still got that Luger. Oh, yes. I can show it to you any time you care to see it. For some reason I've treasured it. It's not a matter of getting it out and having a gloat over it, not a bit. I just like to remember it sometimes and think to myself, you will pass this way but once,

Sydney Faraday, and any good you can do, do it *now*. Well, that was my little bit of good when we was sweeping across to victory in old Monty's wake.'

Nobody asked to see the gun. Victor was thinking of asking when Sydney announced that he would go upstairs and fetch it. The Luger was wrapped in a white silk scarf, the kind of thing men used to wear with evening clothes. Victor's mother asked if it was loaded and when Sydney sneered that of course it wasn't, what did she take him for, handled it gingerly while remarking that it hardly seemed right on Christmas Day.

Sydney wrapped the gun up again and returned upstairs with it. The moment he was out of the room Victor excused himself to go to the bathroom. He went quietly up the stairs. At the top on the left was Sydney and Muriel's bedroom, a big room with a pink flowered carpet and a pier glass in the middle of the floor. Victor glanced quickly in there, then turned down the passage towards the bathroom at the end. Sydney's stooping form could be discerned inside the second bedroom (there were four) lifting up the eiderdown on a brass bedstead. He didn't seem to have heard Victor pass by.

At that time Victor had scarcely thought of needing a gun. Rather, he had reflected that a gun was a precious thing to possess because it was rare and it was forbidden. But in the following May he made an attack on a girl on Hampstead Heath and the girl had had some sort of training in martial arts, which wasn't very usual back in the seventies. She managed to throw Victor and escape. He remembered Sydney's gun.

Sometimes Victor thought how wrong it had been of Sydney to put temptation in his way like that. If Sydney hadn't boasted about the gun and shown it off, he, Victor, would never dreamed of such a thing being in Muriel's house, and in default of that gun, of course, he would never have acquired one. And if he had never acquired a gun . . .

Even then he didn't think much about it until Sydney fell ill and went into hospital. He was suffering from lung cancer, and a year or so later he was to die of it. Muriel had scarcely set foot outside the house for years but she had to go and visit Sydney. Victor learned all this from his mother, who told him how Muriel would only go to the hospital if she went with her, arriving in a taxi at Muriel's door to collect her. For a long time Victor's mother had had a key to her sister's house.

The next time the two sisters were due to go hospital visiting, Victor went to Gunnersbury. He watched the taxi come and his mother climb the mountain path between the alpine plants and horizontal conifers. His mother let herself into the house and came out five minutes later with the obese figure of Muriel clinging to her arm. Muriel had on a big black hat with a wide brim and a black silk raincoat, as if she were anticipating Sydney's death and was already in mourning. A few minutes after the taxi was out of sight, Victor let himself in with the key he had had copied from his mother's. It was a bit stiff and new and for a second or two he thought it wasn't going to move the lock. It did.

He wondered where that key was now, what had happened to it. There was no particular use he could think of for it, but just the same he liked having things of that sort, they made him feel safe and rather powerful. It must have got lost six months later when all his possessions were transferred to his parents' house. What, for that matter, had happened to the gun? Presumably, the police had held on to it, though it wasn't theirs any more than it had been Sydney's. It rightly belonged to the German government, Victor supposed.

He went straight up the stairs, which were of dark polished wood with a runner down the middle of the treads of red turkey carpet. How dark this house always was, even in the height of summer! The gloomy upper floor smelled of camphor and as if the windows were never opened. Victor entered the room with the brass bedstead and lifted up the eiderdown. A stone hot-water bottle and a metal bedpan lay on the bare mattress, but no gun.

Victor looked inside the hot-water bottle and inside the bedpan, he looked through the folded clothes in the chest of drawers, setting mothballs rolling out of sleeves and sock toes. The carpet was blue with a faded pattern round the border of yellow grapes and green vine leaves. He lifted up the carpet, he searched the wardrobe, he opened a wall cupboard full of shoes and boots, its upper shelf containing a small library of western novels in paperback: *The Man Who Rode to Phoenix, The Secret of Dead Eye Ranch*. It was his temper, his anger, which helped him that time. In a rage he kicked at the shoes in their wooden trees, over-turning them. Underneath, a floor-board was loose. Victor could lift the board up with his fingers. Inside was a card-board shoebox and inside the box was the Luger wrapped up in Sydney's fringed white silk scarf. What Sydney hadn't mentioned was that he had also taken off the German officer four rounds of ammunition. Probably that sort of rifling of a corpse would have been harder to explain on grounds acceptable to Sydney's vaunted morality.

Sydney didn't die until Victor had been nearly a year in prison. He had been out of hospital and home again when Victor made use of the gun – totally unaware, Victor often thought, how much he shared responsibility for the maiming of Fleetwood. He and Fleetwood and the girl Rosemary Stanley each had a share in that responsibility: Sydney for taking the gun in the first place, Fleetwood for refusing to believe in its evident reality, the girl for her stupid screaming and breaking of that window. People never thought of how much they might embroil others in their careless behaviour.

He hoped, though, that Sydney had been made to feel something of his guilt when, after the shooting, the police had gone to him and asked about the gun, how he had come by it and why he had given it to his wife's nephew. Even on his sickbed they hadn't spared him but had pest-ered him until he told them everything. That must have been one time, Victor thought, when he hadn't enjoyed boring guests with that particular after-dinner story, when he couldn't have put across all that *spiel* about how moral and caring he was.

*

In an interview he had given to a Sunday newspaper Fleet-wood had talked quite frankly about his life and his feelings, less so to a women's magazine. Or the women's magazine had cut out the bits it thought might make its readers uncomfortable. He spoke about not being able to walk, about foregoing all those athletic activities which had been important to him, running, playing rugger and squash, going on walking holidays. He mentioned – not for the newspaper, only the magazine – how he had become fond of reading. One of the ventures he had begun on was studying for a degree with the Open University. He read novels and biographies and poetry, had joined the London Library as well as two book clubs. Gardening interested him and he enjoyed planning a garden, though he had to have someone else to do the work for him. He was considering as a hobby learning to make musical instruments, an organ perhaps or a harp.

In the middle of the newspaper article, just when the reader might have started thinking that being paralysed and confined to an orthopaedic chair for the rest of one's life wasn't so terrible after all, Fleetwood said, 'I suppose the worst thing is what most people don't think of, that I'm impotent, without sex. I can't make love any more and it's pretty unlikely I ever will. People forget that that gets paralysed too, they think it's solely a matter of not walking. It's the hardest thing to bear because I like women, I used to love women, their beauty, you know. That's all lost to me in a real sense, I have to face it. And I can't marry, I couldn't do a woman that sort of injury.'

In another cutting, which pre-dated the Sunday paper story by some years, was something about how Fleetwood's fiancée hadn't married him after all. There was a picture of her with him when he was fit and well and another picture of her sitting beside his wheelchair. She was slim and fair-haired, very pretty. The magazine the cutting came from wasn't particularly harsh to her or lacking in understanding. It quoted her without much comment, asking its readers at the end of the piece how they would feel in her situation: *Write in and let us know your views.*

'I loved David – well, I still do,' she had told them. 'I started off with high hopes. Good resolutions, I suppose you'd call them. The fact is, I just wasn't a big enough person to take it. I want a real marriage, I want children. I wish I could be a better person, more of what he expected, but I think it's better to know it now, to face up to it now, than to have tried marriage and failed.'

The sickly sentimentality of it made Victor cringe but he went on reading. The cuttings were laid out on the table like a pack of cards for some elaborate patience game. They spanned Fleetwood's life from the day in the house in Solent Gardens to the present, or almost to the present, the latest being dated the previous Christmas. There was the story about the charity concert Victor had read of while in prison. A photograph of Fleetwood accompanied it. He sat in a wheelchair on the stage with, on one side of him, a famous comedian whose name had been a household word for years before Victor went to prison, and on the other, a beautiful long-legged girl in a spangled leotard who leaned over him with her arms loosely about his neck. More photographs were inserted into an account in a magazine of some of the physio-therapeutic treatment Fleetwood had undergone. One of those showed the former policeman sitting in a garden with a yellow labrador dog; another, in a later story, had him at his father's funeral, holding a wreath of pink and white roses in his lap; a third was in the text of an interview with Fleetwood in which he said he was moving out of London, it was even possible he might emigrate to Australia or New Zealand. In all there were fifty-one cuttings on the table – not quite a pack of cards – and the last of them was about Fleetwood distributing presents to children in an orthopaedic hospital. He had travelled to the hospital from where he now lived, in a place in Essex called Theydon Bois.

Victor, who would scarcely have known his own aunt, whose own face in the mirror sometimes seemed unfamiliar to him, would have recognized Fleetwood without any introduction or caption. Once in his life he had seen him, for Fleetwood had been too ill to attend the trial, but he

58

would have known him anywhere. That face was printed on his memory more indelibly than his mother's. It was a firm square solid face with regular features and a rather large long mouth. The eyes were dark (and now mournfully sad), the eyebrows black and very nearly straight, the hair dark, thick and wavy. It was a face not unlike his own. There was no question of a twin-like resemblance, but they might have been taken for brothers. They belonged to the same physical type, as if to the same tribe of tallish, well-built, even-featured people. Victor raised his head and looked at himself in the large oval steel-framed mirror which hung on the opposite wall and saw threads of grey in his hair, an indefinable ageing of the skin, something old and tired and experienced in the eyes which was similar to that in Fleetwood's own. They were each thirty-eight, which was young yet, but Fleetwood had ruined both their lives by refusing to believe an evident truth.

His aunt had come creeping back into the room. She went behind the table, keeping the table between them, as a means of defence perhaps. On the hand which held together the two sides of her dressing gown was a magnificent diamond ring. The clustered diamonds formed a dome half an inch in diameter and a quarter of an inch thick. It was a ring that should have adorned the lily-white hand of youth. Victor thought how rich Sydney must have been, better off than any of them had thought. He said to her, 'What made you save all this lot?'

Her expression was truculent and spiteful. 'Somebody had to.'

It was a senseless remark. 'Why did they? What's the use of raking up the past? I've got to put all that behind me.'

She was silent, looking at him, her tongue moving across the almost closed lips, a habit of hers that he could remember from early childhood. Then she said, 'There's some might say you ought to feel shame for what you did.'

It was useless arguing with people like her. They had stereotyped minds that ran along grooves of stock response and the commonplace. 'Anyway, I don't want this stuff,' he said. 'I'm not interested.'

'I never said you could have it,' she said. 'It's mine. That took me years to do.'

She spoke as of a work of art, a book she had written or tapestry embroidered. Like a child who is afraid of having its hand slapped, she began gathering up the cuttings, casting cautious glances up into his face. A reek of camphor came from her and he stepped back, disgusted.

'I'll see about getting someone to move the furniture. I'll phone you.'

'You'll be lucky if you get an answer.'

'What's that supposed to mean?'

She had put the cuttings carefully away into two quarto-size brown envelopes. Probably she had some secret hidey-hole for them, and Victor shuddered a little when he remembered hiding places in that house.

'There's some funny types phone,' she said. 'You wouldn't believe the things I've had said to me. Me, at my age. So now, mostly, I don't answer.'

'OK, I'll come round and tell you.'

The envelopes were merely tucked in among the maga-zines, halfway down the *Lady* stack. 'It can't be too long for me,' Muriel said, her tone ordinary, mildly disgruntled, not matching the malevolence of the words. 'I'd sooner have your chairs and tables than you, and that's the truth. What you've done's enough to turn a person's stomach.'

Outdoors was becoming familiar to him, less alarming. He had been on a bus and, to the amusement of the other passengers, expressed his amazement at the magnitude of the fare. Returning, he had tried the tube and the tunnels hadn't bothered him or the crowds. For days he had concentrated on getting used to London, to losing the terrible self-consciousness that had made him feel everyone was looking at him and everyone knew. Walking along Acton High Street, he followed a girl part of the way – that is, she was walking along and he was behind her, going in the same direction. She wore spiky heels and a short skirt which made him feel uncomfortable. He wouldn't express it to himself more strongly than that. It made him feel uncomfortable, that was all. Suppose it had been night time, though, and one of the paths crossing Ealing Common rather than this densely populated place, what then? He refused to answer the question.

The shop where they bought furniture and cleared flats was at the bottom of Grove Road. On the pavement outside was a rack of old books no one would buy either for their content or their decoration value, and just inside the window a tray of Victorian jewellery, rings and pendants and buttons. The stuff for sale inside reminded him of Muriel's own furniture, big, ugly, uncomfortable and shabby. A stuffed peacock with its tail feathers spread in a threadbare fan perched on the back of a chaise longue upholstered in horsehair and black leather.

A boy of about eighteen in jeans and a denim jerkin came out and asked Victor if he could help him or did he just want to browse round? Victor said he had some furniture he wanted to sell. It was really a valuation he wanted.

'You'll have to see Mr Jupp,' the boy said.

'All right.'

'Yeah, but he's not here, is he? He's up the other shop. I mean, you could go up there if you felt like it or I could pass on the message.'

'I could go if it isn't far.'

'Salusbury Road – well, sort of Kilburn. You want to go to Queens Park on the Bakerloo.'

Victor didn't realize until he got there and saw the name Harvist Road. Everything seemed to be spelled wrong around here, or spelled in an unlikely perverse way, that made him feel uneasy or as if mocked. But it wasn't that which caused him to pause outside the station, lean against the wall and momentarily close his eyes. Solent Gardens was a turning off Harvist Road. A step or two or three westwards and you were in Kensal Rise.

He had told Muriel he wanted to forget, to put the past behind him, but he was walking along Harvist Road in the opposite direction to where Jupp's shop was and remembering how, ten years before, with Sydney's gun in his pocket, he had been in the park that lay to the right here very early in the morning.

In those days he had got into the habit of roaming London at all hours. Possessing the gun gave him confidence. With the Luger in his pocket he felt invincible, a victor indeed. Had Sydney, home again by then, ever missed it? Had Muriel been told? If they had, no hint of this had filtered through to Victor living up in Finchley in his 'studio' flat, driving cars for Alan to airports and stations. In the mornings he would sometimes get up at five and go out while it was still dark. His hours were strange and irregular anyway, meeting planes as he often did at six in the morning, taking home to Surrey or Kent party-goers who at midnight or later had drunk too much to drive themselves. That morning in the late autumn he had been on his way to Heathrow, due there at nine thirty to meet, in the best of the limousines, an Arab businessman and take him to the London Hilton. What had happened to the limousine? Victor had sometimes wondered since. Leaving home at five, he had parked it round the back here, in Milman Road. And then he had walked about, feeling an excitement rise in him that he couldn't have called pleasant but which he needed to have, the trembling, breathless, choking feeling Cal had told him he felt when he looked at a pornographic photo. Cal hadn't used those words but that was what he meant, and Victor had recognized this as the feeling he had when he contemplated forcing some woman, any woman. At seven thirty he had entered the park that lay to the north of Harvist Road.

The girl was exercising a dog, a very small dog. She had just taken it off the lead and watched it run into the bushes when Victor seized hold of her. He caught her from behind, hooking one arm round her neck and clamping his hand across her mouth. That was to stop her crying out. She hadn't needed to make a sound because she was seen. A man had been in among the trees, having 'stepped in there for natural purposes', they said at the trial, which meant standing up against a bush for a pee. That was just Victor's ill-luck.

He didn't forget the gun but he didn't use it. He ran. He hadn't been certain whether both of them chased him or just the man, but it came out at the trial that it was both, and two or three others they picked up along the way. Like a pack of hounds after a miserable fox. Round those back streets he had run, doubling back and hiding, still thinking then about shaking them off and finding the car and getting off to Heathrow, still hoping. He had found himself in that lane between back gardens, a place of broken concrete pavings and garage entrances and padlocked gates. One gate wasn't padlocked though and he had gone in, up the path, bent double so they shouldn't see him over the fence, ducking down at last into a corner made by house wall and fence. It was then that he had heard the throb of a taxi's diesel engine and a front door slam. The occupants of the house were leaving it, were going out. If they were going out at this time of the morning, he had reasoned, it would be for the day.

He climbed up on to the extension roof and in through a bathroom window that had been left open a crack at the top. It was a sash window with nothing to hold it and it had slid down easily. By then his pursuers were lost or at least were soundless and invisible. He crouched for some minutes on that bathroom floor. Then, because he was sure the house was empty, he went out on to the landing. He crossed the landing and looked through the crack of a barely open door, and because he could see nothing or not enough he pushed the door a little and the girl in bed inside, the girl called Rosemary Stanley, sat up and screamed at the sight of him, jumped up screaming and ran to the window, smashed it with a hairbrush and screamed 'Help me! Help me!' to the outside world.

The strange thing was that the house meant nothing to him as he looked at it now. No doubt it was the same house, 62 Solent Gardens, the end of a terrace, but he would not have recognized it on sight alone. He walked along the opposite side of the street, looking at it. The uneven plaster surface had been painted chalk white and the front door was a different colour – wasn't it? Victor couldn't remember whether he had ever seen the front door. The broken window had been mended. Of course it had, years ago. Yet somehow when he had thought about that house while in prison he had always seen it with the window broken and the wind blowing in and lifting the curtains. That had been one of the most frightening things, that billowing curtain, for each time it lifted he had expected to see a policeman on a ladder outside. And then, at last, he had seen one. He would never know why he had aimed the gun at Fleetwood and not at the policeman on the ladder outside the window.

A woman came out, walked to the gate and leaned over it, looking to the right and then to the left. She was about forty, dark and plump, and there was no way she could be either Rosemary Stanley or Rosemary Stanley's mother. The Stanleys must have moved away. She went back into the house, leaving the door a little ajar. Victor turned round and walked back past the house towards Harvist Road and Salusbury Road and Jupp's shop.

In that room with the girl it had all seemed unreal. This can't be happening, was what he had thought over and over again. The police had insisted he meant to rape the girl but this had never crossed his mind. Indignation was what he had felt, indignation and amazement that all this could have happened, the police outside and police trying to get in, a state of siege in fact, sirens sounding, a crowd gathered and watching – and all because he had put his arm round a girl's neck and run away and tried to find refuge in an empty house . . .

Jupp's shop looked exactly like the one in Acton. There was a trough full of secondhand books out on the pavement and a tray of Victorian jewellery just inside the window. A bell jangled when he opened the door. Inside it was different, with less furniture and a case of pin-stuck butterflies, clouded yellows and commas and red admirals, instead of the stuffed peacock. On a red marble table stood an ancient cash register priced at thirty-four pounds. Victor couldn't imagine why anyone would want to buy it. A dusty green velvet curtain at the back of the shop was pulled aside and an old man came out. He was tall and strong-looking with big calloused hands. His face was the purplish red of morocco leather, against which his mass of creamy white hair, worn rather long, and the yellowish-white shaggy moustache made an almost violent contrast. He had little, bright, red-veined blue eyes.

'Are you Mr Jupp?' said Victor.

The old man nodded. He was one of those people who always stick out their lower lips when they nod. For his age he was extraordinarily dressed in a pair of denim jeans, a red shirt and a black pinstriped waistcoat, which he wore unbuttoned. Victor explained what he wanted, that he had a houseful of furniture to be valued and a buyer found for the items.

'I could come and have a shuftee,' said Jupp. 'Where is it? Not out in the sticks, I hope.'

Victor said it was stored in the garage of a house in Gunnersbury.

The lower lip went out over the upper as Jupp nodded. 'So long as you don't get things out of proportion,' he said. 'I mean, no delusions of grandeur about mum's priceless antiques and all that jazz.'

'How did you know it was my mother's?' said Victor.

'Well, ask yourself, cocky, who else's would it be? Poor old mum's gone at last and left you her bits, which is the last thing you want to be lumbered with, them not being your Louis Kangs or your Hepplewhite, whatever you might wish others to believe.'

'It's good furniture,' Victor protested, beginning to feel aggrieved.

'I daresay. So long as we don't have to hear about *valuations* and *finding a buyer*. What I do is clear flats and houses, right? I have a shuftee and tell you a price, and if you like it I clear the lot, and if you don't you go elsewhere and find a bigger sucker than what I am. *If* you can. Right? You happy with that?'

'OK, but I'll have to warn her you're coming. My aunt, I mean. It's my aunt's place where it is. I'll have to go round and tell her you're coming.'

'Don't break no speed records,' said Jupp. 'It'll be a good fortnight. I'm up to my eyebrows for the next fortnight. How about we say two weeks tomorrow, cocky? You give me the good lady's address and I'll be there three on the dot.'

Victor gave him Muriel's address. Jupp wrote it down and Victor's own name as well. Victor waited for the name to be recognized but it seemed to mean nothing to Jupp, who closed up his order book, took a packet of Polo mints out of his pocket and offered one to Victor.

Not liking to refuse, Victor took a mint. Jupp hesitated reflectively, contemplating the mint on the top of the pack, rather as a man who is trying to give up smoking stares with longing and disgust and doubt and hunger at the next cigarette. After a second or two he gave a small sigh, folded the torn paper over the exposed mint and restored the pack to his pocket.

'Mustn't indulge myself,' he said. 'I used to be addicted to these things something shocking, hooked you'd say. Twenty packets a day was nothing to me and thirty was more like it. Luckily, I haven't got my own teeth or they'd have gone for a Burton. Nowadays I've got it down to five. A steady five and I'm happy, or let's say I can take it, I can live with it. I don't suppose you can understand that, cocky?'

Although he had never been subject to an addiction, Victor could understand it only too well. It made him feel uncomfortable and in a way he wished he hadn't come to Jupp, but he didn't want to have to go searching for another secondhand furniture dealer, so he said he'd see Jupp at Muriel's on Thursday fortnight at three in the afternoon.

This time he avoided the tube and got on to a bus instead. Going over the hump of bridge by Kensal Rise station, he caught sight from the window of a newsagent's

board on which was scrawled: *Acton Girl in Rape Horror*.
He turned his head sharply away but at the next stop he
got off the bus, went into the first newsagent's he came to
and bought a paper, the *Standard*.

5

The story was a short one, at the foot of the page. A girl from Acton Vale had been raped in Gunnersbury Park on the previous evening, her jaw broken by blows, her face cut. A gardener found her after she had lain all night where her attacker had flung her, in a shrubbery of laurels. Reading it gave Victor a strange feeling, a faint dizziness, a nausea. In the past he had sometimes read accounts of rapes he himself had committed during his marauding of London from Finchley to Chiswick and from Harlesden to Leytonstone, one of Alan's cars parked somewhere as, *en route* to fetch a client, he looked for what the more sensational papers called his 'prey'. In those days the police and judges and juries and the general public had been far less sympathetic towards rape victims and far less condemnatory of rapists than they now were. The consensus of opinion had been that the victims asked for all they got and that the rapists were tempted beyond control. High-ranking police officers were not above suggesting that victims should 'lie back and enjoy it'. It seemed to Victor, reading the *Standard*, that things had changed a lot. This had registered with him even while he was still in prison, that what with Women's Lib and women campaigning against the way rape victims were treated and the attitude of the court changing, rape was regarded with a severity unthinkable ten years ago.

Here, on an inside, page, were some figures. He read them as he walked along. Out of 1334 cases of rape 644 men had been proceeded against. A variety of sentences had been imposed on those found guilty. Twelve of the men had been given life imprisonment, eleven of them seven to ten years' imprisonment, and fifty-six had been given two to three years. It was interesting, he thought, that in only three cases had a restriction order been made under the Mental Health Act. Yet, speaking for himself, personally, he knew that the acts of rape he had performed had been beyond his control, had had nothing to do with will, had been as involuntary and as distinct from any decision or purpose of his own as his firing the gun at Fleetwood. Did that mean he was mad when he did these things or at least not responsible for his actions?

Having now walked all the way down Ladbroke Grove, reading his paper and just staring at the blurring print, thinking, wondering how in the future he would control that which admitted no control, Victor got on a bus that would take him home. A faint feeling of regret for the prison he had left took hold of him, a certain nostalgia for that brutish sloth and lack of any responsibility. He had been looked after in there and safe, and if it had often been uncomfortable, always boring, a waste of life, there had been no worries and, later on, no fear. He read the story of the Gunnersbury Park rape once more as he walked up Twyford Avenue, raising his eyes just before he reached the house. Tom Welch was sitting outside the gate in his car. He got out when he saw Victor coming, putting on an over-warm, jovial expression.

'I guessed you wouldn't be long. I thought I'd wait for you.'

It was a week since Judy had brought him here but Victor hadn't bothered to get in touch with the after-care people. They ought to be relieved, he thought, they must have enough on their plates.

'How are things? How have you been getting on?'

Victor said he was OK, he had been getting on all right. Going up the stairs, Tom talked in a very hearty way about the weather and about the neighbourhood, that this was really the best part of Acton and these houses particularly attractive. When he saw the writing about the shit hitting the fan he laughed rather too loudly and said he hoped that wasn't Victor's handiwork. Victor said nothing. When they were inside he made Tom a mug of Nescafé, thinking that later on he would have a drink. At last, after all these years, he would have a drink. Go out and buy himself a bottle of wine, maybe.

'Any prospect of a job?' Tom asked.

Victor shook his head. He had forgotten about trying to get a job, it had seemed unimportant. There were so many other things to think about and handle and live with.

At one time he had felt very differently. After one year at the polytechnic, they had refused to have him back because he had made such a mess of his first-year exams. He had done so deliberately. The course wasn't hard and he was sure he could have taken a good degree but it felt like school and he was sick of school. He wanted to work and make real money.

Jobs were not a problem in the late sixties. He could take his pick. He tried the Civil Service and he tried a bank, but both bored him. His father began to get heavy, making vague threats, so Victor left home and took a flat, paying rent in advance with an insurance policy which had matured when he was twenty-one. He had a new job selling cars. The showrooms were in North Finchley, his flat not far away in what the estate agent called 'Highgate Borders', and he was engaged to a girl he had met at the polytechnic and who was still a student there. If Pauline's temperament had been different in one respect, he sometimes thought, his whole life might have been changed, none of this might have happened. He would be happily married – for didn't all the psychologists say that the children of the happily married had themselves the best chance of happiness in marriage? – he would be a father, a householder, prosperous probably, respectable, content. But Pauline . . . what a piece of ill-luck that this woman of all women was the one he had taken up with! He didn't want to think about her now.

He could see that Tom, who was still talking about employment and unemployment, had his eyes fixed on the newspaper Victor had bought, which lay folded with the page uppermost on which the headline was 'Rape and its Aftermath'.

'You're sure you're all right,' Tom now said. 'There's nothing you're in need of?'

What on earth did he mean by that? What would he say if Victor answered that yes, there was plenty he was in need of? His youth back again, a place of his own far from here, a decent job he'd enjoy doing – and another thing too, something that just at present he wouldn't even name to himself. His eyes strayed to the open newspaper, the word on the page, and he felt the blood go out of his face and a shiver touch the nape of his neck.

Tom said, 'Look, Liz said to tell you to come and have Sunday lunch with us some time. I mean, why not this coming Sunday, Victor? Will you do that?'

Victor sensed the effort behind the invitation. He had the impression Tom had had to conquer an enormous distaste for the task, would have given a lot to forget it, but duty impelled him, social conscience forced him. Of course Victor didn't want to go, he wouldn't go, but he couldn't think of a reason for saying no. He said yes, he'd come, while making a private decision not to turn up when the time came.

After Tom had gone, Victor sat in the window, looking down over the roofs of houses, over the roof of the house where his mother and father had lived, and thought about things. It was seeing the house in Solent Gardens that had brought this about, even though he had resolved not to think about the past. He couldn't help it. It was funny how people expected you to mean the things you said, he thought. Judges and juries and policemen and psychiatrists and social workers and just about everyone took it for granted you meant what you said, though they didn't mean what they said, and of everything that was ever said, Victor estimated, only about a half or less was meant. They had called him a psychopath on the grounds of something he had said while he was in that bedroom with Rosemary Stanley. They took it as evidence of his cold-bloodedness and his intent to shoot Fleetwood.

'I won't kill her,' he had said to Fleetwood out of the window. 'I'll shoot her in the back, in the lower spine.'

Fleetwood hadn't been at the trial to repeat that, but Rosemary Stanley had and half a dozen witnesses. It never occurred to any of them that he hadn't meant it. In fact, he could remember exactly why he had said it. The evening before, at home in Finchley, he had been reading the evening paper, this same *Standard*, only they called it the *Evening Standard* in those days, and there was a piece in it about some old war hero, an ex-airman with a VC, who was paralysed through a spinal injury. And there was a bit by a doctor in the article writing about what happened to you when you got shot down there, in the 'lower spine'. The words had come back to him as he talked out of the window and he uttered them as if by inspiration, as the nastiest thing he could think of just at that moment. It was his bad luck that when he shot at Fleetwood – never having fired a gun before, hardly knowing where and how to aim – the bullet had struck him just where Victor had threatened to shoot Rosemary Stanley. Why he had fired at all he didn't know.

He had been so frightened, so intolerably frightened, in the worst panic of his life. Somehow, he had always thought, if he had been able to make them understand that, they would have let him off. But they never understood. They barely stopped to listen. And yet they must all have known fear, have been frightened out of their lives, just as every day they made remarks and comments, excuses and threats which they did not mean even at the very time of uttering them, which stemmed from fear or boredom or simply from not knowing what else to say.

Victor picked up the *Standard* and read the rape story again. The girl's name wasn't given but she was twenty-four, a hairdresser from Old Oak Road. She was 'recovering in hospital', her condition 'satisfactory'. Victor wondered who it was that had attacked her in that park so near to Muriel's house and where he was now and what he was thinking. He turned the page and his eyes met those of David Fleetwood, sitting in his wheelchair with his dog beside him.

The story was a chatty piece. Fleetwood was writing his

memoirs, in fact had written them, and this autobiography was to be published in the autumn. There was talk of a sale of television rights. The photograph showed Fleetwood sitting in the garden at the front of his house in Theydon Bois, where he had been living for the past three years. Victor thought of the houses which stood in his life like landmarks. It was as if his life were a road and, as this road curved, another house of disturbing or even terrible significance came into view. His parents' house first of all, the one whose roof he could see, then Muriel's grotesque Tudor pile, the house in Solent Gardens with its broken window and the wind blowing in to lift the curtain, now this one, Fleetwood's house in Theydon Bois.

Of the four the latter was the most attractive, part brick, part dark weatherboard, with a gable and latticed windows, a porch over an oak-studded door, a large integral garage, climbing plants, roses perhaps, half covering the wall and now coming into leaf. The front garden was neat and well tended, a garden pretty enough to be on a seed packet or advertising something – a hosepipe, say, or a lawn mower. Tulips filled the bed under the front windows and some sort of blossoming tree was in flower. On a birdbath a pigeon had obligingly perched, or perhaps the bird was made of stone. Fleetwood sat in his wheelchair, his knees covered by a rug, one hand on his labrador's head, the other holding some sheets of manuscript. He had been interviewed by the *Standard*'s reporter, talking about the book mostly, though not mentioning the actual incident that had caused his paralysis. Yes, he did feel pleased about the book; he would be getting a substantial advance from his publishers; but no, he wasn't planning to do any more writing in the future. Marriage? He didn't think so, though of course it was possible. Well, yes, he did have a girlfriend. Clare, she was called, and she had typed the manuscript for him.

It was all right for some, Victor thought, folding up the paper and putting it under the bamboo table out of sight. Money, success, a woman, a nice house – Fleetwood had everything; and what did he have? A furnished room, a sum of money in the bank that was very small by today's standards, an aunt whose property he just might inherit if she forgot to make a will. If she remembered to make one, he certainly wouldn't inherit anything. Muriel, anyway, though she looked a hundred, couldn't in fact be more than in her mid-sixties and might very likely live twenty years.

His youth he had lost. It was pointless looking at it in any other way. Those years he had spent in prison were the best years of a man's life. That was the period of life when the best things happened to you, when you got on and when you settled down. Alan, for instance, who was the same age, would be married now with a house of his own and flourishing business. Victor had slaved for him, sweated his guts out getting up at all hours and often not going to bed at all, worked for him for five years after he got fed up with selling Fords, and Alan hadn't even come to see him in prison, hadn't so much as written. Pauline, he thought, would be married now to some poor devil who had perhaps adjusted to what Victor had never been able to accustom himself to: her icy impenetrable coldness. Well, no, not impenetrable, for he had penetrated on numerous occasions a limp flaccid body which lay passive as blancmange while Pauline studied something on the wall with intense concentration, her mind elsewhere. Once he had observed her counting on her fingers, doing sums. After a while this affected him so that he wilted inside her. Pauline hadn't seemed to notice. That had been around the time when she had begun being more wakeful and active during their sexual moments, wakeful and active to the extent of chatting about what her mother had said to her on the phone that morning and her history tutor's comments on her latest essay. Victor had got up and put his clothes on and gone out into the dark and raped a girl who was taking a short cut home through Highgate Wood. The girl had been terrified and had shouted and fought. It wasn't like doing it to a dead sheep with a chit-chat tape playing. It was wonderful. She had cried out, 'Don't, don't, don't – Oh, no, no, no!' She howled like an animal. 'Oh, no, no, no!'

It took Victor some time – by then he had committed three more rapes – to remember where and in what circumstances he had heard that before. When he did remember, he refused to think about it. It seemed disgusting, blasphemous almost, to think of that. By then Pauline and he had parted. But if she had been warm and loving, greedy for sex as he had read that women in the 1970s inevitably were, if she had been all this and his wife, would he ever have attacked the two women on Hampstead Heath, the girls on Wandsworth Common, Wanstead Flats in Epping Forest? That Christmas, if that different Pauline, that transformed Pauline, had been with him instead of gone five years before, would he have been so interested in Sydney's Luger and a few months later stolen it?

That night he slept badly and dreamed a lot. When Tom had been gone an hour or so he had gone out and bought a bottle of wine and drunk it all. It was the first alcohol he had tasted for nearly eleven years. It made him drunk, which was what he wanted, though he didn't want the after-effects. His dream was an enlarging of that fantasy of his about his life as a road and the houses which appeared as he rounded the bends in it. Only this time, after Muriel's house and before 62 Solent Gardens, there came into view along the road the block of flats in Finchley High Road where he had lived with Pauline and the house in Ballards Lane where he had been renting the top floor at the time of his arrest. He walked on, though the surface which had been smooth was now rough like a cart track, with stones and rocks in his path like the stones in the mountainous front garden at Muriel's. The house in Solent Gardens stood alone, having been lopped off from its fellows in the terrace, and the upper window was still broken, the wind blowing in and lifting the curtain. Why, in his imagination and his dreams, did he always see it from this side, the outside, when from that aspect he had glimpsed it only once, when they had brought him out between two policemen, his hands manacled?

The next house along the road that he came to was Fleetwood's with its gable and its black weatherboard and climbing roses, but it wasn't the last. The last was the prison where he had spent half his adult life, a red-brick sprawl with a forest of chimneys sprouting out of its red roofs.

Why did prisons always have so many chimneys, he asked himself stupidly as he woke up. It wasn't as if they were warm places or distinguished for their cooking or the standard of their laundry. His heart was pounding, his head throbbed and his mouth was bone dry. Because he couldn't go back to sleep again, he got up, drank pints of water straight from the tap, his mouth over the tap, and sat by the window, looking hopelessly out over Acton. It was dawn, pearl-grey and misty, the swell of traffic noise mounting already, birds starting to sing. All the gardens he could see were filled with small trees coming into leaf and flower, green and white and pink, so that a muslin-pale haze of colour lay like a thin printed cloth over earth and brick and stone. Hating the human race, Victor thought with an anger that made him clench his fists how all these householders were so mean and grudging that they wouldn't even plant a tree unless it was a fruit tree they could get something out of.

Why had his life been passed in these dreary suburbs? He had never lived anywhere interesting or different, though there were plenty of interesting places he had passed through on his way to the airports at Heathrow and Gatwick and Luton and Stansted. Like most Londoners born north of the river, he found it hard to contemplate living south of it. The west side of London he had enough of and he told himself he hated the north. Go east then, a long way, to Epping perhaps or Harlow, or as far as Bishops Stortford.

Three hours later he was once more making his way down Gunnersbury Avenue towards Muriel's house in Popesbury Drive. This was the way he had regularly driven to Heathrow. He missed the use of a car. Would he ever have one again? He supposed he could go out to Epping –

if he was serious about that – by bus or coach or all the way to the end of the Central Line.

A lot more trees had come into leaf in the week since he was last here. Over the craggy outcroppings up to Muriel's front door the hanging plants had burst into masses of purple flowers, pink and mauve and purple and puce, so bright they hurt the eyes. Victor could hear Muriel scuffling about inside, fumbling at the door. She knew who it was – she had seen him from the window or she had guessed. The blue dressing gown and the mules she wore were the same, and so was the smell of camphor, but the pink snood with which she had covered her hair had been changed for a brown one. She peered suspiciously out at him, grudgingly easing the door open, widening inch by inch the gap between door and door frame until it was just wide enough for Victor to pass through.

'What d'you want this time?'

He might have been some importunate beggar always bothering her for money or meals rather than a nephew whom she had seen only twice in ten years. Needless to say, Muriel hadn't been to see him in prison either. If she wouldn't set foot outside for her husband's funeral, she'd hardly have gone prison visiting. Yet he had never done her any harm. You couldn't call taking that gun harming her, and if the police had come here questioning her about it and searching the place, no one had blamed her, no one had put her away for ten years. He followed her into the living room, explaining about Jupp and how he would be coming to look at the furniture two weeks from today.

The room was stuffy with a fine fug built up. A large electric fire with two elements was switched on. Muriel had made herself a cosy haven or enclave in front of this fire, an island in the sea of magazines. There was the armchair in which she had been sitting with two cushions in the back of it and a pillow in a dirty white pillowcase, a plaid rug over one arm, a footstool that looked like a hassock pinched out of a church, a table on each side of it, one with a library book on it, a pair of glasses and a bottle of aspirins, the other containing a pile of magazines, a

77

ballpoint pen and a pair of scissors. Instead of returning to her chair, Muriel stood there hesitantly, looking at him with a truculent stare. From a distant part of the house a whistle started up and rose to a scream.

Of course Victor knew quite well what this must be, or he knew within a split second. At the start of it though, he gave a slight jump and for some reason this brought a grin to Muriel's face.

'I was going to make myself a coffee,' she said.

Victor followed her down the passage to the kitchen. Muriel shuffled along, the belt of her dressing gown trailing behind her. For some reason she never fastened the belt but preferred to hold the sides of the dressing gown together with her left hand. The kettle was jumping about on the gas and squealing. Muriel was very slow. She put a spoonful of instant coffee into each cup, calculating that they contained precisely the same amount by studying the individual grains and tipping an extra grain off the top of the second one with a knife. Victor's nerves couldn't stand the bouncing and squealing and he pushed past her to lift the kettle off the gas. She looked at him in resentful surprise. She opened the fridge and removed a small carton of double cream. This went on to a round tray with one of the cups of coffee, a sugar basin and two biscuits on a plate. The biscuits were of the kind made for children called Iced Bears, shaped like teddy bears with coloured sugar on them. On to a second, smaller tray Muriel put the other cup of coffee and pushed it across the table to Victor.

He could hardly believe his eyes. The tray with the cream and biscuits she meant exclusively for herself, she was hugging it to her with her hands round its rim. He didn't even merit a teaspoon. But what was the use of arguing with her? He reached across the table for the sugar, climbing over her hands, so to speak, in order to do so, like someone scaling a fence that surrounds a forbidden park. Taking his cup, he went out into the garage to have another look at the furniture. It was wonderful how material, mere pieces of coloured fabric, could awaken so much in the memory. Covering a bedstead and some sort of chest were the curtains which had hung at his own bedroom windows when he was a boy. They must have been of very good quality to have lasted so long, a pattern of bluish-green and red blocks on a black and white background, postwar and early fifties' fashion. He could clearly remember lying in bed and looking at that pattern, the sunlight shining through and making them transparent, or else they would be opaque when there was darkness outside. He would lie there waiting for his mother to come upstairs and tuck him in and kiss him goodnight. Sometimes, before he could read, he hoped for a story as well. She always promised to come but she seldom did; she was with his father, distracted by his father's greater glamour, stronger desirability. The neglect wasn't bad enough to make him cry, though, and he would fall asleep with the last thing printed on his retina those curtains patterned in bluish-green and red blocks on a black and white background.

Perhaps he shouldn't let Jupp have all this furniture. If he was going to find himself somewhere to live in Epping, he might need it. Suddenly Victor knew he wouldn't be able to live with the furniture which had surrounded him when he was a boy. It was painful even to look at it. The curtain patterns, for some reason, were the worst, but the beds were bad too and that brown velvet settee. The only thing, he decided, he felt all right about was his father's wheelchair, and that was perhaps because he hadn't been there when his father had got it and he had never seen his father using it. Victor drank his coffee and covered up the bed and chest again and asked himself why he was suddenly taking it for granted that he was going to live in Epping. Surely he hadn't decided on that? He had never really been to Epping, just passed through on his way to Stansted, and once of course stopped off in the Forest near a pub called, he thought, the Robin Hood. And there, a good quarter of a mile from the road, in a glade of bracken and birch trees, he had come upon a woman walking alone, not young or pretty or in any way attractive to him, but a woman alone . . .

Victor went back into the kitchen. His aunt had gone. He found her back in her armchair in front of the electric fire in the close camphor-smelling fug, cutting a piece out of a sheet of newsprint with her scissors.

'I've got something to show you,' she said.

'No, thanks. I know what it is.' Out of the corner of his eye he had seen the photographed corner of Fleetwood's house, a section of gable, an inch of chimney stack.

She took no notice but went on cutting, holding the paper and the scissors right up close to her nose. 'He's writing a book,' she said. 'It's going to be all about his past life.'

'I know,' said Victor. 'I've seen the paper. You're not telling me anything I don't know.'

'You'll be in it.'

He felt anger beginning to mount again, hot liquid rising in the vessel of his body.

'There's bound to be a long bit in it about you, with pictures.' She laid the scissors down, folded the cut piece of paper in two. Her face was raised up towards his, the sagging flesh of her neck hanging in a double pleat from her chin. 'It's only what you deserve,' she said.

Victor had read somewhere that walking or any vigorous exercise frees the body of tensions and calms anger. He didn't find this to be true in his own case. Making his way back to Gunnersbury Avenue, he was filled with murderous rage, to the brim now. The lack of understanding maddened him, not just in his aunt, in everyone, all those people who couldn't see why things happened, how things could happen to you almost without your being aware of them, and then – you were punished for ever, and even then they said it wasn't enough.

He would be in Fleetwood's book. Victor wasn't much of a reader, he had always preferred films and television, but if he ever read anything it was biography and memoirs. If Fleetwood were to write a book about his life, indeed had done so, Victor would be in it, with a chapter to himself probably, with photographs of himself. While his trial was going on, newspapers had used a studio portrait of himself taken at his mother's request at the time of his twenty-first birthday. His mother wouldn't have given it to a reporter, so Muriel must have done. Another photograph was the one of him being brought out of 62 Solent Gardens between two policemen. Probably both these would be in Fleetwood's book – unless he could stop it by some legal means, though he didn't know how to go about this and was afraid anyway that it might cost a lot of money.

Could Fleetwood say what he liked about him in the book and he have no redress? No doubt, Fleetwood would call him a psychopath and those words he had shouted out of the window would be quoted again: 'I'll shoot her in the back, in the lower spine!'

When she had stood in the witness box and repeated those words, Rosemary Stanley had cried. She had stumbled over the words and begun to weep – a very effective method, Victor had thought, of getting all the sympathy of the court, as if she didn't have enough already. That would doubtless be in Fleetwood's book, even though he wasn't at the trial. And Fleetwood's book was going to be on sale everywhere, in paperback as well, turned into a film for television. The idea made Victor feel sick. As soon as he was back in his room, he took the *Standard* from the rack under the bamboo coffee table in order to read the article again, to learn from it what he could. But he had left the paper folded so that the Gunnersbury Park rape story was uppermost and a line caught his eye, a kind of subheading in quotation marks: 'Rape is not a sexual act but an act of aggression'. Some psychiatrist had said it. He was wondering what it meant, how screwing a girl could be anything but sexual, when the front doorbell rang. Victor had heard that bell ring before, usually in the evening when one of the other tenants had gone to answer it. Whoever it was it couldn't be for him and he wasn't going to answer it now. The bell rang again. Victor heard footsteps and then voices. Someone had opened the front door and this surprised him, very slightly alarmed him, for he had been nearly certain there was no one in the house.

Footsteps started up the stairs. He *knew* they would go past his door and on up, they had to, there was no one who could possibly want him. There were at least two people coming upstairs. The knocking on his door was like thunder, the kind of thunder that makes you jump because it is preceded by no warning flash of lightning. Victor's calm, his sanity, his euphoria, vanished and he felt panic like a mass of tingling wires. He opened the door, aware of how vulnerable, how helpless, he must look.

Outside stood a woman in a hat and two men in the kind of leisure wear the police thought disguised them. Victor knew the woman must be Mrs Griffiths, his landlady. He knew it from the expression on her face, forbearing, patient, virtuous yet mildly disapproving, the kind of look worn by someone who is socially conscientious enough to take ex-convicts into her house, along with all the inevitable consequences.

'CID,' said the older man, the one in the heather-mixture tweed jacket. 'Can we have a word, Vic?'

6

No one ever called him that. Vic – he hated it, it sounded like the stuff his mother rubbed on his chest when he was a child. And what right had they to call him by his Christian name anyway? He heard the younger one, the one in the distressed leather jacket, say, 'Thanks very much, Mrs Griffiths. Sorry to bother you.' They didn't call *her* Betty or Lily or whatever her name was. But he had been in prison, of course, and therefore forfeited his human dignity, his right to respect for ever and ever.

They came in and Distressed Leather shut the door.

Heather Mixture said, 'Nice little place you've got here.'

Victor said nothing. The palms of his hands tingled, he felt a creeping in his shoulders as if an insect was crawling across his back. He sat down. They didn't.

'Don't suppose you need to go out much. Haven't got a job, have you?'

Replying to this with a shake of his head, Victor wondered if he would be able to find a voice. His throat had closed. He would have liked to ask what they wanted rather than endure all this facetious preamble but he didn't dare experiment with speech. They were both staring at him but at least Distressed Leather had sat down.

'Still, you've been out today, need a breath of fresh air sometimes, no doubt. We're having a nice spring, aren't we? It's often the way after a bad summer. But you wouldn't know about that really, would you, having been – what shall we say – out of circulation at the time? Most people in your situation, Vic, find going out a bit of an ordeal at first. But it hasn't taken you that way, am I right?'

Victor lifted his crawling shoulders.

'No, it hasn't taken you that way,' repeated Heather

Mixture. 'You've been out, you've faced the world. How many times have you been out, would you reckon? Every day, every other day, twice a day? How about last Monday, for instance? Did you go out then?'

His voice came, less than a voice but better than a croak. 'Why d'you want to know?'

Even as he spoke, he knew. Nonetheless, it was a horrible shock to him. On Monday night a girl had been raped in Gunnersbury Park, he had read about it in the *Standard*; he had bought the *Standard* and read about it on his way back from Jupp's. He hadn't been to prison for rape, he had been in prison for shooting David Fleetwood, but once he had been convicted, before sentence was passed, he had asked through his counsel, on his counsel's advice, for two cases of rape to be taken into consideration. This had been done expediently in case the police tried to charge him with these offences once he had served his sentence. Victor's counsel was not to know that those two instances were not the only rapes Victor had committed.

He hadn't wanted to mention them at all, he hadn't wanted to bring it – his nature – out into the open. But he had, he had yielded to persuasion. And now the police knew. He must be on a file somewhere, a file on one of these computers which had taken over the world while he was inside. Victor didn't want to think, now, of the implications of that.

'Let's play it this way,' said Heather Mixture. 'You answer my question first. How about that?'

'I went to see my aunt.'

Heather Mixture's facial muscles didn't move but a grin twitched at Distressed Leather's mouth.

'And where might this lady live?'

'Gunnersbury.'

They went stiff and still. For a moment.

'As to your question, Vic, I think we can forget that, don't you? You know very well what we're on about. You know what you are and we know. It would save a lot of time and trouble if we all got in the car and went down to the police station.'

They wanted to carry out some tests. Heather Mixture had all sorts of amusing euphemisms for being in prison, bringing them out one after another, for the sake of seeing Victor's discomfiture perhaps and Distressed Leather's twitching sycophantic mouth. At first Victor refused, saying he wanted his lawyer. The name of the solicitor who had briefed counsel for him nearly eleven years ago he still remembered, but not the man's office address or phone number. Nor did he have a five- or ten-pence piece for the phone. Heather Mixture said he could have his solicitor, no problem, easiest thing out, he could phone him from the police station. At that Victor gave in because he thought they could probably eventually *make* him go to the police station, though how he didn't know.

The girl's name was Susan Davies. She was in hospital and would be there for a long time. She had described her attacker as being between twenty-five and thirty-five, dark-haired, of medium height. They told him all that. When Victor pointed out that he was thirty-eight, Heather Mixture said most people liked being taken for younger than they were and, anyway, you didn't age so fast when you were sheltered from the world in durance vile.

They told Victor they would like to do a blood test. Victor said he wanted his lawyer. Nothing easier, said a detective inspector Victor hadn't seen before, but when he asked for a phone directory the detective inspector said he couldn't quite lay hands on one just at that moment and why didn't Victor go over to the lab with Sergeant Latimer (Distressed Leather) and have his blood tested while he looked for a phone book? Of course Victor went. He was considerably unnerved. Latimer explained something to him he hadn't known before – perhaps it wasn't generally known or hadn't even been discovered before he went to prison. This was that some men are what are called 'secretors', that is, their blood group can be detected from their semen and other body fluids. There was no knowing whether or not Victor was a secretor without carrying out tests.

Victor now saw that it was very much in his own interests

to have the tests done. He stopped worrying about finding a solicitor. All he wanted was to get out of there and get home – exonerated. He hadn't raped Susan Davies but he could already see that *circumstantially* he wasn't going to be able to prove he hadn't been in Gunnersbury Park at the relevant time. There were no witnesses he could produce that he had been at home. And his Aunt Muriel – if it was imaginable that anyone could get any sense out of her – could only say that he had been with her for a couple of hours in the afternoon. The blood test would prove it. Three quarters of all people were secretors, Latimer said.

They kept him hanging about there until they got the results of the tests. Nothing more was said about a telephone directory and Victor didn't mention it. It was early evening and they had brought him a hamburger and a cup of tea before they told him the results. Well, they didn't exactly tell him, they wouldn't, they merely said he could go home, they wouldn't want to be seeing him again. Like Judy and Tom, only more so, they treated him as if he were sub-human, sub-intelligent. Victor said he supposed he must be a secretor then. That's right, the detective inspector said. What blood group was he, Victor asked, not expecting an answer, expecting to be told this was a police station, if he didn't mind, not a Harley Street consulting room. But the inspector told him, laconically, dismissively. It appeared that he was B positive. Did that mean anything to him? Victor left.

On the way home he went into a wineshop and bought a quarter bottle of whisky and twenty cigarettes. Soon after he went to prison he had stopped smoking, though it was possible to smoke in there at certain prescribed times. But he had stopped. Now he felt he needed something strong and comforting to drink. At least he hadn't succumbed to panic, he hadn't fallen into raving madness and tried to grab, hit or shake them. He congratulated himself on that. The cigarettes and the scotch would take care of this shaking which had taken over his hands and sometimes his knees too from the moment he left the police station.

He let himself into the house. Mrs Griffiths, in hat, coat

and gloves, was in the hall talking to a young woman Victor had never seen before. The young woman looked away. Mrs Griffiths gave him a tight smile which Victor knew meant it was one thing having ex-convicts in one's house but only if they had turned over a new leaf. It was seven years since he had smoked a cigarette. The first puff made his gorge rise and he vomited into the sink. He sat down on the bed shivering.

Things suddenly presented themselves to him with an awful clarity. While it had obviously been in his interest to have those tests done at that particular point in time, taking the long view it was a disaster. They had found out his blood group, they had found he was a secretor, and on top of that was the misfortune that he belonged to a rare blood group. Victor remembered incongruously an occasion years and years ago watching a television show in which the comedian Tony Hancock appeared in a sketch about blood groups. The point was that he turned out to have the rarest known group, AB negative. B positive, which was Victor's group, wasn't as rare as that but still only six per cent of the population belonged to it.

Every time there was an attack on a girl in West London – in the whole of London and the Home Counties, come to that – and there was evidence that the perpetrator was a B secretor, they would come to him. But that was one thing, that could be borne, since there would be few cases. What if he himself were the perpetrator? Victor knew the time would come when he would want to assault a girl again. There was a part of him which said it wouldn't, that he would struggle for his own sake to avoid this, but at the same time he knew that the struggle couldn't be wholly effective.

He poured some of the whisky into one of Mrs Griffith's thick moulded glasses, the kind that are given away with a sale of more than thirty litres of petrol. There was no question of vomiting that up. It warmed him and swam into his head. If the time came when he attacked a girl, *when* the time came, they would do whatever you did do to a computer, type it like a typewriter probably, and up would come a printout: Victor Jenner, 38, 46 Tolleshunt Avenue, Acton, W5, secretor, blood group B Pos . . . And it would, must happen every time, only there wouldn't be 'every' time – there would be the once and the last, for after that he would be in gaol for the rest of his life. He could imagine the judge calling him a 'dangerous animal' who would have to be locked up 'for the safety of the community', a 'wild beast' who, unless permanently restrained, would indiscriminately ravish women and murder men. The thing was that he wasn't really like that at all, Victor thought; he was frightened and panicky and alone. He would have liked help but he didn't know where to get it – certainly not from Tom or Judy, who would offer evening classes and community service.

How different must be the life of David Fleetwood whose fault all this was! Fleetwood was safe, secure, housed, pensioned. His sexual problems had been taken care of in the soundest, most final way. Victor, sitting on his bed drinking whisky in the darkening room, thought he wouldn't mind *that* solution to his own dilemma. Then the desire, the temptation, the uncontrollable urge, would be gone for ever. And most of all Fleetwood had respect. Everyone respected him, positively worshipped and honoured him. If he had had to go to a police station for tests, they would probably have called him sir. It was ironical really. Fleetwood had brought all this about by his obtuseness, yet it was he who had all the glory and Victor who got all the stick, on and on for years. Perhaps Fleetwood had done it on purpose, Victor thought. Human behaviour was incomprehensible, everyone knew that. Perhaps Fleetwood had got himself shot on purpose, knowing he would get looked after for life and that people adored a crippled hero.

Victor walked along Twyford Avenue towards the High Street. He had passed two dreadful nights and a bad day. Both nights he had wakened up with his heart racing and his body all a-prickle. The first time he had lain there weeping, then turning his face into the pillow to muffle the screams he couldn't otherwise control. In the morning he had met a fellow tenant on the landing, a man, who had asked him if he had heard anything in the night, someone crying, for instance, and a noise like bedsprings repetitively jerked. Victor muttered that he had heard nothing. Most of the day he had slept, finding it easy to sleep, escaping thankfully into sleep as a respite from life. But that night the panic came upon him with redoubled force, enclosing him in its straitjacket way, convulsing his limbs with a kind of spasticity, so that he could not lie still but had to jump out of bed and seize and manhandle the nearest object. This happened to be the cane chair, which he found himself grasping and pounding, up-down, up-down, first against the wall and then on the floor. His teeth were clenched and he could hear himself make a kind of growling sound.

One of the legs split off the chair and hung by a strand of raffia. Spent and gasping, Victor flung himself on the bed. Almost immediately someone knocked on his door. Victor took no notice. His heart was beating so hard that it hurt him with its pumping as if it would pump its way out through his chest wall. Whoever had knocked at the door shouted that they wanted to know what the hell was going on. Victor staggered to the door, put his mouth close to it and whispered that it was nothing, it was over. 'For Christ's sake,' said the voice.

Victor had no more sleep. He got up very early and went out on to the landing with a bar of soap and a pot scourer and erased the writing on the wall. There was no point in it any more. It had happened. The shit had hit the fan.

He went to the library to see what he could read up about blood grouping. There was quite a lot of literature about it. Victor knew he was an intelligent person – someone had measured his IQ for him when he was at college and it had come out at 130 – and usually able to grasp scientific data, but blood grouping was too much for him. It was too complicated and abstruse for him to follow. What he did gather was that the ABO system had been discovered as far back as 1900 but that since then a dozen or so other systems had been found, including the Rhesus one, and all these could be tested for, thus fining down even further the possibilities of whose blood was whose. There was the MNS system, the Lutheran, the Kell, the Yt and the Domrock. Why, it looked as if the time would come when everybody's blood group would turn out to be different from everybody else's.

But later he began to think about it more rationally. He had never been charged with rape and rape had never been proved against him. Besides that, he intended never to attack a woman again. If he could survive ten years in prison without attacking a woman, surely he could survive the rest of his life. 'Rape is not a sexual act but an act of aggression,' the newspaper had told him. Was it anger then that made him attack women, and if he could otherwise handle his anger would that make him stop wanting to attack them?

Tom lived in North Ealing, up near Park Royal station. Victor didn't think that the house was likely to be a landmark along his road, it being small, semi-detached and one of those between-the-wars council houses that proliferate in north-west London, though Tom probably owned it. An overturned tricycle lay on the patch of grass in front and beside it a teddy bear face-downwards, looking as if someone had shot it in the back. Victor winced and wondered why he had had to think of that comparison. He hadn't meant to come at all but to spend the day working out some plan for the future, walking first, continuing with the business of accustoming himself to the outdoors, then in his room, calculating how much money he had and how much he could muster. But he had got no further than Ealing Common when the rain began and he went into the tube station to take shelter. It wasn't going to stop, it was coming down in summer tempests. Park Royal was only two stops up the line and at least he would get his lunch cooked for him.

The tricycle was covered with water drops and the teddy bear looked wet, though the rain had now stopped. Tom's children must have abandoned them to run indoors. Victor didn't much like children. A thin woman in trousers and a flowered apron opened the door to him, smiling much too enthusiastically and assuring him in a very hearty way how delighted she was to see him, how she and the children had been looking forward to meeting him. A curious memory came back to Victor as he entered the living-dining room. It was of a newspaper article he had read years ago, long before he went to prison, in which the theory was put forward that no one can be in prison for more than five years and remain quite sane. A psychiatrist had written it, someone who called himself a behaviourist. Victor hadn't remembered that all the time he had been in prison, but he did now, and with a kind of jolt or shock – but he didn't know why he remembered it, there being nothing about Liz Welch or the small shabby cluttered room to bring it to mind.

'Tom's just popped out to get a bottle,' she said. 'Wine, I mean. Would you like a can of beer for now?'

They lived in the kind of hand-to-mouth way, Victor thought, which obliged them to run out to a wineshop whenever anyone came. There was very likely a single can of beer in the house. He had never drunk beer, didn't like it. The Welches were poor. Tom didn't get paid for working for the after-care people, he was a schoolteacher by profession, but Victor didn't feel particularly sorry for him. It seemed to him insane to marry and lumber oneself with all this.

The children came in, subdued, staring. The little girl wore steel-framed glasses. The boy, who was younger, had a bandaged knee through which the blood was beginning to ooze. When he saw the blood he burst into loud cries, was taken on to his mother's lap and comforted. Mrs Welch talked to Victor about the weather, other topics not being safe.

'All this rain day after day,' she said, unwinding the bandage. 'There hasn't been a day in the past week without rain. As bad as last year, isn't it?'

She realized what she had said and blushed. Victor enjoyed her discomfiture. He wondered if it was Tom who had told the police where he was to be found. But Tom didn't know about his history as a rapist, did he? Tom came in while Liz was re-bandaging the child's knee. It had come on to rain again and water was streaming off his bright blue nylon cape. He shook hands heartily with Victor, produced the bottle of Bulgarian red wine he had gone out to buy and said they would be all right now.

Victor suddenly decided against telling Tom he intended to move away from London. The less anyone knew about his movements the better. If they had been alone, he might have mentioned his fears about appearing in Fleetwood's book and asked where he could go for advice about taking legal steps. But he wasn't going to talk about it in front of this woman – he hoped she would wash her hands before she served the food – or this squalling boy or the girl who since she had come into the room had done nothing but stand in front of him and stare.

Lunch came at last. It was roast pork, apple sauce, tinned peas and old potatoes that were boiled, not roasted, followed by a Sainsbury's raspberry and redcurrant tart with custard made from powder. It reminded Victor of better Sunday dinners in prison. Tom talked about television programmes and Victor said he was thinking of renting a television set. This seemed to thrill the Welches because it gave them an opportunity to recommend various rental companies and compare what they knew of rival costs. Tom went outside to make coffee while Liz cleared the table.

Left alone with the children, Victor hid himself behind the *Sunday Express*. As far as he could see, there was nothing in it about rape or Fleetwood. The extraordinary thing was that on an inside page he came upon a photograph of a man on a horse riding in Epping Forest. It seemed to mean something, it seemed as if fate was pointing him that way. And of course it wasn't all that extraordinary. It was well known, for instance that things went in threes, that you had only to come upon a new name or place for it to recur twice more that day. He was startled by a fist banging on the paper from behind and he drew it away, not intending to lower it. But the little girl caught hold of the top of the paper and pulled it down, bringing her face close to his over the top of it.

'What's a lag?' the child said.

Victor muttered, 'I don't know.'

'My daddy told my mum we'd have to have one of his old lags over on Sunday.'

Sometimes Victor thought he had educated himself from magazines. Most of the information stored in his brain seemed to have come from them. Perhaps reading magazines ran in his family or perhaps it was a passion that showed itself only in himself and Muriel, for he couldn't remember his father or mother ever reading anything much. But he could remember Muriel bringing him comics when he was very young, and perhaps the habit had started then.

An article in a magazine had led him to believe he might cure himself of his phobia. This was years ago, before prison, before the house in Solent Gardens, before he took Sydney's gun. The article said that the method it outlined was derived from modern psychotherapy treatment – only you proceeded on your own without the psychotherapist. You began by looking at pictures of the thing you feared. A week or two before this, a nature magazine had been among the ones Victor had bought and the centrefold was devoted to a feature on terrestrial turtles of North America, principally to the courtship ritual of the gopher tortoise. Catching a glimpse of this, barely more than that, Victor had slammed the magazine shut and put another magazine on top of it so that he shouldn't even see the cover. The cover was innocuous enough, being of a butterfly poised on the lip of an orchid, but because Victor knew what was inside, this innocent and in fact very beautiful photograph was enough to start a shiver up his spine. He did not throw the magazine away though, because there was another article in it he very much wanted to read – if he had the courage to touch even the outer pages again. Up till he had read the piece about the modern psychotherapy, he hadn't had that courage. Well, he would try.

In his teens, while he was still at school, they had gone on an educational visit to the Victoria and Albert Museum. In the museum was a Staffordshire teapot of the Whieldon type, circa 1765 – he could remember all that, he would never forget – made in the shape of a tortoise in tortoise-shell-patterned pottery. There it was, in front of him, eyeing him, a totally unexpected sight. Victor had fainted.

No one knew why. He wasn't going to tell them. Imagine letting one's schoolfellows find out about a thing like that. Boys of that age would have no mercy. The teachers who were with them thought he was ill, and in fact the incident had occurred not long after he had come back to school after having had flu with bronchitis. Since that time his phobia had been worse, had grown very slowly but progressively worse, until it reached a point where he not only couldn't look at a picture of the thing, he couldn't touch the book in which the picture was or even approach too closely the shelf or table where the book was. He suffered all this secretly, privately, in silence. Pauline had a tortoiseshell-backed hairbrush which he could touch, he could just touch it, but he disliked it and he didn't care to hear it called by name.

Of course one could pass through life encountering the land-dwelling turtles of the family *testudinae* only rarely. It wasn't like having a phobia for cats or spiders. But fainting in the V and A had really frightened Victor, just as these horrid glimpses in magazines frightened him, or the effect they had on him did. What would happen were he to see a real one?

With the aim of curing his phobia or attempting to cure it, he opened that magazine at the centrefold and made himself look. At first it was a dreadful experience, making him feel shivery, queasy and weak, then starting up a barely controllable shuddering. But he followed instructions. He told himself that this was a harmless reptile, that these were mere photographs of this harmless reptile, rendered in glossy colour on to paper. They could not hurt him and he

94

was free to close the magazine whenever he chose. And so on.

Up to a point it worked. He could look at those pictures. He could get quite blasé about them, though he would experience a great tiredness, a feeling of total exhaustion after one of these sessions. He went to the library, looked 'tortoise' up in the *Encyclopedia Britannica* and obliged himself to fix his eyes on the most awful picture he had ever seen in his whole life: a colour photograph of *testudo elephantopus*, the giant Galapagos tortoise, a huge reptile four feet long and weighing three hundred pounds. Fortunately, the picture of it was very small.

The next step would be to visit a pet shop. His nerve failed him. The article of instructions also failed because what was essential was the presence of the psychotherapist, if only in the role of a supportive human being. Victor couldn't do it on his own. He actually phoned a pet shop and asked them if they had any tortoises – he spoke the word aloud on the phone! – and they said they had and he started to go there, but he was worn out by the effort of it and his spirit was broken. What was the point anyway when you scarcely ever saw the things, or even their pictures, unless you went out of your way to find them?

But he fancied he had never been quite so bad since then. Some progress had been made, some success achieved. He could walk past pet shops now, he didn't have to make detours to avoid them, and he could look at the covers of nature magazines and touch them, despite what might, what just possibly might, be inside. Since his emergence from prison, this slight emancipation he felt he had from his phobia wasn't put to the test until four or five mornings after his panicky crashing about in his room.

Someone knocked on his door at about nine thirty in the morning. It was Mrs Griffiths, whom Victor got a good look at for the first time. She was dressed rather as a woman might have been for a Buckingham Palace garden party taking place some thirty years before: a navy blue suit, frilly blouse, straw hat with a white nylon flower in it, white gloves and very high-heeled white openwork shoes.

Pinned to the left lapel of the suit jacket was a gold brooch in the shape of a tortoise, its shell formed of stones which might or might not have been sapphires.

'There've been complaints about you, Mr Jenner,' she said.

She didn't pull her punches or hesitate or preface her words with an 'I'm afraid' or 'you won't mind my saying'. She charged straight in, speaking in a coarse near-cockney voice very much at variance with her genteel appearance. Victor had given the brooch one glance, swallowed, and now was looking away. But he didn't feel like fainting, he didn't even feel sick. He even thought he would be able to look at it again provided he fixed his eyes on the blue stones and avoided the tiny gold protruding head.

'Banging about in the night,' she said. 'Stamping. Knocking on the wall and I don't know what.' He could see her eyeing the furniture for chips or missing legs. 'What were you up to?'

'I have bad dreams,' he said, his eyes going back to the brooch.

'Just have them lying down in bed next time,' she said and, aware of his hypnotic gaze and perhaps also of the pallor of his face, 'I hope you're all right, Mr Jenner. I hope we're not going to have any trouble. For instance,' she said, 'are the police likely to come back?'

'No,' said Victor. 'Oh, no.'

It would be a good idea to move as soon as possible, Victor thought after she had gone. When he closed his eyes, he could see that brooch, a glowing dark image on a white background, but gradually it faded and disappeared.

7

There was a tube map on the station platform just as there had always been on stations. Victor didn't bother to look at it because the indicator informed him that the next train due would be going to Epping. It wasn't quite at the extreme other end of the Central Line but almost. A small subsidiary line went on to North Weald and Ongar during the rush hours. He stood on the platform with a return ticket for Epping in his pocket, waiting for the train that would go no further than Epping. Later on, in the weeks to come, he was to wonder what would have happened if he had looked at that tube map. Would his life have been utterly changed, have run along a different track, so to speak, an alternate line? Certainly he might have changed his mind about going to Epping that day. But in the long run, probably not. Probably, by then, he was committed to certain steps, to certain inevitable courses, even though these were not known to his conscious mind.

The journey was long and slow, for the line soon entered the tunnel, and would not emerge again till the eastern edge of London. Victor had bought *Ellery Queen's Mystery Magazine* and *Private Eye* to read. The train began filling up at Notting Hill Gate. An elderly woman, very overweight, cast longing glances at his seat and sighed each time she was jostled or someone pushed past her. Victor wasn't giving up his seat to her. Why should he? No woman had ever done a thing for him; they had been positively antagonistic to him: his neglectful mother, that malicious old bag Muriel, Pauline, Rosemary Stanley, who had screamed and broken a window when he threw himself on her mercy, that hard-faced Griffiths woman. He owed women nothing and he felt rather resentful when a man of her own age got up to give this one a seat.

The train finally emerged from the tunnel after Leyton. Victor had never been this far along the line before. This was deepest suburbia, the view being of the backs of houses with long gardens full of grass and flowers and pear trees in bloom running down to the track. Four more stations of this sort of thing and then, after Buckhurst Hill, a burst of countryside, part of the Green Belt encircling London. Loughton, Debden, and what seemed to be an enormous estate of council houses with industrial areas. The train came out into more or less unspoiled country again, slowed and drew to a stop. The station was Theydon Bois.

Victor stared at the name. He hadn't looked at the tube map and it had never occurred to him that Theydon Bois would be in this particular forest corner, adjacent to Epping. Essex, the *Standard* had said, and of course this was Essex, metropolitan Essex but still Essex. It was one of the biggest counties of England, extending from Woodford in the south as far north as Harwich. The effect on Victor of seeing that name, the letters of the two words seeming to stand out and vibrate, was one of sickening shock. He stood up and stared at it, leaning across the seat, resting his hands on the window ledge. The doors closed and the train began to move. Victor turned away and looked unseeing into the face of a fellow passenger, a middle-aged man.

The man grinned at him. 'Theydon Bois,' he said, 'or Theydon Bwah, as the natives don't call it,' and he sniggered at his joke.

Victor said nothing. He sat down again in a daze. This, then, was where Fleetwood lived. Out there, somewhere beyond the station buildings and the trees, was the house with the weatherboard and the gable, the roses round the door and the birdbath in the garden. If he had looked at the tube map, Victor thought, he would have seen where Theydon Bois was and he wouldn't have come. If he closed his eyes he could see that name, Theydon Bois, in dazzling white letters that vibrated a little, that danced. He wished very much that he hadn't come, for he felt nauseous now, a real physical sickness. And what was the point of his coming to Epping anyway? What did he think he would get out of it? He couldn't afford to buy a place and there would be no flats to let here, there never were in places like this. As if he would think of living only a mile away from Fleetwood!

The train stopped at Epping and Victor got out. This was the end of the line anyway. He had hesitated, thinking he might just as well stay in the train and go back again, but it was his feeling of nausea that stopped him. Fresh air would help that. He imagined being sick in the train with people looking.

Epping hadn't changed much as far as he could see. The High Street seemed a bit quieter, if anything, less congested, and there were street signs which seemed to indicate that new roads to divert the traffic, motorways, had been built during those lost ten years of his. The wide market place looked much the same, as did the water tower shaped like a castle with a single turret sticking out of one corner that you could see from miles away, the grey stone church, the big triangular green and the tall shady trees. Victor walked from one end of the town to the other, from the Forest side of the tower up to nearly as far as St Margaret's Hospital. He didn't see much, the process of seeing, of registering what he saw, seemed to have gone into abeyance. All he could think about was Fleetwood and the fact that Fleetwood was no more than a mile or two away from him, over that hillside, to the south-east. Or perhaps even nearer, for when Theydon Bois people went shopping surely they would come here?

Walking back, down the hill, he was aware that he was looking for Fleetwood. There were a lot of cars parked and Victor looked at all of them, seeking the sticker of a pin man in a wheelchair disabled people have on their car windows. If Fleetwood were shopping in the town he would himself be in a wheelchair. Victor caught sight of a wheelchair outside a supermarket and he approached it with a return of that sick feeling. But already, from a distance of fifty yards, he could see that the occupant, whose back was to him, had fair hair. As he passed the seated figure, glancing back, swallowing the saliva which had gathered in his mouth, he saw a boy with drawn-up knees and twisted spastic hands.

It was still early, not yet midday. The rain Liz Welch had bemoaned came back in a sudden squally shower with a rumble of thunder over the Forest. Victor went into a place that was half café half wine-bar and had a cup of coffee and because it was raining and nearly lunchtime anyway, a hamburger and salad and a strawberry yogurt. The sickness was gone. So was the rain, for the time being, and the sun had come out with tropical heat and brilliance, shining on the puddles and wet pavements and making them too mirror-bright to look at.

Victor studied the boards outside newsagents' shops. Several furnished rooms to let were advertised, two or three in Epping itself, one in North Weald and one in Theydon Bois. He noted down phone numbers. The North Weald one said 'inquire within' but when he went into the shop the girl behind the counter said she knew for a fact that room had gone weeks before, months before, they just hadn't bothered to take the advertisement out, she didn't know why.

'Could I walk to Theydon Bois from here?' he asked her.

She looked at him, a grin on her face. 'Maybe *you* could. I know I couldn't.' She thought he was interested in the room advertised on the next card. 'I expect that one's gone too. Most of the stuff's out of date.' She spoke with the indifference to an employer's interest of someone whose job is boring and uncongenial.

He had no intention of walking to Theydon Bois and he had no idea why he had asked the question. As for living there . . .! He left the shop and started to walk in the direction of the station. If he wanted to live outside London, what was wrong with somewhere along the river, Kew or Richmond, for instance, or in the far north on the borders of Hertfordshire? There was a train waiting but it was a long time before it departed. An elderly woman with a carrier bag got into the train. He and she were the only people in the carriage. Victor soon realized that there was something wrong with her, that she was probably more than a little mad, or at any rate suffering from delusions. She wore a long red flowered skirt and a sweatshirt with a number on it like an American baseball player's, highly unsuitable garments for someone of her age, but her shoes and stockings were of the most conventional and she had an old lady's knitted hat tied under the chin with knitted strings.

At first she merely sat, smiling and nodding, shifting her bags about, placing one to the right and the other to the left of her, then both on the right, then both between her knees. The train doors shut, trembled and came open again. She got up, leaving the bags where they were, tripped to one end of the carriage and slid down the window between it and the next, ran all the way down to the opposite end and did the same to the window there. At the open doors she leaned out, looking up and down the sunlit deserted platform. Victor realized that she was playing at being a guard and a cold shiver went down the length of his spine. She was at least seventy. He couldn't remember ever having seen a guard in a tube train even in the old days, though they did have them, they did exist, and she was playing guards. He knew this but it still made him jump when, leaning out, she shouted, 'Mind the doors!'

Either it was coincidence or she knew something he didn't know, but even as she spoke the doors began to close. She sprang inside, rubbing her hands together with evident satisfaction. She said to Victor, 'All aboard for Liverpool Street, Oxford Circus, White City and Ealing Broadway!'

Victor said nothing. He was embarrassed but he felt something worse than embarrassment. He remembered the thought that had come back to him the day before, at the Welches, how the behaviourist had said that prison drove everyone mad who was in there more than five years. He, Victor, had been there twice as long as that. Already he sensed in himself strange currents of behaviour, divergences from the norm and impulses he could barely understand. Would he one day become like this old woman? She was sitting opposite him again, shifting the bags, mouthing whispers, smiling. The train had gathered speed and was heading towards Theydon Bois. She skipped up the aisle between the seats, seized hold of the handle on the door at the far end of the carriage and struggled to open it. The awful thought occurred to him that she might be intending to throw herself out. He didn't know what to do. Her bags remained on the floor opposite him and he saw one of them move. He saw a slight movement inside one of the bags and the top of it seem to swell and sink. There might be some animal inside there – a rabbit? The thing he didn't care to name? – or it could simply have been the plastic of the bag itself responding to temperature changes. But Victor didn't think it was that. He got up and stood by the doors. She came and stood close beside him, looking up into his face.

The train seemed to take hours pulling into Theydon Bois. It came almost to a stop, gathered speed again and finally stopped in the station. The doors opened and Victor got out, tremendously relieved. He meant to run up the platform and get into the next carriage and he hardly knew why he stood there instead, savouring relief. She called out behind him, 'Mind the doors!'

He watched the train depart, taking the madwoman with it. Afterwards he thought he would have got out of the train anyway, his fate or stars or destiny or something decreed that he get out of the train, but for the moment he felt angered by what had happened. He would probably have to wait half an hour for the next train.

It was a waste of money as well as time, he thought as he left the station and gave up the return half of his ticket. Now, when he had finished whatever it was he was going to do in Theydon Bois, he would have to buy a single ticket to West Acton. And what was he going to do? Look for Fleetwood's house, a quiet little voice answered him.

The place was much bigger than he had expected. A huge green space traversed by an avenue of trees filled the centre of it. Around this green were houses, a church, a village hall, and roads from it that looked as if they might lead to more estates of houses. Victor walked along past a parade of shops, feeling vulnerable and wary. He had already noticed a car parked with a disabled sticker on the windscreen. But thousands of people had those. Alan had told him once that they were easy to get hold of. Your doctor would let you have one for nothing much worse than corns or a twinge of gout. There was no reason to suppose that this car, parked outside the shops, belonged to Fleetwood. And there was nowhere to be seen a man in a wheelchair or a man on crutches. Victor caught sight of his own face reflected in a shop window, dark, rather drawn, the eyes feverishly bright but the eye sockets becoming dark as an Indian's, the short black hair threaded with grey over the temples and with grey showing in the combed-back bit above the forehead. A thought that was rather more fanciful than those he usually had came to Victor: that age was like frost which passes leaving a whitening behind it and a withering and a shrivelling, a blight that destroys all the bright signs of hope. Would Fleetwood even know him if he saw him now?

The former policeman, if photographs didn't lie, had barely changed at all. But then what had he had to change him? In and out of hospitals, waited on, cared for, cosseted, he had led a sheltered preserving life, had done nothing and undergone nothing to make him look old. Victor had a momentary vision of that bedroom at 62 Solent Gardens once more, of himself standing with his back to the cupboard, holding Rosemary Stanley in front of him, his arm round her waist, and of the door being thrown open and Fleetwood standing there – Fleetwood, who could have had no prevision that a few minutes only were to pass, two or three at most, and after that for the rest of his life he would never stand or walk again. For two or three minutes only they had looked at each other and spoken to each other before he let the girl go to Fleetwood and she threw herself into his arms. Perhaps it had been five minutes in all before the wind blew the curtain out and under the

103

lifted curtain he saw the man on the ladder outside and
Fleetwood had turned his back and Victor had shot him.
For five minutes at most they had studied each other's
faces, looked into each other's eyes, and Fleetwood had
refused to believe, pinning enough faith on his refusal as
to turn his back and, as it were, challenge Victor. The
challenge had been taken up and the gun had gone off, but
before that they had got to know each other's faces better
than each knew his mother's face, as well as each knew his
own looking back at him from the glass.

Or was it all in his imagination? Was it nonsense and
did he only feel he would recognize Fleetwood with such
ease because he had been reminded of that face by pictures
of it in a heap of newsprint? There had been no pictures
of him for Fleetwood to see since those early ones, himself
leaving 62 Solent Gardens between two policemen and
another that Victor tried to forget: a faceless photograph
that would be no use to Fleetwood for identification
purposes, of the man accused of disabling him hustled into
a police van waiting outside the court, a dark coat flung
over his head.

Victor looked over his shoulder. He saw a woman with
a bandaged leg come out of a shop and get into the car
with the disabled sticker. Looking for Fleetwood's house,
be began to walk the winding roads, the network of roads
where the gardens were pretty with pink and white
blossom, trees spread with veils of green, houses of which
so many were in the style of Fleetwood's, built at the same
time and of similar materials, but which were nevertheless
not the same, of which none was the *one*.

The road he was on was a loop that brought him back
to face the green. Beyond it and its trees were what seemed
in the distance to be more pretty, blossoming, garden-
bordered roads, more houses of brick and plaster and
weatherboard with creepers climbing them and tulips in
their flowerbeds. Victor crossed the road and walked across
the green, feeling misgivings now, not doubting he would
recognize the house when he saw it, but deploring the
method he had chosen of finding it. Why hadn't he done

the obvious thing, gone into a post office or a phone box and looked up Fleetwood in the phone directory? Anyone would be able to tell him where Fleetwood's particular road was, he wouldn't need a plan of the place.

By now Victor had reached the avenue of trees, a metalled road which bisected the green diagonally. It would lead him back to the centre of this village suburb and to the parade of shops. A double row of oaks formed the avenue and Victor had scarcely come within the shade of their branches when he saw something which made his heart give a lurch, then begin a bumpy painful beating. From the far end of the avenue, approaching him quite slowly under the trees and on the crown of the metalled surface, were a man and a girl, and the man was in a wheelchair.

They were a long way from Victor and he could not see their faces or discern much about them except that the girl wore a red blouse and the man a blue pullover, but he knew it was Fleetwood. The girl wasn't pushing the wheelchair, Fleetwood was manipulating that himself, but she was walking close by it and talking animatedly. It was a place where voices carried and Victor heard her laugh, a clear, happy, carefree sound. This would be Clare, he thought, this would be the girlfriend called Clare. In a moment, even if they proceeded at this slow pace, he would be able to see their faces and they his; he would be looking on Fleetwood's square-shaped, fresh, regular-featured, dark-browed face, for the first time in the flesh for ten years, for only the second time ever. Victor made no conscious decision to avoid the confrontation. His motor nerves did it for him, turning him swiftly aside off the avenue on to the grass again, carrying him over the grass on to the main road where the garage was and the row of houses and the pub, so that by the time he reached the opposite pavement he was running, running for the station like someone who has no more than one minute in which to catch his train.

8

In the old days Victor used to buy at least two daily news-papers and an evening, the *Radio Times* and the *TV Times*, the *Reader's Digest, Which?* and *What Car?* and sometimes even *Playboy* and *Forum*, though the former bored him and the latter made him feel sick. Cal's preoccupation with pornography, soft and hard, was beyond his understanding. Driving for Alan, Victor had a lot of waiting about to do, and it was while sitting in cars waiting that he did most of his reading. He even tried really high-powered periodicals sometimes, the *Spectator* or the *Economist*, but after a while he realized that he was only doing this to impress the client, who would be stunned to see the hire-car driver engrossed in literary criticism or polemics. Most days the coffee table in the Finchley flat had a heap of papers and magazines on it, though Victor had never hoarded them the way Muriel did.

A psychiatrist writing in the *Reader's Digest* had said how people's life-style patterns have a way of reasserting themselves even if circumstances have changed and a period of enforced disruption has intervened. That just about described what had happened to him, if you like long words, Victor thought, and the patterns were reasserting themselves, at least the habit of buying newspapers and magazines was. As to other habits and patterns, they could lie low as long as they pleased. He had got back into the way of buying two dailies and an evening paper and reading them from front to back, reading everything that was in them, and that was how he came upon the paragraph about the arrest of a man for raping that girl in Gunnersbury Park. A small paragraph on an inside page, that was all. The man's name was omitted but it said that he was twenty-three, lived in Southall, and that he had appeared that morning at Acton Magistrates' Court and been committed for trial. Victor wondered if he too were a secretor with a not too common blood group. At least it meant the police would leave him alone now – until the next time, of course.

None of the papers had anything in them about Fleetwood. There was no reason why they should have had, for Fleetwood wasn't a celebrity whose every movement was news. Probably there wouldn't be any more until this book of Fleetwood's was published. Victor told himself that it was on account of the book and the probability that he would figure in it that he thought about Fleetwood so much. At first he had bitterly regretted running away at the point when it seemed that he and the former detective sergeant must inevitably meet, though he knew it was panic which had made him run and therefore something over which he had little control. And after a while he told himself it was for the best, for what could they have to say to each other but give vent to anger and recrimination? Yet what of the book? Was he going to appear in the book and in such a light that everyone he met who had read it would shun and hate him?

Tom called round one morning to tell him he had heard of a job going if Victor was interested. A local wineshop owner wanted a driver for his delivery van and Tom had seen the vacancy advertised in the shop window. It was the place he had been out to that Sunday morning to buy the Bulgarian claret.

'You'd have to explain about your background,' Tom said awkwardly.

'Considering there'll be about a hundred people after the job and I'll be the only one who's done ten years inside, I'll be a really likely candidate, won't I?'

'I don't want to seem to take an authoritarian attitude, Victor, you know that, but you do have to think a bit more positively.'

Victor decided that while he was here he might as well ask him. He showed Tom the *Standard* article about Fleetwood's book.

'I'm not qualified to tell you if it would be libel,' Tom said, looking worried. 'I just don't know. I shouldn't think he could just say anything he likes about you but I honestly don't know.'

'I suppose I could ask a solicitor.'

'Yes, but that'll cost you, Victor. I'll tell you what. You could make inquiries at the Citizen's Advice Bureau; they'll have a lawyer come there and give advice for free.'

Instead of the Citizen's Advice Bureau, Victor went to the public library, where they had telephone directories covering the whole country. There he looked up Fleetwood and found him entered as Fleetwood, D.G., 'Sans Souci', Theydon Manor Drive, Theydon Bois. Victor knew that the name of the house was French but he didn't know what it meant. He went over to the dictionaries section and looked up *souci*. *Sans* he already knew. The translation was 'without care' or 'carefree', which was an odd name for a house, he thought. Had Fleetwood given it that name himself and was he without care? Perhaps he was. He had nothing to worry about, no awful past to forget, uncertain future to dread. He didn't need a job, he would have a nice fat pension, and growing older wouldn't make much difference to him.

Victor didn't want to drive a wineshop van, the idea was grotesque. Besides, it wouldn't be driving, or not much. It would be humping great heavy cases up staircases in blocks of flats. But he went by tube up to Park Royal and found the shop, a poky little place with its windows pasted over with cheap offers and amazing bargains. There was no job advertisement, and when Victor went inside to inquire he was told that the vacancy had been filled.

Walking back to the tube, he realized he would have turned it down even if it had been offered to him. Taking that job would have meant staying here, either going on living in Mrs Griffiths's house or finding somewhere else in the neighbourhood. He still wanted to move out, to move a long way away. In his mind's eye he saw Epping once more, the forest and Theydon Bois with its green and the avenue of trees. It was pervaded in his memory by a kind of tranquillity, a soft sunlit peace. But Fleetwood lived there, thus making it impossible for him to live there too, and Victor felt building up inside him a second resentment of Fleetwood, as if the man were again ousting him from the proper course of his existence. His conduct had consigned Victor to prison for the best years of his youth. Now he was expelling him, as from paradise, from the only place in the world where he felt he wanted to live.

Ever since he had come back from Theydon Bois, ever since that long long journey from one outer end of London to the other, he had had a sense of unfinished business. He should not have run away, he should have stood his ground. A strange idea kept confronting him whenever he was walking along Twyford Avenue, as he now was, or sitting in his room or lying on the bed, letting the magazine fall, concentrating no more – an idea that, once he had seen Fleetwood and spoken to him, the spell would be broken. For instance, he would no longer feel unable to find a place to live in Epping or even Theydon Bois itself, for there would no longer remain a fear of running into Fleetwood by chance or of having, each time he went out, to be on the watch to avoid meeting him. Why, it was possible once they had resolved things, that they might meet quite casually in the street or under those trees in the avenue and simply pass each other with a hallo and maybe a remark about the weather. Possible but not too likely, Victor had to admit. There was the book to take into account, after all, and the fact, never to be done away, of the great injury Fleetwood had inflicted on him. No doubt, some would say, most did say, that this had only been tit for tat, and Fleetwood too had been injured. So well and good, Victor thought, but you measured injury surely by its long-term effects and Fleetwood was contented now, a famous, honoured person, soon to be a bestselling author, a man who lived in a house called 'Carefree', while he . . . There was no use going into it all again. Nothing made any difference to the fact of the unfinished business, the business he was never going to feel easy about until he had finished it.

In Mrs Griffiths's house, on the ground floor, in a dark

corner behind the stairs, was a pay phone. A cupboard had once been there and, later on, its walls and door had been taken away, to make more space, Victor supposed. When you stood by the phone and looked up, you could see the underside of the stairs treads, raw wood still, unpainted, though the house was getting on for a hundred years old. Tenants, over the years, had written telephone numbers in pencil and ballpoint on the raw pitch pine of those stairs.

Victor had copied Fleetwood's phone number down on the same piece of paper on which Tom had written the address of the wineshop. Now he wrote it on the wood of the stairs and, on an impulse, 'David Fleetwood' beside it, having a confused idea in his mind of recording it there for future users of the phone to look at and wonder about while they waited for the pips to cease and their calls be answered. He wrote Fleetwood's name and then he dialled Fleetwood's number. He was pretty sure he was alone in the house. At this hour he usually was and by lunchtime Noreen had always gone. The bell began to ring.

It rang seven times and then the receiver must have been lifted, for the sharp repetitive sound of the pips started. Victor, holding the phone with its lead at full stretch, was squatting on the floor, for he did not trust himself to stand – that is, for his legs to support him. He had a ten-pence piece in his hand and he stretched up and pushed it into the slot. A man's voice said, 'Hallo? David Fleetwood.'

Victor had sunk on to his knees. The voice was unchanged. He would have recognized it whatever words it had spoken, without the utterance of that name. The last time he had heard it, in that bedroom, it had said in fainter tones, 'Whose blood is that?'

Now Fleetwood spoke again, on a note of slight impatience. 'Hallo?'

Victor had never used Fleetwood's name. In that room he had naturally not addressed him by name. He spoke it now, but hoarsely, in a whisper.

'David.'

He didn't wait to hear what Fleetwood had to say next. The receiver slipped out of his hand and swung on the length of its lead. Victor got to his feet and replaced it in its rest. He heard himself give a kind of groan and he stood with his forehead pressed against the stair tread that had Fleetwood's name and phone number written on it. Why hadn't he spoken to Fleetwood? What was the matter with him? He should have explained to Fleetwood who he was and, if Fleetwood had hung up on him, so what? It wouldn't have hurt him, it wouldn't have done him any actual harm. Fleetwood probably wouldn't have hung up on him but would have been distantly polite and might actually have agreed when Victor asked if he could come and see him and talk about the book.

The voice rang and echoed in his ears. He went upstairs and lay face-downwards on his bed. Fleetwood's voice continued to speak inside his head, saying the things he had said during the hour that passed between his arrival in Solent Gardens and his collapse on the landing floor, shot in the back. Victor could remember every word that had been said as clearly as if he carried a tape cassette inside his brain which he had only to push into a slot and switch on.

'That's very sensible of you. Come over here, Miss Stanley, please. You'll be quite safe.'

Victor had said that Fleetwood had to make him a promise.

'What, then?' The same note of impatience as on the phone just now.

The request then for escape by means of the bathroom window and for five minutes to get away in – a five minutes' start, like when kids played hide and seek. But Fleetwood had promised nothing, for just at that moment the other policeman appeared at the top of the ladder, the wind blowing the curtain in and up to reveal him.

'Take her downstairs,' Fleetwood had said.

The gun went off in Victor's hand, filling the room, the little house, with the loudest noise he had ever heard in his life, shaking his body with a shock from toe to head, driving shock through him so that he almost fell. But it was Fleetwood who had fallen, sprawling forward on to the banisters, clasping them with his hands and slipping down, down, silent while Victor shouted, a silence and a shouting that seemed to endure for an infinite age, until Fleetwood's calm voice intruded upon it and said, 'Whose blood is that?'

Victor remembered it all, his mind playing the tape. When, then, had Fleetwood told him he didn't believe the gun was real? He must have told him, and over and over again, for it was this which had challenged Victor to shoot him, to prove he wasn't lying, but somehow Victor could not fit these statements of disbelief into the recording. They had to be there, though, for they had certainly been uttered. Perhaps he was too confused now, knocked sideways by the experience of hearing that voice again, to remember properly.

Getting off the bed, he looked at his face in the mirror, pushing his face up close to the glass. He looked pale and drawn, his eyes unnaturally bright and the sockets dark as bruises. A muscle worked at the corner of his mouth. Chorea, it was called, 'live flesh'. He had read an article about it once in the *Reader's Digest*. The mirror had become hateful to him and he took it down, laying it face-downwards on the shelf by the sink. Mrs Griffiths (or Noreen) provided him with a clean towel each week on Mondays, a thin almost threadbare towel, larger than a hand towel but very small for a bath size and always of a sickly shade of pink. Probably the intention was to match the pale pink nylon sheets. Victor took his towel and the piece of soap from the sink and went along the passage to the bathroom. Because he had only two ten-pence pieces left with which to feed the water heater, he got rather a small bath, not the kind you could relax in and be comforted by. He put on clean jeans and the one good shirt he had and the jacket that had been among the clothes he had had in Finchley, a velvet cord jacket in dark green for which he had paid the then enormous sum of twenty-five pounds. It looked a bit shabby and indefinably out-of-date but it was the best he could do.

By now he wasn't panicky or upset or frightened. He

was excited. He was so excited that he had to stop himself running the quarter-mile or so to West Acton station. Although he had walked, although he had made himself walk nonchalantly, and had positively strolled into the station, his voice was breathless and hoarse when he asked for a return ticket to Theydon Bois.

A man serving petrol at a filling station opposite the green told him where Theydon Manor Drive was; pointing to the far side of the green and away up to the left. It was three thirty in the afternoon and Victor had had no lunch, not even a cup of coffee. But he wasn't hungry. The idea of food was slightly nauseating. He began to walk up the avenue of trees.

The weather was much the same as it had been that last time he was here, just a week ago, heavy showers followed by bursts of bright, quite hot, sunshine. Water still lay in puddles at the side of the road. The blossom had blown down during that week and petals lay everywhere in pink and white drifts. Apple blossom was coming out now and white fool's parsley. Victor walked up the avenue of oaks where he had seen Fleetwood and the girl coming towards him. Suppose Fleetwood always went out in the afternoons? Suppose he were out now? If he were out Victor thought he would just wait for him to come back, though the idea of waiting, of any sort of inactivity, was intolerable. He had to stop himself running.

Following the directions the garage man had given him, Victor crossed the top of the green on the right-hand side of a tree-fringed pond. Theydon Manor Drive started here, a road that might have been a country lane and where the houses looked as if they had been built within the confines of a beautiful and varied wood. Tall chestnut trees were in full bloom, each bearing hundreds of creamy-white candle-like blossoms. Wall-flowers, the colours of a Persian carpet, bordered lawns of a rich soft green, and late narcissi and tulips filled tubs and window boxes as if flowerbeds alone were inadequate to support all the flowers people here had to have. The houses were all different, of varying sizes, all standing alone and surrounded by garden. Victor saw Sans Souci ahead of him when he had reached number 20. The road bent a little to the right and Fleetwood's house was facing him diagonally.

It was one of the smaller houses, less grand and imposing than it had looked in the photograph. The front lawn with the birdbath was no more than fifteen feet by twelve. The bird on the rim of the fluted stone font was no longer there, so it had been a real one after all. Fleetwood was no longer there either and nor were the tulips, their heads all neatly snipped off. He must employ a gardener, Victor thought, for all was trim and well kept, the grass cut and the edges clipped, the climbing rose wired to its trellis. Breathless now, though he had not run, Victor stood for a while looking at the house. On the white-painted gate the name Sans Souci was lettered in black but above the front door, an oak door with studs, was the number 28. Victor could see no signs of life, though he hardly knew what signs he expected.

He had come all this way in a white heat of excitement and need, but now he had arrived at his goal, a reluctance took hold of him. Even now there was nothing to prevent him turning round and returning the way he had come. Some idea of the self-reproach and bitterness and disgust this would cause stopped him. He moistened his lips, swallowed, put his hand to the gate. His fingers touched the black letters of the name that were slightly raised above the level of the white board. Although this was a shady place because of the trees and shrubs, numerous and tall, the path that led up to the front door was bathed in sunshine. There was a feeling in the air that a period of settled weather, of summer, was about to begin. The sun fell on Victor's face, deliciously warm. He wondered whether to ring the bell or use the knocker which was of brass, its clapper the figure of a Roman soldier. It was the bell he decided on, drawing his breath in sharply as he put his finger on the push and pressed.

No one came. He rang the bell again and still no one came. Of course, if Fleetwood were alone in the house, it would take him a little time to answer the bell, since he must necessarily propel himself to the door in his wheel-chair. Victor waited, feeling nothing, preparing nothing to say. The air was pervaded with a sweet floral scent that he had smelled before, long ago, but could not place. For the third time he rang the bell. Fleetwood must be out.

Victor looked through two front windows into a comfort-ably furnished room where there were bookshelves full of books, pictures on the walls, flowers in vases. On a coffee table the *Guardian* lay folded with, beside it, a packet of cigarettes, an agate table lighter and what looked like an address book. He moved on round the house but there were no more windows except one that obviously had on the other side of it a bathroom or lavatory. The floral smell was far stronger here as Victor rounded the side wall and came to the back of the house, to the back garden; he saw that it came from a climbing plant covered with a dense mass of pinkish-golden blossom, a honeysuckle perhaps. It hid from his view the whole of the back of the house. He took a few steps further along the path, then turned to look back. On the stone terrace that ran the entire length of the house, at this end of which the honeysuckle hung in a drapery of colour and scent, a girl was standing and staring at him. She was standing behind a circular teak garden table from the centre of which protruded the shaft of a sunshade, its blue and white striped canvas not yet unfurled.

It was the girl who had been with Fleetwood in the avenue the previous week. Somehow, although on that occasion he had seen her only from a distance, he was sure of this.

'Hallo,' she said. 'Did you try to ring the bell? It's not working, there's a loose connection or something.'

He took a step or two towards her, across grass, up to the edge of the terrace. Smiling a little, assuming probably that he was some meter reader or salesman, she bent across the table to put the sunshade up.

'What was it you came about?'

He made no answer, for the canvas sprang into a broad

115

umbrella and the girl stepped aside, thus revealing open french windows behind and on the threshold of them, where a ramp had been built, a wheelchair in which David Fleetwood sat, his hands resting on the wheels. It was clear that he did not at first recognize Victor, for his face wore a look of polite inquiry. Victor was choked and silenced by a curious indefinable emotion, yet in the midst of this, or on another level of mind, he was aware of a pleased feeling that Fleetwood in life looked much older than in his pictures. His tongue passed across his lips. He had not foreseen Fleetwood's failure to recognize him and he was at a loss for what to do. Fleetwood, manipulating the wheels with practised hands, rolled the chair down the ramp and stopped about a yard from the table. Victor said, 'I'm Victor Jenner,' and, 'You'll know the name.'

The girl didn't. She had drawn one of the striped canvas chairs up to the table and sat down in it. Fleetwood's face, squarish, brown-skinned with the black brows and the clear blue eyes, had undergone a slow change. The expression was not so much grim as wondering, incredulous.

'What did you say?'

'I said I'm Victor Jenner.'

'Good God,' said Fleetwood. 'Well, good God.'

The girl looked at him inquiringly. He said, 'Clare, you were going to get us a cup of tea. Do you mind? You wouldn't mind if I asked you to leave us alone for five minutes, would you?'

She stared at him. 'Leave you alone? Why?'

'Please, Clare. Do this for me.' His voice had become urgent, almost as if he were – afraid.

'All right.'

She got up. She was a beautiful girl. With wonder that he should notice such a thing at such a moment, this fact registered in Victor's brain along with all the other wonders. He found himself half stunned, confused, by her looks, by the cloud of blonde hair, the honeysuckle skin, the small perfect features. Those eyes, that were a clear bluish-green, turned doubtfully from Fleetwood to him, then back to Fleetwood. 'You'll be all right?'

'Of course I will.'

She went into the house. At first she moved with hesitation, then more quickly, disappearing through what was probably the doorway to a kitchen. Fleetwood spoke in a calm steady voice. Once a policeman, always a policeman, Victor thought. But Fleetwood sounded as if he were forcing himself to remain calm, exercising that control Victor always envied in others.

'Why have you come here?'

'I don't know,' Victor said and he didn't know, he really didn't know now why he had come. 'I wanted to see you. I've been – out three weeks. Well, a month nearly.'

'I know that,' Fleetwood said. 'I was told.'

He had an air of recalling that he had been told much more than that, that he had somehow been *warned* about Victor's being once more at large, or having been told had warned himself to be on his guard. His strong lean brown hands were gripping the wheels of the orthopaedic chair.

'I didn't expect we should meet – like this.'

Rather desperately Victor repeated, 'I wanted to see you.'

'Was it by any chance you who phoned at lunchtime?'

Victor nodded. He wet his lips, pushed the back of his hand across his mouth. The edge of the table dug into his thighs and he pressed his hands heavily on it.

'Sit down, won't you?' Fleetwood said more gently, and as Victor lowered himself into one of the chairs, 'That's right.' He seemed relieved or as if recovering composure. 'Would you like a cigarette? No? I shouldn't either, I smoke too much, but I feel in need of one now. That's rather an understatement. I'm glad it was you who phoned.'

Victor found himself holding on to the seat of his chair, grasping the corners of the canvas-covered cushion. 'Why – why are you glad?'

'I used to get some pretty unpleasant phone calls. Not so much obscene as, well, violent, insulting. Anonymous letters too. But the phone calls were a bit – well, upsetting. And they've started again lately.'

The girl called Clare was coming back, carrying a tray. 'They're disgusting,' she said. 'They call David "cop" and "fuzz", and the main theme seems to be that it was a pity that thug didn't finish the job and shoot him dead.'

Victor made a small inarticulate sound. It was evident that Clare supposed him to be some friend of Fleetwood from the past before she had known him. And Fleetwood himself was taken aback by what she had said. He drew on his cigarette, exhaled, said, 'This is Clare Conway. If, as I suppose, you found out where I was from the story in the *Standard*, you'll know who she is.' He paused as Victor gave an infinitesimal nod. 'Where are you living yourself?'

The voice had a sort of authority about it, commanding though kind. Perhaps it was this quality which made Victor reply like someone making an application for a job or a document, 'Forty-six, Tolleshunt Avenue, Acton, West Seven.' He added, 'I've got a room.'

Clare was looking puzzled and wary. She passed a teacup to Victor and indicated the sugar basin. Her hands were small and brown, rather plump-fleshed with tapering fingers. She wasn't a thin girl but no one would have called her plump either, well made perhaps, full figured. When she leaned forward to take back the sugar basin and pass it to Fleetwood, Victor saw the tops of her round smooth breasts above the neckline of her white and pink dress. Her eyebrows, like moth wings, were drawn together in perplexity.

Fleetwood lit another cigarette from the stub of the first.

'I will have one,' Victor said. 'Please.'

'Sure,' said Fleetwood, and he pushed the packet across the table.

The first inhalation made Victor's head swim. One of those sick feelings to which he was prone rose up into his mouth. He closed his eyes, bending across the table.

'Come on,' Fleetwood's voice said. 'Bear up. Are you all right?'

Victor muttered, 'I'll be OK in a minute. It's years – years since I smoked.'

Forcing his eyes open, he stared at Fleetwood, and Fleetwood said in a tone that was no longer steady, 'You know, when you first came here and said who you were, I thought, he's going to do what that phone caller said, he's going to shoot me again. He's going to finish the job.'

Victor said stupidly, 'I haven't got a gun.'

'No, of course you haven't.'

'I didn't do it on purpose!' A voice burst out of Victor almost without his volition. 'I didn't mean to. I'd never have done it if you hadn't kept saying the gun wasn't real.'

Clare had sprung to her feet. The blood poured into her face and it was crimson. Victor smelled a heavy wave of honeysuckle scent, as if brought about by the movement of the air, by the energy of them all, for even Fleetwood had moved all of himself he could move, flexing and tensing his upper body, leaning forward with hands upraised.

'Do you mean this is the man who shot you?'

Fleetwood shrugged. 'That's what I mean, yes.' He flung himself against the back of the chair, turning his head to one side away from her.

'I don't believe it!'

'Oh, Clare, you know you do believe it. You only mean it's such an amazing thing to have happened, that he – that Victor – should have come here. Do you think I'm not amazed?'

An extraordinary sensation of warmth touched Victor's skin like the sunlight had on the path, but this warmth penetrated and seemed to fill his body. It was prompted by Fleetwood's use of his Christian name. But even as he felt it he was aware of the girl's eyes on him, of the look on her face, an expression of the kind of hatred and disgust a woman's face might show when confronted by a poisonous reptile. She had even drawn her hands up from the surface of the table and crossed her arms over her breasts, a hand on each shoulder.

On a note of infinite scorn she said, 'What have you come for? To apologize?'

Victor gazed down at the brown polished bars of teak, at the blue china c p and saucer, the cigarette smouldering, its long accumul ion of ash dropping on to the stone paving of the terrace.

'Did you come to apologize for ruining his life? For

taking half his body away from him? For smashing his career? Is that why you're here?'

'Clare,' said Fleetwood.

'Yes, it's Clare and if that means, stop, Clare, control yourself, watch what you're saying, I won't, I can't. If you can't express how you feel, I'll express your feelings for you. I'll tell this thing, this animal – no, because animals don't do that, not to each other, not to their own species – this *subhuman* what he did to you, the pain and the suffering and the misery and the loss, what you've been through, the hopes raised and dashed to the ground, the pain and struggle, the awfulness of realizing what paralysis means, the . . .'

'I would much rather you did not.'

It was steely, the voice, the same which had said, 'I'm not making any promises, mind, but it will count in your favour.' And it repeated her name.

'Clare. Please, Clare.'

Victor had pulled himself to his feet. He stood unsteadily, holding the edge of the table, looking down into the cup at the tea leaves in the dregs, a pattern like islands. His head ached from that all-pervading perfume.

'He went to prison for ten years, Clare. In most people's opinion, that would be payment enough.'

'He sent you to prison for life!'

'That really isn't true,' Fleetwood said. 'That's an exaggeration and you know it.'

'It's what you said yourself last week. Those were your own words.' She moved a little way round the table towards Victor. He had an idea she might be about to strike him and he wondered what to do.

'You've come and you've seen,' she said. 'I hope you're satisfied with what you've seen. He isn't going to walk again, whatever the papers may say, and he knows it and all the doctors know it. Crudeness is what people like you understand, so I'll be crude. He isn't going to fuck again either. Not ever. Though he does still want to. And now you can get out. Get out and don't ever come back. Go!' she shouted at him. 'Go, go, go!'

120

He looked at neither of them again. Behind him she was crying. He had a confused impression that she had collapsed or thrown herself across the table and was crying. From Fleetwood there was no sound. Victor walked back around the side of the house in the sunshine that was hotter and brighter though the afternoon had worn on. A pale-coloured creamy-grey dove with a darker band round its neck sat on the rim of the birdbath, drinking the water. Victor closed the gate that was named 'Carefree' behind him, feeling nothing, feeling drained and empty and weak. But as he made his way to the station, walking on the springy green turf, a tremendous anger, familiar and welcome, invaded his body and filled those empty spaces with a seething heat.

9

Anger fed him and buoyed him up and sustained him. It was a source of enormous energy which he wanted to keep, not rid himself of. There was no real temptation to punch and pummel the bed and the furniture. He sat in his room feeding on his anger, directing it against that girl – that fat, showy, noisy blonde, he called her in his furious mind, that loud-mouthed bitch with her tits sticking out of her dress who used the sort of filthy language he had always hated to hear on a woman's lips. Fleetwood had said nothing, not a word of reproach – supposing he felt he had a reason for resentment – but that girl who probably hadn't been around Fleetwood for more than a year of two, who took it upon herself to sit in judgement on *him*, who raved and screeched . . . Now Victor's anger dictated to him all the things he might have said if he had thought of them, how in front of Fleetwood he might have put her down, squashed her with some well-chosen words that entirely exonerated him and revealed the truth – that no one was responsible, that it was fate, the force of circumstances and destiny which had inflicted such terrible injury upon the man she loved.

That night he dreamed of rape. From boiling energy he was potent and inexhaustible, ravishing women like a soldier sacking a town, faceless women that he seized upon in the dark. And when he had done with them he raised them by the shoulders and battered their heads against the stone ground. He walked among the women, dead or unconscious, despoiled, lying in their torn clothes, their blood, holding a torch in his hand, looking for Clare's face but not finding it, never finding it, looking instead at the worn flaccid cheeks and loose mouth of Muriel and jumping away with a cry of horror.

Whether it was the dream or the night itself or sleep which took away his anger he didn't know, but by the morning it was gone and it didn't return. A certain partial satisfaction replaced it, that he had after all, in spite of everything, seen David Fleetwood and talked to him. David, he said, to himself, savouring the name and repeating it, David. How would it have been if David had been alone and the girl not there, out perhaps or just not existing? Though he could form no very clear idea of what might have taken place in the absence of the girl, he had a profound feeling it would have been good, pleasing to both parties. Each might have acknowledged his personal share in their fates, his imprisonment and David's disablement, admitting that neither was more to blame than the other, but that the good thing which had come out of it was their ability to confront one another and discuss the subject. Of course that hadn't happened because that foul-mouthed blonde bitch had intervened, yet Victor felt it *would* have happened – it was, so to speak, there waiting to happen. The necessary goodwill was present on both sides.

Victor bought a lot of magazines, picking likely-looking ones off the shelves at W. H. Smith's and more from the station bookstall. He also bought a packet of cigarettes, he didn't quite know why, for he didn't really want to smoke and he certainly couldn't afford to. The way he lived, eating out, buying wine and now cigarettes, he wasn't going to be able to live on the DHSS money and soon he would be making inroads on the small capital left to him by his parents. He would have to get a job.

Reading his magazines, he realized he was looking for an article or feature about David Fleetwood. Now he *wanted* to read about David, there was, of course, nothing to read. That was Sod's Law. But David wasn't a singer or an actor or TV personality, only someone who'd been – well, brave, was how you'd put it, Victor thought. There was no doubt he had been brave, though foolhardy was another word, but yes he had shown courage that time at 62 Solent Gardens. Victor had to admit it. They had both shown a good deal of bravery and – what was the word his father used to use? – grit.

Did David know about the rapes? The police had always, as far as Victor knew, assumed, or half assumed, that he was the man responsible for several cases of rape carried out in the Kilburn–Kensal-Rise–Brondesbury districts of London. And he was responsible, there was no doubt about it, for this was a district his route to Heathrow led him through. But nothing had ever been proved against him and he had never been charged with rape. Yet because Heather Cole had told the police, and repeated it at his trial, that he was the man who had taken hold of her in the park, he was immediately stamped as a rapist, *the* rapist. Then, for safety's sake, he had asked for two incidents of rape to be taken into consideration. That perhaps had been a mistake and had added to the assumption that he intended to rape Rosemary Stanley, whereas he had entered the house only to hide and his encounter with Rosemary Stanley had been as much of a shock to him at it was to her. To assault her had never crossed his mind, any more than while in prison or after his release he had thought of rape. A man was not responsible for his dreams, they were something else.

Since he had never been convicted of rape and nothing in that way proved against him, the police had no right whatever to make these assumptions. At his trial, all the time, there had been this undercurrent of belief that rape was behind it all, attempts at rape the underlying cause of what prosecuting counsel had called 'the final tragedy'. The real cause, finding refuge from his pursuers and reacting to David Fleetwood's taunts, was never mentioned. But all this could give him no clue as to whether David knew about the rapes and if he had passed on what he knew to the girl, Clare. He might not know; he had still been in hospital at the time of the trial, and if he were fair-minded, as Victor had begun to believe he was, even if he had heard hints that Victor and the Kensal Rise rapist were one and the same, he might presume a man innocent until he was proved guilty. Not, Victor told himself, that he cared what the girl thought, but David's opinion was another matter. It was so long since he had raped anyone, and he never would again, that it seemed terrible he should be stigmatized for this thing in his past. Shooting David was one thing, that had been an accident, brought about by circumstances, by loss of control and will over his own reactions, by David's own folly, but the rapes were in another category, regrettable, something Victor could imagine he might one day feel remorse over, especially about the girl he had hurt in Epping Forest. He wouldn't like David to know about that, he wouldn't care for it at all.

In vain he looked through his magazines for some note or paragraph about David. He had started going to bed early, there was so little to do, and he lay there reading a short story about an old man, a French peasant farmer, who, instead of keeping his money in the bank, plastered it into the walls of his house, the notes folded up and wrapped in strips of the plastic bag the farm fertiliser came in, thrust between the laths, then daubed and painted over. No night passed without dreams, and in this night's dream he was in a train, on the Northern Line, going towards Finchley. No one was in the carriage but himself and then, at Archway, his mother got in with David Fleetwood. David could walk, but not well; he had a stick and he hung on to Victor's mother's arm. They took no notice of Victor, they behaved as if he wasn't there, as if no one was there, whispering to each other, putting their faces close and then kissing. They kissed each other passionately as if they were alone. Victor jumped up and shouted and protested that it was disgusting what they were doing, it was indecent, that this was a public place, and woke up shouting, sitting up in bed and shaking his fist.

This was the day he was due to meet Jupp in Muriel's house but he very nearly forgot about it. At lunchtime he bought the *Standard* and saw a driving job advertised in it, a mini-cab driver wanted, and the attractive thing was that it said 'car provided'. The firm was in Alperton. Victor went straight up there on the tube to look for the mini-cab company in Ealing Road.

Few people, he thought, would have got hold of the *Standard* before he had, and any who had would probably have obeyed the advertisement and telephoned. It might be that he would be the first applicant to present himself. In his one pair of good trousers, a clean shirt and the velvet jacket, he knew he looked presentable. Before buying the paper he had by a lucky chance had his hair cut. For a while he had considered growing it long again, the way it had been on the day of his arrest, but that was old-fashioned and he, too, was growing rather old for it now. In a few weeks' time he would be thirty-nine.

The mini-cab company he found in half a shop, a very small poky place, not much more than a cupboard, where a middle-aged woman with streaked blonde and brown hair sat answering two phones. He wasn't used to women being bosses, for there had been far less of this when he went to prison, and he knew he had got off on the wrong foot when she corrected his assumption that she was a sort of secretary–receptionist and that the boss was somewhere else. He never found out her name. She wanted a reference from his last job, she wanted to know why he hadn't had a job for ten years. *Ten years?*

'My God, with women it's babies,' she said. 'It can't have been that with you, where were you, in gaol or something?'

She was joking but he said no more. So angry he could have leaped on her and seized her by the throat, he made a mammoth effort at control, turned round and left the place, slamming the door with all his strength behind him. The shop shook. The shop next door shook, and an assistant came to the window to see what the noise was. Victor looked back and saw old furniture, a brass bedstead, vases, a plant stand in the window behind her. With a jolt it reminded him of his appointment with Jupp – at Muriel's house in Popesbury Drive at three. It was ten to now.

At least he could sell that furniture and get some money by this means. He got back into the tube at Alperton and it took him down to Acton Town, the nearest station to

Muriel's. If anything, the purple flowers which overhung the rock slopes of Muriel's garden were even more purple today and their stems had grown longer, so that the stone ornament Victor avoided looking at was entirely concealed. He stared defiantly in its direction, feeling nothing. Since he was last here a laburnum of a particularly violent acid yellow had come into bloom. Two women chatting on the pavement were examining the laburnum and saying how lovely it was, what a wonderful sight, but Victor didn't think it was lovely or that flowers were inevitably beautiful just because they were flowers. Somewhere inside his brain he seemed to smell that honeysuckle once more, though none of the flowers here was scented and the only smell was a faint one of diesel fumes.

A van with J. Jupp printed on the side of it was parked on the ramp that led down to the garage, backed up to the garage doors. Victor went round the back way, through the side gate, into the area between the garage and the back door of the house. The rear garden was a wilderness, blossoming apple trees rising out of grass that reached halfway up their trunks. Victor tapped on the back door, tried the handle. To his surprise it wasn't locked. His aunt and Jupp were sitting at the kitchen table, drinking tea.

What had Jupp said or done to put Muriel so unusually at ease, to get into the house and make his way to the kitchen? Victor seemed to have interrupted a conversation, at least an anecdote of Jupp's, to which Muriel listened avidly. They both seemed rather sorry to see him. Muriel had her pink hairnet on and the left-hand earpiece on her glasses, which had apparently been broken, was done up with pink sticking plaster. At last Jupp got up and, saying this wouldn't buy the baby a new frock, followed Victor out to the garage. Today he had on the trousers of the suit of which the black pinstriped waistcoat was a part and with them a black tee-shirt and long ginger suede jacket with fringes. His long hair and walrus moustache looked thicker and more luxuriant, on account perhaps of recent shampooing. He took a Polo mint from his pocket and put it in his mouth.

'Remarkable woman, your aunt,' said Jupp. 'Had a fascinating life. It's not often you'll find a person frankly admit they married for money. I call that honest. Been a good looker too – there's what you might call remnants of it still.'

Victor said nothing. They might not have been thinking of the same woman.

'Pity about her never going out, though. If you don't mind me saying so, you ought to make an effort there, get her moving, put a spot of salt on her tail, eh?' Victor did rather mind him saying so. He began to unlock the door. 'What was she doing then, storing all your stuff for you? You been away?'

The only reason Muriel wouldn't have told him the truth was because she hadn't yet had the chance, Victor thought. When he was a little boy, very small, he had hated his parents talking about a time before he was born. That there had been a time when he didn't exist he hadn't been able to bear, and he had cried and stamped when his mother spoke of it. It was the first memory he had of outbursts of anger. Because that time of non-existence was intolerable to him, he had started saying he had been in New Zealand. When his mother spoke of 'before you were born', he corrected her and said he was in New Zealand. He said it now to Jupp.

'I was away a long time. I was in New Zealand.'

'Really?' said Jupp. 'Nice. Very nice. Let's have a look-see then. Let's have a shuftee at some of the movables.'

He pushed his way about among the furniture, pulling off the curtains, the gold folkweave and the green rep, and Victor's bedroom curtains with the red and green squares on the black and white background, pulling them off and tossing them aside, peering under table tops and tapping surfaces with a rather long fingernail. Victor wondered if he was checking for woodworm. The wheelchair he pushed back and forth like someone trying to get a child off to sleep. Victor noticed that the wheelchair was the same make as David's, though his looked like a later model. Jupp stuck out his underlip.

'I tell you what, I'll give you four hundred pound for the lot.'

Victor was disappointed. New furniture, he had seen from looking in shop windows, was very expensive. Secondhand furniture too had rocketed in price. Why, when he had wanted a few bits for his flat, the dealers couldn't give old sideboards and dining tables away. Things had changed. The three-piece suite alone was surely worth four hundred pounds.

'Five hundred,' he said.

'Now wait a minute. I've got to pay a fella good wages to come over here with me and clear this lot. I've got to pay for juice and maintenance of the van. I've got to lose half a day in the shop.' He took another mint, looked at it and put it back in his pocket.

'I reckon that wheelchair's worth a hundred,' said Victor. 'Look at it, as good as new.'

'There's not exactly a boom in the wheelchair market to be honest with you, cocky. Suspending an invalid carriage on a chain from your lounge ceiling hasn't caught on in Acton, it's not what you'd call chic, right? Four hundred and twenty.'

They compromised at four hundred and forty pounds and Jupp said he would come back and pick the stuff up next Wednesday. He looked at the thigh-high grass in Muriel's garden and said what a wicked waste when there were lionesses and cubs looking for homes. Victor went back into the house. Muriel was washing up cups and saucers. She washed a cup, rinsed it, dried it on a teacloth, put it inside a cupboard, then began on the process with a saucer. Saying he needed to go to the bathroom, Victor went along the passage and up the staircase with its runner of red turkey carpet. It would not have been true to say nothing had changed when he had made this same journey just a little less than eleven years ago in search of Sydney's Luger. The house was much dirtier. Had it been Sydney who did the housework? Or was it simply that Muriel had done none since he died? The once polished edges of the stair treads lay under a layer of grey fluff and the carpet itself was coated with a mat that consisted mostly of hairs, Muriel's hairs presumably, shed and left to lie over the years. The sun was shining outside, even as it had been on that evening when he had let himself in with the key he had had cut, when Muriel and his mother had gone to see Sydney in hospital, and as on that evening the interior of the house was dark. It was gloomy and still and dark and everything was now coated in dust. Perhaps the windows had never been opened all those years. The camphor smell was still there and allied to it, mingling with it, the sharp sour choking odour that is the smell of dust itself.

Once it had been a handsome house, for it had been built at a time when materials were relatively cheap, when fine hard woods were plentiful and when, somehow, there had been more time and more skill and craftsmen to create panelling and carved wood and unusual mouldings for cornices. And yet the builders or maybe the architect had gone too far so that the thickly leaded windows excluded more light than they let in and the curtains completed the job, curtains that some big store – Whiteley's, he guessed, or Bentall's – had made to order and hung themselves, swatches of thick velvet or heavy slub silk, lined and interlined, pleated and flounced and looped back with tasselled cords. They had never been cleaned or even brushed, and dust and powdered cobweb lay in their folds. Victor gave a twitch to one of the curtains in the room where he had found the gun in the hiding place under the cupboard floor. A cloud of dust flew out into his face, making him cough. The dust lay so thick on the carpet that you could no longer see the pattern of yellow grapes and green vine leaves; only a vague impression was received of a bluish-grey pattern.

The western novels were still on the shelf, undisturbed for more than a decade. He left the room and went into his aunt's bedroom. A big mirror, framed and swinging, mounted on two uprights, stood in the middle of the pinkish flowered carpet. Pink and white crêpe-paper roses filled the fireplace, a decade of soot having fallen on to and spotted their petals. The bed, unexpectedly, was made and in the middle of it lay a pink fluffy dog, the zip fastener in its belly open and revealing the white nightdress which must be the one Muriel put on when she took off the nightdress she wore by day.

The story of the French peasant in his mind, Victor thrust his hand under the pillows, between under-blanket and mattress. He pulled open the drawers in the bedside cabinets, opened the doors of the wardrobe, which he found full of Sydney's suits. A search of the pockets afforded him nothing. A section of the side compartment of this wardrobe was crammed with old handbags, navy and black and wine-coloured and white, cracked and split, their metal fastenings tarnished, their clasps broken. Victor pulled a black one out, it was imitation crocodile skin, and felt inside. The crackle of notes made him catch his breath. But he had been up here too long, he would be back next week when Jupp took the furniture. Without counting the money, he helped himself to a handful of whatever colour those notes were, closed the bag again, shut the wardrobe door and ran downstairs.

Muriel was sitting by her electric fire, busy with her scissors, with copies of *Country Life* and *Cosmopolitan*. She seemed to be compiling a scrapbook of events in the life of the Duchess of Grosvenor.

'You were a long time,' she said to Victor.

She had a way of looking at him which was similar to the way a mouse looks emerging from its hole: wary, suspicious, sharp, perceptive and entirely self-absorbed. He could almost see her nose twitching, whiskers vibrating, eyes making quick nervous movements. The ring that was a dome of diamonds was on her finger; perhaps she never took it off.

His hand in his jacket pocket, he could feel the crisp notes there, one, two, three, four – at least four, maybe five, it was hard to tell. They might be tenners.

'I want to tell you something,' she said.

He moved across the room, he stood by the window. It was just as stuffy there, the dense smell of mothballs and old unwashed clothes, of ageing newsprint and dust burned on the heater element, was just as strong, but you could see daylight, you could even feel the warmth of the sun struggling through the dirty diamond panes. The long yellow plumes of the laburnum hung against the glass.

Muriel said, 'I never fancied making a will. I'm superstitious, I suppose, don't want to tempt providence.' She looked up from her cutting, up at the ceiling, as if God had taken up his residence in her bedroom and had his ear to the floor. 'But there comes a time when you have to do what's right and not what you want, and I knew the right thing was to make sure you never got hold of anything that was mine.'

'Thanks very much,' said Victor.

'So I made my will the day after you was here last time. Jenny next door that goes to the shops for me, she got a will form and took it to my solicitor and he's done what I wanted and I've got it signed and witnessed. You can see a copy if you want. I've left the lot to the British Legion. That would have pleased Sydney. I said to myself, poor old Sydney devoted his life to pleasing you, Muriel, and now you can do this to please him.'

Victor stood staring at her. He could feel that pulse beginning to beat at the corner of his mouth, the twitch of live flesh. His hand in his pocket felt the money and he rubbed his fingers over the notes.

'The Legion do a lot of good,' said Muriel. 'They won't waste it. Sydney would turn in his grave if you got your hands on it.'

'He was cremated,' said Victor.

It was the only time he had scored with a parting shot, uttered it at the right time instead of thinking of it afterwards. He slammed the front door behind him like he had slammed the door at the mini-cab place. Walking home by the back streets, up towards the Uxbridge Road, he took the notes out of his pocket. There were five of them, two twenties, one ten, two fives. The possibility that there might be twenties among the notes hadn't occurred to him and his spirits rose. Losing Muriel's house and her money was hardly a misfortune since he had never counted on getting them. The malevolence of her glare and her words grated on him, though. The attitude she had taken towards him, a combination of fear and dislike, made him glad he had taken the money and wish he had helped himself to more.

Victor had never stolen anything before, unless you counted chocolate bars nicked off the counters at Woolworth's when he was still at junior school. Everyone did that and it was more a game than delinquency. As an adult he had rather prided himself on his honesty. He and Alan and Peter, the other driver, had had a system whereby they shared their tips, which were sometimes substantial, and Victor had almost always rendered his up in full for the share-out. Once or twice the temptation had been too much for him – as, for instance, when that American, on a first visit, had confused pounds with dollars and given him twenty-five – but generally he had been honest. He told himself that, if Muriel's something she had to tell him had been different, had been, say, the very opposite of what she had told him, that she had made a will in his favour, he would have taken that money back upstairs and restored it to her handbag. Now his only concern was that she might miss it. What if she did? She was hardly likely to call the police in over her own nephew, however much she might hate him.

On the strength of what he had from his parents, was going to get from Jupp and what he had taken from Muriel, Victor went into one of the High Street shops half an hour before it was due to close and bought a television set.

Since he had come to Mrs Griffiths's house Victor had received virtually no mail. All he ever got were communications from the DHSS. Letters and cards were spread out on the table in the hall by whoever came out first and picked the mail up off the doormat. On Friday morning he had been promised delivery of his television set and when ten o'clock had passed with no sign of it – between nine and ten was the time named – he came downstairs to check that the doorbell was working. Electric doorbells can go wrong, as he had recently learned. He only looked at the mail on the table because there might have been a card from the TV people explaining why they hadn't come or saying when they would come. Between two postcards of foreign seaside places lay an envelope addressed in a strong upright hand to Victor Jenner, no 'Mr' or 'Esq.' or anything. The postmark was Epping.

Victor forgot about the television. He took his letter upstairs. His throat drying, the tension that preceded nausea getting a hold on him, he sat down on the bed and split the envelope open. The letter was typewritten on both sides of a single sheet and signed 'Clare Conway'. Victor read:

Dear Victor Jenner,

You will be surprised to hear from me after the way I spoke to you on Monday. May I say that you took that very well? A lot of people would have shouted abuse back at me and I think you would have been justified if you had done that. This letter is in part an apology. I had no business or right to speak to you like that, I wasn't involved, the injurer or the injured, I was just being as I often am a bit too partisan.

I am trying hard to say what I have to say but it isn't easy. I'll try again. David and I think it was very brave of you to come here, a very brave thing indeed to do because you couldn't know what sort of reception you would have, and in fact you had about as bad a one from me as possible. You didn't say why you came, though of course it was obvious you did so because you felt you wanted to make some sort of restitution to David. I imagine you as having been haunted by events and feeling the need to take some positive action as soon as you could.

I'll admit here and now that I wouldn't be writing to you if it was your conscience only that was in question. You have to deal with that in your own way. It's David I'm concerned about as I have been almost since I first met him nearly three years ago. David is a wonderful person, easily the most just and honest and generous-minded, the most *complete*, person I have ever known, which seems an odd thing to say, since physically of course he is anything but complete. You can't be aware – no one can except those who are very close to him – how, in spite of being able to forgive and accept, he is still as haunted by what happened in that house in Kensal Rise eleven years ago as I suspect you are. He dreams of it, every possible association reminds him of it, the memory of it comes back to him every day, but the worst thing is that he can't resign himself to it as having been inevitable. He *regrets*. I mean that he is always thinking of what might have happened, what might have been avoided rather, if he had acted differently or maybe said different things.

The point is, though, that since seeing you and talking a little to you last Monday, in spite of everything, in spite of *me*, he seems easier in his mind. At least I think he seems easier. And when I said I was going to write to you he welcomed the idea and said he would like to see you. You see, I am convinced that if you two could talk a bit more and tell each other what you felt, really talk this thing out, a lot might be resolved. David might at last be able to resign himself to what his life is going to be for the rest of it and you – well, it might solve things for you too and bring peace of mind.

I hope this doesn't sound too high-flown – or worse, like some sort of psychotherapist. If you have read this far you will have guessed what I'm going to ask. Will you come and see us? I know it's a long way for you, so please come for the whole day, a Saturday or Sunday, and please make it soon. I'd like to think it was a good destiny that made David keep your address in his head. He has a good memory – too good, I sometimes think.

In the hope that we shall see you,
    Yours,
    Clare Conway

Victor couldn't remember the last time he had been really happy. It must have been before he went to prison, for certainly there had been no happiness since, not even when he knew he was going to be released and was released; resignation, yes, and a degree of contentment, the relative calm that came between bouts of anger and panic, but happiness never. The last time was probably when he knew he had got the Ballards Lane flat or when, six months before he took Sydney's Luger, Alan had promised him a future partnership in the business. It was an unfamiliar feeling but he recognized it: happiness. Like anger, only differently, without the burning pain and the beating heart, it filled the vessel of body and mind with the effervescence of a sparkling wine. It reached his lips and made him laugh aloud, he had no idea why.

There was no phone number on the letter and he had thrown away Tom's piece of paper. When the television man had been, he would have to go back to the library. He went down to the hall, stood looking at the phone, wishing he could remember David's number and then, turning his head, he saw it. He had written it on the raw wood of the underneath of the stair treads and David's name beside it: David Fleetwood.

His hand was shaking and he had to grasp his wrist in the other to steady it. Because of that tremor in his fingers, he couldn't be sure he had dialled the number correctly but he must have done, for when the pips sounded and he put his ten pence in, Clare's voice answered.

He said, his voice uneven with excitement, 'It's Victor.' They weren't likely to know another Victor, so there was no need to say his surname.

'It's good of you to get in touch so quickly.' She had a beautiful voice, low and measured, a little formal, things he hadn't noticed when she was abusing him. 'I feel,' she said, 'a bit embarrassed talking to you. I was so awful.'

'Oh, forget that.'

'Well, I'll try. I do hope this call means you'll come. When will you come? When would it suit you? We'd like it to be soon. I've a job, and David sometimes has to go to hospital for checks, but apart from that we're always here, we don't go out much. It's complicated for David to go out – we have to make so many arrangements in advance.'

'I could come any time.'

The doorbell rang and he knew it must be the television man but it seemed no more than a distant nuisance, something he wouldn't allow to be an intrusion.

'Could you come tomorrow?' she said.

10

Sixty pounds didn't go very far these days when you were buying clothes. Having parted with almost all of what his parents had left him on the purchase of the television set, Victor had decided to spend the money he had 'had' from Muriel on a pair of trousers, a shirt, a pair of shoes. He preferred to put it like that, what he had 'had' from Muriel, rather than what he had 'taken'. It was Ealing where he went shopping, the district being rather more upmarket. Half the money went on the trousers and half on the shoes, a shirt as well being beyond his means. He was more than ever convinced that he needed a job, and a long way away from here, where so much reminded him of Muriel and Sydney, of his parents and his youth.

Victor had never really had any friends. This was probably because his parents hadn't had any. Of visitors to the house he could only remember Muriel and later, once or twice, Muriel and Sydney, a neighbour who occasionally came to tea and a married couple called Macpherson whose society his mother lost because she did not, as his father put it, 'keep friendship in repair'. She had never cared for intruders into the unit formed by her husband and herself. They were all in all to each other, as Victor once heard her tell Mrs Macpherson, and besides this, she found entertaining, even in the most modest way, too much for her, it made her hysterical. When Victor was at school she didn't encourage him to bring other boys home and because of this he seldom got asked back to their houses.

It was for his ninth birthday that the idea of a party was mooted. He would never forget the circumstances but he could no longer remember whose idea it had been, his mother's or his father's. The birthday was in June but plans for the party were made weeks ahead. Victor's mother thought invitations ought to be sent out but she didn't know how to word them, so although a great deal of energy was expended on worrying nothing was actually done. If it was a fine day the party could be held in the garden, but who could tell, in England, if 22 June would be a fine day or not? Victor's mother didn't want all those little boys – there were no prospective little girl guests – in her house. She wasn't a houseproud woman but she could not contemplate the idea of all those little boys running about. Victor had not been allowed to say anything about the party at school. He had been forbidden to issue invitations by word of mouth, but of course he had hinted that a party would be held. Then there was the food. It was really a question of which kind of food would be least messy and least trouble to prepare. Victor had been to a party where the children threw the food at each other and he had been unwise enough to mention this at home. His mother talked about the party every day and she talked about it as if it were a watershed on this side of which lay unimaginable stresses and anxieties and problems and on the far side, if it could ever be attained, a glorious peace and freedom. Sometimes she cried about it. One evening – it was the first week of June and no invitations had been sent – she burst out crying and asked why had they ever considered having a party, what had got into them, were they mad? Victor's father calmed her down and cuddled her and said they didn't have to have a party if she didn't want to. This made an amazing difference to Victor's mother, who dried her eyes and smiled and said they really didn't, did they? She immediately became happy and put the radio on and made Victor's father dance with her. She danced and sang 'Mr Sandman' and they never had the party.

When Victor was older he sometimes found himself on the perimeter of one of those groups which are formed of a nucleus of two friends with two or three lesser friends and a few hangers-on. Victor was one of those hangers-on. He never had much to say but he wasn't a good listener either. Silent or laconic, he lived in a world of his own, as one of his teachers said in a school report. If a girl at his school didn't have a boy to go out with by the time she was fourteen, she felt less than a girl, inadequate and unattractive, but no such stigma attached to a boy with or without a girlfriend. At the time he went to the polytechnic Victor had scarcely spoken to a girl and he had certainly never been alone with one.

Pauline chose him, not he her. His mother, who didn't like her, said she wanted someone to get married to and wasn't too particular about who it was, as long as he was young and nice-looking and with a potential for making a good living. Victor had been very nice-looking in those days, everyone said so. He was somewhat vain of his appearance and was glad when the fashion came in to grow one's hair long.

Pauline had friends but he never got on with them. Women's voices irritated him, the pitch of them, their flexibility and rise and fall. Nor did he feel much need for a male friend. Alan was the nearest he ever had to a friend, but they seldom saw each other out of working hours and working hours were spent in separate cars. They had nothing in common but age and sex. Alan had a wife and child in Golders Green, a girlfriend in Camberwell, and was obsessed with vintage cars and rugby football. Victor could take an interest in the cars but that was about all. It wasn't much of a friend, he thought, who deserted you when you were down on your luck, never even wrote you a postcard. He had never had a friend but now perhaps that was about to change. The novelty of it excited him. As he put on his new trousers, his new shoes, he began to feel new himself, a person in the process of being re-made, his past shadowy this morning as if it had all taken place in a previous life – in New Zealand, in fact.

And yet, of course, without that past he would never have got to know David. A pretty costly way of making a friend, he thought, as he got into the train, and a picture of prison came before his eyes, notably the night when Cal and the other three had raped him. Why did he have to think of that now? Settling in his seat, opening the first of the magazines he had bought, he wiped it away.

It was a beautiful day, the best day they had had since he came out. The sun was as hot as late summer, though it was still only May. Clare had said 'about one' but he intended to be punctual, he intended to get there on the dot of one. Too late it occurred to him that in some circles it was considered polite to take flowers with you on these occasions or maybe a bottle of wine. Flowers would be like coals to Newcastle. Perhaps he could give them *New Society*, *Country Life* and *Time* Magazine, which still looked quite new and as if unread.

There were people all over the green, throwing balls about and playing games and exercising dogs. Victor loitered, for it was only a quarter to. He remembered the room at Theydon Bois he had seen advertised on the newsagent's board and he wondered if it were still vacant. The place was so green and peaceful, the air so fresh compared to London, and yet London was only about fifteen miles away. He started walking slowly towards Theydon Manor Drive, feeling the sun on his face, thinking how impressed they would be by his appearance, his trim haircut, his new clothes. The scent of the honeysuckle he could smell all the way down the street and it quickened his excitement, his alert feeling of expectation.

He had supposed Clare would open the door to him. This time he didn't make the mistake of pressing the bell but rapped with the Roman soldier door knocker. No one came and he waited. He waited, knocked again, and held his breath, afraid. The door was opened by David, which accounted for the delay. David had reached from his wheelchair and opened the door and sat there with a smile on his face.

'Hallo, Victor. Is that right or would you rather be called Vic?'

'I'd rather Victor,' said Victor.

He put the magazines down on the hall table. It was the first time he had set foot inside the house, which was cool and rather dark, but not dark in the way Muriel's was, for there was a feeling here that these rooms were a kind of refuge from the sunshine, but that if you wanted it you had only to throw open doors and windows and curtains for light to pour in. The hall floor was carpeted in a glowing ruby red. On the stairs was a lift, which ran on a rail above the banister and which was large enough to accommodate David's wheelchair.

'It's good of you to come.'

Victor couldn't think of a reply to that. Just when he could have done without it, when he needed to make a good impression, the chorea had come back, making his left eyelid twitch. He followed David into the room with the french windows. David was wearing the same baggy slacks he had had on last Monday but on top he wore a tee shirt and he said to Victor to take off his jacket if he wanted to. And help himself to a drink, the drinks were on the sideboard. Victor poured himself a measure of whisky, rather a large measure. He needed it – both to help him talk to David and for the confrontation with Clare which would surely happen at any minute. David, watching him, was lighting a cigarette.

'What about you?' Victor said.

He shook his head. Victor felt he was being subjected to a fascinated examination. David seemed to be watching his every movement with a compulsive interest as if he were wondering how it was that this man could perform routine tasks like other men, pour liquid from a bottle into a glass, walk across a room, seat himself. Perhaps he was imagining it, though. Perhaps David was silent, smiling now, only because he too was at a loss for words.

Inspiration came to Victor.

'Where's the dog?' he said.

'Mandy?' said David. 'Oh, she died. She got old and died.'

'I saw her in the newspaper photograph,' Victor said.

'She wasn't a puppy when I had her. She was two. They don't usually live past eleven, those labs. I miss her. I keep thinking I see her, you know, in a doorway or lying up against my chair.'

Victor didn't say any more because Clare came in.

He wondered how he could ever have called her fat, even when he was hating her, when nothing was too bad to think about her. She was one of those women who are both slim and plump. Her figure was perfect. It was just that she wasn't one of those stick-insect girls who pose (he had noticed) in designer clothes in magazines. She wore a dark blue skirt and a white shirt and her face was without make-up. You could see it was without make-up in this midday light; those colours, the rosy-gold and the soft pink and the feather-brown brows were natural.

She had written to him and spoken to him on the phone, she expected him to come and knew he had come, but when she saw him her face reddened. She blushed and smiled slightly, putting one hand up to her cheek as if she could wipe the blush away. He held out his hand to her, though he hadn't done this to David. She shook hands with him and he thought how this was the first time he had touched a woman for years and years . . . Only it wasn't, for he had touched Muriel, held her and shaken her, when first she showed him the cuttings about David.

'Victor, we thought we'd eat our lunch outside, if you'd like that. We get so little summer, it seems a pity not to take advantage of it, but if you hate eating outside please do say.'

He couldn't remember that he had ever tried it but he wasn't going to admit to that. Clare had gin and tonic and David white wine mixed with Perrier water, and Victor showed some interest in the Perrier water, which had hardly been around when he went to prison – or at any rate wasn't the universal drink and mixer it had since become.

'Not before you-know-what,' said David and the ice was broken. You could almost hear the tinkling of it as it broke.

'Well, a lot of things have changed,' Victor said.

'I know. I was – out of the world too for quite a while. In and out, anyway. And when I came out I'd always find something new people were talking about or eating or drinking.'

'Or saying or singing,' said Clare. 'Five minutes away and you lose your grip. But you were ten years away, Victor, and you haven't.'

The compliment pleased him. 'I read a lot,' he said.

They had lunch. It was cold soup, white and green and lemony, and an onion and bacon flan with a salad. Clare had done the cooking and she was a good cook, which somehow he hadn't expected. The whisky had had an effect on Victor, which the wine they drank reinforced. His tongue was loosened and he talked about the room in Mrs Griffiths's house and Acton and Ealing, which, after all, were his native heath, but he added how he would like to move away, move outside London. He'd got a job in marketing coming up, he said, for he couldn't bear them to think him indefinitely unemployed and without prospects. A proper flat was what he would really like with a kitchen of his own so that he too could cook. In fact, he had scarcely cooked anything ever beyond scrambled egg and cheese on toast but as he said it he believed it, and he told Clare what a good cook she was, as from one culinary expert to another.

'You'd think he'd marry me, wouldn't you, Victor? I've proposed to him often enough but he always turns me down.'

Victor didn't quite know how to take this. He looked sideways at David.

'I've been living with him for two years now. It's time he made an honest woman of me.'

David said gravely, 'I've never made a dishonest woman of you.'

A chill seemed to fall across them. It was as if the sun went in. Victor thought he understood what was implied but he wasn't quite sure.

Clare said rather brightly, 'After we've had coffee we thought you might like to go out for a walk. I mean, we'll all go. The forest is beautiful in May, it's the most beautiful time.'

For a moment he was alone with David once more while she cleared the table. The ice seemed to be forming again

and Victor sought desperately for words that would dissolve
it. He fancied that, though silent and calm, David kept his
eyes on him unblinkingly. The scent of the honeysuckle,
still overpowering, was past its best, sickly now, cloying,
a rotten sweetness.

'Up there on the horizon,' David said suddenly, 'at night
you can see the lights of the new motorway. I say "new"
but it's been there three years now. Yellow lights go all
the way along it and they're on all night, like a kind of
phosphorescent yellow ribbon winding over the fields. It's
a pity really, it spoils the rural character of the place. You'll
see later on. Sometimes I think of leaving here, of going a
long way away – well, of emigrating.'

'I thought of emigrating, but who'd have me? I'd have
to be open. Anywhere I'd want to go to, they wouldn't
have me, with my record.'

David said nothing. He had clasped his hands together
and was holding the left hand tightly in the right, making
white knuckle bones. Victor began to talk about getting a
job when you had a record, about having to tell the truth
to a prospective employer, and then he remembered how
he had said he had a job lined up. But before he could
correct the impression he must be giving David, Clare came
back and asked him if he would mind helping her with the
dishes. Victor was rather surprised, for he had never done
anything about the house while Pauline was living with
him and he had never seen his father lift a finger to help
his mother. But he followed Clare because he didn't know
how to refuse. It was a well-appointed kitchen, full of the
usual equipment and gadgets and a lot more unusual ones
besides, the kind of bars and ramps and handles specially
designed and installed for the convenience of a disabled
person. Clare, of course, hadn't always been here to look
after David. She handed Victor a tea towel but there
weren't many dishes to do as David had a machine which
Clare had already loaded.

'I wanted to be alone with you for a moment,' she said.
Bending over the sink, she kept her face turned away
from him.

'I have to tell you that when I wrote to you and talked to you on the phone – I did that to please David. I wanted to kill you. It seemed unreal, your coming here, I mean *you*, the man who actually shot David and maimed him for life. And yet at the same time it seemed too real, the right thing, the only possible right outcome – and I couldn't handle it. Do you understand what I mean?'

Victor wasn't sure that he did, though he thought she must be praising him for coming here, congratulating him, and he was conscious of a warm feeling of pleasure.

'I thought,' she went on, 'that when you came here I wouldn't be able to keep it up, I mean being nice to you, treating you politely. I've been crazy with worry ever since we spoke on the phone yesterday, wishing I hadn't asked you to come, anything but that. But now you're here, as soon as I saw you in fact – I knew it would be all right. I suppose I'd seen you either as a sort of monster or else as a – well, an instrument of evil, I suppose. And then I saw you again and of course I realized you were just a man, a human being, who must have done what he did because he was unhappy or afraid.'

'The gun went off by accident,' Victor said. *Had* it? He could no longer remember. 'It just went off in my hand, only no one believes that.'

'Oh, I can believe it,' she said, and she turned to look at him. 'I sometimes think life is all like that, a matter of random happenings and chance and accident.'

'You're right there,' he said with feeling.

'Take me meeting David, for instance. I'm a radiographer at the hospital in Epping, so you'll say that's not chance, that's one of the obvious ways people meet. He must have come to me for X-rays. But he didn't, he's never been to St Margaret's. All his treatment's been at Stoke Mandeville – he's going back there in a couple of weeks time. We met in the dry cleaners in Theydon. The wheels of his wheelchair got locked on the step and I freed them for him – it's wearing out, that wheelchair, he needs a new one. But the point is, it was just chance we met. I passed the shop, not meaning to go in, but the sun had come out and it was warm, and I thought, why don't I take off this jacket here and now and get it cleaned? And I did and David came in and we've been together more or less ever since. That was two years ago last September.'

'Do you live here, then?' Victor asked her.

'Oh, yes.' She laughed. 'I'm pretty committed. I've thrown in my lot with David, there didn't seem an alternative. I told you he's a wonderful person.' She looked at him defiantly. 'I'm lucky.'

Every inhabitant of Theydon Bois was out for a walk this afternoon, it seemed. Most of them knew David and spoke and smiled and even those who didn't know him gave him looks of sympathy and admiration. Victor wondered what it must be like to receive people's regard in this way. He walked along on one side of the wheelchair with Clare on the other, past the pond, across the green and up the road that led into Epping Forest. Clare said she thought it one of the most beautiful parts of the forest because it was hilly and with open clearings between the groves of trees. There were silver birches everywhere with pale spotted trunks and a covering of new green leaves like a sprigged veil. The whole place looked as if newly made because of the freshness of the young foliage, the brilliant thick green grass and the flowers that grew among it, yellow and white and star-like. Yet the birches, the preponderance of them, awakened in Victor an uneasy memory which increased the further they walked. For a moment, for more than a moment, the panicky idea invaded him that David and Clare knew, that every detail of his past in all its circumstances was known to them and they were bringing him to the scene of the rape he had committed here to test or mock him. For it was here, on this very spot, that it had happened.

The girl had been ahead of him in her car on the Epping New Road, heading north. He was on his way to pick up a couple and their daughter at Stansted airport but he was very early. Where the girl was going he didn't know, but he followed her car round the Wake Arms roundabout, out by the second exit and down this road. He had had no idea that it led to a place called Theydon Bois. But here, at this point where Clare was suggesting they leave the road and follow one of the clay rides among the trees, she had parked her car and left it, to walk her little dog. The dog was too small to help her. Victor recalled how its yapping had maddened him. It was this as much as anything which had made him beat the girl so badly, the only time he had ever done this, punching her face, clasping her head in his hands and pounding it against the ground, finally stuffing her own tights into her mouth. The dog had yapped and then howled, staying by its owner's unconscious form, while Victor drove away, hearing those thin reedy howls in the distance behind him. In the papers it said that the dog had saved the girl's life, for a passer-by heard it and came to find her. By that time Victor was stowing the Stansted passengers' baggage into the boot of the car.

He could actually recognize one of the trees here, a gnarled oak with a hole in its trunk shaped like an open screaming mouth. He must have fixed his eyes on that hole in the tree trunk while he was raping the girl and the little dog howled. Sarah Dawson, her name had been. Victor realized by now that Clare and David had no idea of the associations of this place for him. It was simply a place they liked to come to. The rape of Sarah Dawson had taken place at least twelve years ago and they had probably never heard of the case. Why, Clare wouldn't have been more than about fifteen herself then, he thought.

How could he have done such a thing? What had impelled him to harm that girl, to cause her such pain and terror, to beat her until her jaw had been broken and she had to have operations and orthodontic treatment? Victor had never before asked himself such questions, they were a novelty to him, and he felt stunned by the inquiries he was making of himself. But they were too much for him and he shirked deeper probing. He knew only that these events were long in his past, far away, never in any circumstances to be repeated.

'You're a very quiet man, aren't you, Victor?' Clare said as they sat down for a while on a smooth grey beech log.

He thought about it. 'I've never had much to say.'

'I must seem an awful chatterer to you.'

'It's all right when there's something worth talking about.'

'David and I talk all day long,' she said.

She smiled at David and he reached for her hand and took it in his. They *had* been talking all the time, Victor realized, on about the people they knew, and the forest and plants and trees, and where they would go for their holiday, and Clare's job and the people she worked with. It mystified him a little, for such conversation was unfamiliar to him. David began asking him if he liked it here and he said he did, that he thought of living here and looking for work. Victor felt disappointed because neither David nor Clare said they thought this a good idea or that they would help him to find something and keep their eyes open.

But when they were back at the house and Clare had left them alone together – to prepare a meal, Victor thought, but afterwards he wondered – David asked him if he would mind if they talked a little about that morning at 62 Solent Gardens . . . Victor said he didn't mind. David, who hadn't had a cigarette all the time they were out, lit one now and Victor had one too, just to be sociable.

'I've never been able to confront what happened that day fairly and squarely,' David said. 'I mean, I've resented it and raged about it. I've lamented my fate, if that doesn't sound too melodramatic. Well, even if it *does* sound melodramatic. It was a melodramatic thing that happened there that morning. But what I'm saying is, I've never had a long cool look at it and tried to re-live it. I've never talked it through – even to myself.'

Victor nodded. He could understand that David might feel like this.

'I've simply assumed I did it wrong. I've assumed I handled it badly – well, I handled *you* badly. Do you remember every detail of it like I do?'

'I remember it all right,' Victor said.

'I was in the front garden and I said to you that if

you murdered Rosemary Stanley you'd get life. Do you remember that?'

Again Victor nodded. He found he was pushing out his lower lip the way Jupp did.

'And you said you wouldn't murder her, you'd just . . .' David's voice broke off and he wet his lips. He leaned forward in his chair and seemed to be trying to speak.

Victor thought he ought to help him out. 'Shoot her in the lower spine,' he said.

'Yes. Yes, you do remember. At the time I – we – all of us – thought it was a terrible thing to say. It was so cold-blooded. I suppose it was what someone told me counsel said at your trial: 'a statement of cruel intent'. And then, of course, later, you actually did do that to me. I'm finding this extraordinarily hard to say, Victor. I thought I would and it isn't any easier than I expected. The thing is, I felt you meant all along to – well, *do that to someone* – and the someone happened to be me.'

'I didn't mean to,' Victor said. 'It was just something to say. I'd read something the night before in a magazine about – what's it called? – paraplegia and being injured down there. I do read a lot. It stuck in my mind.'

'And that was why? Is that really true?' David's voice was full of wonder.

'Of course it is,' Victor said.

'You only made that threat because of something you'd been reading? So if, for example, you'd read about shooting someone in the shoulder and disabling their right arm, you might have threatened that instead?'

'Right,' said Victor.

Clare came back then and they had supper. It was cold stuff on a tray, pâté and cheese and different kinds of bread, a fruit cake and apples and grapes and a bottle of sweetish flowery German wine. They drank that bottle and David opened another. The evening remained warm and they sat around the table on the terrace, the air pervaded with the heavy scent of honeysuckle, a violet dusk closing over the garden. To protect them from the mosquitoes, Clare had set up a 'zapper' and against this glowing blue ring the insects cast their frail bodies to be electrocuted with a snap and a hiss. Victor was rather amused by this effective method of control and said, 'There goes another!' with great satisfaction each time the device hissed, so that David's attitude astonished him. David couldn't stand it. He said that, if it was a choice between sitting out here and listening to this slaughter and going inside with the windows shut, he'd rather go inside. For an ex-policeman that was almost unbelievable, Victor thought.

They did go inside and Clare played records, country music and then some English folk songs, and the dark came down and at last Victor said he ought to be getting back. It was late – though not too late for the last train – and the idea was forming in his mind that if he hung it out long enough they might ask him to stay the night. He wanted to see what the place looked like first thing in the morning, hear the dawn chorus of birds, the garden when the sun came up. He imagined having breakfast here, Clare in her dressing gown perhaps, he imagined the smell of the coffee and the toast. But when he said he must be going neither of them suggested anything about staying the night, though Clare did say they would let him know if they heard of any flats or rooms going and she gave him a copy of the local paper to look at the accommodation page.

When he left, they came part of the way with him to the station. The wheelchair set up a squeaking and again Clare said it was wearing out.

'He charges about so much, Victor, he wears them out like other people wear out shoe leather.'

Victor thought this a bit tactless but it made David laugh. When they were down on the green, David pointed to the horizon and the crest of yellow lights that spanned the length of it, the bright necklace of the motorway that strung out the whole length of the skyline. It brought London nearer, it made Victor feel Acton wasn't all that far from Theydon Bois. He shook hands with David and then he shook hands with Clare, though this seemed strange with a woman, but it would have been stranger still to have kissed her.

He turned back twice and the first time they too turned and waved to him. The second time he could still make out their shadowy figures in the distance but although he looked for a long time, watching them recede into the dark, they didn't turn their heads again.

Victor was sitting in the almost empty train, reading the paper Clare had given him, looking out occasionally as Leytonstone was passed and Leyton and the train entered the tube tunnel, when it came to him that he had forgotten all about David's book. He had forgotten about the book and had never mentioned it or whether he might figure in it.

11

His mother used to say that you only needed to write thank-you letters to people if you stayed with them overnight. It wasn't necessary just for a meal or a party. How she could make these rules Victor hardly knew, for he had never known her eat a meal (apart from those Christmas dinners at Muriel's) away from her own home, still less stay the night in someone else's house. All day Monday he thought about writing to Clare or David or both of them but he didn't know how he should address the envelope. 'Mr David Fleetwood and Miss Clare Conway' looked clumsy and perhaps tactless and anyway perhaps the 'Miss' should come before the 'Mr'. Nor could he think of anything to write except 'thank you for having me', which was what kids said when they had been to tea. In Victor's life were huge gaps, empty spaces, where other people had social experience. He was only now aware of it. He could phone them but then they might think he was trying to get another invite for himself. He was, but he didn't want them to realize it.

The accommodation page in the local paper had afforded him nothing – or nothing that was attractive to him. Only one advertisement looked hopeful but, when he phoned the woman who had a two-room flat to let, she asked for a thousand pounds' deposit. Victor, having put the phone down, thought that of course once Jupp had paid him for the furniture he would be in a better position, but it was essential then that he made no more inroads on his capital. If he didn't hear from Clare or David by the end of the week, and so that they didn't think he was on the cadge, he would invite them to have a meal with him. There must be good restaurants in the neighbourhood, there always were in places like that, and Clare drove a car – well, a Land Rover. He hadn't seen the Land Rover, it was shut up in the garage, but she had told him that they had one and that it was specially equipped to take David's wheelchair. If he hadn't heard from them by Friday, that was what he would do. There were ways of paying for the meal without breaking into his inheritance.

Jupp was already there when he got to Muriel's on Wednesday morning. He and Muriel were having coffee in the dining room and a man whom Jupp said was his son-in-law was starting to load furniture on to the van. For once Muriel was properly dressed with a skirt on and a flowered blouse, stockings and lace-up shoes instead of nightdress and dressing gown. She had combed her hair and smeared some red on her mouth. The only thing unchanged was the camphor smell. She had taken a fancy to Jupp, he could tell that, and they were having digestive biscuits with their coffee and a chocolate Swiss roll.

Victor said he would go out and give the son-in-law a hand. Instead he went quietly upstairs and into Muriel's bedroom. This room was over the living room, not the dining room where Muriel and Jupp were, so they were less likely to hear him. At their age they were probably a bit hard of hearing anyway.

Muriel had been too busy dressing up for Jupp to make the bed. Two nightdresses, grubby nylon entrails, sagged out of the unzipped belly of the pink toy dog. One of the windows was open, a fanlight. Much more of this and she would be behaving like a normal person. Victor opened the door of the wardrobe and a draught from the window blew the skirt of Muriel's black silk raincoat up into his face. That was the coat she had worn on the evening Victor's mother took her in a taxi to the hospital, and in their absence Victor had gone in and taken Sydney's gun. Perhaps he could get hold of another key of Muriel's and have another one cut from it.

The handbags were there in the shelf section in just the same positions as he had left them last time, the black imitation crocodile one at the front. Now, with Jupp keeping Muriel occupied downstairs, he had more time – time to look as well as feel. He unclasped the bag and saw the notes inside, neatly arranged, a wad in each of the bag's stiff corded silk compartments. The familiar feeling of sickness rose into his throat. He tried to breathe deeply and steadily. Why shouldn't he take David and Clare out somewhere really nice, buy them a really good meal? The reading he had done in the past weeks had taught him that a really good meal for three people, even out in the outer-most outer suburbs, might cost getting on for a hundred pounds. Why shouldn't he spend a hundred pounds on them?

He pulled out one of the wads, emptying the compart-ment. Some of the notes were fifties, rich-looking, golden-green. He couldn't remember that he had ever seen a fifty-pound note before – they were new, or new to him. This must be Muriel's accumulated pension, he thought, that Jenny next door fetched for her as her accredited agent. There must be some sort of form she had to fill in to appoint an agent to fetch her pension. He should be so lucky! Then what did she use to pay for her shopping and all those magazines? Cheques to the paper shop, no doubt, and maybe cheques to a grocer. Why not? He didn't wonder why she hoarded all this money in cash. He knew why. It made her feel safe having plenty of money about the house, money in every cupboard for all he knew, in every drawer, stuffed inside shoes and the pockets of coats as likely as not. He understood because, in her position, in any position where cash was plentiful, he would do the same.

Sydney had left her a lot. The pension was superfluous, icing on a rich cake, but the kind of icing you take off and leave on the side of your plate. She wouldn't know how much cash she had and she certainly wouldn't know how much was missing. He took all the notes out of the next compartment and then distributed all that remained between all the compartments, counting as he did so. The next bag he opened was empty but a red leather one with a lot of gilt decoration on it contained a bundle of tenners fastened together with a rubber band. Victor took twenty notes out of the bundle. That made five hundred pounds. He could hardly believe it.

No doubt, later on, he would be back for more and he would want to know whether she had touched the bags in the meantime. His own belief was that she had packed as much into these particular receptacles as she intended to and had moved on to another 'bank', a shelf or drawer or box perhaps not even in this room. He pulled a hair out of the crown of his head and laid it lightly across the clasp of the black crocodile bag. There was no way now that anyone could move those bags without dislodging the hair.

Downstairs he heard Jupp's voice. He and Muriel were coming out of the dining room and Jupp, of course, would go straight to the garage where Victor was supposed to be. It probably didn't matter too much but he had better go down. Inadvertently he caught a glimpse of himself in the pier glass. The furtive look on his face, mean, sharp and calculating, took him aback. He drew back his shoulders, squaring them. He raised his head. If Muriel hadn't said that about leaving her property and money to the British Legion, he wouldn't have helped himself to her money. Or at any rate he would have put back what he had taken if the reverse had been true and she had announced she was leaving it to him. Never would he have thought of coming back for more. It served her right. In a properly constituted legal system there would be a law compelling people to leave their property to their own flesh and blood.

Jupp didn't comment on his absence or ask him where he had been. He was about to put Victor's father's wheelchair into the van, was pushing it up the ramp. Almost everything was gone and the curtains lay in a crumpled heap on the floor. Victor had a wonderful idea. David's wheelchair was wearing out, Clare had said so twice. Why shouldn't he give David this one? It was a good wheelchair, anyone could see that, and his father had only used it for about six months. It was an Everett and Jennings orthopaedic chair, leather and chrome, and Victor thought what a marvellous present it would make for David. Of course

David had that house and nice furniture and obviously didn't want for anything, but he would only have some sort of disability pension to live on (not a great hoard of inherited capital like Muriel) and no doubt couldn't just go out and buy a new wheelchair when the fancy took him.

'Want a mint, cocky?' said Jupp, holding out the packet.

'You can give me one,' said the son-in-law. 'I reckon I do you a favour every time I take one of them things, like when a person takes a smoker's fags. It's a kindness to them, keeping them off their poison.'

'I'm not as bad as that, Kevin,' Jupp said humbly. 'I'm a thousand times better than what I was. You wouldn't call me addicted, would you? Dependent maybe, but addicted, no.'

'He's a mintaholic,' said the son-in-law, laughing. 'Joseph Jupp MA, Mintaholics Anonymous.'

'I don't want the wheelchair to go,' said Victor. 'I've changed my mind and I'm keeping it.'

'Now he tells me,' said Jupp. He pulled the wheelchair out from where he had stowed it between a bookcase and a pile of cushions. 'I shall have to knock a bit off the purchase price. No doubt you've taken that into account. Four hundred.'

'Four hundred and twenty,' said Victor.

Jupp gave the chair a shove and it careered down the ramp. 'Four hundred and ten and that's my final word. Do you think your auntie'd come out for a drink with me? Or maybe the cinema?'

'She never goes out.'

Another mint went into Jupp's mouth. He had finished the packet and he screwed up the paper wrapping and threw it into the back of the van. 'She never got dressed either, did she? But look at her this morning. Quite the glamour girl. I think I shall go and try my luck. Faint heart never won fair lady.'

'Christ,' said the son-in-law.

'Don't be like that, Kevin.' Jupp's hand went to his pocket but the supply was exhausted. He said to Victor,

'I'm a widower, by the way, in case you was thinking it wasn't all above board.'

'It's nothing to me,' said Victor. He held out his hand, palm uppermost. 'I'm a bit pressed for time.'

Jupp wrote him a cheque. He was left-handed and he wrote slowly in a sprawly round hand. The cheque smelled of mint. What with his mints and her camphor, they would make a fine pair, Victor thought disgustedly. He let Jupp go back into the house and, leaving Kevin seated on a spur of rock among the purple trailing flowers, he went round the house to see if a key might be concealed somewhere under a loose paving stone or flowerpot. But there was nothing.

On the garage floor lay the brown checked travelling rug that had always been draped over one end of the settee. To conceal a cigarette burn made by his father, Victor had discovered when he was about eight. On an impulse, he picked it up, folded it and put it on the seat of the wheelchair.

'That'll have to come off the purchase price,' said Kevin, winking. 'No doubt you've taken that into account.'

Because Kevin meant to be funny, Victor managed a smile. He said goodbye and went off, pushing the wheelchair. Instead of going the direct way home, he crossed Gunnersbury Avenue and walked along Elm Avenue towards Ealing Common. There was no one about, it was very quiet, a dull weekday morning with rain threatening. Sure he was unobserved, Victor sat down in the wheelchair and covered his knees with the rug. Manipulating it looked easy when David did it. He thought he would have a go and see how easy it was. The wheels had chromed metal hoops attached to them of slightly smaller circumference. These you pushed forward and they drove the larger wheels round.

There was something quite pleasant and gratifying about making the chair move along. Victor took one of the paths across the common. He felt rather like the way he had when he had first mastered the technique of riding a bicycle. It brought a new dimension to daily life. A woman was

157

coming towards him with a retriever on a lead. Victor's first thought was that he must get out of the chair because this woman would think it odd or be shocked by what he was doing, but immediately he realized that of course she wouldn't be. She would simply take him for a handicapped person who was obliged to use a wheelchair. And this, in the event, was what happened. It was interesting to observe her behaviour. Although Victor was on one side of the path and she on the other and a good six feet separated them, she drew in the dog's lead, shortening it to less than a yard's length, gave Victor a quick searching glance, then looked away with an assumed indifference as if to say: Of course I know you are a cripple, but to me, sophisticated creature that I am, you are no different from anyone else and I shan't commit the social solecism of staring at you, so don't imagine I am wondering what is concealed under that rug or what brought you to what you are now.

Victor was sure he could read all this in her reactions, and it intrigued him. There was no doubt that in a wheelchair one was the centre of attention. He met and passed several more people and the feeling he often had when on foot, that he might as well not be there, that he was invisible, that no one took a bit of notice of him, was replaced by a sensation that in this new guise he affected everybody. No one who saw him was immune from his effect. It might be pity they felt or embarrassment, resentment, guilt or curiosity, but they felt something, those who stared, those who ostentatiously did not stare and those who stole at him sideways glances. When he came to the lights at the big crossing where the Uxbridge Road crossed the North Circular a big man came up to him and said, 'Don't you worry, mate, I'll see you over,' and when the lights changed and the traffic stopped, shepherding Victor, walking along by the side of the chair, 'Let them wait, that won't do them any harm.'

Victor thanked him. He was enjoying himself. Something else he realized was that he had always hated walking, though he had never confessed this before, even in his innermost thoughts. One thing about prison, exercise might have been compulsory but there had been nowhere to walk to. For the most of his adult life, prior to prison, he had had a car to drive. The wheelchair was hardly a car and it would be out of the question in bad weather, but in some ways it had advantages over a car, it had attractions, Victor acknowledged, as two gossiping women jumped aside to let him pass, that cars didn't have. He caught himself up on that when he realized the enormity of his thoughts – a man with the full use of his legs wanting to be confined to a wheelchair!

It wasn't easy getting the chair up the stairs at Mrs Griffiths's, but there was nowhere to leave it downstairs. Victor thought how good it would be if the phone under the stairs were to ring at this moment and for it to be Clare. He would tell her about the wheelchair being a gift for David and she would be delighted and probably come over as soon as she could in her car and take him and the wheelchair back to Theydon Bois, and this time perhaps he would be asked to stay the night. The phone didn't ring, of course it didn't. Clare would be at work, doing her radiography at St Margaret's Hospital.

The wheelchair was more comfortable to sit in than anything provided by Mrs Griffiths. Victor sat in it by the window, looking at the roof of his parents' house and reading *Punch*. The roof was all that could be seen of the house for the leaves were thick on the trees now and the spotty green and pink and white veil had become a blanket of foliage. In the garden below, weeds had grown up as high as the woodpiles and oil drums: nettles and thistles and a pink flower as tall as a man. Victor counted his cash. With his last social security payment he had just on a thousand pounds in hand. The magazines he had bought contained plenty of advertisements for restaurants recommended in the *Good Food Guide* or by the AA or Egon Ronay. Victor sat in the wheelchair reading them and wondering where it would be best to go. If he hadn't heard from David and Clare by Saturday, he decided, he would ring them on Saturday morning and ask them to have dinner with him that evening. He had never taken anyone out to dinner before, apart from eating in cafés with Pauline and once or twice going to the steak house in Highgate with Alan.

Victor thought he wouldn't go out at all on Friday. It would be awful if he were to go out and David were to phone and there was no one here to take the message. At various times throughout the day, which was very long and passed slowly, he told himself that he had no reason to believe David would phone, he hadn't said he would phone. Probably he and Clare were waiting for him, Victor, to phone them and thank them for last Saturday. At three in the afternoon, when he was bored and sick with waiting, Victor went down and dialled David's number. There was no reply. He sat in the wheelchair reading last Sunday's *Observer* colour magazine for half an hour and then he went back to the phone and tried again. Still no reply. He would leave it for two hours, he thought, and at five thirty he would try again.

On the stairs, coming down at twenty past five, he heard the ringing begin. He ran down and lifted the receiver. It was Clare.

Her voice had a strange effect on him. He didn't want her to stop talking, her voice was so lovely, warm and rich and with an accent few women in his circle, such as it was, had possessed. She spoke rather slowly and precisely, yet with a kind of breathlessness that was very charming. He was listening to the tone of her voice and its quality, not the sense of what she said, so he had to ask her to say it all over again.

'It's a flat, Victor. Not here but at a place called Epping Upland. The house belongs to someone my mother knows. Her husband has died and she wants to let part of her house. She's going to advertise but she won't for a week or two, so now's your chance. I haven't said anything to my mother. I thought I'd wait until I'd asked you.'

Victor said he would like to see the flat and Clare said he could fix that up with Mrs Hunter himself. She would give him Mrs Hunter's phone number and address. Victor realized she wasn't going to invite him to Theydon Bois or even say anything about seeing him again. The beginnings of nausea cramped his chest.

'There's just one thing I'd suggest, Victor. I'm not advising you to be dishonest – I'm sure you wouldn't take that sort of advice anyway – but I wouldn't say anything about the past to Mrs Hunter if I were you. It's not as if – well, what you did you're likely to repeat. It's not as if you did something likely to affect a person letting you a flat, I mean stole something or – well, committed a fraud or anything. Please forgive me for mentioning it.'

Victor swallowed. He said, 'That's all right.'

'David and I have talked it over and we agreed we wouldn't say anything about who you were even to my mother.'

'Thanks,' Victor said, and, 'I thought of changing my name,' though he had not in fact thought of this until that moment.

'That might be a very good idea. Well, fine. Now let me give you Mrs Hunter's phone number. Have you got a pen?'

He wrote it down mechanically. Epping Upland was probably miles away from Theydon Bois, almost the other side of Essex, very likely. They wanted him a long way away. Had he done something he shouldn't last Saturday? Had he blown it in some way?

'Right, I'll have to ring off now,' she said. 'We're going out.'

'Clare,' he said, his mouth dry, 'I'd like to – I mean, would you and David have dinner with me tomorrow? Somewhere nice, somewhere out near you. I'd really like to take you out but I don't know any places.' He felt spent with the effort of making this long speech.

'Well . . .' she said. That single word sounded doubtful. Did it also sound pleased? 'We couldn't tomorrow.'

Disappointment was an actual pain. He crouched down on the floor, doubling up his body in an effort to ease it.

'Victor? Are you still there?'

'I'm still here,' he said hoarsely.

'Would a night in the week be possible?'

161

'Oh, yes. Any night. Monday?'

'Let's say Wednesday, may we? And shall I book some-where? Would you like that? I'll have to arrange with them about getting David's chair in. We always have to make sure restaurants can do that.'

The best place, Victor said. The best place she knew, she mustn't worry about expense. He would call for them, would that be all right? He would rent a car. Why not?

'Of course not, we'll go in ours. Come early, come about six.'

He asked her to remember him to David, please to give David his best regards. She sounded surprised when she said she would, surprised and a bit puzzled. Amazed he could afford all this hospitality, he thought, as he returned to his room. Epping Upland wouldn't be all that far from Theydon, very likely no more than three or four miles. He thought he could remember noticing a signpost to it on those trips he used to make to and from Stansted. When he was living in Mrs Hunter's flat he would be able to ask Clare and David over for a meal. By then, of course, he would have a new name. He wondered what he should call himself. His mother and Muriel had had the maiden name of Bianchi. Their grandfather had been Italian, from southern Italy, which accounted for Victor's own darkness of hair and eyes. He didn't fancy calling himself by an Italian name. Faraday then, after Sydney? Pauline's surname (doubtless changed long ago) had been Ferrars but he didn't want to be reminded of her. It would be easy enough to pick a name out of the phone book.

Victor phoned Mrs Hunter, giving the name of Daniel Swift and saying he was a friend of Clare Conway. She said he could come and see the flat on Wednesday if he wanted to. Not knowing how far Epping Upland might be from Theydon Bois and wanting to be absolutely sure of getting to David's by six, Victor said he would come in the morning. He would come at eleven thirty. He forgot to ask what rent Mrs Hunter would want or when the flat would be available.

On Tuesday he went out shopping, this time to the West End. He couldn't wear the green velvet jacket yet again. To go out to dinner surely you needed a suit. If only he had a car of his own! The possibility of ever owning a car seemed remote. He went into the men's department at Selfridge's and bought a dark grey suit. It cost him two hundred pounds. To go with the suit he bought a grey and cream striped silk shirt and would have got a grey tie, only the assistant told him flatteringly that this was rather dull for a man of his age and recommended instead a rich leaf green with a single diagonal cream stripe.

Dressed in his new clothes, he set off early on Wednesday morning – too early, for he was at Epping by eleven. A station taxi took him to Epping Upland and Mrs Hunter's house. It was rather a long way and Victor hadn't seen any sign of public transport, though there must be some, and he disliked the idea of walking all this distance. He asked the taxi driver to wait and was glad he had done so, for it turned out that, although she had said nothing of this on the phone, Mrs Hunter wanted a married couple for the flat and help in the house in lieu of some of the rent. Victor returned to Epping, the whole empty day stretching before him.

At any rate, dressed like this and with money in his pocket, he could buy himself a good lunch in one of the hotels. It was a very good lunch he had and he found himself very respectfully treated, no doubt because of the suit. Victor realized, as he was eating his crème caramel and drinking the last of his wine, that it was nearly two weeks since he had been in a panic or felt angry. Those great angers that took hold of him and took control of him, changing him physically so that his skin burned and he felt literally as if his blood was boiling, they seemed remote. So did the panics that enclosed his limbs in an electric suit that tingled and shocked where it touched. He was changing. As he thought this, he was aware once more of a feeling that must be happiness and with it came a gentle luxurious calm.

Beginning at the tower end of the town, Victor went into

every estate agent to ask what they had in the way of unfurnished flats to let. There was none, but some had furnished flats and houses on their books, their owners protected by leases which stipulated strictly limited tenancies. The DHSS would, of course, pay his rent but would they pay *any* rent? A hundred pounds a week, for instance? It seemed unlikely. Victor decided he must ask Tom or Judy about that. He bought a local paper, though it was nearly a week old. He had a look at a newsagent's board, not the one he had been to before, and wrote down two phone numbers, both with the Epping exchange.

By the time he had tried these two numbers – one advertising a flat, the other a room – and had got no reply from either, it was nearly three thirty. If he walked slowly to the station and got a train and then walked slowly to Theydon Manor Drive, surely he wouldn't be too early at David's? Well, he would be early but only about an hour and David wouldn't mind.

Just as a journey can be very long when one is late so it can be accomplished with amazing speed when one has time to kill. The train was waiting and as soon as Victor got into it the doors closed. Last time he had travelled from Epping to Theydon Bois that old woman had been in the compartment with him, the one who ran up and down playing guards and had some live thing with her in a carrier bag. This afternoon he was alone. About an hour ago the sun had come through and it was quite hot, the carriage full of almost static motes of dust suspended in the rays of light. It was still only ten to four when he got to Theydon.

He walked very slowly across the green, not wanting to sit down on a seat, still less on the grass, for fear of marking his suit. At ten past four he could bear it no longer. He could feel his calm threatened by a strange stretched feeling that was part boredom, part exasperation with the dilatoriness of time, part an undefined fear. Unwilling to let it mount any further and destroy his new self, he began to walk rapidly towards Sans Souci.

The garage doors were open and the garage was empty. Victor knocked at the front door, a smart double rap with the Roman soldier. No one came, so he walked round the side as he had done that first time. The honeysuckle smell had grown stale and petals lay everywhere. On the terrace, in his chair, David sat fast asleep, his head hanging forward at an awkward angle. For a moment or two Victor stood watching him. Hanging like that, David's face looking puffy, the cheeks pendulous. He looked old and sick and sad.

Victor moved quietly towards the table and sat down in one of the blue and white canvas chairs. Almost immediately, though Victor was sure he had made no sound, David woke up. He woke up, blinked, and seeing Victor there, made an involuntary movement of recoil. It was a flinch, made with shoulders and head, and at the same time he rolled the chair a foot or two back towards the french windows.

'David,' Victor, said, 'I know I'm early. I thought you wouldn't mind.'

David took a moment to recover. He passed his fingers across his forehead. He blinked again. 'That's all right. I was fast asleep.'

Victor wanted to ask him if it was he that he was afraid of, that he had flinched from, or if anyone would have had that effect. He would have liked to ask but of course he didn't. David's cigarettes and lighter were on the table and an empty cup that had had coffee in it. Victor didn't look at David but at the wall behind him, where a rambler rose climbed, its stems laden with clusters of creamy buds.

David said, 'You look very smart, what my father used to call "Sunday-go-to-meetings".'

'My father called it that too,' said Victor, though he had no memory of his father actually ever saying this. He began telling David about the flat and David said it was pity Mrs Hunter hadn't thought to mention that bit about a married couple to Clare's mother.

'I've got something I want to give you,' Victor said. 'A present. I want you to have it. I couldn't bring it with me though, it's too big and awkward.'

'I'm intrigued. What is it?'

'A new wheelchair. Well, it's not absolutely new, it was my father's. But it's hardly been used.'

David looked at him, a steady blank stare. In a way that gave the impression of stiff lips, of lips frozen perhaps, he said, 'I've got a new wheelchair, this one. Didn't you notice? I got it at the end of last week.'

And then Victor did notice it, the shiny chrome, the smooth new grey upholstery. He passed his tongue across his lips. The glassy stiff expression on David's face had crumpled and he was smiling. He was smiling in the way people do when they don't want to seem to be smiling, yet at the same time want the person they are talking to to see there is cause for amusement.

'*You* wanted to give *me* a wheelchair?'

'Why are you smiling?' Victor said.

'You lack a sense of humour, Victor.'

'I expect I do. There hasn't been much in my life to be humorous about.'

'Never mind, then. It was the irony that struck me, but never mind.'

It took Victor a moment or two to see what David meant but he got there, he did see. He got to his feet and stood, holding the edge of the table.

'David, I didn't shoot at you on purpose. It was an accident. Or rather, I lost control through you taunting me. I wouldn't have shot you if you hadn't kept on saying the gun wasn't real.'

David breathed deeply, looking at him eye to eye.

'I said that?'

'Over and over. You kept on saying the gun was a replica, that it wasn't real. I had to *demonstrate* – can't you understand?'

'I never once said the gun wasn't real,' David said.

Victor couldn't believe it. He would never have thought David capable of lying. An abyss seemed to open before him and he held on to the table to stop himself from falling in.

'Of course you said it. I can hear you now. "We know the gun isn't real," you said. Four or five times at least.'

166

'It was Superintendent Spenser who said that, Victor. From the front garden.'

'And you said it too. When we were in that room, you and me and the girl. You've forgotten, I can understand that, but I haven't. That's why I shot you. It wouldn't – it wouldn't do you any harm to admit it now.'

'It would do me a lot of harm to admit to something that never happened.'

'Unfortunately, there's no way of proving it.'

'Yes, there is, Victor. I have a transcript of your trial. Detective Bridges gave evidence and so did Rosemary Stanley. Both of them remembered very clearly what was said. Counsel asked them both if I ever asked if the gun was real or suggested it might not be. Would you like to see the transcript?'

Silent now, Victor nodded.

'If you'd like to go into the living room, the room at the front of the house, you'll find a roll-top desk on the right-hand side of the door. It has three drawers and the transcript is in the top one.'

The house smelled of lemon polish and faintly of David's cigarettes. It was cool and very clean. The living-room door was held open to the extent of about a foot by a stone doorstop that from a distance caused Victor a tremor of alarm but it turned out to be a crouching cat. Victor went into the living room. On one side of the fireplace, its grate laid with a pile of birch logs, was the desk, and on the other, on a low table, stood a photograph of Clare in a silver frame. She wasn't smiling but seemed to be looking at whoever looked at the photograph with a rapt mysterious gaze. Victor opened the top drawer of the desk and took out a blue cardboard folder to which was attached a label with the typewritten words: *Transcript of trial of Victor Michael Jenner.*

Presumably, David meant him to read the relevant part of the trial proceedings outside in his presence. Victor went back to the garden where David, having rolled the chair closer to the table, was lighting a cigarette. He sat down opposite David and began to read. It was quite silent in

167

the garden but for the irregular throbbing hum made by a bumble bee drawing the last pollen from the honeysuckle. Victor read Rosemary Stanley's evidence and James Bridges's evidence. He could remember nothing of any of this. It was a blank to him, the trial no more than a blur, a confused memory of injustice and persecution. David sat smoking, his eyes fixed on the far end of the garden, which was enclosed by trees and a hedge of blossoming red may. The familiar sick feeling was taking hold of Victor, combined with a tingling he knew to be the start of panic. That afternoon, finishing his lunch, he had spoken (or thought) too soon. He forced himself to re-read the evidence. He re-read the cross-examination. An exhalation of smoke from David, a rather harsh sighing sound, made him look up. He became aware, perhaps for the first time, of the angle of the other man's legs, their utter useless *deadness*. They were like the limbs of dead men seen in battlefield pictures.

Victor jumped up. He stood trembling.

'Victor,' David said.

Almost without knowing what he was doing, Victor had crashed his fist hard down on the teak slats of the table. Again David rolled the chair back.

'Victor, here's Clare now,' he said. 'I can hear the car.'

Saying nothing, Victor turned away and went into the house. It seemed extraordinarily dark in there. He walked blindly across the room and came up against a wall and stood with his forehead pressed against it and the palms of his hands. It was something that had hardly ever come to him before, to understand that he was wrong, that he was at fault. The floor and ceiling of his world had gone and he hung in space, he hung on the wall with his forehead and his hands.

Victor let out a low animal moan of pain, turning blindly. He felt his body come up against another body, his face touch skin, soft warm hair veil him, arms enclose his shoulders. Clare had come in and without a word taken him in her arms. She held him lightly at first, then with increasing tender pressure, her hands moving on his back, up to his neck and head, to bring his head into the curve of her shoulder. His lips felt the warmth of her skin. He heard her murmuring gentle comforting things.

Holding her now, letting her hold him, indeed pressing his body into hers with a voluptuous abandonment as he had yielded it in the past to warm water or a soft bed, he felt the last thing he would have expected, a swift springing of sexual desire. He was erect and she must feel it. There was no embarrassment, he had gone too far into despair and horror and now a kind of joy, too far into intense emotions, for anything so petty. He was aware only that his feelings, here and now, were new, never before experienced in quite this way or for this reason. He held her hard against the length of his body and, raising his head, moving his face against hers, across the soft skin with a sensuous trembling delicacy, would have brought his lips to her lips and kissed her had she not, with a whispered something he couldn't catch, disengaged herself and moved away.

12

In the next two weeks Victor saw David and Clare several
times but Clare never put her arms round him again or
kissed him or even touched his hand. They all knew each
other well now, they were beyond shaking hands, they were
friends, or so Victor expressed it to himself. He had lost
his shyness about arranging meetings. It was better for him
to phone them anyway. He could hardly hear the phone
bell when he was up in his room and most of the time there
was no one else to answer it.

That evening at the restaurant in the old part of Harlow
where they had had dinner, Victor hadn't said much. He
had listened to the other two talking. Silence had always
seemed to come naturally to him, and when he spoke he
used clipped sentences, merely stating facts. He liked the
sound of David and Clare's voices, the rhythm of them,
the rise and fall, and he marvelled that they could talk so
much when they really had nothing to say. How was it
possible to go on and on like that about a piece of roast
duck and where you had had it done like that before, or
about something called 'cuisine naturelle' and something
else called 'tofu', or the appearance and ages and
professions – all guesswork this – of the couple at the
next table? After a time he scarcely heard their words. He
thought about David and what he had done to him and
how David had forgiven him. Why, all these years, had he
convinced himself he had been goaded into shooting David
by David himself? Perhaps because he had never quite
wanted to admit to himself that he could lose control
without provocation. Whatever David said to him or
proved by that transcript, he, Victor, was still left asking

himself why he had done it and what that provocation could have been.

Their talk, though, had brought him closer to David. And much closer to Clare. Victor couldn't help wondering quite what he would have done, how he would have coped. if Clare had not come in at that moment and comforted him. He had no words, or few, to say to her when they were together but at home he talked to her. He carried on a silent inner conversation with her all the time, something he had never done with anyone before. She never replied but that was somehow unimportant. Her replies were implicit in what he said to her and the questions he asked. He sat in the wheelchair, looking out over the green rustling treetops, talking to her about his parents' house and his parents and the exceptional devotion they had for each other. He asked her if she thought he ought to go out more, take more exercise. It would be better for him to read books, wouldn't it, rather than all these magazines? And then, getting up and going out, he would ask her in the newsagent's which magazine to buy today.

Another remarkable thing was how he kept thinking he saw her. She never came to Acton – in fact she had told him she had never once been there – but time after time he fancied he saw her ahead of him in the street or in a shop or getting into a tube train. It was always someone else, of course it was, some other pretty girl with fine-spun flaxen hair and golden-pink skin. But for a moment . . . Once he was so sure he called her name.

'Clare!'

The girl who came down the library steps didn't even turn her head. She knew he was calling someone else.

It was funny how David had receded into the background. Of course he *liked* David tremendously, he was his friend, but he didn't think about him much any more. One way and another, Victor had got hold of a good many ideas about the mind and the emotions, among other things by reading *Psychology Today*, and he wondered if he had, so to speak, *exorcized* David by the talks they had had, by the revelation that had been made, by 'talking it through'.

It was possible. He realized now how much he had thought about David, how exhaustively he had been obsessed by him, between leaving prison and going for the first time to Sans Souci. Now, when he wasn't thinking about Clare and talking to her, his mind dwelled on his parents and particularly on the love they had had for each other. Once, he now understood, he had resented that love, had been jealous of it perhaps, but he no longer felt like that. He was thankful his parents had been happy together and when he remembered the settee embraces it was with indulgence rather than distaste.

He sat in the wheelchair most of the time he was at home. It was comfortable, and if he was going to have to keep it in his room it might as well be put to use. Once or twice he tried an experiment. He sat in the wheelchair and pretended he couldn't move his legs, that he was dead below the waist. This was very difficult to do. He found it easier if he covered his legs with the travelling rug. Then he attempted to lift himself out using only the power of his arms, talking all the time to Clare but unable to decide whether she approved or not. Once he fell over on the floor and sprawled there, lying immobile until he told himself that of course he could get up, *he* wasn't paralysed.

The first time he went to Theydon after the three of them had had dinner together it was to take them a present – well, a present for David really since it wasn't Clare's house and Clare wasn't married to David or even a girl-friend in the usual sense of the word. Since it wasn't possible to give David the wheelchair – and he saw now that this had been a tactless idea – he must give him something else. That was what you did. If you suggested a present to someone and it wasn't acceptable, you found an alternative. What the alternative must be was obvious – a dog. David's dog had died and he missed it, so he must have a new dog.

Victor bought *Our Dogs* magazine. There were a great many advertisements in it for yellow labrador puppies. He was amazed at how expensive dogs were, a hundred pounds was the norm and, for certain less usual breeds, two hundred, wasn't uncommon. Victor rang up the nearest dog breeder to advertise and, when he was told puppies were available now, went up to Stanmore. Fortunately, the tube went there, the Jubilee Line that had been enlarged and changed its name since he had gone to prison. He found that you couldn't just buy a dog the way you bought a TV set. The breeder wanted all sorts of promises and guarantees that the ten-week-old bitch would be going to a good home. Victor told the truth. Objections melted away when the dog breeder heard that his puppy's new owner would be the heroic policeman David Fleetwood whose case he remembered well from eleven years back. Victor paid for the dog and arranged to pick it up on Wednesday. It wouldn't be of much benefit to Clare, he thought, in fact might be rather a liability, so he went to the perfumery department at Bentall's and selected a whole range of St Laurent Opium, eau de toilette and talcum and bath stuff and soap, but when he told the salesgirl that Clare was young and blonde she persuaded him to change to Rive Gauche. The dog cost him a hundred and twenty pounds and the perfumes not far short of a hundred. Victor still had his driving licence and it was still valid. He went to the car-hire place in Acton High Street and rented a Ford Escort XR3.

By a piece of luck David had wheeled himself round to the front of the house and with secateurs was clipping the dead heads off those spring flowers which were within his reach. Again Victor was early. He had allowed himself two hours to get here from Stanmore and thanks to the motorway had done it in less than an hour. The puppy, in a wicker basket shaped like a kennel that Victor had bought specially, cried all the way.

David propelled the wheelchair up to the gate.

'Victor, you've got yourself a car! You didn't tell us.'

It's on hire, Victor was on the point of saying. But the admiring light in David's eyes – admiring of him surely, as well as the Escort – he didn't want to see go away and be replaced by that more usual patient polite look.

'It's not new,' he said, remembering the B on the licence plate.

'Well, maybe not but it's very nice. I like that shade of red.'

Some explanation was necessary, Victor felt. Suppose David were to think he had stolen the car or the money to pay for it!

'My parents left me a bit,' he said.

'What's in the basket?' David said.

The puppy must have fallen asleep. It had been silent for the past ten minutes. He lifted out the kennel basket and at that moment Clare arrived. The Land Rover looked shabby beside the Escort, and Victor felt sorry for her and David but proud at the same time.

'It's not our birthdays, Victor,' she said when he gave her the package wrapped in coloured paper.

Savouring his surprise, Victor opened the top of the basket, lifted out the plump, cream-coloured, velvet-skinned puppy and put her into David's lap. Afterwards he knew he must have imagined their looks of dismay. He *was* a pessimist and a bit paranoid sometimes, he knew that; he did tend to think people distrusted him and disliked the things he did. Anyway, within seconds David was cuddling the little dog which snuggled up to him, and stroking its head and saying, how lovely, what a beautiful animal, and, Victor, you shouldn't have.

In the back garden the dog gambolled about, examining everything, digging a hole in a flowerbed. Clare said, though she was smiling, 'I don't know how we'll ever train her with me out at work all day. Mandy was trained when David got her. But oh, she is sweet, Victor! What will you call her, David? How about Victoria?'

'Her proper name is Sallowood Semiramis.'

'I daresay,' said David, laughing. 'Dogs should have simple, ordinary names. Sally will do very well.'

Victor decided to keep the hire car for a few days because he would be coming back to see them during the following week. In the meantime he drove about the outskirts of London a good deal, looked at two flats in metropolitan Essex, one in Buckhurst Hill and one at Chigwell Row, and rejected both. He imagined Clare sitting beside him in the passenger seat and he talked to her as he drove, though without moving his lips or making a sound. He asked her if she thought he ought to buy a couple of pairs of really good shoes, a raincoat and a spare jacket, and he sensed that she thought he should. Not much now remained of the nine hundred and ten pounds.

Returning to Mrs Griffiths's house, Victor passed Tom, who was on foot as usual, a long way from West Acton station but evidently bound for there. It struck Victor for the first time how shabby Tom always looked. He was wearing trainers not real shoes, a thin pale blue nylon zipper jacket and badly worn Lois jeans. Tom turned round as Victor pulled up alongside and called his name. His pale puffy spectacled face peered out between black fuzzy beard and black fuzzy hair.

'Hop in. I'll give you a lift.'

'You *have* come up in the world,' said Tom.

Victor said he had a job, out in Essex. He was commuting at present but soon he would move. As soon as he had said this, he realized he could no longer ask Tom about whether the DHSS would pay the rent of a hundred pound a week flat for him.

'You're looking well, Victor. Work obviously agrees with you. What's the job exactly?'

Victor told him a lot of lies. The gist of them was that he had been taken on by an estate agent's in Epping, where business at this time of year was brisk.

'Do you want me to jot down your business address in case you move before I see you again?'

Victor pretended not to hear. 'Here you are. West Acton,' he said.

While he had the car he had another errand to perform. He drove down Gunnersbury Avenue in the stream of airport traffic but, instead of taking the car right up to 48 Popesbury Drive, he parked it round the corner and approached Muriel's house on foot. The idea came to him that he would find Jupp there, a permanent resident perhaps, at least Muriel's steady friend, a 'boyfriend', if that wasn't too grotesque a word. Muriel might even marry

Jupp and then it would be he and not the British Legion who came into her money.

An unexpected sight met his eyes as he came in view of the house. Jupp's van was nowhere to be seen. The front door was ajar. Where Kevin had perched himself, on a broad flat grey stone that protruded from the rock plants, squatted a man in jeans and a vest with a pair of shears in his hands. He had been cutting back the grey attenuated seed heads which were all that now remained of those millions of purple flowers that had hung over the stone ridges like a drapery of thick fuzzy cloth. Victor hung about, not wanting to be seen. The man gathered up armfuls of cut seed heads, laid them on a barrow which he had lugged up on to the cliff top, and humped the barrow away over the stones in the direction of the garage. He went round the side of the house, leaving the side gate swinging behind him. Victor cast a quick glance in the direction of the lowest stones but the shearing hadn't progressed so far and they were still covered. He ran up the steps and in at the front door.

There was no one in the hall and the doors to the ground floor rooms were shut. The chances were that Muriel was behind one of them. Victor went upstairs and into a bedroom he could not remember ever having entered before. Like the one where, under the floorboards, he had found the gun, this room contained a bed, a chest of drawers and a chair. The differences were that a wooden-framed swinging mirror stood on the chest of drawers, the curtains were a dull yellow-gold and the carpet gold with a dark brown border. Dust covered everything, gathered in fluffy nests in the folds where the curtains were looped back, lying so thickly on the top of the chest that it took a moment or two to see that the wood was partly covered by an embroidered runner. Victor pulled open the top drawer. It was empty, lined with brown paper, on which the activities of woodworm had left small pyramids of sawdust. The second drawer was the same but contained a man's underwear and socks. The bottom drawer was full of money.

Not full, that was an exaggeration. At first it looked like the other, empty, lined with brown paper. But it was too shallow. Victor lifted up the sheet of paper that lay at the bottom and the money was underneath, not in bags or in any way wrapped, but in neat stacks of pound notes and fives, hundreds of them, arranged in blocks as carefully as Muriel's magazines.

He skimmed the top. He took a quarter of an inch or so from the top of each of the twenty stacks and filled his pockets, glad he was wearing the padded cotton jacket, fashionably bulky, that he had just bought. You could have stuffed pounds of paper into those pockets without it showing. Out on the landing once more, he remembered the hair he had placed over the clasp of the mock-crocodile handbag. It would be as well to check. The house was silent, he could hear nothing. Muriel had made her bed today but for some reason the pink dog, zipped up for once, plump and glassy-eyed, had been placed on the pink satin dressing table stool, from which vantage point it seemed to watch Victor's movements. He opened the wardrobe door, knelt down and looked at the bag. The hair was till there.

What would Clare think if she could see him now? The thought came to him uninvited, unwanted, as he crossed the landing. When advising him not to talk about his past to Mrs Hunter, she said, 'It's not as if you stole something . . .' The circumstances were different, though, he thought. It wasn't stealing in the usual sense of the word, for if he had not been sent to prison unjustly, for something which had been an accident and not deliberate, Muriel would certainly have willed him her money and probably given him some of it in advance as people did (he had read in the *Reader's Digest*, in an article about Capital Transfer Tax) to avoid death duties. If, if . . . If Sydney hadn't happened to look into that ditch outside Bremen in 1945, if his attention had been distracted, for instance, by a low-flying aircraft or a vehicle on the road, he would never have seen the dead German officer with the Luger in his hand, so the gun would never have been under the floorboards here and Victor would never have taken it in preparation for it to go off in his hand and paralyse David for ever . . .

He had reached the foot of the stairs and was in the hall when the living-room door opened and Muriel came out with a young woman who looked just like Clare. Or so Victor thought for about ten seconds. Of course she wasn't really like Clare at all, being ten years older and twenty pounds heavier and with a face that was Clare's pushed about and melted and remodelled. But just for a moment, the colouring, the hair, the green-grey eyes . . .

Suddenly Victor knew how Muriel would introduce him. She would say that this was her nephew who had been in prison. But he had misjudged her, she didn't introduce him at all.

'This is Jenny from next door.'

The voice was about as different from Clare's as could be, shrill but lifeless, with a false warmth.

'And you must be the nephew I've heard so much about.'

Heard? What could Muriel have said about him?

'I expect you'll be wanting to do a bit for her now you're back. We do the best we can, I pop in and out, but it's a drop in the ocean really and we've got our own lives to lead. I mean, you need a *team* in that garden, not just one man, but now you're back you'll want to pull your weight.'

'Back?' he said, waiting for it.

'Muriel told me you'd been in New Zealand.'

Victor couldn't look at her. Was it, could it be, coincidence? Or did Muriel remember thirty-five years back, visiting her sister, and hearing her sister's little boy insist that there was never a time when he wasn't alive, only a time when he was in New Zealand? Certain it was that Muriel was ashamed of his, Victor's, past and didn't want to associate herself with that past. She didn't want her acquaintances, Jupp, this woman, to know.

Jenny had taken from her a shopping list so long that the items on it covered both sides of the sheet of paper. With it Muriel handed her a blank cheque which was made out to J. Sainsbury PLC and signed Muriel Faraday. I should be so lucky, thought Victor. Had she seen Jupp again? Had she been out with him? She was dressed – or undressed – as before, in nightdress and dressing gown, brown snood and pink mules. Victor thought she wasn't going to say a word to him, but he was wrong.

Her nose twitched, mouse-like. 'What did you come for?'

'I thought I might get you a bit of shopping in,' he said.

Jenny chipped in at once, luckily cutting off whatever retort Muriel was preparing. 'Oh, that's all right, no bother, I promise you. I'm not saying that once you get to know the ropes, I mean, once you've settled back and got into a routine, I mean, then you're at liberty to do your bit. But just at the moment – I mean, Brian'll run me to Sainsbury's in the morning and, to be perfectly honest, I do such a big shop there myself that her little bits and bobs don't actually make an iota of difference.' She and Victor had moved towards the front door together while she was talking. Muriel followed them only so far. Not only did she not go out, but she seemed to fear contact with fresh air or even the sight of outdoors from inside. She hovered in the background clutching with both hands the two sides of her dressing gown. Jenny said, 'Bye bye now. You can expect me like six-ish tomorrow, so mind you have the sherry ready and the dry roasted peanuts.' She winked at Victor, pulling the door closed behind her. 'What a life! Might as well be in the tomb already. I never miss a thing, I don't mind telling you, there's nothing goes on down here I don't see from my windows, and I can tell you that, until you came home and that old boy that eats the mints started coming, she never saw a soul but us from one year's end to the other.'

'Have you seen me come, then?'

'This is your fourth time in as many weeks,' said Jenny with alarming accuracy. 'If you want to get past me, you'll have to come Saturday lunchtime. That's when Brian takes me to do my big shop, isn't it, Brian?'

Looking around him at the garden, Brian said, 'I've not even skimmed the surface, not the surface.'

'If I'm going to start doing a bit for her, I'll have to have

179

a key,' said Victor. He felt awkward but he pressed on. 'Could I have a loan of your key to get one cut?'

'We haven't got a key, Vic, not one of our own, that is. Don't you know where the key lives? Well, you wouldn't. I should leave that now, Brian, you'll only overdo it and I shall be up with your back half the night.' She pointed towards the hedge. 'Under the tortoise, Vic. The key's under the tortoise.'

22 June would be Victor's birthday, his thirty-ninth. He couldn't remember ever having celebrated his birthday beyond receiving presents from his parents in those early years. The time his mother and father had talked about a party for him and his mother had grown distraught at the prospect, they had in fact taken him to Kew. There isn't much in botanical gardens for a boy of eight but his mother was fond of Kew. She quoted something about wandering hand in hand with love in summer's wonderland, and she and his father did wander hand in hand, smelling the flowers and saying how beautiful it all was. Victor said to himself, as he drove past Woodford Green where the chestnuts had blossomed and shed their petals, that this year he would celebrate his birthday. He would do something with Clare and David before David had to go back into hospital.

The car he had kept for a further day – well, the weekend, for he would return it to the hire company on Sunday evening. He wore his new cotton padded jacket, two shades of grey, dove and slate, with slate binding, Calvin Klein jeans and, not to seem too exclusive, a dark red Marks and Spencer sweat shirt over the grey and cream striped shirt. On the back seat of the car were two bottles of German wine, Walsheimer Bischofskreuz, and two hundred cigarettes. A breeze was blowing and the sun was shining. It wasn't a bad day, warm enough to have the window open on the driver's side. Victor had never been one to play the radio in cars. He liked silence. From the drawer in the chest in Muriel's second spare bedroom he had helped himself to four hundred and sixty pounds. Unable to bear the prospect of waiting, he had counted the notes the moment he was back in the car. How much cash did that mean Muriel actually had in the house? Thousands? As much as, say, ten thousand? It was a well-known fact, one was always reading about it in the papers, that old people stashed away huge sums in their homes. It wasn't unusual, it was more normal than otherwise.

The hair had not been moved from the clasp on the handbag, so therefore Muriel had no idea as yet that any of her savings were missing. But suppose she did get that idea, suppose she found out, would she do anything about it? By this, Victor confessed to himself, he meant tell the police. Her behaviour led him to think she wouldn't. She had said nothing about his past or his prison sentence in the presence of either Jupp or Jenny next door, and this must mean she wanted to keep it dark, for she was malicious and uncharitable and there was no way she would have been discreet out of consideration for his feelings. If she discovered that he had been helping himself to the contents of her bags and drawers – to a fraction of what they contained, in fact – the chances were that she would berate him, would demand it back, but would do nothing more. The respectability of her family, as it appeared to other people, was important to Muriel.

If only he could acquire a car, Victor thought, he could start his own car-hire company, doing for himself that which in the old days he had done for Alan. He could buy a new car for six thousand pounds or two secondhand ones and take on another driver . . . With these ideas running pleasantly through his head (a flat in Loughton, for instance, a phone-answering service, journeys to the three London airports a speciality), he took the second exit out of the Wake roundabout and drove down the hill, through the forest, to Theydon.

It was a Saturday, so Clare would be at home. Victor's thoughts turned away from David and towards her as he drove into Theydon Manor Drive and he was aware of a mounting apprehensive tension, with a sick edge to it. Last night he had dreamed once more of the road that was his path through life with the significant houses on either side of it. There had been no temptation to enter any of the houses until he reached Sans Souci, which came into view round a sharp bend in the road. The part of the road that bent also passed through a dark wood of fir trees planted very close together in regular rows. Beyond the wood Sans Souci lay bathed in sunshine. Victor went into the front garden and helped himself to the key which was kept under the birdbath. He let himself into the house and called their names. 'Clare!' first and then 'David!' For a while there was no sound and then he heard someone laughing, two people laughing. The living-room door opened and Clare came out with David beside her, only David wasn't in his wheelchair, he was walking. He was well again, not paralysed, and he was walking.

Clare said, 'Look, a miracle!'

A terrible feeling of sickness and despair had come over Victor, for he knew, he couldn't tell why, that now David could walk again he had lost them both. But almost immediately he had woken up and the relief was tremendous, the knowledge of reality after that strange and frightening dream.

He didn't want to remember it now. He parked the car and walked round the side of the house. David had said he would be sure to find them in the garden if it was a nice day. The honeysuckle smell had been replaced by a scent of roses. Clare was mowing the lawn with an electric Flymo on a long lead and David was watching her from his wheelchair under the blue and white umbrella. She switched off the power and came towards him.

'Hi, Victor!'

Smiling, David raised one hand in a kind of salute. They were easy with him now, they accepted him, he was almost like a family member. Clare was wearing a cream-coloured cotton dress with an open shirt neck and big puffed sleeves. The dress was held in at the waist by a wide belt of saddle-stitched leather in a shade of deep tan. She had on flat sandals with thongs. Her hair, newly washed perhaps, instead of hanging to her shoulders, stood out in a shimmering gauzy cloud. In his dream she had been much less beautiful than this and when he thought how he had found a resemblance between her and Jenny next door he felt that somehow he had betrayed her.

The little dog Sally was on David's lap but she jumped off when she saw Victor, uttering surprisingly mature barks which made them all laugh.

'You shouldn't bring us all these things, Victor,' Clare said when she saw the wine and cigarettes.

'I like to. I can afford it.'

'You're wasting your substance on *our* riotous living,' David said. 'One day you're going to need that inheritance of yours.'

That inspired Victor to tell David about his plans for a car-hire company. David seemed to approve of this, but he thought it wisest for Victor to start in a small way, with just one car.

'We'll employ you when David has to go to Stoke Mandeville,' Clare said.

'Especially if you arrange to have the kind of vehicle the size of a large van with a ramp for taking a wheelchair up and an anchorage for the chair when it gets there and a specially designed seat belt.' David was smiling all the while he said this and Victor didn't think he was mocking him. How could he be? David really did need all those things and Clare's Land Rover did have them. He, Victor, was being over-sensitive and had doubtless imagined the sideways look Clare gave David and the very slight warning frown.

Lunch was salmon with a mayonnaise Clare had made green by putting finely chopped herbs in it, cucumber salad and French bread. Victor had never had that sort of salmon before, only the tinned kind and once or twice the smoked. Then they had strawberries and cream. David lit a cigarette.

'Would you mind fetching me something, Victor?' he said. 'You'll find it on the table where Clare's photograph is. In a brown envelope.'

'It's his book,' said Clare.

'There goes my surprise!'

'But, darling, Victor must know about your book. It was the article about your book that told him where you lived.'

'So it was,' said David.

His steady gaze rested on Victor and that small ironical smile was again on his lips. David's face had that heavy jowly look today that Clare said it had when he had slept badly the night before. Victor got up and went into the house, into the living room, pushing back the reclining cat doorstop. Clare's eyes met his from the silver photograph frame. He would like to have that picture, he thought, and he wondered if there was any way he could contrive to take it. But it was in such a prominent place and David evidently valued it . . .

The feeling he had was comparable to his sensations when they had taken him for that walk in the forest – that, contrary to all outward evidence, they were in fact mocking him, conspiring together to be revenged on him, leading him to this place only to confront him with the most despicable aspects of his past. Again he felt it as he picked up the large brown envelope. In some form or other inside here was David's book. Was David going to ask him to read it (even read it aloud?) in order to discover terrible revelations made about himself? Was he, Victor, pictured inside and described as a 'psychopath', 'a cold-blooded criminal', 'a sex maniac'? Suppose it were so, what was he to do?

He stood, holding the envelope, realizing that he dreaded looking inside. There was a sudden temptation to leave the house by the front door, taking the envelope with him, and drive away. He went back through the house and out into the garden once more. The little dog had fallen asleep on the lawn. Clare was bending over David's chair, her arm round his shoulder, her cheek against his. For one who had boasted that he didn't know the meaning of loneliness, Victor felt very alone, an outsider, lost. He thrust the envelope at David.

'Have you ever seen galley proofs before?' David said. 'I must confess I never had. Fascinating!' He was smiling and Victor knew that he was tormenting him. 'I'm supposed to read these and mark them for the printer – find typographical errors, you know, and maybe mistakes of my own.'

They were just the pages of a book, page one and two, for instance, on one side of the sheet and three and four on the other. In the text a word had been circled in red and a hieroglyphic made in the margin.

'How do you know what to do?' Victor said.

'*Pear's Encyclopedia* has all the proofreader's marks.'

There were no pictures, of course, and no cover or jacket, just this thick mass of printed pages. On the first page was the title: *Two Kinds of Life* by David Fleetwood. Their eyes on him, feeling sick, Victor leafed through the pages, but haphazardly, and blindly, seeing nothing but a dancing mass of black and white swirls.

Clare spoke gently. 'Victor, there's nothing to worry about.'

'Worry?' he said.

'I mean, there's nothing about you in there. The book's just what it says – two kinds of life. The life David had as a police officer and all that involved and the life – well, afterwards. It's really to show people life isn't over because one becomes a paraplegic, it's about all the things David has managed to do: get his Open University degree, for one thing, travel, go to concerts, learn to play a musical instrument. Did you know he not only plays the violin, he learned to make violins? That's what the book's all about, it's cheerful and forward-looking, it's full of hope.'

'Poor old Victor,' said David. 'What *were* you afraid of?'

Once Victor had hated and feared him. A wave of that old hatred broke over him now, of bitter resentment, for he knew that David had followed his thoughts every step of the way to this end. David had known how he felt and had kept him tantalized, believing perhaps that Victor had been screwing himself up to ask about the book ever since their first meeting a month before. Little could he have known that Victor had been too happy in his new friendship even to give the book a second thought till now . . .

'Look,' Clare said. 'Here's the only bit that mentions Solent Gardens.'

Victor read it. The thoughts he had had about David evaporated. Perhaps it had all been in his imagination. He knew he was sometimes paranoid, prison made one paranoid, said those supposedly in the know.

> The siege of Solent Gardens – never much of a siege and of very short duration – has been described too often elsewhere for me to say much about it. In a few words then, I was shot and the shot crippled me for life. These days, now that times have changed, some would say for the worse, the police engaged in that exercise would almost certainly have been issued with firearms and the likelihood is I would not have been shot . . .
>
> But 'jobbing backwards' is a useless and destructive practice. The past is past. I was shot in the lower spine, my spinal cord was severed, and my body below the waist permanently paralysed. My last memory for a long time was of lying in a pool of blood, my own blood, and asking, 'Whose blood is that?'
>
> The next months of my life, my second kind of life, were passed in Stoke Mandeville Hospital, which is what the following chapter is about.

'There's to be a foreword by a senior police officer,' said David, 'in which he is going to outline the siege. But without mentioning you by name, we decided on that.' He grinned at Victor. 'My publishers didn't like it, and that's the truth. They were scared of libel, I think. So no pictures, Victor, and no hard words, right?'

That might be true, about the publishers, Victor thought, but it was true too, he was sure of it, that David intended him no malice. David understood that it had been an accident. Why then did his eyes, lingering on Victor more constantly surely than usual, hold always that glint of irony, that tolerant amusement? Why did he seem to be watching Victor as if he were waiting – yes, that was it – waiting for him to do something terrible again, to have perhaps another disastrous accident of which he, David, would be the victim?

He replaced the proof sheets in the envelope and turned his eyes on Clare, his look full of gratitude. She it was who had read his thoughts and interpreted his anxiety, she who had given him comfort before he asked for it. Her ringless hand lay on the table, the hand on which David refused to place an engagement ring, a wedding ring. Victor longed to cover it with his own and hold it, but he did not dare.

13

The birthday was still two weeks off. Victor had cunningly ascertained that David and Clare were doing nothing in particular that Sunday night but would be together at home as usual. He said nothing about his surprise, only taking care to tell them it would be his birthday on that date, for he was confident they would all meet during the next fortnight.

Driving home – very late, in the small hours of Sunday morning – he made up his mind that he would leave it to them to phone him. Of course they could get hold of him if they wanted to, he was nearly always at home in the evenings, and if he left his door ajar he could hear the phone. Perhaps it had been a bit over the top going to see them twice in one week; he must be careful not to overdo things at this early stage. Why, they all had years and years before them. It would probably take a whole year or more to become really close friends. Victor wondered as he drove along the empty road between the beech woods, past the dark slopes and the paler clearings of the forest, if the day would come when they might all live together, sharing a house somewhere. The idea was an attractive one, he running his car-hire business and, if it were as prosperous as he thought it might be, Clare working for him, entering into partnership with him, while David, whose book was bound to be a success, entered on a third kind of life, the life of a writer. He wished, though, that he had that photograph of Clare. He could have asked her to give him a photograph. Why hadn't he? Fear of looking silly, he thought. Next time he saw them he would give them a photograph of himself and ask for pictures of them. That way they wouldn't know it was specially Clare he wanted a photo of.

Dressed in his new suit, Victor went a few days later to a photographer who had his studio at Ealing Green. The photographer seemed rather surprised by his request and assumed at first that Victor wanted his picture taken for a passport. Apparently it was rare for grown men on their own, without wife or child, to want portraits of themselves. And Victor sensed a real disappointment because he didn't smoke a pipe and wouldn't hold a dog or a golf club. However, the photographs were taken and Victor was promised a selection of shots from which to make his choice within the next few days.

He bought the *Tatler*, the *Radio Times*, the *TV Times*, *What Car?* and *House and Garden* and sat in the wheelchair reading them. In the evening he watched his new television set with the sound turned down and the door open so that he should hear the phone. On the Friday Clare did phone – to ask him if he realized he had left his sweater behind. She had parcelled it up and sent it to him by recorded delivery that morning. This was the red Marks and Spencer sweatshirt she was talking about and Victor hadn't missed it for the weather had been very warm, but he wished it had been his jacket he had left behind, or something with a more exclusive label on it.

Clare didn't invite him over but she did say, just as she was ringing off, that she would be seeing him. Victor liked that, the casual acceptance of himself as a friend, nothing formal about it, no need to say how enjoyable last Saturday had been, how lovely his wine, how they looked forward to meeting again. That was past, they were beyond that. And he told himself he was glad *not* to be asked. If he went there this weekend the birthday celebration might be made that much more difficult. There should be pauses in friendship, he thought, there should be breathing spaces. But after she had rung off he stood there in the darkening hall, still holding the receiver in his hand, and then speaking aloud into the mouthpiece what he had not said to her when she was at the other end of the line: 'Goodnight, Clare. Goodnight, darling Clare.'

That was not a word he had ever used to anyone before in his whole life. He picked up the pencil off the top of the phone box and wrote on the wood beside David's name and phone number: Clare.

In the food hall at Harrod's Victor looked at delicatessen, cheeses and cold meats and fish and salads. He looked at cakes and fruit, pricing items, unable to make any sort of selection in the face of this plenty, this excess, this amazing choice. But he would come back here next Saturday and buy everything he wanted for his birthday dinner. He would hire the car again. It was a pity he couldn't hire a refrigerator.

The prints arrived from the photographer, who stressed that they were unfinished, they were rough yet, just a guide. Victor thought that even in their present state they were quite good enough for him. He had not known that he appeared so young. His good looks were less marred by those prison years than he had thought. It was a serious, handsome, rather reserved face that looked back at him, the mouth sensitive, the eyes with their sombre experiences alone betraying that the man in the portrait was past his twenties. In one he was in profile, in the other two he was facing forward with his eyes slightly turned. Should he have the picture for David and Clare framed or simply give it them in the cream-laid deckle-edged paper folder the photographer would provide? He put the question to Clare in his thoughts but as usual she did not answer him.

Muriel had a refrigerator. Indeed, she had a very large refrigerator with large freezer compartment, necessary for someone who lived as she did. But Victor was loth to ask her if he could keep the food he was going to buy at Harrod's in her fridge overnight. She was quite likely to say no. Besides, he had a curious feeling that now he had begun using her house as a kind of bank there could be no relationship between them any more. They had ceased to be aunt and nephew. She had seen to that really by her aggressive attitude towards him.

In a way Muriel's house was like a bank with a machine on the outside (they didn't have them before he went to prison) where you stuck in a card and dialled a secret number and your money came out. Only here you merely needed the key and a certain amount of nerve. At the moment he didn't need any more money, he had enough to tide him over the next week or so. Victor walked along Acton High Street, pausing to look at refrigerators in a showroom window. Once he had his flat he would certainly need a fridge but at present he had scarcely room for one, the wheelchair took up so much space.

Returning, he passed Jupp's shop. In the middle of the window, behind the tray of Victorian jewellery, stood his father's writing desk. The price ticket, hanging from a string, was turned so as to be invisible from the street, a technique common to antique and secondhand dealers. But in this case it hadn't been turned quite enough, for by dint of bending his head down almost to touch his knees and twisting his head round, Victor could read, writen in biro, the sum: £359.99. And Jupp had given him only £410 for the whole lot! He must have known even then that the desk was an antique. And if the desk was worth so much, what about the rest? Probably his furniture had been worth nearer four thousand than four hundred pounds.

He understood though, as he looked at it and at his mother's pair of matching brass candlesticks which stood on top of it, that it was too late to do anything about this now. But he went into the shop just the same. The doorbell jangled. Prominently placed, some few feet inside, was the brown velvet settee on the arm of which someone had put the stuffed peacock, its clawed feet concealing the cigarette burn his father had made. It was not Jupp or the boy but Kevin who came in from the back.

'He's making a packet out of me, isn't he?' Victor said. 'He's asking nearly as much for that desk as he gave me for the lot.'

'Absolutely. It's daylight robbery,' said Kevin cheerfully. 'Well, he's not in it for his health, is he? And talking of health, you'll never credit it but he's given up them mints. Given them up total, cold turkey.'

Victor wasn't interested. The entire contents of his parents' house were spread around Jupp's shop, but for a few items which Victor supposed he had already sold or else transported to the place in Salusbury Road. He walked about reading price tickets: £150 for the dining table and six chairs, £25 for his parents' double bed (scene of so many love transports and cries for more, masked as distress), £10 for the buttoned satin bedhead, £75 for a bookcase and £125 for a glass-fronted china cabinet.

'D'you fancy a coffee?' said Kevin, coming in from the back once more. 'You may as well.' Victor followed him, ducking under the looped-up curtain. A saucepan was starting to boil over on an electric hob, white froth bubbling up and leaping over the sides before Kevin could reach it. 'It's no use crying over spilt milk,' he said.

The room was furnished like a kitchen but with armchairs and an ironwork table with a marble top of the kind you sometimes see in pubs.

'Do you live here?' Victor said.

'Are you kidding?' Kevin handed him a mug of boiled milk and water with half a spoonful of powdered coffee in it. 'Sugar? He's been giving your auntie a bit of a whirl, if you can credit it. I don't know what's come over the old Joe of late. He's been taking her out.'

'She never goes out.'

'Well, it's a manner of speaking, innit? "Taking out" – what does it mean? Anything from buying a chick a half of Foster's to screwing her out of her brains. He's got to have something to take his mind off his withdrawal symptoms.'

'He lives here then, does he?' Victor was determined to stick to the point.

'Nobody lives here,' Kevin said patiently. 'The wife and me, we live up in Muswell Hill, and old Joe's got a maisonette over the shop down Salusbury. Satisfied? So why do we have them chairs and a fridge out the back here? On account of if you're in this business you may have long periods of the working day, to say the least, when not a sod comes in. Right?'

'Can I put something in your fridge to keep overnight? Over Saturday night, that is.'

'What's wrong with your own?'

Victor explained that he hadn't got a fridge. Kevin took some convincing. Apparently, it had simply never occurred to him that there might be people – ordinary people living around him, not aboriginals or Amish – who didn't possess refrigerators.

'Would you credit it?' he said, looking at Victor with new eyes, and he began talking about the refrigerator he shared with Jupp's daughter, the largest and most efficient on the British market, of vast cubic footage and equipped with freezer, ice-maker and compartment for chilling drinks and dispensing them from a tap. At last Victor managed to elicit from him that the shop would be open until six on Saturday and he, Kevin, would be 'unofficially' opening it until midday on Sunday. 'Strictly against the law but highly favourable to the tourist trade,' he said.

Victor was prepared to point out that Jupp owed him something, the way he had practically stolen his furniture, but Kevin needed no more persuading. They never kept anything beyond milk and maybe half a dozen cans of beer in the fridge here. Victor was welcome.

'About twelve on Saturday then,' Victor said.

Suppose Jupp were to *marry* his aunt? Stranger things had happened. And after all it must be this which Jupp had in mind, for he could hardly be interested in her for sex or company. It must be her money. Victor let himself into Mrs Griffiths's house, into the warm musty silence, the quiet of the long day when he would be alone there. The parcel on the hall table was for him, addressed in Clare's hand. The sweatshirt, of course, and with it a current copy of the local weekly paper. Victor hoped for a letter as well, but the enclosure was a postcard with a drawing on it of a statue and a square and some buildings he thought Clare might have done herself but which said on the back: *Versailles*, Raoul Dufy. She had written: 'I thought you might need this in case we don't meet for a while. Love, Clare.'

He took it upstairs with him. He put the sweatshirt on, though it was rather too warm to wear it, and sat in the wheelchair, studying the note again. What did 'for a while' mean? A few days? A week? A month? Of course it didn't really matter what it meant as he would be going over there on Sunday to surprise them anyway. She had put 'love' when she might easily have written 'yours'. Last time she had written 'yours'. She could have put 'yours sincerely' or 'yours affectionately' or even 'yours ever' but she had put 'love'. You didn't write 'love' unless you had quite a strong feeling for a person, did you? He couldn't imagine writing 'love' to anyone – except her . . .

The sweatshirt had been handled by her, folded by her. He could smell her on it, a definite though faint scent of the Rive Gauche that he had bought her himself.

Advertised in the paper was a likely-sounding flat. It had probably gone by now, Victor thought, but he phoned the number just the same, standing in the hall with his eyes on Clare's pencilled name on the underside of the stairs. The flat was still available, fifty pounds a week and in Theydon Bois itself. Victor imagined seeing Clare and David every day. They would call in on him on the way back from their walks and sit outside with him under a striped sunshade, drinking white wine. It was a ground-floor flat, large bedsit with 'patio', kitchen and bathroom. A garage was also available for rent, if desired. Victor arranged to see the flat on Sunday afternoon. Without thinking very much about what he was doing, just doing it because it seemed right and what he wanted to do, he bumped the wheelchair down the stairs and out of the front door. Once he was in Twyford Avenue he got into the wheelchair and sat down and covered his legs with the brown checked travelling rug. It was a warm day but not warm enough to make the rug look silly.

Victor made his way on to Ealing Common. In the distant past such places had been attractive to him because of their potential. There he could find women alone. There, no one was in earshot of their cries. Dogs he had always found singularly ineffectual in coming to the aid of their owners, though it was also true to say that he had never attacked women accompanied by large dogs. He parked the chair under some trees. A child playing with a ball was called sharply away by its mother – in case it should be a nuisance to the handicapped man, he thought. The rapist he had once been seemed like a different person, and this was not simply because he was currently in the role of a disabled man. Rape itself had become as alien to him as to any normal ordinary citizen. Why had he done it? What had he got out of it? He asked Clare, who was listening sympathetically, but as usual she didn't reply. It was because he was always angry, he thought, and now he wasn't angry any more, nor could he imagine a cause of anger.

He turned round and went home. A young girl who looked a lot like Clare came to help him over the crossing at the Uxbridge Road, walking beside his wheelchair and holding the back of it. His arms were tired by the time he reached the corner of Tolleshunt Avenue, but when he got out of the chair to push it back to Mrs Griffiths's house his legs felt stiff from disuse.

Next day he had the hire car again and by a piece of luck managing to get the same one. He parked it in Harrod's car park, securing the last vacant space. In the food hall he bought asparagus and raspberries, smoked trout and quails, which he hoped Clare would know how to cook, tiny English new potatoes, the first of the season, herb butter, clotted cream, *mange tout* peas, brie and Double Gloucester and a goat's cheese that looked like a swiss roll with icing on it. He bought champagne, Moët et Chandon, and two bottles of Orvieto.

It cost nearly a hundred pounds. Victor hadn't known you could spend a hundred pounds on such a small amount of food. He drove to Jupp's shop. Jupp himself was there, trying in vain to sell an ugly *art nouveau* lamp to a woman who had obviously come in only to look round. Kevin, of course, hadn't bothered to tell him about the arrangement he and Victor had made.

'Bit of a peculiar request, isn't it?' he said lugubriously to Victor. 'A bit bizarre?'

'Your son-in-law said it would be all right.'

'I daresay. He thinks he owns the place, reckons he's monarch of all he surveys. You do as you like, cocky, make yourself at home.'

Jupp was wearing his jeans and the striped waistcoat but an incongruously formal white shirt and tie with a regimental crest. With the tip of his finger he removed something from the underside of a mirror frame and slipped it into his mouth. Victor went back to the car and fetched the box of food, noticing as he came back that his father's desk had gone. Munching his chewing gum, Jupp stood holding the fridge door open. He eyed every item Victor put inside and at the sight of the champagne his shaggy white eyebrows went up.

'Didn't I tell you not to spend it all at once, cocky?'

'You're making enough profit out of it, I should say,' said Victor.

Jupp slammed the fridge door. 'All's fair in love and war.' He didn't explain how love or war entered into a straight commercial transaction. Victor said he would be back for the food next morning, and left.

In fact he went back quite early, before ten, because he had wakened up in the small hours with the awful thought that suppose they didn't open the shop this particular Sunday, suppose Kevin simply forgot? Kevin, however, was there. He helped Victor re-pack the food, having peeled off and flung away a gob of gum he found adhering to the fridge door handle.

'Disgusting, innit? He's got an addictive personality. He'll be smoking next.'

This reminded Victor to buy some cigarettes for David. He also got a packet of Hamlet cigars. Back at Mrs Griffiths's house, he dressed carefully, casual today in a new dark blue tee shirt he had bought, dark blue cord jeans and the two-tone grey padded jacket. It was when he was lacing up his new shoes, perfectly plain fine grey leather, the most expensive pair he had ever owned, that he remembered it was his birthday. All this was in honour of his birthday yet he had forgotten the occasion in the complexity of preparations. He looked at himself in the mirror. Thirty-nine today, his fortieth year entered upon. No one had sent him a card – but who was there that knew his address except David and Clare? He was aware though of an uneasy feeling, a slight feeling of let-down, but he refused to let himself think about the reason for it: that David and Clare, who had been told it was his birthday, had not sent him a card.

At noon he set off, the box of food in the boot of the car, and in a stout brown envelope on the seat beside him the portrait photograph of himself which had arrived by yesterday's post. Victor had four hundred pounds in the pocket of his jacket, all that was left of the money he had drawn out of his 'bank' at Muriel's.

He had lunch in an hotel at Epping and drove down Piercing Hill to Theydon Bois. It struck him that he was living in the kind of style he had always aimed at and never quite achieved before: driving a smart new car, well dressed, lunching in good restaurants, about to choose a new and attractive home for himself, then to entertain his friends to a luxurious meal. The past was there still but it wasn't even like a bad dream, being too distant and impersonal for that; it was like someone else's past or something he had read about in a magazine.

The flat was part of one of the older houses adjacent to the forest. It was very small, a single room with french windows that had been converted into three. The 'patio' was a little bit of concrete outside these windows with trellis round it, overhung by a clematis at present covered by myriad creamy-white flowers. The woman who owned the house and whose name was Palmer told him it was a clematis and that the blue flower in the narrow border was bugle and that the iron table and chairs were new and of the best quality. Victor didn't think much of the chipboard furniture, the broken wash basin and the haircord carpet, but he imagined living here and eating out on his patio and having David and Clare drop in several times a week. On the phone, remembering what Clare had advised, he had given his name as Michael Faraday and now he repeated it, quite liking the sound of it. Mrs Palmer wanted a deposit of a month's rent and a reference. Victor handed over two hundred pounds and promised a reference, thinking that perhaps Clare would help him there, it being she after all who had suggested the assumed name and discarding of the past.

It wasn't yet four. Victor thought David and Clare might still be out for their walk, if indeed they had gone today. Bright and sunny when he left Acton, it had clouded over and grown colder, and as he drove slowly alongside the green a few drops of rain dashed against his windscreen. He hung about till half past, sitting in the parked car reading *Time Out*.

Rain was falling steadily by the time he drew up outside Sans Souci. They wouldn't be out in the garden today. He rapped on the front door with the Roman soldier knocker, the box of food and bottles at his feet. A curtain in one of the front windows moved and Clare peered out. He couldn't conceal from himself that, at the sight of who it was, her face was overspread with a look of blank dismay. The smile which replaced this was unnatural and forced. He felt suddenly very cold.

Clare opened the door. She was wearing white cotton trousers and a blue shirt that made her look very young and holding the puppy in her arms. Clare always looked young, she *was* young, but now she looked about eighteen. She said, 'Victor, what a surprise!'

'I meant it to be a surprise,' he said, speaking in an awkward mutter.

She looked at the box. 'What have you brought this time?'

He didn't reply. He picked up the box and took it into the house and stood there, aware of something different, aware of a sense of something missing or lost.

'I'm afraid David isn't here,' she said. 'They asked him

to go into hospital a week earlier than arranged. They specially wanted it and it was all the same to him. He's coming home tomorrow.'

Then Victor knew what was missing, the smell of David's cigarettes.

'Don't look so disappointed!'

'I'm sorry. It was just . . .'

'You'll have to put up with me instead. Come and meet Pauline.'

He had a horrible feeling of a possible trick again. She had arranged it, she had fixed it, and Pauline Ferrars was waiting behind that door for him, fetched from her hiding place, discovered, brought here to confront and taunt him. But of course it was quite some other Pauline, some friend or neighbour, a girl of about Clare's own age, dark-haired, pretty, wearing a gold wedding ring.

They had been drinking tea and the teapot was there and two mugs and biscuits on a plate. While Clare went away to fetch another mug he tried to talk to Pauline. He said it had been a nice day but it wasn't any more. She agreed. Clare came back and began talking about David, the treatment he was having, some kind of electric shocks to the spine that was still really in its experimental stages. She was going to fetch him home herself, would be taking the day off to do so, because he liked that better than going in the kind of ambulance that had been provided before.

Victor felt more than disappointed. He was bowled over and stunned. In this woman's presence he found it impossible to speak and he had already convinced himself that she had come for the day, for the evening. The absurdity of his plan, his 'surprise', unfolded before him and he saw how stupid it had been, indeed how childish, not to phone and check that they would both be at home and free. But when Pauline got up and said she must go – it was nice to have met him, she said. How could it have been? – he felt marginally better. He felt something might be retrieved and, though he was embarrassed, he was also rather pleased when Clare came back from seeing Pauline out to say that she couldn't help noticing the champagne in the box and what were they celebrating?

'My birthday,' he said, and because he couldn't resist it, 'I did tell you.'

'Oh, Victor, of course you did! I do remember. It was just that all this with David and him going to hospital early and getting things ready – it went out of my head.'

'It doesn't matter.'

'You know it does. You know it matters a lot. I think I know what's in the box. Things for a celebration dinner, is that it? Wine and food and lovely things?'

He nodded.

'Come on. Let's unpack them and see.'

Victor suggested they drink the champagne while they did this.

'Wouldn't you like us to save it till David's home? You could come back one day in the week and we could have it then.'

'*Today's* my birthday,' Victor said.

She was kneeling on the floor and she looked up at him with a sudden smile that was joyous and somehow conspiratorial, perhaps in appreciation of the childlike directness of his reply. She wrinkled her nose. He hadn't felt much like smiling but he managed it. The things that came out of the box made her gasp.

'We couldn't possibly eat all this anyway, just the two of us!'

Victor opened the champagne. She had two glasses standing ready. It hadn't been his lot in life to open champagne very often and when he had done so in the past there had been something like an explosion followed by a mess but now the operation was smoothly done and every foaming drop caught in Clare's glass.

'Can you cook all this stuff ?' he said.

'I can try. They do look pathetic, the quails, rather like four and twenty blackbirds baked in a pie.'

'Cooking will make a lot of difference,' said Victor.

'It had better.' Clare lifted her glass. 'Happy birthday, Victor!'

He drank. He remembered her face of dismay appearing at the window when first he knocked at the door. A layer of paranoia seemed to peel itself off his mind; he saw something more rational beneath and all kinds of understanding became less remote.

'If you wanted to be on your own this evening,' he said, 'if you'd rather I went, I wouldn't mind. I really wouldn't.'

She put out her hand and laid it on his arm. 'I'd like you to stay.'

It was clear that she meant it. He was very conscious of her touch, of the weight of that small brown hand, though it lay lightly, almost hoveringly, on his sleeve. He had a curious impulse to bend his head and press his lips to it. She took her hand away, sat back smiling at him.

'Of course I want you to stay. We owe you a lot, Victor.'

He stared, sensing sarcasm.

'I know that sounds strange, considering – well, if it hadn't been for you, David wouldn't have been in this state in the first place. That's true, of course. But we're different people at different stages of our life, don't you think?'

Didn't he! Passionately, he nodded, holding his fists clenched.

'The man who shot David isn't the man who's here with me now, he isn't the man that David can talk to and – well, somehow straighten things out, get things into perspective. And even that first man, David doesn't see him as a monster, as evil, any more. He's beginning to understand. Victor, there was a time when I thought David would go – mad. He was heading for a complete breakdown. He couldn't talk about the shooting, he certainly couldn't have written about it, and that's really why it's not in his book – not because of compassion for you, if that's what you thought. And then you turned up. First he thought you'd come to kill him and then, believe it or not, he thought he'd like to kill you.'

Silently Victor listened, watching her face.

'Then he started to *like* you. There is something – I must find the right word – *lovable* about you. Did you know that? I think it's because you seem very vulnerable.'

201

It might have been the champagne, though Victor didn't think so, but something seemed to move and tremble and unfold inside his body. Her words repeated themselves on his inward ear.

'Yes, lovable,' she said. 'I know David feels it. Forgive me if I say I don't think he quite trusts you yet, not entirely, but think how he has been hurt. He will, he will come to it. He'll adjust himself to life finally through you.'

Victor felt as if she had given him a magnificent birthday present. There was nothing material she could have given him to please him half so much. He would have liked to say so but he was unable to express these thoughts, they stuck on his tongue and he was struck silent. He packed the food back into the box and carried it out to the kitchen. The windows were awash with rain, the green and flowery garden a distorted blur through glass than ran with water. She came in carrying the champagne, took his hand and gave it a squeeze.

'Clare,' he said, holding her hand, 'Clare.'

In the end they decided not to eat the quails but to keep them in the fridge for when David got back. Clare cooked the asparagus and they ate the trout and then the raspberries with cream. They ate at the kitchen table and Victor loved the informality of it, the red and white check cloth Clare laid on the pine table, the red candle in a pewter candlestick that it was dark enough by eight to light, so wintry and twilit did the rain make Theydon Manor Drive that evening.

He told her about the flat he had put a deposit on. Clare said what he had fantasized she might say, though had not truly imagined she would.

'We'll be able to drop in when we're out on our walks.'

Victor said, 'He's back in hospital now – is there, does that mean there's a chance they'll cure him? Can he get better?'

She lifted her shoulders. 'Who knows, one day? It's not a subject I know much about. David knows everything about it, you'll have to ask him.' She smiled at his incredulous look. 'Yes, I mean it. It would do him good to talk.

But a cure . . .? Not at present, not at this stage of – well, knowledge. They experiment on him a bit – with his full consent, of course. By his desire even. That's why he's there now. But no miracles are going to happen, Victor. I'm not going to go there tomorrow morning and be met by a reception committee of joyous doctors with David walking in the midst of them. At best his reactions may be giving them some ideas to work on.'

He wondered if her mention of the following morning was a hint to him to go. But these suspicions he knew to be symptoms of a paranoia he was beginning to shed. She had asked him to stay, she wanted him here. He helped her with the dishes. He opened one of the bottles of Italian wine.

It was curious that, until then, he had really felt no desire for her. Several times he had remembered how she had caught him in her arms that afternoon when David had shown him the proofs of the book, and how he had responded to that embrace. But desire of that kind for women was something he had hardly ever felt, not since Pauline anyway, and to compare Pauline with Clare was a travesty. He recalled his response to Clare as an isolated phenomenon, interesting and even pleasing but something he might never feel again. When she had touched him, laid her hand on his arm and held his hand, he felt something that was distinct from desire, something he might define as mysteriously involved with what she called his vulnerability, his quality of being lovable. Yet things had now changed and he was aware as they moved about the kitchen of an alteration of consciousness, a shifting of his relations with her. He wanted her to embrace him again.

She blew out the candle and they went into the living room. The television set was there and he expected they would watch television. He had come to think of this as what you did in the evenings, what everyone did as a matter of course, a way of life. Clare put on a record instead. It was the sort of music he had always told himself he didn't like, sounding old and alien, *historical* music played on instruments no one used any more. She handed him the sleeve to read and he saw it was a harpsichord suite by Purcell. The cold sweetness of it poured into the room and his contentment went and he was filled with unhappiness, with grief almost and a sense of waste, with loneliness.

He said, 'Can I have that picture of you?'

'Can you have it? You? You mean have that photograph in the frame?'

He nodded. Then he remembered. 'I've got something for you. Something else, I mean. I nearly forgot.'

The envelope containing his photograph he had left on the passenger seat of the car and he got it out but he didn't re-lock the door. He would be going soon. The rain had stopped and the air was bluish, cold, very clear. A white moon had risen, screened by a nimbus, and on the horizon the yellow ribbon of the motorway could be seen, the lights sending a bright shimmer up into the dark sky. She got up as he came in and took the photograph from his hands. The music had changed, was warmer, a dance it sounded like, though still from a long way in the past.

'Did you have this taken specially?'

Put like that, it made him sound a bit of a fool. He nodded.

'Thank you,' she said. 'You can't have that picture of me, that's David's, but I'll give you another.'

He watched her search through the desk. A conviction formed itself and strengthened and became absolute that he couldn't drive home that night. It would somehow be beyond his powers. The loneliness that would sit beside him would overpower him and take over; like some hitch-hiker bent on violence, it would attack and subdue him and leave him for dead. He could tell her some lie, he thought, like not being able to start the car, anything, any subterfuge in order to stay.

Without turning her head, reading his mind surely, she said, 'It's late, Victor. Why don't you stay the night? I'll have to leave very early in the morning but you won't mind that.' She laughed, spun round in her chair. 'To tell you the truth, I don't much like being here alone. Pauline's been staying with me but her husband's back from a trip and she's had to go.'

He tried to sound casual, offhand, as if it were he doing her the favour. 'I could do, no problem.'

The picture she gave him was different from the one in the frame, taken longer ago, a young, almost childlike Clare. He sat staring at it, staring as he would hardly dare to gaze at the living woman. She'd give him the spare room where Pauline had slept, she said, David's room being so full of gadgets and aids for the handicapped. Her voice, he noticed, had taken on a strange, strained note. She had drunk rather a lot of wine, more than he remembered she had permitted herself at other meals he had shared with her. Her cheeks were flushed and her eyes seemed very large. He thought, she will kiss me again when she says goodnight to me.

A need to postpone that parting took hold of him. He was looking at her in silence, gazing now as he had gazed at her picture. She had been talking, conventionally enough, about tomorrow's trip, the long drive across country, and he entered into this, asking her questions about the route, offering to drive her himself – an offer which was rejected – and all the time keeping his eyes on her face with a yearning that increased to a nearly physical reaching towards her. At the same time he was aware of a reciprocal reaching in her towards him. He thought he must have imagined this but he wasn't mistaken, he couldn't be, and he remembered she had said he was lovable. Inwardly he trembled, though his body and his hands remained steady. His feelings were quite different from what they had been that time she embraced him, more diffuse, more tender, less rapacious.

This was the word he used to himself and it made him shudder. He said suddenly, harshly, 'What do you know about me? My past? What has David told you?'

She said steadily, 'That you were in a house with a girl, a sort of hostage, and David had to go in and rescue her and you shot him. Do we have to talk about it?'

'Is that all?'

205

'I think so.' She got up and he too rose. She stood looking at him, just standing there, her hands by her sides. 'It's late. We don't have to talk about that tonight.'

The hungry anxious look she had that he couldn't define. He had never seen it in a woman before. He had never before taken a woman in his arms and cupped her head in his hand and brought her face to his and kissed her lips. It was his thirty-ninth birthday but he had never quite done that before. The feelings it aroused in him were unexpected and new, tremendous, overpowering yet not somehow clamouring for immediate swift satisfaction.

She responded to his kiss quite differently from that last time, for he felt she was as desirous as he. Her kiss explored his mouth and her body pressed its curves into his hard muscles and vulnerable nerves. And then she twisted away, stood for a moment gazing at him in a kind of panic, the back of one hand against her lips. Puzzlement made him silent, left him at a loss. In these matters he had no experience. She left the room and when he followed she had disappeared. The hall was empty. He looked into the kitchen but there was no one there, only the little dog Sally curled up in her basket. He switched off the lights and went up the stairs where the railway for David's lift spanned the banisters.

Upstairs he didn't know the rooms, didn't know where to go and went into David's by mistake. Violins in various stages of construction, one finished, lay on a pine bed. A wide arch led into a shower room big enough to take the wheelchair under the water jets. He turned back. His heart was beating painfully and he half wished he had gone home, even through the cold moonlight, even with loneliness for a companion. The house was silent. Through a landing window he could see the golden thread of the motorway draped across plains and hills.

He drew a deep breath and opened a door and saw her waiting for him, sitting naked on the side of her bed, lifting her eyes to meet his, extending her hands to him without a smile.

14

In the night they both awoke at the same time. Victor woke and found that they had slept embraced and now her eyelids moved and her eyes opened. He couldn't remember putting the light out but he must have, for he saw her face now by white moonlight. Her breasts were very full and soft and he held them in his hands, which was another thing he had never done before last night. Lovemaking for him before had been an attack and a swift pumping, an explosive discharge, a gasp and a rolling off; and this not only with the women he had assaulted – that was still something else, something even further removed and less sexual – but with Pauline, who had somehow embarrassed him, had made him treat her body as a hole with a bit of flesh round it. Clare had not had to teach him to make love – he would not have liked that from a woman, any woman – but making love had come naturally with her, came naturally now, as he explored her body with his hands, the delicate tips of his fingers, his tongue and a murmuring stroking whispering of his lips. And he could not have anticipated the rewards, the sensation of her melting and flowing under his touch, of unfolding around him and receiving him with a kind of sweet loving gratitude.

She was not an active woman, the kind he had read of in magazines. A thrashing of limbs, a manipulation of his flesh, a riding and exultant cries he could not have borne, could not have coped with, nor any demanding initiative. Easily, with a dreaming reserve, thinking not of present gratification but of a lifetime of rarefied pleasure, he postponed his climax until he felt the pressure of her hands tighten on his back, until her lips joined to his whispered, 'Now!' The night before it had not been quite like that, not as perfect for her as for him, not an absolutely shared moving of the world. Years of dismay and bewilderment tiptoed away. His body filled with light and he knew that precisely the same thing had happened to her, the blood in their veins different, recharged.

'I love you,' he said, unfamiliar words that he had read but never thought to utter.

She was gone when next he awoke. The curtains were pulled back and it was a white-grey morning, dull of sky, a white rose, paler than the clouds, blossoming on a rambler, framed in one of the window panes. Clare came in, dressed, bringing him tea, sitting on the bed, dressed like someone's efficient secretary in a grey flannel suit and a red blouse with a bow. She kissed him and pulled away smiling when he tried to take her in his arms.

'Let me drive you. Let me get up and drive you.'

'No, Victor. I have to fetch David on my own. You must see that.'

Of course he saw. He could see plainly in her face what she was thinking, nothing changed her affection for David, her loyalty to him, any more than it could change Victor's. She had made a promise and she must keep it. After all, in a way she *was* David's secretary, his nurse or a loving sister.

'I'll get up and make myself scarce,' he said. 'I'll get off home.'

She nodded. 'We'll meet soon. I'll phone you.'

'I'd like to see David, you know.'

She seemed surprised. 'Yes, of course.'

He heard the Land Rover move out of the garage directly below his bed. He heard it move away, the change of gear, the pause as the bigger road was reached. When he could hear it no longer he got up and dressed and tidied up, washing their cups and her breakfast plate and the teapot. Eating didn't appeal to him, he didn't want breakfast. In the living room he found the photograph of herself she had given him. Clare, he said to the picture, Clare. He gazed at it, sitting in an armchair and holding the photograph in front of him and gazing. Why hadn't he understood all these weeks that he was in love with her? Because it had never happened to him before. His parents' need for each other's exclusive company he now understood and he wondered why he had been so blind and so deluded.

He slipped the photograph inside the envelope in which his own had been contained. He left his own lying on the table. Originally, he had been going to write across the corner of it, the way famous people do, write a message to both of them and sign it. He couldn't do that now, so he just left it.

It was still not eight o'clock. He went out to the car and heard a heavy distant hum like aircraft. It was the motorway, laden with morning traffic. The needs of the day and its pressures began to close on him, ordinary life coming back. He was due to return the car this morning but there was no way now that he could get it back by nine. He would have to pay for an extra day. Mrs Griffiths too must be given notice that he was leaving and perhaps Tom or Judy told. He thought about these things and then Clare, the image of her, the memory of her voice, drove them away. He drove back to Acton with his head full of Clare, his body intermittently excited by awareness of certain aspects of her, but not daring to think too intensely of what she looked like naked or the things they had done together. Even to remember her eyes opening in the moonlight made him tremble and a long shiver run the length of his spine.

And what next? They had said nothing about telling David, though Clare had agreed when Victor said he would like to see David, understanding what he implied by this. David himself would probably understand what had happened. He might even be pleased. After all, he might be very fond of Clare, he might share his house with her and depend on her for so much, but he couldn't be her lover, he could never give her what he, Victor, had given her last night. If he were really fond of her he would want her to have a love life and probably be glad it was with someone like Victor who would really love and cherish her and care about her.

Victor took the car back and because it was only ten past nine they didn't charge him for the extra day. He walked home to Tolleshunt Avenue, feeling strong and fit and young, in spite of having been thirty-nine yesterday and drinking nearly two bottles of wine. Upstairs in his room he sat in the wheelchair, imagining what it must be like to be David, alive only above the waist, capable of thinking and speaking and eating and drinking and moving the wheelchair but not of much else. Of course if he couldn't do it because the nerves or whatever it was down there were dead, it stood to reason that he couldn't want to do it. Victor knew he wanted to do it because he got erect whenever he even thought of Clare like that. Sitting in the wheelchair he was erect now, a bulge holding out the brown check travelling rug that he had pulled over his knees. How ridiculous and grotesque! He jumped out of the wheelchair and lay face-downwards on the bed but the bed brought her image to him again and suddenly there came a fierce painful longing for her to be here, painful because there was no hope of that today. Or was there perhaps? When would she get back? When would she phone him? He imagined her driving through June-green England, up the motorways, on the little winding roads through villages, thinking of him surely as he was thinking of her, a gold-skinned girl with paler gold hair in a secretarial suit and red blouse with a bow . . .

Presently he made himself get up and sit at the table with the bamboo frame adorned with cigarette burns and write to Mrs Griffiths. A week's notice only he would give her. She wouldn't be the loser, for the DHSS were paying her. He calculated that Clare would just about be there by now but when the phone rang downstairs he thought he had miscalculated and she was already home. As soon as she had got home she was phoning him! He ran downstairs and took off the receiver and a woman's voice asked if that was Curry's. A wrong number. It would be better to go out somewhere than sit here waiting for the phone, but he knew he wouldn't go out.

Committing himself utterly to her, he thought about

what they would do, where they would live. In the new flat for a while, presumably. He would have to get work, start the car-hire business he had already had ideas about. Would she, he asked himself, would she – one day – *marry* him?

Although it brought a kind of havoc to mind and body, causing him a physical torment of a kind he had never known before, he was unable to keep himself from thinking of how she had responded to him, with such sweet abandonment, almost with *relief*, as if this was what she had been aching for for a long time. She had given herself to him, old-fashioned expression he had once heard his mother use, though disparagingly – 'She gave herself to him and of course she regretted it.' Clare, he was sure, would never regret it, but it was true that she had given herself, making a joyful loving gift of it, the better to receive. He loved her and she loved him. There was a rightness about it all which had begun the day he saw the name Theydon Bois on the station and after that had begun the search for David. A lucky day for Clare, who had been rescued from a life that was no life for someone as young and lovely and capable of giving love as she was.

In the evening she phoned him. It was quite late, about ten, and he had given up hope of hearing from her that day. In a way he hadn't expected to hear and he wasn't unhappy or anxious. But the phone ringing and then her voice, that was a bonus.

'Victor? It's Clare. David's asleep. He's had an exhausting day.'

'When can I see you?'

'David's been asking about you. He wondered how you'd feel about coming over on Saturday.'

'I mean, when can I see *you*?'

She was silent, thinking. He began to understand that there might be difficulties. At first there were going to be difficulties. Of course it wouldn't be all plain sailing.

'I don't suppose you said anything to him, did you?'

'Said anything?'

211

'Well, told him.'

'No, Victor, I didn't tell him.' He could see her face as clearly as if this were a phone with a television screen. It swam in the darkness of the hall like a spirit face, a beautiful floater on his retina. On the underside of the stairs her name was written: Clare. 'Do you want to see me before Saturday?'

'Of course I do. Don't you want to see me?'

'Yes.'

His heart, which had been a prey to doubts suddenly, to terrible groundless fears, leaped with joy. He couldn't sing, had scarcely ever tried, but he would have liked to sing now. Tenors in operas, crowing with love and happiness, grief and tragedy, he could understand them now. 'When, Clare?'

'Not tomorrow. I can't. Wednesday, after work, five thirty in Epping. Could you manage that, Victor?'

He could have managed Wednesday at five thirty in Marrakech, he thought.

'Not a pub. It'll be too early anyway. On Bell Common, we could meet there, Victor. I'll park the Land Rover in Hemnall Street, just in from the High Street at the common end.'

'I love you,' he said.

It was an awful dream he had – 'unnecessary', he told himself. Why was it necessary for him to be visited with a nightmare like that? Of course, whatever the psychologists might say, you could account for dreams by what had happened to you on the previous day. And on this day, in the *Standard* he had bought himself, along with *Reader's Digest* and *Punch* and *TV Times*, was a paragraph that, though tucked away, leaped to Victor's eye. Things about rape always did, even though it no longer concerned him. This said that the man they called the 'Red Fox' – because he had red hair? A red face? – who had raped a seventy-year-old woman in Watford had now made a similar assault on a teenage girl in St Albans. How did they know it was the same man? Because of the descriptions which the women had given?

Victor didn't think about it. Or he thought he didn't think about it. Who knew what went on in the unconscious mind? If you knew, it wouldn't be unconscious, and that was the catch. Before going to sleep he read an article in *Reader's Digest* about the unconscious mind. And then, very soon after sleeping, it seemed, he fell into this dream. No road this time and no houses. He was in the wheelchair, out for the evening, crossing a common on which were areas of woodland. At one point he came to a bridge across a stream. It was a narrow bridge, of wooden planks, precarious and rickety, with a handrail made of rope on each side. A man on the far side, a kind of bridge keeper, came across to help Victor, walking backwards himself and pulling the wheelchair, telling Victor to close his eyes and not look down over the edge. Victor thanked him and continued along the path, which now entered one of the small dark woods. A woman was walking among the trees. She wore a long duster coat or mackintosh of black silk and over her head an embroidered black veil like a mantilla.

When she saw Victor approaching she turned to look at him, standing in an attitude of pity, of yearning sympathy, with both hands clasped in front of her. Victor jumped out of the wheelchair, ran towards her and, seizing her in his arms, threw her to the ground and tore at her clothes. She wore a mass of petticoats, layers and layers of stiff lace petticoats, and he tried to rip them away, burrowing in the starched crackling stuff with his hands, pushing with his face, his nose, like a snuffling pig. There was nothing there, nothing beneath, no flesh, only a clothes prop of wooden sticks. He tore off all the clothes, a wardrobe full, and the veil which was not one veil but two, three, a dozen, a wad of silky dusty black gauze, and underneath, under the last filmy layer, lay the photograph of Clare, her eyes looking up into his.

Nightmares recede quickly. Who had ever been troubled by a bad dream for more than an hour or two after waking? Nor could the dream spoil his feeling for the photograph. He took it with him down to Acton High Street and found

213

a shop that did framing three or four doors up from Jupp's. They said they could do it on the spot and Victor chose an oval frame of walnut-coloured wood – perhaps true walnut. In Jupp's window, among the Victorian bric-a-brac and jewellery pieces was a gold locket shaped like a heart with a delicate chasing on it of flowers and leaves. He would have bought it, he would have gone in there and bought it for Clare, even though that meant putting more money into Jupp's pocket, but as he pushed the door open an inch or two and the bell began to jangle he noticed that the brown velvet sofa now had a label with 'sold' in red attached to it. Jupp came into the shop from behind the curtain, masticating gum, but Victor had turned away. He would buy a present for Clare elsewhere. Gold lockets, or gold anything come to that, were thick on the ground in London junk shops.

It was a pity that he couldn't have the car, but when he went to the car-rental place all they had available was a small Nissan van, the red Escort being out on hire. Besides, he was getting short of money again and after he had bought Clare a present it would be time to return to the 'bank'. A distaste for these transactions of his now began strongly to affect Victor. He didn't want to deceive her any longer about his possession of a car or lie to her about the source of his income. The idea that she might find out about his raids on Muriel's house appalled him, for he sensed that the justifications he made to himself would weigh nothing with her. 'It isn't as if you went to prison for stealing,' she had said. A vague unformed vision was slowly taking shape in his mind that Clare would lift him out of his past, just as knowing her had already absolved him from anger and panic and violence.

By mistake he got into a train that was going no further than Debden, and there he had to get out and wait for the Epping train. It was a warm white-skied day, sultry, the air full of flies. There had been a big blue-bottle buzzing against the windows of the carriage, trying to get out, seeking the sun. Victor had read in a magazine an article about how insects, searching for freedom or a way home, look to the sun to guide them. He had been glad to get out of the train, away from that frantic buzzing.

For some reason he fancied that Clare would want to see him dressed as he had been on his birthday, which he thought of and expected always to think of as the day they had found each other. He wore his dark blue cords and the same dark blue tee-shirt but it was too hot for the padded jacket so he carried that slung over his shoulder. Sometimes he caught sight of himself reflected in windows and he thought how much younger he looked since he had come out of prison, how much weight he had lost, and how his good looks, which he had once been proud of, had returned. There was no doubt that he looked years younger than poor David with his jowls and his excess couple of stone. In the train he had been thinking about David and thinking too that there was an alternative way for him to react. He might be bitter and resentful, he might say that Victor had ruined his life and now compounded the injury by stealing his girl. Uneasily, Victor remembered how Clare had said that David liked him but hadn't quite learned to trust him – yet.

A train had come in. It wasn't the shuttle service but another train from London, this time going all the way to Epping. Victor got into an empty carriage, the second from the rear. The doors were starting to close when the mad old woman came through them, holding in front of her a covered basket.

She put the basket on the floor between the long seats but, instead of sitting down herself, went up and down the carriage opening the windows. Victor looked at the basket, which was covered over with a piece of torn green towelling and which was distinctly moving up and down, a welling and subsiding movement, as if some culture worked underneath. It was the same uneven motion that had caused the shuddering of the carrier bag on that previous occasion. Victor could not keep from staring at it, though he did not want to. No culture, no activated yeast or fungus, could writhe with such vigour. It was as if she kept a pair of snakes in that basket.

The train drew into Theydon Bois and Victor got up to go into the next carriage. But the old woman blocked his egress – though surely not purposely – standing between the open doors with her arms in ragged red cotton sleeves spread wide to span them, calling out in accents which were a mimicry of an Indian's sing-song, 'Mind the doors! Please to mind the doors!'

He sat down again, too late to reach the other door. What did it matter? She couldn't harm him and in two or three minutes they would arrive at Epping station. He tried to read the *Essex Countryside* magazine. She was kneeling up on one of the seats at the far end writing something in a tiny cramped hand on an advertisement for mouthwash. Victor's eyes wandered back to the covered basket. There was no longer any movement under the green towel and it might have been eggs she kept in there or a couple of cabbages.

Why cover it with a towel then? Perhaps there was no accounting for the actions of the insane. He read a few lines about Morris dancers in Thaxted, then looked, because he could not control his eyes, back at the basket. If it was what it might be under that towel, if it showed itself or part of itself, what would he do, what would become of him? To be shut in this confined space from which escape was impossible with the object of his phobia, at this old creature's mercy too, when once she *knew* – that was the stuff of which his worst nightmares were made. For know she would, once she saw his reaction. Control would be impossible. Breaking into a total body sweat, he stood up. His eyes were on the basket but from the corner of the right one he could see her, kneeling there, looking at him.

The towel moved, slipped back. He gave an involuntary cry. It was a guinea pig's furry snout that appeared, waffling, a guinea pig whose coat was ironically in the colours and combination they call tortoiseshell . . . He breathed. The train drew in to Epping and the old woman picked up the basket, flinging the towel over the guinea pig with the swift quelling gesture of someone blanketing a parrot's cage. Victor tore off the return half of his ticket.

Somehow he didn't think he would be needing it but, on the other hand, if David was sore with him . . .

This business of always being early was something he would have to get out of. Whenever he wanted to be somewhere very much, he was about an hour early and that hour, passing it, was like getting through a day. He walked up from the station, taking it slowly, remembering the last time he had been here, before he knew Clare, when he scarcely knew she existed. If he turned right at the top of the hill he could go along to St Margaret's Hospital and wait outside the gates for her. But the main gates might not be the only exit, he thought, there might be other ways. He wandered through the town instead and in a little antique shop, much smarter and prettier (and more expensive) than Jupp's, bought Clare a Victorian ring of gold clasped hands on a silver band. The shopkeeper put it in a blue velvet box lined with white satin.

To kill time he walked Bell Common from one end to the other. The forest looked deep and dense, all the pale green of beech and birch darkened by summer, the grass under his feet starry with white and yellow flowers. In the still heavy air languid insects moved.

The Land Rover he saw in the distance, parked along a curve in the road, under chestnut trees. It had arrived while, for a moment, his head had been turned away. He wanted to run to her, though he would look a fool if he ran, but he ran just the same. The passenger door swung open. He climbed up inside and took her in his arms almost before he saw her. She was in his arms and he was kissing her, smelling her skin and tasting her mouth and pushing his fingers through her hair, before he could even have said whether she had make-up on her face or her dress was pink or white. She struggled a little, laughing, gasping, and then he was more gentle, taking her face in both his hands and looking at her, eye to eye.

Afterwards he could not remember how she had begun what she had said, the first words she used. Not precisely. And this was a merciful dispensation, for it was bad enough remembering what came later. He could remember only from the onset of his anger.

'You love me,' he said just as the anger began. 'You're in love with me. You said you were.'

She shook her head. 'Victor, I never said that.'

He could have sworn she had. Or was it only he who had kept saying it? Who had kept saying, I love you. 'I don't understand any of this.'

She said, 'Could we get out of here, please, and sit on the grass or something? Sitting so close to you, looking straight at you, it makes it hard.'

'I'm repulsive to you, am I? You could have fooled me.'

'I didn't mean that. You know I didn't.'

'I don't know anything any more,' he said, but he got out of the car into a wilderness of dead white sky and stuffy fly-laden air and dry grass. They walked in silence. She dropped suddenly to the ground, hid her face in her hands, then turned to him.

'Will you believe me when I say I honestly didn't know you felt like this? I know you said you loved me but people do say they love people. It's emotion makes them say it, being happy, it doesn't mean much.'

'It means the world to me.'

'I thought you felt the way I do. I like you, Victor, you're attractive too, very physically attractive. And I'm . . .' She looked down at the ground, the grasses and the flowers, her fingers pulling a daisy to pieces, stripping petals from the yellow calyx. 'The kind of lovemaking David and I do – it's all right, it's fine. Sometimes though, it's just not enough. I've got to learn to make it enough and I will. I've never,' she said very quietly, 'broken down, weakened, whatever you like to call it, before.'

He was horrified. 'You and David – make love? How can you? I don't know what you mean.'

She said a little wearily, 'Think about it, Victor. Use your imagination. His hands aren't paralysed. Or his mouth. Or his senses, come to that.'

'It's revolting.'

She shrugged. 'Never mind anyway. It isn't your

218

concern, is it? I was attracted by you. Still am, come to that. You were attracted by me. We were looking for comfort too and it was raining and – well, we had too much wine. We were alone together and frustrated and we fancied each other. I'm trying to be honest and not shirk things so I will say that I knew – well, I knew on Monday morning, we wouldn't just pass it over, forget it, I knew there'd be repercussions. That's why I got up so early. I was a bit aghast at what I'd done, Victor. For it was what *I'd* done. I know very well you wouldn't have touched me if I hadn't – instigated things.'

'Too right I wouldn't,' he said.

Ignoring that, she said, 'You're not really in love with me, Victor. You don't know me. You know scarcely anything about me. We've met just six times, and five out of those six times David's been there too.'

'What has that to do with it? I knew I loved you,' he said, believing it himself, 'from the first moment I saw you.'

'When I was so horrible to you?' She was smiling now, tried a laugh. 'When I abused you and used foul language? I'm sure you didn't, Victor. I don't – well, I don't make a practice of sleeping around casually, I've already said that, I think, but this time . . . Victor, can't we just say that we do like each other very much, we are attracted, and that Sunday night was good and lovely and we'll always remember it? Can't we do that? Look, it's six now. Let's go into the Half Moon and have a drink. I *need* a drink and I'm sure you do.'

Anger, at this stage, made him cold and condescending. 'You've already said you drink too much.'

'I don't think I quite said that.'

'In any case, it doesn't matter. None of this matters because I don't believe any of it. You couldn't pretend about something like this. You weren't *pretending* on Sunday night. It's now you're pretending so as not to hurt David, you're sacrificing yourself for David. Well, I won't have it. D'you hear me, Clare, I won't have it! Aren't I as important as he is? Hasn't my life been spoiled as much as his?' An idea came to him. 'I suppose you haven't dared tell him, is that it?'

She turned her head away. 'I didn't think it would be necessary to tell him.'

'Look at me, Clare. Turn round. I want to see your face.' He saw that she had become rather pale. 'Of course you're afraid to tell him. I'll tell him, I don't mind. You wouldn't spoil both our lives for the sake of ten minutes' unpleasantness, would you? Sticks and stones can break my bones,' he said, 'but hard words can't hurt me.'

'You don't understand at all.'

'I understand that you're nervous and you don't want a fuss. Look, why don't you take me back with you now and we'll both talk to David, we'll talk to him together.'

'That's impossible.'

'All right. You go. You go home now and just act as if nothing had happened and I'll follow in an hour. Don't say anything to him, I don't want you upsetting yourself. This is between David and me anyway.'

'Victor,' she said, 'can't you see we're worlds apart, you and I? The way we talk and think, the way we look at life?'

'What does that matter?' he said. 'That's not important. We didn't think like that on Sunday night and we won't again.'

'I would rather you didn't come tonight,' she said carefully.

'When then?'

'Oh, Victor, what's the use? Can't you *see*?'

'You go back to David now,' he said, 'and I'll follow in an hour.'

He smiled encouragingly at her. Her eyes were on him and she had a trapped look. Well, that was understandable, seeing what lay ahead of her. He slammed the door and she started the Land Rover. It occurred to him she must think he had his car with him, could get to Theydon without trouble. That was what he wanted her to think, wasn't it?

Momentarily the feeling came to him as he watched the Land Rover turn out into the main road that he would never see her again. That was ridiculous, she wasn't going to run away. It was a quarter past six. There was no need to take that stipulated hour too literally. Anyway, it was he who had stipulated it. He felt excited and energetic, tingling with excitement, but not afraid. David couldn't do anything to him beyond saying a few hard things. It would take him an hour to walk to Theydon and he decided to walk, the alternative being the train.

The motorway disappeared into the ground here, came out on the other side of the hill and wandered away, bearing its load across the meadows. But all you could see of it was the wall on top of the tunnel that might have been enclosing someone's garden. Victor walked down a winding country lane without a pavement, green-hedged and overhung with trees, past a golf club, the garden gates of big houses, through a bit of forest, coming out into Theydon by the church. The sun had come out and it was going to be a fine evening. Theydon Manor Drive was full of roses, hedges of white and red, circular beds of roses in many colours, roses climbing over porches and pergolas. Everything is coming up roses, he thought, another expression which he couldn't remember from before he went to prison.

Faint heart never won fair lady. Who had said that? Jupp, he remembered, going courting Muriel. It rather annoyed him to think of Jupp – and of Muriel, come to that – in this connection; the comparison with his own case was grotesque. At the gate he paused, though. There was a precipice on the other side of that front door. Clare had put the Land Rover away and shut the garage doors and for some reason that troubled him. He would have expected her to leave it out in the street. But of course she thought *he* had a car . . .

He went up to the front door but he didn't knock. He lifted the knocker and, instead of letting it fall, restored it quietly to its original position. Not looking in at the windows, he walked round the side of the house, came into the back garden, which seemed full of roses. On Sunday it had been raining too much to notice them. He turned his face slowly towards the house. The french windows were open. Inside the room, just inside the open windows, David was sitting in his wheelchair with Clare very close beside him in another chair. There was an impression that they had retreated in there from outside, for on the garden table was a jug of water with melting ice in it, a glass and David's cigarettes. Victor couldn't remember seeing David and Clare sit like that before, close together, holding hands. The way they were sitting was curious, as if they were waiting together for something awful to happen, for death or destruction, for the ultimate disaster. He remembered a picture he had seen years before, in a school history book. It was of the Goths or Huns or someone coming to Rome and the members of the senate waiting for them, sitting with impassive dignity for a horde of barbarians to come and bring desecration with them. Clare and David reminded him of that.

He said, 'David,' and, 'I expect Clare told you I was coming.'

David nodded. He didn't speak but his eyes moved from Victor's face down his body. Victor had his hands in his pockets, having placed them there because they had started to shake. David was looking at Victor's right hand in his jacket pocket and Victor knew at once, sensed beyond question, that he thought he had a gun there.

Clare had got up. Her face was pale and her eyes seemed very large. She was wearing the cream cotton dress with the big sleeves. Had she been wearing that in Epping when he kissed her? He couldn't remember. He took his hands out of his pockets. They were steady now. Taking a step or two forwards, he came up to the table, as to a barricade set up for battle, and lowered himself into one of the chairs.

'Clare has just said she'll marry me,' David said.

Victor shook his head. 'No.'

'I refused to ask her. You know that. She asked me again just now and I've said yes.'

'There are a few things I have to tell you,' said Victor, 'which may make you change your mind about that.'

'I've already told him the few things, Victor,' said Clare.

'Did she tell you I fucked her? Not once, on and on, all night.'

'Of course she told me. Don't be so melodramatic. That may happen again in the years to come – Oh, not with you, there's not much chance of that. With others. She says so herself. I know my limitations, Victor, and she knows them. Neither of us pretends life is what it isn't – unlike you.'

'I want to marry David,' Clare said. 'It's what I've wanted ever since I first got to know him.'

Victor trembled. He had a sensation all over his body of vibrating needles in the flesh.

'What did you tell her,' he said, 'to make her change her mind?'

'She hasn't changed her mind.'

Victor wouldn't have said it if he hadn't been so angry.

'Did you tell her I'd raped women?'

'No.'

Clare made that flinching movement that was like Judy's shrinking away when he had stood beside her at the window.

'I don't believe you,' Victor said.

'Is it true?' said Clare.

'Ask him. He's poisoned your mind against me. I should never have let you go back to him. I knew what he was, I always knew, and I thought – I thought we could be *friends*.'

He got up and moved, watching with pleasure as David tried to remain still and upright, to hold his ground. But David couldn't keep himself from shrinking, from drawing his hands back and gripping the wheels. Clare made a movement of protest, half shielding David with her arms. Victor saw red. He crashed his fists down on the table and the glass flew off and shattered on the stone. Victor picked up the water jug and hurled that on the ground too. Water flew on to David with splinters of glass and he covered his face with his arm.

'I wish I'd killed you,' Victor said. 'They couldn't have

done worse to me than what they did if I'd killed you. I wish I had.'

Somewhere in the house the puppy had begun to bark like a real watchdog.

15

When he left David's house Victor walked for a while aimlessly, having no idea of destination, unable to think of anywhere he wished to be. Prison might be the best place for him, the only place, and if he killed David he would go back to prison. He hadn't a gun but it was possible to get a gun. It was possible to get anything if you knew how, if you had money. He found himself heading for the forest, passing the house where he had paid a deposit on a flat. He would never live in Theydon now, never set foot in the place again except to see David once more. His head full of images of David shot, David bleeding, David sprawled on the floor, he went up to the door and rang the bell.

Mrs Palmer behaved in rather a frightened way. After-wards Victor thought this must have been because he had acted wildly and talked wildly, he must have appeared scarcely sane to her. Clare had receded from his conscious-ness and David's image filled it. The woman didn't argue, she said he could have his deposit back and gave him a cheque. Victor thought he would spend the money on a gun.

He began to walk up the hill that led through the forest, by means of a steep winding hill, towards the junction of main roads. It was a little after half past eight. Anger had started to boil up in him, taking the form of a fierce energy. He could have walked for miles, he could have walked all the way to Acton, and still not have used up that rage-stimulated energy. It was not Clare he was angry with, it wasn't her fault; she had simply bowed to a greater strength, as women must do. If she hadn't been there, he thought, he would have taken David by the throat and strangled the life out of him. But what power David had!

What power a man could have from a wheelchair, a man who was only half alive!

Occasionally a car passed him, going up to Loughton or down to Theydon. Once he saw a man walking in the depths of the forest with a big grey gambolling dog, an Irish wolfhound. There were stretches of open green in the forest here, of fine cropped turf, and wide areas where only the unfurling fronds of bracken grew, branched, tall, green as the trees, and there were copses of birches with thin white trunks and trembling leaves. The sun set in a smoky red glow and the sky grew briefly pale, greenish-gold as if stripped, as if peeled of cloud. Victor was angry and full of energy and now he was afraid, because he asked himself what could become of this anger, how could he live with it? What happened to you if anger conquered you?

Then he saw the girl in the forest.

First he saw the car, which was empty. It was parked at the entrance to one of the rides which lead through the forest, in mud ruts, now dried, made previously by a much heavier vehicle. She was sitting, with her back to the parked car and the road, on a log of wood among the bracken. Victor, who would not have thought of things in this way even a week before, decided that she was waiting to meet a man. Clare had waited to meet him in the same sort of way, an illicit way. This girl too had a possessive jealous commanding man at home, so she had to meet her lover secretly, in a lonely, unwatched place.

Only it wasn't unwatched. She was dark and thin, not at all like Clare. It was nine fifteen and she was early perhaps, their arrangement being for nine thirty, but he didn't reason or work things out, he was beyond that. She was quite unaware of his presence, unhearing of his footfalls on the grass behind her, for he could see now what absorbed her. In the dusk she was making up her face. With her handbag open and a small mirror propped on it, she was pencilling her eyelids. Hardly daring to breathe, he stood a yard behind her and watched the red-tipped fingers take hold of the implement that would mascara her lashes. This was an operation to be postponed until she got here, an act that would arouse suspicion if carried out at home.

He came a step closer to her, hooked his left arm round her neck and pressed his other hand across her mouth. A scream tried to burst out of her into the palm of his hand. The contents of the handbag went flying. She struggled like a creature in a net, wriggled like a landed eel. He was immensely strong, his own strength amazed him. It was easy to hold her, to manipulate her, to throw her to the ground in a nest of bracken and stuff into her mouth the scarf that had fallen from that handbag. He was erect like a brass rod, hot as fire and painful with anger. His free hand fumbled with his fly but she was limp now, her head and neck twisted to one side, her hands not fighting him but pressed under her body. He dragged down her tights, his fingers going through the filmy stuff as fragile as a cobweb.

Dimly he was aware of something cracking. He heard a sharp crack and thought it might be a breaking bone, she was all bones, iron hard and unyielding. He pushed against cold dry resistant flesh and felt, suddenly, a sharp excruciating pain in his chest. It was a stinging blow he felt and he lurched off her body, seeing blood, *smelling* blood. He cried out in pain and disgust. There came more pain, as of needle pricks, and he heard the roar of a car's engine, wheels crunching on dry clay, the rev of a motor whose driver gives the accelerator a final flip before he brakes. Victor leaped to his feet. Blood was running down his chest. The girl, her mouth full of scarf, red silk trailing from her mouth like more blood, held a triangle of broken mirror in her hand. Underneath her body, on a stone perhaps, she had contrived to snap that handbag mirror and use one of the slivers as a weapon.

He plunged for the cover of the trees, doing up his clothes as he ran. Behind him he heard a man's voice call, 'Where are you? What's happened?'

A cry, a sobbing, silence as she was caught, held, comforted. Victor didn't dare to stop, though he could feel blood flowing out of the largest of the wounds, pumping out even, a pulse throbbing and a darker stain spreading out over the dark blue tee-shirt. He ran deeper in among the trees, having no idea where he was heading. It would be dark soon, it was nearly dark now. Running in the forest wasn't easy if you left the paths, for underfoot it was all brambles and stinging nettles and the endless bracken. And all the time he was listening for pursuers. They would follow him, he thought, just as, on the day he took refuge in Solent Gardens, Heather Cole and the man in the park had followed him. The brambles caught at his trousers and he stumbled and righted himself, but next time he fell, plunging forward into a damp hollow full of thorny tendrils.

Victor knelt there, listening. His hands stung from contact with nettles. He was sure he was still bleeding. There was no sound behind, no sound anywhere but the faint buzz, insect-like it was so far away, of a distant aircraft. Big splayed chestnut leaves, vegetable hands, damp and cold, touched his face. He got up, still listening. No one was following him and then he knew why. The couple were illicit lovers, each of whom, probably, had given false excuses as to where they were going to a husband and a wife or to other, more legitimate or accredited, lovers. Chasing him, telling the police about him, would be to blow their cover, to bring down the wrath of those others on them, perhaps to end their affair. He shivered with the relief of it. But fear took over almost immediately. How badly had she hurt him? Suppose he bled to death?

It was too dark in here to see anything. He could feel the blood on his chest, though, its warm wetness. The sky above him was still visible as a pale glowing greyness, but the tops of the trees were black bunches, festoons of black leaves. There must be a path somewhere, places like this were always traversed by hundreds of paths. It wasn't really country, more like a big park really, not much wilder than Hampstead Heath.

The segment of forest he was in, he calculated, must be bounded by the Theydon road he had come from, the road from Loughton to the Wake Arms, Clays Lane and Debden

Green. Once, a lifetime ago, he had had to drive someone from Debden Green to Cambridge and he had some idea of the neighbourhood. He couldn't go back the way he had come; in spite of his reasoning, that would be too risky. It was too dark to see what time it was, perhaps no more than ten. David had brought him to this. Why hadn't he killed David that time in Solent Gardens?

After a very long time had passed Victor did reach some sort of path or ride. By then he had revised his view of Epping Forest being a kind of outer London park. It was huge and dark and confusing, a maze. He followed the path he had found, or perhaps it was another path, an offshoot of the first one. He had no idea where it went. It seemed to him that he was covered with blood, not only on his body but on his hands, for while groping his way along, he had tried to hold the sides of the worst wound together and staunch the flow. At least he had succeeded in staunching it. The blood had clotted and he could feel the crust of it mixed with forest dirt. He put out his hands to touch the obstruction ahead of him, thinking it might be yet another huge smooth trunk of a beech tree, and came up against a man-made close-boarded fence.

Feeling along it, he came upon a gate. It wasn't locked. Victor went through it and found himself in someone's back garden, a vast garden of lawns and trees, shrubs and glistening in the middle of it a pond, a smooth sheet of water in which the stars were reflected. At the far end of the lawn, up by the house, light from a bedroom window fell on to this lawn in the form of two yellow rectangles. With a sense of horror, he thought: I could climb up there and go in and find Rosemary Stanley in bed, and she will scream and break the window and David will come . . .

To reach a road, a way of escape, he would have to pass the side of the house. Victor was afraid to do this, he had had enough, he was aware all of a sudden that he was tired to exhaustion point, he was worn out. Adjoining the fence, by the gate where he had entered, was a wooden shed. The door had a padlock on it but the padlock hung loose and the door came open when he turned the handle. Inside it was dry and stuffy and smelling of creosote. It was also pitch dark but Victor could just make out, lying on the floor, what he thought was a pile of netting, the kind of thing gardeners use for protecting fruit bushes from birds. He shut the door behind him and flung himself face-downwards on the pile of nets.

By four it was light. He had no idea how long he had slept, perhaps as much as five hours. Very bright pale light from a newly risen sun was coming in through a small window high up under the eaves of the shed. Victor looked at his hands. He tried to look at his chest but the largest wound was too high up to see and, besides, his tee-shirt was a mess of matted blood sticking to skin and hairs. A way must be found of cleaning this up before he got into a bus or train.

Leaving the shed and then the garden itself by the gate in the fence, he came out on to a forest path which led to a road. He saw how near he had been last night to one of the main roads. Not that it would have been of much use to him at midnight. On the other side of this road was a pond, one of the forest ponds which once were gravel pits, its surface clear and brown with long flat leaves floating on it. A truck went past, then, in the opposite direction, a car. But there was very little traffic yet. Victor crossed the road and, kneeling down, bathed his face and hands in the water of the pond. It wasn't cold, nor was it very clean, but brown, rather oily, stagnant. It more or less served his purpose and he dried himself as best he could on the lining of his jacket.

The road downhill seemed to lead towards houses and away from the forest. After about half a mile he realized that he was in Loughton, approaching the High Road. The traffic was just beginning and there were one or two people about. He stopped a man and asked him the way to Loughton station and the man told him, not eyeing Victor in any particularly curious way, so he guessed he must be presentable and not a figure of horror.

*

A scar would always remain. The wound should have been cleaned and stitched, for it was more than an inch long with sides which still gaped and showed dirt inside. Perhaps, even now, it wouldn't be too late to stitch it, but Victor knew he wasn't going near any doctor. The girl might go to the police, there was always that possibility. If she and her boyfriend could think up some story for her being there, she might go to the police. In any case, Victor thought, he could be wrong. She could have been meeting him there because she lived at home with her parents and he lived at home with his and there had been nowhere but the forest to make love.

She had made a nasty mess of his chest. Apart from the major wound there was a mass of smaller cuts. It had been painful getting his shirt off. In the end he had given up and lain in the bath to soak it off and the bath water had gone brown as with rust. His jacket would have to be cleaned. He emptied out his pockets and found the cheque and the blue velvet box containing the ring he had bought for Clare.

His anger was still there, for he had done nothing to assuage it, but it was simmering indignantly rather than exploding. Also he was now able to reason out how he should have behaved, where he had gone wrong. Of course he should have gone back to Sans Souci with Clare in her car. His mistake had been his own pride, he could see that. Had he sacrificed his happiness and hers out of a refusal to admit that the red Escort was a hire car which had had to go back? If they had gone in there and confronted David together, how different things might have been! David only understood violent action, force, for once a policeman, you were always a policeman. Victor knew he should have gone with Clare and he should have done the talking, told David some home truths, forcibly removed Clare. What could David have done – from a wheelchair?

The little ring with the joined silver hands on a gold band – he wouldn't throw it away, he would keep it, Clare would wear it yet. Victor put sticking plaster on his chest and then he dressed, the striped shirt, denim jeans, green velvet jacket. He sat in the wheelchair and counted his money. Under sixty pounds remained, though he had this week's social security payment to come. Still, there was the cheque, his deposit on the flat returned to him, two hundred pounds. He unfolded it. She had made it out to M. Faraday.

When he came back from taking his clothes to the cleaners, Victor phoned David. It amused him to remember how shy he had been of phoning David that first time, how unable to speak beyond uttering his name when David had answered. Things were very different now. He dialled David's number and waited impatiently, tapping with his fingers on the underside of the stairs.

'Hallo?'

'David, this is Victor. I just wanted to say that thanks to you I had a pretty horrendous night, missed the last train and all that. I'm lucky to be alive, what with one thing and another. I don't think I handled things very well last night but that won't matter in the long run. You'll have to make up your mind, you know, that Clare and I are going to be together, she wants me and I want her and that's the way it is. Right?'

David didn't say anything but he hadn't rung off.

'I shall be talking to her later today and making arrangements, but I think we ought to be civilized about this. I think you owe it to me to give me a hearing. Anyway, I'd like to talk the whole thing through with you. You know it helps us both to talk things through.' It cost Victor something to say this and he didn't really mean it anyway. It was a sop to David. 'I'd like us to go on being friends. I know Clare will want to go on being your friend.'

'Victor, let's get this straight,' said David. 'It was a mistake our meeting in the first place. A lot of harm's been done, maybe irrevocable harm. The best thing we can do now is try to get back to where we were before, pick up the pieces. We shan't be seeing each other again.'

This superior attitude made Victor furious, in spite of his determination to remain calm.

'You've lost her, David,' he shouted into the phone. 'Make up your mind to it, you've lost this war. You're defeated.'

He crashed down the phone before David could replace his receiver. Upstairs again, sitting in the wheelchair, he counted the money once more, contemplated the ring. Maybe he could sell it to Jupp. Their love, his and Clare's, had no need of rings, of material bonds. He read the magazines he had found in a wastepaper bin, the *Sunday Times* colour magazine and something called *Executive World*, and the *Standard*, which he had had to pay for. The man they were calling the 'Red Fox' had raped a woman in Hemel Hempstead but there was nothing about a girl being attacked in Epping Forest. He watched Wimbledon on television until six and then he dialled David's number, resolving to put the phone down if David answered.

It was Clare who said hallo.

'Clare, darling, you know who this is. Have you been all right? I didn't like leaving you with him but what was I to do? I should never have left you to face him alone. We won't make any more mistakes, we'll do the right thing from now on.' Victor thought he had never talked so much or so articulately in his life before. He was proud of himself. 'I'm longing to see you. When can we meet? I'm going to be perfectly honest with you and confess something. That car isn't mine. I only hired it. I just let you think it was mine because – well, I suppose I wanted you to think well of me.' The words streamed out, it was easy. 'Am I forgiven? Well, I know you won't care about that, not really. And you know I'll come any distance to meet you if I have to walk every step of the way. We'll have to face it, it's going to be tough for the next few weeks, making him see reason among other things. But we'll be together and we'll come through all right.'

'Victor,' she said in a small distressed voice, 'this is my fault. I know that, I'm sorry.'

'Sorry?' he said airily. 'What have you got to be sorry about? Absolute nonsense.'

'David didn't want me to speak to you, he said it was

233

better not, but that would have been such a cowardly thing . . . I still have a lot of explaining to do. I shall always feel guilty if I can't say them.'

'You can say anything you like to me, darling, everything. When shall we meet? Tomorrow? In that Half Moon pub of yours?'

'Not tomorrow,' she said. 'Monday. Six o'clock. I'll tell David what I'm going to do. I know he'll think it's the right thing.'

'I love you,' Victor said.

He replaced the receiver, well pleased with the result of his call. Someone unlocked the front door and Mrs Griffiths came into the hall. She was wearing white gloves and a different navy blue straw hat, this time with a small spotted veil.

'Oh, Mr Jenner,' she said, 'you've saved me a climb,' as if his room was up Ben Nevis or on the tenth floor of a liftless tower.

He stared blankly at her, his head full of images of Clare.

'Some policemen were here again yesterday, asking for you. At about five in the afternoon.'

His heart missed a beat and then steadied. Five o'clock was four or five hours before he had encountered that girl in Epping Forest.

'It isn't pleasant, Mr Jenner.' Mrs Griffiths looked about her, craned her neck to peer up the staircase, said in lowered tones, 'Mr Welch and those after-care people, they did give me to understand there wouldn't be any trouble. However, I do understand from your note that you're leaving and what I wanted to know was – well, precisely when?'

Victor had forgotten that he had committed himself to leaving. Writing that letter she called a 'note' seemed so long ago, so much had happened since. He had nowhere to go.

'At the end of next week,' he said, and corrected himself. 'No, this coming Monday.' He wouldn't let Clare go back to Sans Souci this time. He and she would go to a motel, the Post House at Epping, for instance.

'Do you know you're bleeding through your shirt?' said Mrs Griffiths.

The wound had come open again. Exulting at the sound of Clare's voice, at her calling him by his name, he had flung his arm out wide, expanded his chest. He bathed the wound at the sink in his room, put a fresh piece of plaster on to it, drawing together the sides of the cut. Sitting in the wheelchair, he watched Wimbledon on television, an exciting women's singles.

It was one of the tortoise dreams he had that night. He was back in the shed at the bottom of that garden in Loughton, lying on the nets, aware, though it was dark, of a pile of stones in one corner. One of the stones came alive and began to walk, to approach his bed. Victor saw the scaly feet moving rhythmically like very very slow clockwork, the shell swaying, the head that was a snake's yet stupid, myopic, wobbling from side to side as if attached to a rusty pivot. He shouted and tried to get out but the door of course was locked and the window inaccessible, so he backed against the wall and the thing came nearer, dull-eyed, slow, relentless, and Victor screamed and woke up screaming, the sound coming not in a thin cry as was so often the case with nightmare screams but as yells of agony and fear.

Footsteps sounded on the stairs and someone banged on the door. It was the same voice that had protested once before, the time Victor had pounded on the floor and walls.

'What's going on in there?'

'Nothing,' said Victor. 'I had a dream.'

'Christ.'

He got up, had a bath and changed the dressing on the cuts. At nine, when he knew Clare would have left for work, he phoned David.

'Hallo?'

David sounded wary. He probably had a good idea who it was and he was scared.

'Yes, it's me again, David,' Victor said. 'I don't know if Clare told you I'm meeting her on Monday and that'll be it. She won't be coming back to you after that, she'll be

235

coming away with me. I think it's best to be perfectly honest about this and keep you informed about everything we plan to do.'

'Victor, Clare isn't planning to do anything with you.' David spoke in a patient slow way as if to a child, which annoyed Victor. 'Clare is going to stay here with me and marry me. I think I've already told you this.'

'And I've already told you Clare is meeting me on Monday and coming away with me. Are you deaf or something?'

'Clare and I will both meet you, Victor, and we'll try and talk sensibly about all this.'

'If you come with her on Monday,' said Victor, 'I'll kill you,' and he rang off.

He went out and collected his social security money, his clothes from the cleaners, and, passing Jupp's shop, took the ring out of his pocket and looked at it. There was nothing in the jewellery tray priced at more than fifty pounds, which meant that the most Jupp was likely to give him for the ring was twenty-five. The brown velvet sofa had gone and Kevin was lugging out from the back a rather battered green and gilt chaise longue to put in its place. Victor stood there for a moment, watching him stand the peacock on top of the big gilt scroll that ran along its back.

Victor got into the train at Ealing Common and went up to Park Royal. Not to Tom's this time but to the shop next to the wineshop which he remembered from his previous visit and which was called Hanger Green Small Arms. In the window were all sorts of weapons, it was an armoury of a kind, but Victor knew that very little but the shotguns and rifles were real. He went in and asked about a replica Luger. The man hadn't got one but he offered Victor a Beretta instead, the kind James Bond used to have, he said, before he changed to a Walther PPK 9 mm. It was a large heavy automatic pistol, precisely and in every detail the twin of a real one, but it fired nothing, it wasn't even equipped to fire blanks. The price was eighty pounds, which would leave Victor with just four pounds to live on till the next social security came through. But he didn't hesitate. He had had an idea about cashing that cheque.

On the way home he bought a magazine called *This England* that came out quarterly. He couldn't afford it, he could barely afford food, but there was an article inside about Epping Forest. What had become of all the leftover food from Sunday, he wondered. The quails, for instance. Probably David had eaten them. He wasn't going to demean himself by inquiring but he would phone David again just the same. He might as well use up all the coins he had left on phoning David.

'Hallo?'

'It's Victor,' said Victor. 'As if you didn't know.'

'I don't want to talk to you, Victor. We've nothing to say to each other. Please don't keep phoning like this.'

'*I*'ve got plenty to say to *you*. I'm coming over to see you tomorrow when Clare's at home and this time you won't get the chance to attack me with broken glass. I think you understand me.'

'*What*?'

'You heard,' Victor said. 'If I went to a doctor and showed him the wounds on my chest, you could be charged with causing grievous bodily harm. I'll phone Clare later. Just leave her to answer, will you? Have the decency to do that. It'll be about eight.'

He rang off. Five ten-pee coins remained in his pocket and a pound note and a pound coin. There was half a loaf of bread in his cupboard, a can of tomatoes and about a quarter of a pound of Edam cheese. Tomorrow he would go and see Muriel. He went out and spent the pound note and the pound coin on twenty cigarettes, a pint of milk, a bar of chocolate and the *Standard*. There was nothing in it about rape, either in Hertfordshire or Epping Forest. He sat in the wheelchair smoking and watching television. When the tennis went off and the news came on, he removed, with considerable pain, the dressing from the biggest wound on his chest and covered it with a fresh strip of sticking plaster. Of course he didn't really think David had made those cuts, he wasn't mad, he knew very well they had been made by the thin dark girl in the forest, but he wanted David to think he thought it. David might begin to believe it himself.

Waiting till eight to phone Clare was impossible. He ate some bread and cheese and smoked a cigarette, went downstairs and dialled David's number. It was twenty-five past seven.

David answered, though Victor had warned him not to.

'You've no right to stop her speaking to me when it's what she and I want.'

'It isn't what she wants, Victor. And I may as well tell you this is the last time you'll be speaking to me because I'm going to have the phone number changed.'

Victor started to laugh, he couldn't help it, because David was going to all that trouble when he, Victor, couldn't phone anyway because he hadn't any coins left.

'Victor,' said David, 'listen to me a minute. I don't bear you any ill will, you must believe that. But I think you need treatment, you're sick. For your own sake you need treatment. You need to see a doctor.'

'I'm not mad,' said Victor. 'Don't worry yourself about me. If prison couldn't drive me round the bend, you won't. And I do bear you ill will, a hell of a lot of ill will. Don't think you've seen the last of me. You can tell Clare I won't let her down, I'll never give her up, right?'

But David never answered for the pips started and Victor hadn't another ten-pee piece to put in. He put the receiver back and with the pencil that was kept on top of the phone box blacked out David's name and phone number that he had written on the underside of the stairs. Of course it was Clare's phone number too but that didn't matter because by now he knew it by heart . . .

Tomorrow, he thought, when he had some money, he would go to Theydon Bois and take the Beretta with him. David had been very foolish, last time, refusing to believe in the reality of a real gun, but once bitten, twice shy. This time he would believe. Just as he had once before failed to believe that that real gun was real, so this time he would not fail to believe a fake gun was real. While Victor held

David motionless with the gun, Clare could make her escape from the house. They would go in the Land Rover. He was glad now that he had confessed to her about the red Escort only being hired and about the rapes too, come to that. She knew all about him, he had no secrets from her, which was the way it should be . . .

16

He was going to have to lift that thing up, move it to one side and take the key from underneath it. Fearfully he glanced in its direction and then quickly away. Once more he climbed over the rocks and looked in through the diamond panes. Muriel was still asleep in her chair and no amount of ringing at the doorbell, the shrill clanging made by tugging at the iron bellpull, would awaken her. He even wondered if there might be something wrong, if she had perhaps had some kind of seizure.

There might be a chance of getting in the back way. Victor went round the side of the garage and tried the back door. It was locked, of course. The back garden had become a hayfield which the wind ruffled and made paths through. Once he had done what he came for, he was going to take the tube to Theydon and remove Clare from that house at gunpoint. The Beretta was in the pocket of his grey padded jacket, heavy, weighing it down a bit on the right-hand side. David had confessed that first time that he was afraid of him, afraid he had come to 'finish the job'. Victor didn't anticipate much resistance from David. The pressing thing was to get into this house. It was already two o'clock and he had been hanging about, ringing that bell, trying door and windows for nearly an hour.

Muriel slept on, an empty plate and cup on one of her side tables, magazines, scissors, a paste pot on another. It was a warm day, even the wind was warm, but she had one element of the electric heater on, a single bar glowing red. Victor couldn't smell it out there but he could imagine the stench of burning dust.

He climbed over the stones and stood on the one also shared by the rabbit and the frog. Frogs he didn't mind, or snakes, come to that, or crocodiles even. He could cheerfully have touched the skin of a toad. He moistened his lips, swallowed, forced his eyes on to the stone tortoise. It's stone, he said to himself, it's just a lump of stone. They made the thing in wax or clay and then they made a mould round it and then they cast it. They pour some sort of mortar or fine concrete into the moulds. Hundreds, thousands, they make like that, they're mass-produced. Telling himself all this didn't make much difference. I'll have to work on it again, Victor thought, try and finish what I started all those years ago. Clare will help me, Clare's used to healing. Meanwhile, he had to get into the house, therefore he had to take the key from under the – thing. Tortoise, he said, tortoise.

The flesh on his upper lip began to jump. He tried to hold it still with his hand. Then he imagined that his finger was a scaly leg pressed against his mouth and a shudder went through him, actually jerking his body. If I touch it I will faint, he thought. Suppose he were to go next door and ask Jenny or her husband to move it for him? That was full of difficulties. They would want to know why. Then when he'd got the door open one of them might come in with him and he didn't want that. He knelt down and closed his eyes. Why did he immediately think of those last moments in the house in Solent Gardens and of David thrusting the girl down the stairs and turning his back? Because of the picture of the praying hands on the stairwell wall? Perhaps. He was kneeling now, with his eyes closed, in a ridiculous attitude of prayer.

He told himself to think of anything rather than of what he was doing, about to touch a stone facsimile of the object of his phobia. Think of David, think of those last moments, of the gun going off. Those were bad things but infinitely preferable to this thing. He leaned forward, holding out his hands, clasped the thing, feeling the stone coruscations on its shell. It was surprisingly heavy, which helped. The real thing would not have been as heavy. Holding his breath, he set it down, felt for the key and found it. To replace the thing on the spot from which he had removed

241

it was beyond his powers. He stood up, clutching the key, and retched. His stomach was empty, luckily, he hadn't wanted lunch and was without money, anyway, to pay for it. Twice he heaved and retched, shivering with nausea, but recovered enough to feel the whole street must be watching him. It seemed as if the operation had taken hours but when he looked at his watch he saw that his sufferings had endured for a little over one minute.

He unlocked the front door and went in. She awoke immediately, or perhaps was awake before he even put the key in the lock. She called out, 'Is that you, Joe?'

Victor thought how he might have saved himself a lot of anguish. He walked into the living room. The heat was stifling, the smell of burning dust as he had imagined it. Muriel had her brown hairnet on but she was dressed, in a flowered silk dress which should have had a belt but didn't and stockings rolled down to her ankles and fur-lined bedroom slippers. She contorted herself into that peering attitude, hunched forward, head on one side, looking up with nose twitching.

'What are you after?'

A gust of anger swept through Victor, or, rather, swept upon him and remained. It seemed to grow, to mount, like yeast working, bubbling up. What had she done to herself, he thought, to make her look so like his mother? It was a resemblance he had scarcely noticed before. If his mother had lived, without his father, would she too look like this now? The notion was almost unbearable. There was something about her face. The jawline was fuller and firmer. She didn't have false teeth, as far as he knew, but she didn't have many of her own left either. It must be a plate she wore, that she should wear all the time, but had put in because of Jupp, to present a more attractive appearance for Jupp. He remembered why he had come.

'I needn't go into details,' he said, 'but I gave this woman to understand my name was Faraday and she's given me a cheque made out to M. Faraday. All I'm asking is for you to sign on the back of it for me.'

'The police came here again,' she said.

'What do you mean?' he said. 'When did they come?'

'When was the day it rained? When Joe was here.'

'How should I know? Monday? Tuesday?'

Before his night in the forest, he thought, breathing again.

'They'd been to you,' she said, 'but you weren't there. For rape, they said. It made me go cold all over, it turned me up. The Red Fox they're looking for and maybe that's you, they said.'

The Hertfordshire rapist. That was why they had been to Mrs Griffiths's then.

'Your poor mother,' said Muriel.

'Never mind my mother. My mother's dead.'

His mother's face looked at him, aged, distorted, whiskered, twitching like a mouse, blear-eyed, but still her face. Victor, convulsed now with anger, had the curious sensation that Muriel was a subtle tormentor placed here by some higher power to torture him in most refined and subtle ways, in ways specifically designed to suit him, as if details of what most flicked his raw places had been fed into a computer and the resultant print-out had been presented to Muriel as a guideline. Only Muriel wasn't Muriel but an avenging angel or devil elaborately disguised. Why hadn't they fed in the worst thing? Or had they? Would she, in a moment, open a cupboard and show him . . .?

As if to follow the course of his fantasy, she got to her feet. She lifted up the cup and saucer in her left hand, put two fingers of her right hand into her mouth and drew out a dental plate with seven or eight teeth on it from the lower jaw. Victor, watching in horror, heard himself make a sound of protest. She dropped the teeth into her teacup.

'That's better,' she said, and her face wasn't his mother's any more, but the eyes were, suddenly pale blue and sparkling. Victor closed his own. 'What was it you wanted?' she said.

Again he tried to explain about the cheque, but he gagged on the words, anger closing his throat.

'Speak up,' she said, the cup in her hand, the molars all grinning out of it. 'What did you tell them my name for?'

He couldn't answer.

'Two hundred pounds. There's some swindle going on, I daresay. It's bound to be crooked if it's you.' She came very close, head turned, peering up. 'What stopped you forging my name?'

What had? He had never thought of it. He took her by the shoulders to thrust her away and she cringed under his touch.

'Don't you . . .!' she cried. 'You'd better not . . . Oh, no . . .'

Immediately and with horror he understood what she meant. It was rape she feared. Broken old creature that she was, his ruined mother that she was, she feared rape at his hands and, while dreading it, her eyes nevertheless sparkled. She trembled, tense and fascinated. She peered into his face, reached up to take his hands away, shuffled backwards, one step, two steps, the cup with the teeth falling on the floor, rolling across the carpet.

He was aware for the first time since entering the house of the gun weighing down his pocket. He put his hand into his pocket and took out the gun and struck at her with it. It struck the side of her head and she reeled, screaming out. Victor struck again and again, raining blows with an automatic hand, energy flowing out of a great bowlful of anger in the centre of his body, running down his right arm in a charge of very high voltage. The blows struck at his mother and at all women, at Pauline and Clare and Judy and Mrs Griffiths. From the first blow he was blind, dealing out anger mindlessly and unseeing, doing what all the rapes had been about.

Muriel's screams became moans, then grunts. It was when they ceased, when the silence came, that he opened his eyes. He continued, however, to beat the gun against its target, though that target was no longer solid but a pulpy mass. He was aware, too, that in order to continue this frenzied pounding he had fallen on to his knees. A warm sticky wetness covered him and his hands were glutinous with it. He rolled on to the floor, rolled away from her, both hands clutching the wet slippery gun.

The first thing he did was cover up the body. It was a dreadful sight. He couldn't bear it. He picked up the hearthrug that lay in front of the electric fire, a thin worn vaguely Turkish-patterned thing, and threw it over the bloody mass that had been Muriel. When she was hidden from his sight he felt less as if the end of the world had come. He was able to breathe again. But as he stood there, holding on to the back of the chair Muriel had always sat in, he did ask himself how it was possible for men to do murder and afterwards not die or go mad but carry on with their lives, making their escape, covering their tracks, denying, forgetting. He asked himself and he had no sooner asked than he was doing these things, turning off the electric heater, closing the door, climbing the stairs.

In the pier glass in Muriel's bedroom he caught sight of his reflection and gave an involuntary cry. He had known there was blood on his hands and he meant immediately to wash, but this he had not expected. The sight of himself frightened him. He was splashed with blood and soaked in blood as if he had plunged his arms and face into a bowl of it like some wallowing butcher. The cotton padded jacket was dark with blood, his shirt red with it, and a great dark stain spread across the front of his jeans as if from a wound in his own body. It was so horrible that there and then he began stripping off his clothes, feeling the kind of panic that made him in his haste rip cloth and tear off buttons. The blood had seeped through to his skin, thin, pale and dabbled like meat juice. He staggered down the passage to the bathroom, retching and sobbing.

Washing would be ineffectual; only a total cleansing by immersion would do. He filled the bath, kneeling on the floor with his head pressed against the cold enamel while the water flowed in. Whatever device heated the water in this house Muriel had kept turned low and it was a tepid bath that he had, shivering as he soaped himself. Rubbing his body dry on a thin grubby towel, he thought of clothes, he must find clothes to put on.

The bloodstained heap in the bedroom sickened him again. It was as if a second body lay there. He began pulling open drawers, finding only women's underclothes, pink corsets, their elastic sides stretched out of shape, brown lisle stockings and tan-coloured silk stockings, locknit knickers, bloomers rather, in pink and white, petticoats with wide straps and deep round necks. His own nakedness was horribly alien to him, awkward, embarrassing, a source of shyness. Naked, he moved and walked clumsily, and he realized that he had hardly ever in his life been naked for more than a moment or two, except during those hours with Clare. The thought of her made him shut his eyes and clench his hands on the hard edge of the chest of drawers.

Muriel's dressing table contained no male underwear but in the top drawer was a jewel case. Victor left the drawer open and the lid of the jewel case open. He went into the bedroom where he had found the greater part of the money. The chest in this room had Sydney's underwear, what remained of it, in its third drawer. Victor put on old man's white cotton underpants, yellow with age, reeking of camphor, an Aertex vest, a pair of matted navy blue socks darned with brown. The bottom drawer was still half full of money, mostly pound notes. He took them. In the next bedroom he emptied another drawer of five-pound notes. Back in Muriel's bedroom he opened the wardrobe and emptied out all the handbags. They contained hundreds of pounds.

Victor dressed himself in a suit of Sydney's in light brown tweed and a cream cotton shirt he found hanging on a hanger with the price tag still on it. How ancient must it be, yet never worn? Sydney had paid two pounds nine shillings and eleven pence three farthings for it. Dressed, Victor felt better, he felt clean and sane and as if to continue with life, some sort of life, would be possible. In Muriel's jewel case the ring with the dome of diamonds lay on top of a pile of gold chains and glass bead necklaces. He put it in his pocket and replaced the case in the drawer. The money he stuffed into his pockets until they bulged with it. The nightdress case dog, pink nylon viscera looping out of its belly, watched him with dead glass eyes.

Why shouldn't he clear the house entirely of money? He might as well have it all now. From the cupboard where the gun had been he took a small brown leather case of the sort that his father had used to call an attaché case and stuffed the money into it. He searched all the bedrooms, the fourth one as well, the one he hadn't been into before, and he found notes everywhere, in a plastic carrier bag under a pillow, two tenners under the base of a lamp, a bundle of fivers in the firegrate basket, tucked under a soot-powdered silver paper fan. There was almost too much money to go into the case and it was with difficulty that he fastened the clasps.

The house had grown dark, darker than its normal daytime twilight. Victor had forgotten about time but he thought it must be evening. He looked at his watch and saw that it was not quite three. All this earthquake had taken place in less than an hour.

It was pouring with rain, a dense glittering rain, straight as glass rods. Victor went downstairs, noticing when he reached the bottom how, on his way up, he had left bloody footprints on the hall carpet, footprints which faded and grew indistinct as they mounted the stairs. The rain would wash his shoes clean, cleanse the pale leather of those dark splashes.

The hallstand was hung with coats piled one on top of the other. It had been like that for as long as he had known it. Mixed up with and supported by the coats were a couple of umbrellas. By unhooking the topmost coat, Victor caused the whole accumulation to subside, sinking in a heap to the floor. From among it he pulled a man's raincoat, Sydney's presumably, left here when it was taken off for the last time a decade ago. It was a trenchcoat, black and shiny, of some plastic or rubberized material, and Victor chose it because it looked totally waterproof. He put it on and did the belt up. It was a bit long for him but otherwise it fitted.

He remembered the key, though not where he had left it. Among his clothes? In there with the body? To replace it under the tortoise would in any case be an impossible task. He also remembered the gun. With closed eyes he opened the living-room door and when he opened them he knew that, contrary to the laws of nature and experience, he had hoped to see Muriel sitting in her chair, scissors in hand, the electric element on. As it was, the rug hid the worst of it, and no blood splashes had reached the walls. He crept across the carpet past the dental plate and the teacup, picked up the gun by its barrel between fastidiously extended forefinger and thumb. It was gummy with clotting blood. This was, in a way, the worst part of all, closing the door again, carrying the gun to the kitchen and washing it under the cold tap, seeing the clots swirl in the water and stick at the plug hole, thinking inescapably that it was of this stuff that he too was formed.

'Whose blood is that?' – my own.

He hadn't wanted to remember those words. He pushed them away, dried the gun on Muriel's grubby teacloth, stuck it into the raincoat's right-hand pocket. The rain made a glass wall beyond the porch. Victor stepped outside, put up the umbrella and closed the door behind him. Jenny next door's car was parked outside her house, which it hadn't been when he came. Victor remembered something, that it was Saturday and Jenny and her husband went shopping on Saturdays. No doubt they had been at the shops when he arrived and had returned while he was – upstairs. They would have things with them they had bought for Muriel, as soon as the rain stopped would come to look for the key . . .

Probably they had already seen him. Jenny had told him she missed nothing of what went on in the street. Standing by the gate, at the foot of the stone hillside, Victor understood that it was too late to cover his tracks. As soon as anyone entered that house it would be known who Muriel's killer was. He felt calm, caught in an irrevocable destiny. All he could do was postpone the discovery of the body.

He mounted a similar flight of steps, through similar

escarpments, spars and outcroppings, pulled a similar bellpull, though setting this one in motion resulted in a chime such as a clock makes at the half-hour. Jenny came to the door. He saw the look of Clare again, a debased, spoiled Clare, and he had a sensation of something falling out of his body, leaving him hollow.

'Hallo, Vic, I didn't recognize you for a minute. You do look smart. All got up like a dog's dinner.'

Sunday-go-to-meetings . . .

'She said to fetch the stuff you got her.'

The days of finding an ability to express himself were over. He was inarticulate again, half dumb.

'There was only teabags and a Swiss roll, Vic. You want to come in a minute? OK, if you're pressed for time.' She was away a few seconds, came back with two paperbags. 'Here you are then, but I can easily pop them in later myself.' He saw that she was looking at his shoes, grey shoes into which the blood had soaked in great black patches.

'She's not too good. She doesn't want to be disturbed.'

'Right. I can take a hint. On your bike, Vic. I'll be seeing you.'

Because she might be watching he took the two paperbags round the back of the house. And left them on the kitchen window sill to the depredations of the rain. Tomorrow or the next day, he thought, Jenny next door would find Muriel's body. He walked home, carrying the suitcase full of money, and it wasn't until he was nearly there that he asked himself what he was going back to Mrs Griffiths's house *for*?

From the corner of Tolleshunt Avenue he saw the police car. Victor was calm still and he knew very well nobody could yet know about the murder of Muriel. The police had called on him for some other reason, the usual reason. They were still pursuing inquiries about the Red Fox, or else the woman in Epping Forest had complained. He hesitated and as he waited two men, one of them the detective constable he had dubbed Distressed Leather, came out of Mrs Griffiths's house and got into the car. Even then he thought it wasn't going to move off, but at last it did, sending up a spray of water out of the overflowing gutter.

They would be back, of course, and very soon. He dreaded meeting Mrs Griffiths or the man who complained about his violent nights. But there was no one. Victor climbed the stairs and let himself into his room. There he changed his shoes, uncaring of the grey ones which he left behind for the police eventually to find. He opened Sydney's attaché case and put into it the one thing he cared about taking with him: Clare's photograph.

No, there was one other thing – the wheelchair.

Victor folded the brown blanket and laid it on the seat. He banged the door behind him, having taken a last look at the cigarette-burn pattern round the bamboo table, the ravioli linoleum and the green rugs, the television set on which most of his parents' money had gone. He bumped the wheelchair down the stairs. Outside the front door he got into it and covered his knees with the rug. The rain had thinned to a drizzle. Victor propelled himself along the street towards Twyford Avenue, down the wet puddled pavement, under the dark green heavy-foliaged trees that dripped water denser than raindrops. The suitcase with the money in it and Clare's photograph were on his lap under the rug.

Just as he reached the corner the police car came back, slowed, and passed him. He was not Victor Jenner but a handicapped man in a wheelchair. About a mile from Mrs Griffiths's house, when he had manoeuvred the wheelchair to the limit of his strength, he got out of it and noticed something he had not seen before, that had not occurred to him before. It would fold up. He folded it up and, when a taxi came, took the folded wheelchair into the back with him.

17

Victor lay on the bed in his hotel room. This was in Leytonstone, about halfway between Acton and Theydon Bois. The taxi driver had refused to take him any further and Victor had been too tired to think about hire cars or tube trains. While he had been in prison tourism in London had vastly increased and hotels like this one had been opened all over the inner and outer suburbs, conversions of big old houses they mostly were, charging much lower rates than those in central London. Not that the cost need have bothered Victor. He was carrying with him thousands of pounds in his suitcase – how much he didn't know, he was too tired to count. Enough, anyway, more than enough, to find a place for him and Clare to live in, to set up a business or to go abroad if she would prefer that.

There was a phone in this ground-floor back room but it was useless phoning her. David would be sure to answer. Much better to leave it till tomorrow, when he would go there with the money and the gun. It was still early in the evening but he had stripped off Sydney's suit and lay in Sydney's curious old underwear, wondering if he ought to dress again and go out to eat, but each time he thought of food he remembered rinsing the clots of blood off the Beretta and nausea came up into his throat.

His three possessions furnished the room: the gun, the wheelchair, the attaché case full of money. The hotel management had provided a built-in cupboard, a built-in counter with mirror, bed and television set. Victor lay watching television. The news came on, and two or three hours later came on again. But there was nothing about Muriel, nor would there be until Jenny next door went in

– perhaps not till next Saturday, he thought. He rolled over and fell asleep.

David's phone number had gone out of his head and the only record of it he had he had blacked out on the underside of Mrs Griffiths's staircase. Directory Enquiries gave it to him and Victor phoned the number at about ten in the morning, resolving to replace the receiver if David answered. But no one answered. He wrote the number down on the inside of the attaché case. They were out for a walk probably. It was a fine day, the clouds and rain of Saturday dispersed, the sky clear and the sun shining. Victor looked out of his window on to old London suburban gardens, shorn weedless grass, pear trees, a yellow brick wall. He couldn't bring Clare here.

One of the wounds on his chest had gone a purplish colour and the area around it was swollen. A bit of glass was probably inside there but it hurt too much to squeeze. If he got blood poisoning, David would be responsible, he thought, and in his mind's eye he saw David leaning forward out of that wheelchair, lunging at him with a sliver of glass. But he needn't worry about it, for that was something Clare would deal with as soon as they were together. He asked Directory Enquiries for the number of the Post House Hotel at Epping, phoned them and booked a double room for that night.

Trains were less frequent on Sundays and he waited twenty minutes on the platform at Leytonstone, holding the folded wheelchair, carrying the attaché case, the raincoat slung over his left shoulder, for it was too warm to wear it. On the village green at Theydon children were playing ball games, people were walking dogs. He looked for David and Clare, thinking they might be walking Sally but then he remembered that Sally mustn't go out yet, not until she was past her hardpad and distemper immunization.

Victor wheeled the chair along. It was too heavy to carry. He laid the attaché case, the brown travelling rug and the raincoat across the seat. Although it was a hot day, all the windows in Sans Souci were closed. He looked through the windows, looked through the side window of the garage and saw that the Land Rover was gone. At the back of the house the french windows were closed and the blue and white sunshade furled. He noticed something else. It upset him disproportionately, yet there was no reason to be upset by something which he could remember his mother once telling him was normal for this time of the year, for the end of June. There were no flowers out. The spring flowers were over and the roses cut, the summer ones and late roses not yet in bloom and the garden was all green, just green.

Victor banged on the french windows to make the dog bark but there was no sound from inside. So they had taken her with them wherever they had gone. He decided to go back to Leytonstone and wait there, come back again this evening. The wheelchair was a nuisance but he couldn't very well just leave it in the street. At a newsagent he bought two Sunday papers and read them in the train. In a pub in Leytonstone he had sandwiches for lunch, a glass of wine and then another, aiming to sleep the afternoon away. The idea of getting mildly drunk appealed to him and he had two double whiskies in a pub further along the High Road, a place where urban blight and perhaps a threat of road widening had closed shops and offices and where abandoned houses had their windows boarded up. There was something desolate about the place on this hot sultry day, few people in the streets but lots of traffic and a reek of engine vapours. A long way in the distance, perhaps over Epping Forest, thunder rumbled.

The mixture of drinks went to his head, bringing him a carefree feeling. He passed a woman in a wheelchair being pushed along by an elderly husband, so he got into his own wheelchair, covered his knees and propelled himself along. People got out of his way, cast him the familiar looks of sympathy, embarrassment, guilt and fear, took a self-conscious pride in assisting him across roads. Because he was confused and muzzy-headed from the drink it never occurred to him to wonder (until he was inside there) what the people at the Fillebrook Hotel would think about the man who walked out of their front door that morning and returned in the afternoon a cripple. But a different staff was on duty. The girl in reception reacted of course, but not with astonishment or anger, rather by rushing to open further an already open pair of glass doors and running ahead of him to unlock his room door as if he had lost the use of his hands as well as his legs.

He lay down on the bed and slept off the drinks he had had, waking with a headache, the kind that seems to prick the inside of the scalp. Before he went to sleep he must have switched the television on, for it was on now, a congregation of devout, earnest-looking people singing hymns. He switched channels on to London Weekend, got what appeared to be a detective series and turned the sound right down. Dialling the Theydon Bois number, he thought that the best thing might be to ask the hotel the name of a local minicab company, then get them to drive him out there and pick Clare up. The phone was answered and David said hallo. Of course he wouldn't think it was Victor because for the first time he wasn't calling from a pay phone.

'I'd like to speak to Clare Conway, please.' Victor put on a higher pitched, 'posher' voice than his own and David, though suspicious, seemed deceived. 'This is Michael.'

'Michael who?'

'Faraday,' said Victor.

There was silence. He thought it was working all right and then he heard a whispering and Clare's voice say, 'My God!'

Victor felt the corner of his mouth begin twitching with live flesh. Clare came to the phone and her voice was strange with a tremor in it.

'Victor, where are you? Please tell us where you are.'

Us? He said nothing. His eyes had wandered to the silent television on whose screen had appeared Muriel's house, a Tudor keep standing like a fortress on its rocks, but not a fortress, not inviolable, its front door standing open. He moved the receiver slowly away from his mouth, his arm gradually falling, Clare's voice speaking out of it his name over and over.

'Victor, Victor . . .'

The picture on the screen had been replaced by another, by his own photograph, the one he had given to Clare.

Her betrayal stunned him. For quite a long time he was unable to move. He was just capable of putting the receiver back into its rest but not of turning up the sound on the television. What more could it tell him, anyway, beyond the facts that Muriel's body had been found and the police were looking for him? Clare must have given the police his picture. No doubt David had compelled her to do this but just the same . . . He would have died before he gave up hers, Victor thought. That was where she and David had been all day, with the Acton police, for Muriel's body must have been found either last night or this morning.

Could they trace his call? Victor didn't know, though he had a vague idea calls from private phones couldn't be traced. Was a hotel number private? He put on the raincoat, got into the wheelchair, covered his knees with the rug and laid the attaché case on the rug. In the right-hand pocket of the raincoat the Beretta felt heavy and bulky. It wouldn't work but it was a comfort to him.

Something told him that this would be his last chance to make a phone call for a long time. He dialled the Theydon Bois number, knowing they would answer, knowing they were longing to talk to him. It was David again.

'You know who this is.'

'Victor, please listen to me . . .'

'*You* listen to me. I've got a gun and it's real. You'd better believe me. It's a Beretta and it's for real. You make them believe that if you don't want someone else getting what you got.'

He crashed down the phone. The photograph he had given Clare – the memory of that giving made him wince with pain – was an excellent likeness. He had a sudden mental picture of the reception girl watching the London Weekend six-thirty news in some back office, seeing that face and then coming out into the hall and seeing it again. The wheelchair protected him, of course; in some subtle way the wheelchair even changed his face. He emerged from the room. The hall was empty. With no idea of where to go, Victor bumped the wheelchair down the single step and out on to the pavement and, turning in the opposite direction from the trains, the railway underpass and the High Road, wheeled himself into a hinterland of Victorian streets that led nowhere he knew.

After a time he came to the forest. He had vaguely known that Epping Forest reached all the way down here and he understood that he was facing the southernmost tip of it, urban forest with little grass and no flowers, and only brown trodden earth underfoot. He began propelling the wheelchair along the Whipps Cross Road in a westerly direction. A police car passed him quite slowly. Victor now remembered that he had checked into the Fillebrook Hotel in his own name and understood that it would only be a matter of time, perhaps of minutes, before the management realized who their last night's guest had been. He must get out of the district, think where ultimately to go and what to do. The money would take care of him. With money you could do anything, go anywhere.

Taxi drivers who had been out all day wouldn't have seen television. Victor was afraid to get up out of the wheelchair in the open like this. It would be a suspect act, drawing attention to himself. He turned into a side street, got out of the chair and folded it up, dragged it behind him out into the Whipps Cross Road and hailed a taxi. The driver looked at him indifferently, without interest. He seemed disappointed that Victor wanted to go to Finchley and not central London.

If he showed signs that he knew or suspected, Victor thought, if he spoke in a suspicious way on that radio phone of his, he would press the barrel of the gun into his back and command him to drive to some deserted country place. But nothing like that happened. It had become a gloomy grey evening, stuffy and close. A fork of lightning flickered in the heavy clouds on the horizon that Victor thought was Muswell Hill. That sharp point sticking up was the spire of St James, Muswell Hill. He would go there. No one would expect him to go there.

The storm broke late that evening. In the hotel Victor had found in Archduke Avenue, Muswell Hill, television sets were not provided in the rooms, nor were phones. But they had ground-floor rooms vacant in a single-storey annexe at the rear. Victor checked in as David Swift. The management were solicitous, helpful, opening doors for him, running ahead to check that the room door was wide enough to admit the wheelchair.

Everywhere up here, even ground-floor rooms, had panoramic views over London. He sat in the wheelchair and watched the storm fight its way across a sky of cloud plains and cloud mountains. He hadn't eaten since lunchtime but he didn't want to eat. A feeling of malaise had begun to take hold of him in the taxi and was still with him, not the nausea he so often felt in times of stress, but a light-headedness, something like fever. Perhaps it was only that he had drunk too much at lunchtime. He was aware too of a rapid pulse. Before he went to bed he felt in the pocket of the raincoat to make sure the gun was there but he must have felt in the left-hand side, for there was nothing in the pocket but a half-used packet of mints. The gun was in the other side all right.

Victor slept and dreamed of David. David was well and walking again, back in the police force and put in charge of the hunt for Muriel's killer. He didn't suspect Victor, in fact he wanted to discuss it in all its aspects with Victor, talk it through. The case must be concluded by tomorrow because David was getting married tomorrow. His bride came into the room in her wedding dress but when she lifted her veil and showed her face it was not Clare but Rosemary Stanley. Victor woke up with a feeling of stiffness in his neck and jaw. It must have been the way he had been lying on this hard mattress and latex pillow. There was something ridiculous, he thought, in a man dreaming of weddings. Only women dreamed of weddings. He slept again, but very fitfully, and got up at seven.

257

The stiffness in his face and neck was still there. It was probably something to do with this chorea he had been having, though there were no jumping muscles this morning. His pulse still raced. He dressed in the same underwear and shirt, having no other, but making up his mind to go out and buy some as soon as the shops opened. It had rained all night and the day was heavy and humid, cold-looking.

He had no desire to eat and fancied anyway that it might be a painful process, the way his jaw felt. On the table in the hallway lay the morning papers. Victor, slowly propelling himself in the wheelchair, took a *Daily Telegraph* back to his room.

The murder had made the front page. There was a photograph of Muriel as Victor remembered her from when he was a teenager, at the time of her marriage, a moon-faced smiling Muriel wearing thick make-up and pearl studs in her ears. Jupp had found the body. There was an account of some of the things he had said, such as that he had been going to marry Muriel, that he was 'devoted' to her. On Saturday night he had gone to her house – to see her, yes, but principally to fetch something he had left behind last time. He had a key to the house and had let himself in at about eight in the evening. The first thing he saw was a footprint in blood on the hall floor, only he hadn't of course known then that it was blood.

Victor wondered what it was that Jupp had left behind and why the *Telegraph* didn't say what it was. Surely it would have been more usual to say 'left my umbrella behind' or 'left my scarf'. Perhaps it *had* been an umbrella and that was the one Victor had taken and abandoned in Mrs Griffiths's house.

His knees covered, the attaché case with him because he was afraid to leave it behind, Victor manoeuvred the wheelchair along Muswell Hill in search of underwear, socks and a shirt or two. Shop assistants were attentive, polite, one rather embarrassed. He bought the clothes he wanted but the buying of them brought him none of the pleasure he had felt when he had spent money on his grey jacket, his suit and those grey shoes. His head throbbed and he felt as if he were at a remove from reality, out of touch somehow, his grasp of life lost. Even the realization that Clare was gone from him for ever, that he would never see her again, brought him a resigned sadness rather than pain. Perhaps this was insanity, that might be what it was, the prison years they said drove you mad catching up with him at last.

At the pedestrian crossing in Fortis Road opposite the cinema he waited with four or five other people for the traffic to stop. Then a terrible thing happened. Coming towards him from the other side as soon as the cars had pulled up were a man and woman arm-in-arm, and the man was Kevin, Jupp's son-in-law.

He glanced at Victor, then stared hard. Victor had no choice, there in the middle of the road, but to move towards him. They came up to each other, eye to eye, but there was no recognition in Kevin's face. He had thought Victor was Victor – and then thought better of it. The wheelchair had disguised him, had kept him from discovery, would save his life. Kevin didn't even look back. He said something to the woman Victor supposed was Jupp's daughter, and the two of them went into a shop. Victor remembered now that Kevin had told him he lived in Muswell Hill.

Being in the wheelchair made him invisible or, rather, changed him into someone else. He understood that for safety's sake he must confine himself to it, become a handicapped person, as David was.

18

Back in his room, Victor counted the money. There was something over five thousand pounds. He had been right in guessing that Muriel kept thousands of pounds in the house; probably there had originally been as much as seven thousand. He couldn't be certain of the exact sum he had brought away with him, for he seemed to have lost his powers of concentration. Whatever ailed him it couldn't still be half a bottle of wine and two whiskies from lunchtime yesterday. If you could get flu in July, it might be flu he had, for he felt hot and then shivery by turns. He put the money back into the attaché case but set Clare's photograph up on the table by his bed.

It would soon be twenty-four hours since he had eaten, yet he had no desire for food. He shivered but he felt hopeful, cheerful even. The money would last a good while, so long as he got out of these hotels and found a room. It would have to be a ground-floor room, of course, and the work he got would have to be work suitable for a disabled man, but there were schemes catering for such people, he had read. Getting a job as a handicapped person might be *easier*, life in this wheelchair as David Swift might be altogether easier and happier.

Victor didn't dare have a bath. It would be too complicated and dangerous trying to get the wheelchair along the passage, down steps, into the bathroom. Instead he washed standing up at the basin. The wound on his chest had an ugly inflamed look about it and the edges of it gaped open, ragged snarling lips. He knew he should have had it stitched but it was too late now.

There was no mirror over the basin, the only mirror was

on the inside of the clothes-cupboard door, so he dressed in his new underwear and shirt before starting to shave.

When he opened the cupboard and looked in the mirror he got a shock. It wasn't just on account of the wheelchair that Kevin had failed to recognize him. His face had changed. There was something skull-like, rigid, about it, while the eyeballs seemed to start from his head. His dark skin could never have become really pale but it was livid rather, olivine, deathly sick. It was no wonder after what he had been through, he told himself, no wonder at all.

The evening paper would be on the street by now. It was midday. Although it was warm, Victor was shivering with cold and he put the raincoat on. He told himself that he must not only look disabled but think himself into the *persona* of a disabled man, resigning himself to the confinement of the wheelchair, allowing no possibility of separation from it. It must become as much a part of his mobile self as his shoes were.

Fear of meeting Kevin again made him turn the wheelchair in the other direction, towards Highgate Wood. He came to some shops, one of which was a restaurant where he thought he might have lunch. In the newsagent's next door he bought the *Standard*, *What Car?* and *Here's Health*, this last because he thought his condition might be due to not eating properly and it might tell him what he ought to eat. He manoeuvred the wheelchair a little way into the wood and sat reading the *Standard*. It said that the police were very anxious to interview Victor Michael Jenner, Muriel Faraday's nephew, who had left his home in Tolleshunt Avenue, Acton, and spent the night following the murder at an hotel in Leytonstone, E11. Victor remembered that he had registered there as Michael Faraday, seeing this now as reckless behaviour. However, he was safe enough here, protected by the wheelchair. A lengthy description of him followed, so lengthy as to be continued on an inside page, but Victor didn't bother to turn the page. The print danced and formed black and white wavy patterns, chevrons and parabolas. His hands felt too feeble to make the effort of holding it and it slid from his lap.

Victor watched it fall on to the ground and the magazines after it and he let them lie, lacking the strength to retrieve them. This area of woodland, though dusty and buzzing with flies, yet reminded him of the forest at Theydon where he had attacked the girl long ago, where David and Clare had taken him, where he had tried to rape the woman who sat making up her face and who, breaking the mirror under her in the leaf mould, in the fibrous, spore-ridden, mealy earth, had stabbed . . . Or had David done that in the garden? Or Clare, with a sliver from the broken water jug? Or he himself? Victor couldn't remember. His eyes closed. He saw before them feverish images, curtains blowing ceiling-high at a broken window, his mother's face and Muriel's, blending, separating, a train roaring out of a black tunnel, and he fancied he could smell honeysuckle. A stuffed peacock perched on a sofa screamed and his mother's voice crooned to Mr Sandman to bring her a dream . . .

He awoke and forced himself to move, though he was weak and disorientated. Eating would be impossible. The little restaurant was called Terrarium and he could see a big green glass tank inside which probably contained trout from which customers chose one to be caught and cooked for them. It seemed to Victor a distant outlandish prospect, a custom from another world. Wearily and slowly he made his way back to the hotel. It was no more than two or three hundred yards but it seemed a mile and sometimes he had the illusion he was travelling backwards, as in one of those frustrating dreams, the kind in which everything is geared to stop you going where you want to go and attaining what you want to reach.

The television was on in a kind of lounge place, watched by a single old woman. For a moment he thought it was the old woman in the train, the one who played guards and travelled with a guinea pig, for she was dressed the same and wearing the same woolly hat. But when he looked again his vision seemed to clear and he saw that he had been quite mistaken, that she was even smart with pretty white hair and a blue dress on. He was steering the wheelchair towards the open door when a woman's voice called, 'Mr Swift!'

How strange that there should be a real Swift staying here, he thought.

'Excuse me, Mr Swift.'

The receptionist spoke it almost into his ear this time. She must think him deaf or mad.

'We found this on the floor of your room.'

It was a diamond ring. He was going to deny ownership but, as he stared at the dome of diamonds, he seemed to see Muriel's hand form around it, her dirty-nailed wrinkled finger slipped through it. Hadn't he once thought it should adorn some fair young hand?

'Thanks,' he said through jaws that had grown stiff. He was beginning to find it difficult to open his mouth.

When he was counting the money he must have pulled the ring out of the attaché case with the notes. He sat for a while, gazing unseeing at the television, his head throbbing with pain. Now he was aware of a kind of spasm in his chest, though a long way from the wound itself. Perhaps he should lie down, try to sleep. A young man had taken over from the girl receptionist while Victor was in the lounge and Victor fancied that he gave him a long and searching look.

'Everything all right, Mr Swift?'

It was the kind of question a hotel manager would ask a disabled guest and Victor decided he had been imagining things. He nodded and went on to his room. The wound looked the same, angry, festering, swollen. It must be blood poisoning he had, so what he had said to David had not been far wrong. That would account for the racing pulse and the fever. His forehead felt burning hot and there was sweat on his face. He wondered what his temperature was, very high no doubt, a hundred and two or three, as it had been long ago when he had had scarlet fever and his mother had laid her hand on his forehead like this. He lay on the bed and tried to concentrate on future plans, ignoring his fluttering heartbeat. If he moved out of London and used half the money to buy a car, once the fuss had died down he could leave the wheelchair and set up in the minicab business. Was it possible, even now, that Clare might join him? If only he could see her, if only he could *explain* . . . Her photograph seemed to grow very large, her face to float out of it with that mysterious smile, that gaze fixed on a point far beyond him.

He wasn't well, of course, hence these delusions, imaginings, near-hallucinations. Perhaps it was due to malnutrition. He read an article in *Here's Health* about harmful food additives and another one about mineral deficiency in contemporary diets. Not much the wiser, puzzled by his own physical sensations, never before experienced, he fell asleep.

The sky had been growing dark with storm clouds before he lay down on the bed and when he woke up it was raining. Victor looked at Muriel's diamond ring, which he had put on the bedside table beside Clare's photograph. That would have been a better ring to give Clare than the little one with the clasped hands but he couldn't see his way to giving it to her, he couldn't even think at the moment of an approach to her. What dim light there was in the room the cone of diamonds caught and flashed, twenty diamonds and a large single one in the centre, Victor counted. There had been nothing in the *Standard* about a missing ring (or, indeed, about anything missing from Muriel's house) so it might be quite safe to sell it. What a piece of luck if it should turn out to be worth a lot, thousands and thousands, say.

Victor felt stiff all over, not just his face. He must expect that, he thought, as the result of sitting in the wheelchair all the time and exerting muscles in his arms hitherto not much used. In time he would get used to it, he would adjust. It probably wasn't improving things to starve himself either. He must eat. He must force himself to eat even if he didn't much want to.

The temperature had dropped and it was cold for a July evening. Victor put on the raincoat, wondering for the first time what had possessed Sydney to purchase and wear such an unlikely garment. It was plastic, presumably, not leather, a grainy-ridged surface to the black shiny fabric, and no doubt absolutely waterproof. Sydney had surely been no more than five feet nine and it must have come down nearly to his ankles. Victor came out of his room, finding the propulsion of the wheelchair rather heavy-going. People went in for races in these things, he had seen them on television – how could they do it? His arms felt weary.

The girl receptionist was back on duty. In the lounge the old lady and a couple of German tourists, a man and a woman, were watching the weather forecast that followed the six o'clock news. Frontal systems moving across the Atlantic, a deep depression to the west of Ireland, more rain to come. Between the reception desk and the front door was a circle of wicker chairs with a glass table in the middle of them covered with papers. A man Victor hadn't seen before sat in one of the chairs, reading the ABC London Street Atlas, or at any rate looking at it. He glanced up indifferently as the wheelchair passed.

Under the dripping trees Victor proceeded up the Muswell Hill Road towards the little restaurant called Terrarium. It had been a chambermaid, he supposed, who had found Muriel's ring on the floor of his room. How much more of his property had been examined, investigated? Had she, for instance, found the gun? It had been in the raincoat pocket, hanging up at that time inside the clothes cupboard. Victor put his hand into the right-hand pocket and felt the gun there. He manipulated the wheels, rhythmically pushing on the hoops of chrome, decided he had better transfer money from the attaché case to his pockets before he entered the restaurant, not risk drawing attention to himself by revealing all those wads of notes while seated at a table.

The doorway was only just wide enough to admit the wheelchair. A waitress pushed furniture aside so that he could reach a table. Victor felt in the left-hand pocket of the raincoat where he had put two ten-pound notes and his hand encountered the half-used packet of mints. Immediately he knew whose this raincoat was. It hadn't belonged to Sydney but to Jupp. This was the item Jupp had left in Muriel's house and had gone back to fetch on Saturday evening, had forgotten on a previous occasion because it had been raining when he arrived and not when he left. The newspaper had not specified its nature because the raincoat was so distinctive-looking, because they guessed that Muriel's killer would wear it and could be identified by it.

Victor broke into a sweat and his body was seized by cramps as in some immobilising dream. Luckily he was alone in the restaurant but for two girls who sat studying the menu. His instinct was to take off the raincoat but this could only be done with great difficulty while sitting down. Victor asked the waitress where the men's room was. Through that door, down the passage, there were just two shallow steps. The smell of food made him feel sick, he knew he would be unable to eat anything. He must remove the raincoat, hide it, go. As he began to move the chair again he felt something terrible happening to his face, the jaws clamping shut, his eyebrows dragged up as a frown corrugated his forehead.

In the men's room he struggled out of the chair, took off the raincoat and tried to roll it up. He transferred the gun and the notes to his jacket pocket and left the raincoat in a heap on the floor. The mirror above the washbasin showed him his frowning face and his teeth bared in a ferocious grimace. I am going mad, he thought. Why do I look like this? As he willed his face to relax, the rigid muscles of his neck to slacken, his body went without warning into a violent convulsion. His back arched as if it would split in two, his arms and legs shot in all directions. Victor gasped with pain and tried to cling to the edge of the washbasin. It was awful the tricks fear and shock could play on you.

Trembling and tense, shuddering, he had seated himself once more in the wheelchair when the door opened and the man who had been sitting in the hallway of the hotel reading the London Atlas came in. He nodded to Victor and said good evening. Victor tried to nod but he couldn't speak. Back in the passage, moving towards the door that led into the dining area, he wondered if he should try to see a doctor. If he saw a doctor privately there would be no need of medical cards and National Insurance numbers. With the footrest of the wheelchair he pushed the door open, entering the restaurant for the first time from this angle. Ahead of him, on a table that divided the diners from the cash desk, stood the green glass tank, lit from behind by bright tubular lights, furnished with feathery fronds and weed streamers, swarming with green reptilian shell-backed creatures.

He closed his eyes. He drew a long noisy breath.

'They're terrapins,' he heard the waitress say.

A kindly tone, a gratuitous piece of information offered to the disabled, who from the look on his face was also very likely mentally wanting. Show the poor man our menagerie, out terrarium . . .

He curled his fists on the chrome hoops. She was moving the chair nearer to the tank to show him. Victor had no control left. He staggered to his feet out of the wheelchair, hearing gasps, hearing one of the girls in the corner give a cry. The waitress was staring at him open-mouthed, her eyes round, her hands still on the handles of the chair. He grabbed the attaché case in his left hand. The door from the passage opened and the man who had been in the hotel foyer came in, stopped, took in everything, understood as only a policeman sent there to understand could do. He said, 'Victor Jenner?'

Victor pulled out the gun and pointed it at the waitress. She gave a whimpering cry. She was a small dark girl, Indian perhaps, or partly Indian, olive-skinned with black eyes in dark eye sockets. The policeman side-stepped between the tables, wary-eyed, tense.

Victor said, 'It's a real gun. You'd better believe me.'

That was what he tried to say. Something else came out, some broken mumble, some gagged jerky grunting that was all his locked jaw would allow to escape. But it didn't matter what he said. The gun spoke for him, the gun was enough. Behind him, behind that swarming dreadful green tank, he was aware of more people coming, standing, their breath audible. The two young girls had got under their table, under the overhanging cloth.

'Put that gun down, Jenner. That isn't going to do you any good.'

Because he knew he couldn't, because it was all right to make this threat this time, Victor said, 'I'll shoot her in the back.' The words came out as a series of grinding jerks. He turned the girl round, spun her with a stiff left hand, stuck the barrel on the Beretta into her thin back, her young knobby spine. 'Out of that door,' he said, and because she couldn't understand, pushed her with the gun towards the passage door. There was no way, ever, he could pass that tank, not if his life depended upon it.

Not one of the others moved. They believed in the gun. The waitress was crying with fear, tears flowing down her cheeks. She stumbled to the door, sobbed because she had tried without success to push it open.

'Pull it, pull it!' a woman screamed.

Her mother? Her employer? Victor pulled the door himself, spun round because he thought he sensed the policeman make a move. Everyone was still as statues, the woman who had shouted crying, a man holding her. Victor prodded the girl through the doorway, pulled the door shut behind him and turned the key. He said to the girl, 'I need a doctor, I have to see a doctor,' but God knew what sound came out, not that, not what he had said.

She stumbled on, holding her hands up now, like a hostage in a film, an old film, kicked open another door that led into a room full of metal chairs and trays. There was a way from here into a back yard, through french windows, bolted top and bottom, and beyond the yard rain falling, a grey board fence, the tree trunks and gloomy aisles of the wood. Victor said to the girl, 'Open those doors, windows, whatever you call them. You open them.'

He turned her round to him, pointing the gun. She gave a terrified gasp.

'Do it. Didn't you hear me?'

268

'I can't understand you, I don't know what you're saying!'

'Don't move.'

He could hear sound now, pounding feet, a shaking of the house, the sound of someone running at a door, using powerful shoulders on it. With the gun he motioned her to a stack of chairs. She shrank up against it. Keeping the gun pointed at her, Victor knelt down to undo the bottom bolt on the french window. A muscular spasm, unheralded, convulsed his body, throwing his arms out and arching his back. He cried out through forcibly clenched teeth, tried to get up and was felled to the floor by his own muscles fighting him.

His back leaped, bounded, jack-knifed, and he thrashed about the floor, still keeping hold of the gun until the most powerful spasm he had yet known snatched it from his hands and flung it across the room in a high arc, where it encountered the glass of one of the windows, smashed it and passed through. Victor reached out, grabbing empty air. The girl crept towards him, whispering. His back arched, whipped, coiled like a spring and his limbs danced. The girl knelt beside him, asking him what was wrong, what was happening to him, what could she do, and the tears she was still shedding fell on to his twitching leaping face.

The door opened just as the series of spasms passed and the policeman who came in stood over him, looking in a kind of hushed horror at the man on the floor whose flesh was fighting him to death.

19

The tortoise moved up the garden path at a steady, measured, unvaryingly slow pace, from where it had spent the afternoon under the shade of the rhododendrons. It had seen or smelt or otherwise sensed the small pile of cos lettuce leaves placed for its delectation on the lowest of the stone steps. The little dog watched it but she was used to it now. Patting its shell and seeing head, limbs and tail recede into the horny dome had ceased to amuse her. It might as well be a mobile stone for all she cared. With renewed vigour she applied herself to her marrow bone.

David Fleeetwood reached down over the side of the wheelchair and patted the dog's head. He and Clare were fast accumulating a menagerie: first Sally, then this tortoise that had wandered in from nowhere two days ago, and this morning a neighbour had offered him a kitten. But Clare had put her foot down there. The gnats were bothering him and he lit a cigarette to keep them off as much as anything. The evening was very warm, the air already taking on that dark blue look of a midsummer dusk. A big white moth had spread its wings flat on the house wall, waiting for the outside lights to come on, waiting to burn itself to death on the sizzling glass.

Clare came out of the house by the french windows. He thought she looked pale and rather tired, but you couldn't really tell in this light. She had a glass in her hand containing what looked like a stiff whisky. She drank too much, not much too much but more than she should. Someone had told her that the other day, she had said, but she hadn't said who.

'Do you want one?'

He shook his head, pointed at his half-empty beer glass.

'Are you going to ring the hospital?' he said.

'I already have.'

Her face told him. She sat down at the table very close to him and took his hand. He didn't look at her. He looked at the tortoise nibbling lettuce leaves.

'Victor died this afternoon,' Clare said. 'About three this afternoon, they said. If he'd got through today there might have been some hope. Apparently people with tetanus sometimes recover if they survive the first four days.'

David said rather violently, 'How the hell did he get tetanus?' He lit another cigarette from the stub of the first. 'That was nonsense about my stabbing him with a piece of glass. I never touched him.'

'I know. It's a mystery. Perhaps it was something which happened that night after he left here. He did tell you he'd had a horrendous night and was lucky to be alive, whatever that meant. If he cut himself somehow . . . They say the soil round here is full of tetanus. I looked up tetanus in a book on bacilli at the hospital. The poison itself is one of the deadliest known. It's excreted by the bacterial cells and carried in the bloodstream to the spinal cord . . .'

David shuddered. 'Don't.'

'There is a sort of irony there, isn't there? If you choose to see it that way.'

'I choose not to. It was the merest accident. It has all been accident, Clare. Victor's shooting me, his seeing my photograph in the paper, taking the train to Epping and seeing where I lived, coming here that night when I was away . . .'

She looked beseechingly at him but it was too dark to see her eyes.

'All accidents. For all we know, his killing the old woman was an accident – or started off that way. There's no answer to it, no pattern. If I've been over it once I've been over it a thousand times, the events that took place in that house in Solent Gardens. I even thought of getting Victor to do a reconstruction of it with me, the two of us trying to re-create the situation in a similar set of rooms with other actors . . .'

He peered closely at her, trying to gauge her response. Her face was in repose, wondering, sad, a little lax and vague from the whisky she had drunk. She held his hand in both hers now.

'I'm serious. I meant it as a catharsis for him as well as me. I thought of us getting together with Bridges maybe, wherever he is now, and perhaps finding Rosemary Stanley, and furnishing the place just as it was down to the pictures on the walls.'

'The pictures on the walls?'

'Oh, yes. It was a nicely furnished house, it was pretty. You know I said, Whose blood is that? because I didn't know it was mine then, I thought what a shame to stain that pale cream carpet, what a waste. There were little pictures all the way down the stairs and on the landing walls. Birds and animals mostly, reproductions of famous prints and engravings. Durer's *Praying Hands* and the one of the hare and of cowslips, and Audubon and Edward Lear.'

'I thought he wrote limericks.'

'He did lithographs as well, of animals in menageries. There was that bat of his, I remember, and the turtle.' David glanced at the tortoise that was making its slow way back to shelter beneath the rhododendrons. 'That one was right in the centre with the praying hands just above it. When I fell I had my eyes fixed on those praying hands. I had this elaborate idea of reconstructing all that, only I wanted to wait until I felt I could – trust Victor. And that time never came.' Gently David disengaged his hands. 'Put the lights on, Clare, will you?'

She got up and went inside the dining room and switched on the lights, one on the edge of the terrace, one on the house wall among the honeysuckle leaves. The moth fluttered off the wall and came to the light to burn its tender white feathery wings.